QUEST FOR THE SINGING STONES

CLOUDWATCHER

Registered U.S. Copyright Office
All rights reserved.

No part of this Publication may be reproduced or transmitted in any form by any means, Electronic or mechanical including photocopying, recording, or any information technology or information storage and retrieval system without permission in writing from the author.

This is a work of fiction. All the characters and events portrayed in this novel are either fictitious or are used fictitiously.

DEDICATION

This book is dedicated to Edda who showed me what true strength and courage really is. And to the Taylor family- Debbie, Tara, Brian, Cassidy, and Grayson for their love. And C.T.

Thank You

Cover artist: Le Annette Presciti
Tech, book layout and design help: Raymond Maugere
And you, the reader.

To Contact: questforthesingingstones.com

QUEST FOR THE SINGING STONES

1

Haunting. Mysterious. A little unnerving in the nighttime gloom. The desert-glistening under a light layer of snow-and its many buttes, mesas, plateaus, and mountains echo with the screams and cries of the hunter, or hunted.

Waning moonlight and passing cloud shadows conspire to make it all feel even more ominous and cold. Like restless spirits overhead, the shimmering stars try to send their ghostly silver glow to the rugged cacti filled world below. A heavy blanket that offers no warmth, darkness clings to the uneven, rocky ground.

This is the land of the Hohokam and this is where they have lived for over a thousand years, (AD-1450BC).

Safely tucked in at the foot of a silhouetted butte, called Flat Top, rests an adobe village. Inside, almost everyone is peacefully sleeping despite the howls, screams, and shrieks that occasionally emanate from just outside their walls.

A twisting apparition: a vaporous exhale of breath slowly rises in the eerie light. It languidly floats then abruptly dissolves in the still wintery air. When brother coyote, hidden deep within shadow, lifts his battered head to continue his song, time…

With a surge of warning racing up and down his spine, soon to be leader, seventeen-year-old Hugumki, jerks himself awake. Is it the

Thunder God, unwelcome visitors, or something worse that has his able body rigid in anticipation of what might come next?

"Kani," Hugumki quietly swears to himself as the rest of the all too familiar howl of his favorite coyote starts to fade away into the frosty night. "It's only Short Nose."

After releasing his death grip on the flint knife he always keeps close, Hugumki sits up in his warm bed of cotton blankets and rabbit skins. After taking a couple deep breaths of chilly air, he asks himself, *Did the only singer that sounds worse than me wake..? No*, he smiles, hearing the heavy breathing coming from his sleeping life-giver in the small, dark room they have shared for as long he can remember. In the next room, the rest of his extended family also seems to be sleeping peacefully.

With the residual heat from their communal fire long gone, Hugumki pulls his blankets tighter around himself. After a few more, deep, not so relaxing breaths, he lies back down on the padded earthen floor. Trying to hold off the inevitable, Hugumki rubs his weary and over-filled head to calm down. To no avail. Once again, the many questions and doubts about his own impending leadership come rushing back into his tired mind like a raging debris filled flash flood.

Of all nights to have such a restless sleep. I need sleep. Ahh. Everyone is counting on me. I am the only one that knows we are really going on long hard quest for treasure and not just a coming-of-age test like they all think we are.

What if...no...no more doubts so I will think about those going. Maybe that will help me, oah, fall back asleep faster.

Bird-Like a young walking stick. Always seems to have some sort of fear fluttering around in his eyes. His doubts have the wings of a hummingbird. Enough to hold him up, not enough to move him forward.

Two Bows-Big, strong. I hope we will only need your bow for hunting.

Sky Eye-Don't forget to look around long enough to see the beauty and danger that will constantly surround us.

Rabbit-special in ways I will never know. Will this test help you find out who you want to be, like you said...

Ah Ki Wami-Always unpredictable and... Maybe this journey will help you find your way too.

Ooha-Our singer. Too good looking or not good enough to make it?

Sleepy, who did I forget? Deerhead and his muscles, funny Ista, young but... Turtle? Next, the leader... me, Hugumki. Someday, I will be chief. The greatest chief. I can doo... this. I know I am ready. I just hope.... I fall asleep... before...

2

The fraying hem of the dark, late winter sky starts to brighten, revealing a yellow tinged, jagged edged horizon. Little by little, the landscape of black shapes and shadows morphs into a landscape of grayish blue shapes and shadows. The creatures of the night that made it through the night quickly start looking for places to hide before they are revealed in the rapidly encroaching light.

Taking his time, Father Sun slowly rises so He can share his majestic might with this magical land. As He climbs a little higher, the massive rock formations that are spread about are slowly turned a rich, deep burning red. In the adobe village that is now visible at the base of Flat Top butte, the first of the morning fires are starting to have that same bright glow.

On the east side of the sunward village gently flows the river that brought Hugumki's people to this desolate area many years ago. Carrying her new clay pot, the blanket covered, "Early One" is heading to the water that resembles a winding blue ribbon laid across the crimson terrain.

Constructed from the surrounding red tinted earth and clay, this village of the Hohokam has become a smoldering pink in the early light. Its walls of thick adobe keep out the bite of winter as well as the heat of a long hot summer. Surrounding a small, raised ceremonial courtyard, the glowing, soon to be bustling village contains at least forty-five interconnected square rooms. Some of them are stacked three stories high.

You can barely see the ends of some of the ladders the villagers use to get up and down from here. Oh look, someone is hurrying down on that one over there.

The first floor is used mainly for storage, refuse, and their holy room, which all have doorways. They use the ladders to get up to where they live on the second and third floors and they enter those rooms by way of small square holes in the roof and a short ladder waiting inside. The south side of the village has a larger courtyard surrounded by a low retaining wall.

On a normal day, the village, simply called home, would still be very quiet in the early chill. But not on this very special day. Mixed in with the smells and crackles of the morning fires are the smacking sandal sounds and eager voices of ten, overly excited, coming of age youth.

After you add the additional sounds of their younger brothers, sisters, older family members and other villagers, you can be sure that no one is sleeping in this morning. Well, maybe, except for the oldest member of the village, Gona, who can't hear a thing. That has been proven by the little ones of the village who would creep up behind her and clap their hands. It is almost as if they expected her rear end to answer them, which sometimes it did, to their dismay or delight, depending on how close they were.

Scattered around the inside of the larger courtyard, the boys, who range in age from thirteen? to seventeen, in their earthen shaded ponchos, yucca sandals, breechcloths, and headbands are eagerly picking from the provisions for their test that have been laid out in piles for them. There are small mounds of rabbit and deer jerky, dried fruits, various seeds, and different kinds of very dry bread.

As they bend over and pick from the different piles, the zumis hanging from their necks catch and hold the early morning light. Their zumis are made from different kinds of stones and are carved into the shapes of the various animals that live in the desert: snakes, turtles, birds, wolves, and bears, etc. The more translucent they are, the better, for the capturing of the light represents its ability to hold onto and share its power with whoever wears it.

Like a monstrous impatient heartbeat, a mighty thump cuts through the building din.

It is Turtle starting to stomp to a beat only he can hear. "We should be dancing now," he declares, lifting his other sturdy leg.

As Bird gets out of the way, he points, "Turtle, your flapping poncho looks like it wants to leave right now."

The passing Hugumki reaches over to pat Turtle's shoulder. "There is no time for dancing. It is kind of cold anyway, I think all the drummers want to keep their hands warm for later."

"For what," Bird quietly asks.

"Nothing," Hugumki answers.

Once the usually joking Ista looks Turtle's way, he can't help but laugh. To his credit, he does try to make it seem like the only reason he is laughing is because his playful dog Rock is jumping and slobbering all over him, not because Turtle's already large head looks even bigger after his recent haircut.

"Don't laugh at me Ista," Turtle mutters with a pout on his chubby brown face that makes him look younger than he is. Turtle is glad that his thirteenth cold season is almost over. He doesn't remember his first, but he has heard stories about how he was accidentally dropped into heavy snow then. He was momentarily lost from sight until his struggling on his back opened a hole in the snow. And that is how he got his name: Turtle.

Ista puts more supplies in the thick cotton pack with woven yucca straps that he is taking with him. "At least I did not cry like someone I know did. Down Rock. I still have more to do, and yes, I hope you can come along to."

Rock looks like a large dark gray and white coyote, but he still plays around like a puppy. Will that keep him from being the lucky dog that is chosen to go along on the test as both protector and friend?

Recalling that even Ooha-their handsome singer-had trouble letting go of his long raven hair, Turtle reminds Ista. "I was not the only one that was upset."

"Before the cutting ceremony, I thought Rabbit would be the one that would cry while his hair was being cut. Here comes Sky Eye, he thinks he knows everything, so I will ask him my question. Sky Eye, tell us again why we had to cut our hair?"

Ista studies his blanket covered, long-headed friend who is usually thinking about something, whether it is in front of him or not.

"First Ista, there is the tradition," answers Sky Eye, whose nervous energy is making it look like he is dancing in Turtle's place. "Doing it is meant to show that we are changing from wild boys to men, hoa, and our shorter hair will be easier to take care of while we are away from home."

Ista shakes his eagle egg-shaped head. "Now my hair falls all over the place, even with my headband on. See what I mean?"

"My head does feel lighter," Turtle shakes his head around too. "It feels like nothing is up there now."

"Did you think Rabbit would let Che Wah cut his long hair?" Ista asks, looking around to make sure that they will not be overheard.

Some of the younger ones going have tried to make up their own secret language, but it is not many words, and they do not include Rabbit, or haircuts.

Sky Eye reaches down to carefully adjusts his swinging breechcloth. "He may be different, but he is still one of us. To cut his hair was his way of showing that."

"Che Wah did not cut our hair," Turtle scrunches up his face remembering the pull of his hair as Che Wah, the aged medicine man, slowly sawed back and forth with his dull knife and shaky hand. "It felt more like he was pulling it out. Like he was mad at me."

"Hoa, you were crying even before that." Ista's lopsided grin is so big it can be seen across the whole courtyard.

"Like Ooha said, 'it has been with me my whole life, and now it is gone.'"

Sky Eye offers encouragement, "Turtle, it will grow back if you want." He reaches up to run his fingers through his own freshly cut hair that barely touches his shoulders. "If we ever finish packing, and start the test, we won't even think about it anymore," he intones. With a glance at the rising sun, then at the piles of supplies that he has yet to pick from, he can't wait to get going so he can start learning about something new or unexpected.

"Sky Eye, will you miss your lessons when we are gone?" Turtle looks down, trying to decide what he needs to grab next.

"Like my teacher says. 'You can learn all you want, but if you do not know how to use what you have learned, what good is it?'"

Turtle also checks to see if besides being the slowest runner going, is he also the slowest packer. "What have you learned that you can use on our test?"

"I have learned about some of the different things we may need once we leave the village. What I like the most is when we go outside at night and watch the stars as they move across the sky and how they change at different times. Cansake says if we study them long enough, we will learn secrets from them that we could never learn from looking at the ground. I can't wait until I can compare the stars here to the stars that are wherever we are going, even if it is not that far." Sky Eye's face momentarily goes blank when he tries to remember a particular star that they will need for guidance.

"Why does Cansake always act so strange?" Ista asks as he imitates Cansake's funny way of walking, side to side, while still somehow moving forward.

"He just acts like that around everybody else because he wants me to know that I don't need to be so serious all the time. When we are alone he is a different person, most of the time."

Ista scans the courtyard, "Turtle, do you want…?"

"No, but we can say we did." Turtle loves that answer because it saves him time and energy.

"If you let me have your pinion nuts, I will let you have my pumpkin seeds." Ista bares his shiny white teeth to show how much he dislikes pumpkin seeds.

"No. Sky Eye, how much can we take again?"

"Three or four big handfuls of each."

Turtle partially covers his mouth, "I don't like..."

"Take as much of everything you can because you will need it," Hugumki comments as he slowly passes by again.

Hugumki, the leader and oldest is the first to finish filling his pack and once at the courtyard wall, he places his pack that is filled with jerky, pinon nuts, edible seeds, dried berries, clothes, and other provisions by his feet. Interestingly, he has also packed two pairs of tiny buffalo hide sandals. Who could they be for?

At the bottom of his pack is a small bag holding a strong strand of yucca rope that none of the others going know about.

He also has another small pack with cloth inside that is just waiting to be filled with something magical and wonderous, tucked away, as do all the others going, though they probably think it is only for collecting memories of their test.

Also lying close by is a bow, some arrows in a quiver that is to be shared, and his two botos: deer bladders that hold water.

Once the test has started everyone will add their own personal touches to their botos. It could be a smear of color, a charm, or something interesting that will eventually be hanging from their straps.

Gently touching the bear zumi hanging from his neck, Hugumki turns his blazing black eyes on the others and tries to patiently wait on them to finish with their packing.

"I wonder how the rest are feeling right now?" he asks his maternal clan leader I Ku Ehi, who has come to stand beside him for a moment.

"It looks like Ah Ki Wami is having trouble with his mother. She keeps crying and trying to pull him closer than he wants her to."

"Maybe the mark he got is itching like mine is." Hugumki resists the urge to scratch the identifying tattoo he and Ah Ki Wami have recently received. "Still, when I look in Wami's eyes, I see some bad things."

"Like what?"

"A lot of anger, some sort of inner fire I don't understand."

"Is that what you really see, or what you think you see?"

"I don't know, but I am glad he seems to like me."

"Have you ever tried to talk to him?"

"He is kind of hard to talk to."

"Now is your chance Hugumki. Take your time. Don't push him. Wait to see what happens. As for the others, they only look excited and ready to go. See you soon," she whispers, before silently moving away to blend into the noisy crowd milling about.

Hugumki smiles as he stretches out his neck, remembering his experience with his own mother earlier.

A scraggly haired Shadow comes over to give Hugumki some encouragement. Though not much older, he passed his own test three years earlier, so he knows what he is talking about. "Being a man is so much fun. See you soon Gumki." Like his namesake he too quickly blends back into the crowd.

Across the courtyard Hugumki can barely see Ista, chattering to anyone who will listen, getting the last of his supplies together.

Faster than a heartbeat, Hugumki's smile vanishes when he spots Gray Wolf and Rabbit's older brother, Che Eh Oh Se slinking across the courtyard toward him. He knows they will say negative things to him like they always do when no one is around to hear them because Gray Wolf is mean-spirited, and Rabbit's brother is as sneaky as a starving snake.

"Keep on dreaming Gumki," Gray Wolf's puckered face looks as angry as his words sound. "You will never be chief. It is not your blood right. It is mine! Just because you are leading this little test means nothing. You are not even a man yet, like I am."

Hugumki does not react to Gray Wolf's hate filled words, or the shifty eyed Che Eh Oh Se, who sneers in agreement. But inside, he laughs to himself because by his own admission, Gray Wolf has revealed that he does not really know the true purpose of the test. He has no idea that it is so much more than just a coming-of-age test this time, which is a very good thing.. Instead of responding, Hugumki just smiles, which only infuriates them more.

"What are you grinning at?" Che Eh Oh Se hisses like the snake he seems to be becoming.

"Leave him," Gray Wolf snarls. "When Gumki fails and comes back to the village with little boys all hurt and broken, we will be the ones laughing. He's no leader. He doesn't know what he is doing."

With a last grunt of disgust through their curled upper lips, Gray Wolf and Che Eh Oh Se skulk away so they can find somewhere private to brood and plot.

After they finish filling their packs, Two Bows the tall hunter and scout, and Deerhead the muscular tracker, along with Deerhead's younger brother, Little Bean, join Hugumki at the courtyard wall to wait on everyone else to finish packing so that as a group they can all walk to the river with their families. Once at the river, they will take a chilly sacred bath that is meant to wash away all their negative energy before they leave to start their test. That way, it is not taken with them where it can fester, and cause problems later for everyone.

Shuffling his sandal clad feet in anticipation, "Can you believe this day has finally come Gumki?" Two Bows asks as calmly as he can.

"After the night I had, I did not think it would ever come," Hugumki answers around a yawn. "How about you two, are you excited yet?" he asks his friends who are both staring off into the distance doing their best to look bored.

With a subtle nod at Little Bean who is also shuffling his feet, Deerhead replies. "I am not saying much right now."

"Two Bows, are you ready?"

"Gumki, you know I am always ready," the scout answers back. "What I want to know is, why are so many of us going on this test?"

"That's right. Why Turtle, Ista, and the delicate little Bird? They are barely more than babies." Deerhead's low voice sounds like a growl filled with discontent. "Just because we had to wait on them to get old enough does not mean that they are ready yet."

Two Bows, takes a moment to stretch out his long arms from under his poncho. "I don't want to be mean but look at Ista and Bird over there. They are both so small they almost look like little girls. I wouldn't be surprised if some of the girls in the village are tougher than they are."

"How about Turtle?" Deerhead asks. "He is almost as round as he is tall."

"I have been watching them these past few days," Two Bows turns his head back and forth as he smiles, then frowns. "One time they are happy, next time they are sad. What fun they will be to have along."

"Gumki, have you heard their made-up words?" Deerhead gives his head a not-so-subtle shake.

Hugumki does his best to keep the building irritation out of his voice. "Let them have their fun, they will need it."

Reaching down and pinching Little Bean on his chubby cheek, Deerhead laughs, "I hope that toughness comes from more than just the body."

"I'm tough," Little Bean claims, with a proud smile on his small round face.

"Why them?" Two Bows inquires again.

"Kani," Hugumki swears sharply, his lack of sleep showing on his proud face. Usually, Hugumki's eyes are deep, warm, and mysterious in a face that is rugged at first glance, and handsome on the second. For the moment, his gleaming orbs just hold annoyance. "You know I did not make the decision on who or how many could or could not come. The elders must have their reasons." *Which I can't tell you about*, he reminds himself.

Trying to loosen up his thick neck in preparation for his job later, Deerhead cocks his head, "They did not tell you?"

"How about this question then, Gumki. Who do you think will be the first to fail this test?" interrupts a sneering, wiry, Ah Ki Wami, upon joining the waiting group.

Even on his best days, Ah Ki Wami always seems to be just one thought away from anger. It's as if he wears it around himself like an extra poncho.

Ah Ki Wami's question puts the fire back in Hugumki's eyes. "If anyone fails, I fail, and if I fail, we all fail," is all that he needs to say to express the seriousness of the test for all of them. Deep inside, Hugumki is fighting off more questions. *How am I going to do this? How am I going to keep everybody together as one because we will all need each other? The age difference is going to make it harder.*

When the younger ones start heading their way, along with Rabbit and Ooha, Two Bows makes a soft clicking sound to signal their approach.

"I can tell you one thing already," Hugumki watches the approaching group. "If he gets a new name, I know Rabbit will never be called anything to do with getting up early. He is moving so slow right now you would never guess he can run fast.

Hugumki yawns again, then shakes his head to clear it. Once his eyes have stopped bouncing back and forth, he notices his friend Esan is saving an open spot for them further along the courtyard wall. "Put everything over there by Esan. He will keep an eye on everything for us without eating all the jerky. Right Esan?"

Even though he has his heavy coat on, Esan is both enjoying the warmth of the sun and observing everything that is going on around him.

"Hi Esan" Turtle says with a slight grunt as he bends his legs to carefully put his loaded pack down. Turtle's short legs are sore from the running and walking he has done lately in preparation for his test, unlike some of the others going. Even though they all already have strong legs from climbing up and down the ladders their whole lives, none of that is going to make one bit of difference when the desert literally starts sucking the life out of each one of them.

When Ista and Rock approach, is that bemusement dancing in Esan's eyes? Does he know something they don't?

"Let's go," Hugumki orders to test out his leader's voice.

3

Emerging from the frigid river freshly cleansed, both physically and spiritually, each boy urgently looks around. They quickly walk naked and dripping-their chattering teeth sounding like dueling woodpeckers-to where his parents, parent, or elder, is proudly waiting with their breechcloth, a deerskin shirt, and a wide open soft warm blanket.

After they are all fully covered again, including Little Bean, who is doing everything his big brother does, they start heading back along the short path to the village. Once they are back in the village they will be given the Running Bird Blessing which will imbue them with both speed and strength on their upcoming test.

They will also receive everyone's advice, which they may or may not want or need.

Turtle shivers as he tries to hurry along the path. "The water was so cold it should have been frozen."

"Hoa. I went in and out so fast I don't know if I even got wet," Ista says and laughs at the same time.

"Are you two ready for our test? How hard can it be? When will we leave?" their quivering friend Bird asks without waiting for answers when he quickly passes them by with his mother in tow.

"Hard enough to make us grow up," Ista answers to Bird's back. He then grips Turtle's arm and walks a few steps pretending to be an elder's, elder.

"I hope none of the older ones are mean to us," Turtle quietly says.

Thinking about potential conflicts ahead, Ista's forehead wrinkles up like the old man he is pretending to be. "Like Wami?"

"Any of them," Turtle's face and eyes bear the pain and sadness that only constant teasing can cause. "We are all part of the same group even if some of them did not want all of us to come along. Did you see the way they were looking at us earlier?"

Remembering a conversation he just happened to overhear, "Gumki told my mother that he will watch over us," Ista answers back.

"It looks like everybody is waiting for us to re-enter the village," Turtle points ahead. "Did they do that for the last group that had this test?"

"I think it's because we have more going this time."

"Is that? I can't tell who that is, up on top of the roof, but you can see them waving and yelling from here," Turtle waves back at somebody.

"Look at everyone climbing up and down the ladders," Ista bobs his head, before laughing.

You would think at a time like this, those taking the coming of-age test would be serious or at least try to act serious in front of everyone else, especially with their elders spread all around them, and others watching from on high. Instead, Ista taps Turtle on his blanket covered shoulder. "I will beat you, last one back is a baby forever."

With his head slightly bowed, Hugumki slows down his pace to let everyone else walk ahead of him, or run, if need be. He knows that even though he has prepared the past sun cycle for all aspects of this quest, right now will be the last time he can relax until they all return safely home. Feeling the sun on his back, Hugumki is more than aware that one of the most challenging things he must deal with is the weather of the cold season changing into the warmer season. One day it can be freezing, and the next day, it can be quite warm, if not outright hot, especially where they are going, and then cold again.

Water or lack of water is the next issue he will face. Water is always needed but extremely scarce in the middle of the desert. On a journey like theirs, that could prove to be a problem for all of them. That is, if you think of a long, drawn out, anguished death, as merely a problem.

Another concern that once again weighs heavy on Hugumki's mind and spirit is that only he, out of all of them, knows the real reason for what they are about to endure. As he has been told, over, and over again, their journey is not just a test, it is also a quest for treasure. Only he knows where their real destination is. Only he knows that they will be following the rarely traveled path of Father Sun on their way to the great waters. The great waters that they have all heard about in stories since they were babies.

Just as important to him as everything else, he knows that if he does not bring everyone back home safely, he has shown the elders that he is not a good leader. If that were to happen, it would cost him any chance of ever becoming chief.

Hugumki's face breaks into a much-needed smile. He has started thinking about what the coming-of-age test really means, too most of them.

They know that once they pass, they are men and eligible to start looking for mates, wherever they may be, if they want too.

Ooha seems to have already sung his way into the young Squash Blossom's heart, or did she work her way into his? Just the sight of her long black hair, shy sparkling eyes, beautiful face, and budding lithesome body is making it harder and harder for him to think straight. Even though he has known her ever since they were both young children in the village, the sight of her has always made his heart jump. Lately, it has been jumping very high.

As for Rabbit, he has yet to decide or at least tell anyone what he wants to do, or be.

Before they reach the village, Bear, who is filling in as chief, walks up to Hugumki and places his large hand firmly on his shoulder. Bear is taking the place of the real chief, Hunter, while he is away on his own very important journey. Bears new responsibilities are evident in the recently etched lines on his already, weather-beaten face.

"Hugumki, don't forget we need all the people, that way," he says, turning south, "to stay our friends in trade. As you know, Hunter and his sons are also going that way but even further because they are going around the great waters. They are going to where it is said that the land is greener than a cactus. No one should be on the move out there this time of year, but if you see anyone, be the wind and move away unseen. If anyone does see you, sign, or signal to them that you are looking for a couple of lost elders or that you have gotten lost. Then hurry away while giving them, a wrong path, in case they follow you. You are going to be walking on trails that have not been used for a long time. At times, use the old trade or animal paths. Other times if you have to you can make your own. Some of the old trails follow the way that Father Sun takes this season toward the great waters. The reason those trails are not used anymore is because our people no longer travel there to do the Sun Ceremony like they did in days past. Don't ask me what they did because none of us have a memory of something that happened so long ago. Hoa, you can always check the rocks, maybe a picture will tell you what happened. As we have told you, there are secret trails and hidden ways through the mountains and wastelands that very few people know about. So do not worry if you see a mountain right in front of you blocking your way. Even though you cannot always travel straight like an arrow, be certain that there is a way as long as you stay by or between the things we have told you about. You will see tall mountains, flat mountains, worn down ones, and piles of sand, but do not fear for you can be sure that there is a path that will lead you to the water."

Bear smiles at the confused look on Hugumki's face. "When you get there you will know what Hunter and I mean by piles of sand. Practice your footstep tracking there. Near the great water follow the curve of the river that is there and then turn at the only large rock around. Keep walking for a short distance and then you will be right where you need to be.

Most of the boys have tried to get ready, but make sure you run and walk them hard so they will not get in trouble."

When he turns toward Hugumki, his sudden laugh sounds as warm and big as a real bear's might.

"I wish I could see the great waters, but I am glad I do not have to watch out for nine younger ones. Treat them like they are all important and they will act that way, we hope. Don't forget to keep Wami busy so that he will not build up anger so quickly."

"Yes elder." Hugumki shrugs his shoulders imperceptibly. He could already tell that Ah Ki Wami, who was usually cranky anyway, was not in a very good mood after all the loving he had received earlier.

Knowing that this is his last chance, Hugumki glances around, then asks the question that has been troubling him for too long. "Bear, why are we really doing this? Hunter told me that the treasure is something that our village will need someday soon. But what is it? Shouldn't I know? And why do we have to go so far to get it?"

Once again placing his hand on Hugumki's shoulder, but now, in an almost gentle way, Bear takes a moment to collect his thoughts. "I don't know if you have noticed yet, but something is changing around here Gumki. I don't know what it is but for the past few seasons our crops have been acting sick. The food you are taking with you has taken longer to collect because we did not have two good harvests this season like we used to have before.

Bear peers at Hugumki with a look that is as somber as it is proud. "Hugumki, as you know, the treasure you have, to cross the desert for are what we call singing stones. What you don't know is that they have the power to change into different shapes and things, as we have recently learned. The reason they are called singing stones is because if they bump together, they will sing their song. Hunter and his sons are going to talk to the people where it is said that they know how to turn the treasure into

Gods. Where you are going is the only place we know about where we can get the treasure that we can turn into Gods. Hugumki, we need our Gods to come back before all our crops dry into dust before the wind. That is why we need you to do this important task. You must help save our village by bringing the treasure that can be changed back with you."

Hugumki shakes his head in disbelief so hard that his headband flies off, "Gods can't be made! How can something that isn't even alive be a god?"

"I kind of feel the same way, but nothing else has worked so maybe we should try something different. Here you go. Hunter and some of the others think the same way I do because we are all desperate and don't know what else to do. We have tried everything and every prayer we can think of. Now that you know how precious the treasure is, just remember what you have learned and no one will know you have passed their way. Don't forget to have everyone hide their kani every time they empty their bodies and don't wear that worry on your face. I know you can do this." Bear raises his hand and smacks Hugumki's back. "You will succeed."

Hugumki opens his mouth to reply then closes it because he knows that words mean nothing when you are heading out into the middle of the barren desolate desert and whatever waits beyond.

Once the full impact of how important their quest is hits him, Hugumki is humbled and even more determined to accomplish his special task. But he is still curious about one thing.

"Do you like being Chief? Is it different?"

"What is different is that all of a sudden you feel like you are all alone."

"Why."

"Because everybody starts acting different around you."

"Ahh."

4

When Hugumki, barely visible inside his blanket, and Bear, who is wearing only his breechcloth and deerskin shirt reenter the village, the scene before them is one of jubilant chaos.

The younger women are wearing their colorful ceremonial clothes; the men are relaxing inside their favorite ponchos. Scattered about in clusters, the older villagers have their multi-colored blankets draped over their shoulders to keep them warm in the crisp morning air. In small groups they are all milling around each boy offering them advice and tokens for their upcoming test.

The girls of the village, including Squash Blossom and her friends, Kiete and Rain, shyly stand off to the side of the boisterous crowd. They too want to see the boys one last time before they become men. Their long shiny hair has been freshly combed and they are all wearing their fancy dance clothes of reds, yellows, and blues: a cotton shirt tucked into a long skirt and a colorful shawl. Around their delicate young necks hang the shell necklaces that visitors from afar had brought for special occasions like this. When they start shuffling along with the crowd as everyone starts heading toward the outer courtyard, you can hear the light tinkling of the copper bells they are wearing around their ankles.

When the noisy crowd enters the larger courtyard, the teens are eventually given enough room so that they can start getting in a row to receive their blessings.

Two Bows glances impatiently at Hugumki. "Will we ever get going?"

"Only when you are fully blessed and extra ready to leave," Hugumki replies with a mischievous grin on his face.

Two Bows stands out by the way he carries his tall, lean, muscular body, and his penetrating black eyes. His eyes are open, honest, and intense. A face assured. His posture bears the confidence of someone who will spend a good portion of his life scouting for danger or hunting for something to kill. Right now he is puzzled and intrigued by Hugumki's last words which have brought back the tickle of a memory, he can't quite recall.

Ista, having trouble keeping quiet while his furry friend Rock once again jumps and slobbers all over him, smiles up at the taller, imposing, Ah Ki Wami. Ah Ki Wami, next to him in line, just silently glares back down at him as they all try their best to reverently wait on Che Wah.

Che Wah, the elder.

Che Wah, the medicine man.

Che Wah, the interpreter of dreams.

Che Wah, the bad barber/haircutter.

Before long, Che Wah, whose face looks even more worn than the surrounding landscape slowly enters the courtyard wearing his colorful feathered headdress. Che Wah's headdress is made up of bird feathers from the south. It is a symbol of his stature and power in the village. He slowly makes his way over then stands in front of each of the fidgeting-some still shivering-youth for a moment so he can look them over one last time before they leave to start their test, and quest. When he begins to pray for the new day, the crowd finally quiets down.

Si ziane ayagoh.

Ah ho heimi yagoh.

Si zeane ayagoh.

Ah ho heimi yamei.

"Oh giver of life.

Thank you for this life.

Oh giver of life.
Thank you for this day."

He chants four times to the four directions.

When he is finished, Che Wah shuffles over to stand in front of Turtle at the far end of the restless, taut line. "This day, I give you the Bird Blessing from the fast bird that does not fly."

"Blessed be this day.
Blessed be this life.
May you run fast today.
May you run fast for life."

Che Wah chants two times for the two directions they will be taking on their quest.

When he hears those words, Ista can no longer keep quiet. Even as he is being murmured and shushed, Ista and all the others turn toward Turtle knowing full well that Turtle, short and stout, is the slowest runner of them all.

Turtle tries not to pay attention to their teasing looks or noises.

After the verbal blessing has been given, Che Wah puts a small smear of corn pollen on Turtle's nose. Turtle does his best not to giggle or wiggle his nose when Che Wah lightly rubs it with his trembling hand.

Turtle watches Che Wah move on to bless Ah Ki Wami, Ista, and then Ooha, who like usual, is posing in his singer's stance, along with everyone else. When Che Wah is finished, with Hugumki being the last, those that know what is about to happen, prepare to receive their extra encouragement, if such a thing is possible.

The crowd, now numbering eighty or more villagers moves in and surrounds each of the warriors in training, again. Some of the older elders try to hide their latest fears with a tough glint in their eyes. Then, on a hidden cue, most of them start striking the boys where and when they can with the walking/planting sticks that they have been slyly hiding in the folds of their blankets or ponchos.

"Safe journey." Whack.

"Run hard." Whack, whack.

Then they move on to the next one.

"Safe journey." Whack

"Run hard." Whack, whack.

Just when it feels like their young bodies can take no more, as one, the female and male elders raise their sticks high and surprisingly start shouting words of praise at the cringing boys.

"The Chosen!

They are the Chosen!

They will succeed!

They will become men!"

They then all slam their sticks on the ground with an audible smack.

After watching and hearing the elders do that four-times in a row, the newly named Chosen are so worked up and ready to go that they can't help but start uttering eager grunts of anticipation.

Slyly observing from his second story roof, Gray Wolf's ears perk up. "Chosen for what?" he wonders out loud.

Looking as proud as they are sad, the family members of each boy, gently, very gently, hugs and kisses him one more time while saying, "We will see you soon."

Of course, not every one of the Chosen is only saying goodbye to family members. One of them might even break into a song for his true love.

"I will miss you so much Squash Blossom," Ooha gushes, causing Squash Blossom and her clinging friends to titter, and a couple of his nearby friends, to snicker.

"I have something for you to keep you safe on your test," Squash Blossom shyly responds, running her hand through then flipping her long black hair into the sunlight. When she does that, her prominent cheekbones, strong nose, and beautiful bright eyes explain why she has Ooha so smitten.

"I want to sing one last song for you before we leave." Ooha is captivated watching Squash Blossom's hair shimmer and shine.

With a haughty huff she responds, "I know those going. If you sing something to me now they will think it is funny to sing that back to you every day you are gone. Do you want to hear that?"

In the ensuing silence, Rain adjusts her colorful dance shawl as she leans toward Kiete. "Do you think one of them will want to be our mate when they return?"

"I know one will want you. You are pretty and growing up. To most of them I am still a girl. I think that the only one that would ask me is…"

Ooha, who can see the beauty in every female looks at each of them. "You are all beautiful in your own way. Any of my group would be happy to have you as mates when you are ready."

"When you all return after being out in the desert for days, even Gona and Che Wah will look young again," Keite jokes with her face aglow in the morning light.

Seizing his opportunity, Bird, whose mouth suddenly turns as dry as the desert he is about to enter, casually heads toward Kiete. He tries his best to say something clever and heartfelt. Instead, all that comes out of his mouth is a sound that resembles the croak of a frog more than words. With his face on fire, Bird quickly scampers away from the ensuing laughter.

"See what I mean, that is who I was talking about," Kiete laughs to hide the fact that she enjoyed Bird's bumbled attention more than she is ready to reveal to her friends.

After Squash Blossom finishes giving him his gift, Ooha proclaims. "Squash Blossom, you know you are the only one for me."

When he pulls her into his body to whisper in her ear, "Sseee yyoouu ssooooon," Squash Blossom is dealing with feelings that have become so strong lately that it almost feels like a sickness whenever she is around Ooha. And now, after that hug, her feelings have got even stronger, deeper. Then, just like that, the cause of her affliction is leaving on what could be a dangerous and deadly test, if the rumors are true.

Before she loses him in the crowd she stares at Ooha to hold him in her memory. She knows that he must come back to her now, in order, to make himself whole again.

The first thing Deerhead notices is encroaching shadows, three abreast that cut off the light, an unexpected eclipse.

Three heavy pounding steps in unison. Then three more.

Same stride.

Same attitude.

Same purpose.

Keep Deerhead in their sights in more ways than one. Buffalo is in the middle with Star and One Water on each side of her. Each of them is wearing…

Is that sheer terror that washes over Deerhead's face when he catches the flash of red across their left shoulders?

No, it can't be! The red sash of courtship.

Deerhead tries to quickly get away only to have his new sandal slide a little instead.

"I already told you I am not ready for a mate yet," he grouses. "And not three at once."

His dark eyes start searching for the safety of Hugumki's side.

As Deerhead makes his quick escape, the maidens faces shows how each of them feel about the one that barely got away.

One Water's pretty, oval face reveals patience and experience. "I will be waiting when you get back." she calls after him, hands on her swaying hips. With a sound somewhere between a purr and a snarl she adds, "By the time he gets back, I will be his dream."

Star's wide, fifteen-year-old face cannot hold anymore sadness and she is trying her best. She looks as if she will never have another chance at love. Ever.

"With Deerhead, I would always have had fresh meat," she mournfully says. Then, just like that, her face breaks into a smile. "Maybe I should try Two Bows instead."

She sets her sights on the tall scout if she can spot him in the crowd before he leaves.

Buffalo, who looks like a walking doorway filled with her beautiful self, pats Star's shoulder, puckers up her face in a frown, snorts, then kicks some dirt in the direction Deerhead took.

"Did I do good? Did we scare him?" Buffalo double shakes her shakes with laughter because she had just come along for the fun of it.

From a distance, it appears as if Deerhead is racing Che Wah as they each seek out Hugumki's side.

Scanning the crowd for Bear, Hugumki is surprised to see Che Wah quickly heading toward him. The old, medicine man is almost breathless as he roughly whispers, "We need to talk when you get back. I need your help but now is not the right time," Che Wah turns to see Deerhead approaching, "I must go now. Have a safe journey."

Hearing the urgency in his voice and seeing the worry in the old medicine man's eyes, Hugumki knows that when he returns he will do all he can to help Che Wah, regardless of what kind of problem or problems he is having.

With all the commotion going on around him, Hugumki fails to notice that someone he does not like has observed the worried Che Wah and him whispering together.

It is Thornotse, better known as Thorn, whose mean scrunched up face shows that she is more than willing to live up to everything her nickname implies. She is Gray Wolf's mate and she is with child. Sad to say, her condition does not seem to be making her any more caring or loving. As she rushes, the best she can, to find Gray Wolf, she looks like she could use more than a spiritual cleansing in the river.

While everyone's family members and friends finish up with their teary goodbyes, Bear and Hugumki start checking to make sure that each of the Chosen has properly packed for a test that will last much longer than they expect it to.

There's a mid-sized pack containing clothes, bedding, and food for each of the younger ones: Bird, Turtle, Ista and Sky Eye. They also have two empty boto's and one flint knife each.

The older ones also have their larger packs filled with clothes, a blanket or two, and more dried food. They are bringing along their two favorite bows as well as a small quiver of arrows, and a couple of walking spears to be shared among them along with two empty botto's and a flint knife. They are, Ooha, Ah Ki Wami, Rabbit, Deerhead, Two Bows, and Hugumki.

In addition, all ten have their zumis and medicine pouches in which they have various potions, remedies, and tokens for whatever they may encounter in the harsh and unpredictable desert. In their pouches they have one thing that may be surprising but is very necessary. It is mint leaves to help keep their breath fresh. Since they don't have toothbrushes yet, they will chew on roughage when needed, to clean their teeth. And believe it or not, some cacti needles make very good toothpicks, if you are very, very careful with your tooth picking. Each of them also has some dried-out yucca root, which is their soap once it is mashed up and mixed with water, when they can find it. They also have the smaller pack filled with cloth which is now folded and buried at the bottom of their packs. Why? Only Hugumki still knows the real reason and he has not said anything about it, so far.

In front of Ooha, Hugumki stops and laughs. "Do you want the whole desert and all of the legends to hear us coming?" he teases, bending down to remove a tinkler from Ooha's ankle. They both know it is from Squash Blossom, but the upcoming test is not the time or place to be wearing something that makes any kind of noise.

After spending time with his family, Sky Eye waits for one more goodbye. Finally, in his ear, he hears the voice he has been expecting.

"Have a safe journey Sky Eye. I can't wait for you to get back so that you can tell me about all the things you see and experience. I am a little jealous of you because I have never been to the…," Cansake abruptly stops talking then starts coughing to cover up what he almost said by accident. He then winks at Sky Eye, gives him a hug, and starts walking away while looking skyward exclaiming, "The stars, the stars, it's full of stars."

Sky Eye smiles watching Cansake wobble away.

Rabbit and Ista shake their heads in bewilderment. "He is so strange," Ista laughs.

5

Taking a private moment to change out of their heavier clothes, the boys, glowing with the blessed light of youthful anticipation, regroup, then silently signal to each other that they are ready. At last it is time to leave and begin their test. Out of all of them, Hugumki is still the only one that knows it is really a quest. A long hard quest across the perilous desert for singing stones.

As one, they conceal their medicine pouches and zumis under their ponchos. The heavier deerskin clothes or blankets that they were wearing after they got out of the river have been stored away in their bulging packs which look like they could burst open at any moment.

After tucking their knives into their buffalo leggings they start helping each other put on their packs. Once loaded, they check each other's straps to make sure that the yucca fiber bindings are snug and secure and they throw their empty botos over their shoulders so that they are within easy reach when they get to the river. They will strap them on later when they are full. Since Two Bows is their best hunter and scout, and Deerhead is their tracker, they have been honored by being the first to carry the two walking spears they are taking with them.

In each of the Chosen's faces you can see a mixture of caution and outright excitement, tempered by determination.

Now ready in mind, body, and spirit, they head to the edge of the village. Not one of them voices out loud what they all can't help but wonder deep down inside. *Will I ever pass this way again?*

As they start on their life-changing journey they can feel all the different eyes gazing upon them. Many appear sad, some glad, and one lofty hidden pair seems quite mad. They belong to a woman standing in a shadow intently watching the preparations that have been going on down below. She has concealed herself on a nearby roof top that is three rooms high.

Of an unknown age, is she ignored, unwanted, or simply unseen?

She appears to be all alone, but in her harried mind, she is surrounded by talkative spirits which she thinks of as her invisible friends. When the Chosen start to silently leave the village and head out into the vast desert for their test, all her friends begin discussing who is going along.

Turtle, Turtle, Turtle, she thinks. *What a perfect name for someone so slow and round. Is there any way he can make it? I know he won't. He can't, can he?*

Squawk, squawk, little Bird. Too small and fragile for what lies ahead. Do any of you think he has a chance? I see a broken wing in his future.

Ista, the funny little one with that crooked smile. Before long they will get tired of your foolish games.

I eye Sky Eye, hehehei, You think you are so smart with that long face and your elder ways. Will you see the things that happen around you or will you just keep your eyes to the sky, Sky Eye?

Ooha, oh oh yes. Doesn't he have the sweetest voice? Not yet big, but he is so pretty. Will you only sing instead of helping. They won't like that very much.

Run Rabbit run. Too mixed up inside. With his special body and ways, can he take it? He will never make it. That's what we all say about the lazy one.

Hahe haha

With the spirits flying free in her mind she is having so much fun making her predictions.

A little mountain called Deerhead. He is so thick and strong, will he lead them wrong?

Ah Ki Wami, mean, mean. He has a face like a vulture and don't forget about that scar. Still, we will leave you alone so you can burn in your own fire.

One bow, Two Bows. Thin, tall, but so strong, and those eyes, those beautiful eyes. Will you take them to faraway places? Hunter said this is the special time.

Hugumki. our next chief? We miss you already.. Does Che Wah need your help too?"

"Don't look up here at me," she unexpectedly yells at those passing below. "I am waiting on Hunter to return,"

"Watch out!" Ah Ki Wami jumps backwards, and sideways, in one quick motion.

Two Bows glances up, "I don't know what is scarier. The way she is looking at us or her spit falling like rain on us."

With the love and well wishes from most of the villagers filling their hearts, the Chosen are drawn together into a tight group. As one they begin to leave their village, ready to face everything the desert can and will test them with.

Oh no. It looks like a very important member of the group is missing. Or is he? He is usually around but not always seen. His sandals are already packed because he is also one of the Chosen. But where is he?

Hugumki whistles. *Esan. Where are you? It's time to go.*

6

In a flash, Esan, the color of night is leading the Chosen and a small group of younger boys: Little Bean, Willow, River, and Jatz, along with their furry friends on the path leading away from the village. Is Esan in front because he is excited to be the one picked to come along, or because he has two extra legs?

Esan's bark can say hello in the friendliest of ways or it can be a warning to stay away unless you want to lose something precious, and probably, irreplaceable. He is also very smart, strong, tough, and loyal which is why he was picked over all the other dogs of the village to come along as a member of the Chosen.

When the noisy group reaches the river they slowly start heading north. They are walking on the path that runs along the village side of the flowing water. A path that holds many pleasant memories but is now leading them away from home, which for some of them, will be for the first time.

"How long will we be gone Deerhead?" Little Bean asks his big brother. "If you let me come I can carry things for you."

Deerhead gestures around, "We will be gone as long as it takes, but you are too little to join us."

With a snot speckled face and scratchy voice, Jatz, who has a much longer name but still a small frame for his age, looks up at Ista and asks,"

Will you be a man when you get back? Will you have some hair on your face and a stronger voice?"

"My voice is already like a man's," Ista squeaks.

Willow, like always, is paying attention to everything but is as quiet as a mouse, or he would be, if he didn't have hiccups from being so excited.

"Will you hunt bear and buffalo Deerhead?" River asks, touching one of the bows.

"When I am hungry, nothing will be safe out there River."

Sky Eye reaches over and runs his fingers through River's thick, uncut, black hair. Apparently, he is missing his long hair more than he had let on.

7

Before they know it, the boys, some talking, laughing, shouting, all of them making noise, reach the area where the upcoming spring floods will leave good ground for the village to grow its crops of corn, squash, beans, onions, tomatoes, cotton, and pumpkins, etc. With its protruding land area this is where the Chosen will cross the river.

First, Hugumki turns to the excited young boys tagging along and tells them that they have come far enough. It is time for them to head back to the village. River, Jatz and Willow immediately stop walking even though their faces hold a pleading look. They have no real desire to go out into the desert without their mothers, yet.

But Little Bean, who is dressed just like Deerhead in his umber-colored poncho, leggings, and breechcloth begs to go along.

" Deerhead, I got my hair cut just like yours. I'm ready for the test. I really am," Little Bean starts to sob.

Deerhead smiles as he looks down at his brother whose hair has not fared well under the shaky hands of Che Wah.

"I think you wiggled around too much."

After one gasping sob too many, Deerhead takes a deep breath and pulls Little Bean off to the side. He gently squeezes his brother's shoulders then wipes Little Bean's damp, puffed up cheeks.

"I know you want to go with us."

"Why can't I?" Little Bean's eyes fill with tears again.

"Because when you came back you would be a man. Are you sure you are ready for that?"

Little Bean reaches under his poncho and gives his bear cub zumi a squeeze in the hope that it will work its magic on his big, but not so scary brother, at least to him. "I am ready to be a man."

"Are you really sure?"

"Yes." Little Bean takes a swipe at his runny nose.

"That means you can't play all day, or eat food whenever you are hungry. When you get back there will be lots of things that need to be done in the village."

"They don't let me eat all the time like I used to. What would I have to do?"

"The planting of the crops. The washing of the walls."

Little Bean bites his quivering lip. "I can't reach very high yet."

Deerhead yawns so wide he almost hurts his jaw. "Just thinking of all the hard work ahead makes me tired." He does not mention hunting: he knows that will just start Little Bean crying all over again because Little Bean loves to hunt. Just ask the ground squirrels that have learned to seek cover whenever Little Bean and his small, but fearsome bow are lurking about.

A shadow flies across Little Bean's damp face. Deerhead looks up and sees brother eagle soaring wild and free on the wind.

A good luck sign for sure.

He turns back to Little Bean who is tugging on his arm.

"Deerhead, I will stay." He throws his arms around Deerhead's thick legs and holds tight.

"That's a good idea Little Bean. Have fun with your friends while we are gone. You will be a man soon enough." Deerhead smooths Little Bean's hair the best he can. "I will miss you too. Now let's go back to the others."

When he sees Deerhead, Hugumki again tells the younger boys that they must return to the village, but if they learn their lessons well, before they know it, it will be time for their own coming-of-age test.

What he does not tell them is that it might be a long time before this special kind of quest is undertaken again, if ever.

Both groups tell each other again. "See you soon," while Esan and a couple of his furry friends sniff their goodbyes.

After watching to make sure that the younger boys are safely heading back to the village, Hugumki utters the simple words that will eventually be more loathed than loved. "Eyes ahead, eyes around, let's go."

8

From the moment they start crossing the shallow river the Chosen seem different. Is it the way they are moving through the water? Their tone of voice as they call out to each other? Or is it simply the intense determined look inhabiting their black shimmering eyes? As if the water itself has transformed them, they start to resemble young warriors, even Bird, before he almost falls over in the light current.

Once they reach the other side feeling more energized than cold, they pause by the sandy area that they love to use for swimming during the hot season. It is the perfect place to start filling up their botos without too much mud getting in the water. To every one's surprise Hugumki tells them to fill up both, their botos. When the murmurs start, Hugumki holds up two fingers to stop any question because he wants them to get used to the weight of their two full bottos. When he starts thinking of Che Wah and the real reason for their quest, he also checks to make sure that no one is spying on them, like Gray Wolf, or any of his equally sneaky friends.

Once they start their first and easiest task by the river's edge, some of the Chosen start acting like they already have sore muscles. Or is it more than that?

Flexing his shoulders and legs, "Why do they do that?" Ista asks Two Bows before he starts filling his first boto.

"Who and what?"

"The elders. Why do they try to beat the kani out of us?"

"I know what you mean," Sky Eye agrees. "I think some of them were enjoying it a little too much."

"It seems like they waited a long time to do that," Bird says from the other side of Sky Eye.

Two Bows studies his slightly battered companions. "Were any of you really hurt? Is anything broken?"

"That is another thing, they only hit us where nothing would get hurt," Sky Eye says, while moving a reed out of his way with one hand and dipping his boto with the other.

Hugumki tries to hold back a laugh. "We may be sore for a day or two, but I know all of you could not leave the village fast enough."

"Other than his voice, Turtle's body made the softest sounds," Ista taunts.

"Hoa, you're so funny. Let's see how funny you feel next day when I can't feel it anymore and you will still feel sore where they hit you."

Rabbit stops filling his boto to check his tender body for any visible bruises or marks by pulling his poncho up to his chin. "It must take practice to hit us without really hurting us."

"I wonder, will we be like that when we get old?" Sky Eye asks before falling over when his wet sandals stick in the sand.

"Like what?" Bird laughs, trying not to laugh.

"Just waiting around for something exciting to happen. Now I have, to move or wait for the water to settle."

"I am hoping right now that not very much happens. Turtle don't push Ista in the water! See what I mean?" Hugumki shakes his head in Sky Eye's direction. "Squeeze the air out first so they fill up faster," he suggests upon noticing that some of the others are having trouble filling their botos. "And don't forget, once they are full, make sure you tie them tight so that they don't leak too much. Now that I have thought about it, the first thing I will change when I become chief is that part of the ceremony where the elders give out their extra, whatever you want to call it. There is no reason I can think of as to why it takes that to get somebody ready for this dangerous test. Is there?" All at once nine unkept heads are bobbing around like ducks.

After a quick glance around, Ah KI Wami quietly asks Rabbit. "Did you see the twins before we left home?"

Taking a moment to stretch out his long neck, Rabbit looks more like a brown, graceful swan than a duck at the water's edge. "They must have still been sleeping or probably fighting somewhere like they always do." Rabbit's face clouds over when a worrisome thought enters his mind. "Aren't they young for you to be interested in them?"

Ah KI Wami's narrow face almost flashes what could be called a smile. "Don't be foolish. I am just curious about them. They look the same on the outside but are so different on the inside. Ash is always so happy and Meechi can almost seem evil sometimes, but I have never seen one without the other."

"I know what you mean," Two Bows agrees. "It Is almost like they have the good and bad spirit of one person split up into two bodies."

Noticing an odd movement next to him, Ooha looks at Ista to be sure that he saw what he thought he saw.

Feeling Ooha's eyes on him, Ista takes his finger out of his mouth. "Now that they are softer from the water, I am just getting my fingernails short and ready for the test."

Ooha checks his own nails. "How about your toenails. Are they ready too?"

"I did those earlier," Ista looks down at his sharp looking toes. "Can't you tell?"

A slight groan of disgust escapes Rabbit's lips. To him, using your mouth for personal nail grooming instead of a knife, especially on the feet, is something only a wild animal would do. "Are you some kind of desert beaver?" he asks under his breath.

"A what?" Ista bares his teeth.

Once he has filled his first boto, Bird pauses to scratch his nose. His eyes bulge out when he realizes he may have just done something to seal his fate, and not in a good way. "Tell me that I did not just wipe all the pollen off my nose?"

"Don't worry, I still see a little bit there," Ooha says.

Sky Eye thinks a moment before asking. "Would it really matter anyway?"

Rabbit looks at all of them warily. "My Brother…"

Hugumki knows they will have plenty of time to talk about those kinds of things, eventually, so he interrupts Rabbit. "For right now, anything that can help us, will help us."

Turtle closes his eyes. Softly he says the word that cuts each of them to their very core. "Home. I have never left home before."

With something to think about besides their sore bodies, they go back to filling up their botos.

When everyone is finished, they climb to the top of the barren riverbank. They take one last look at Flat Top butte, their adobe village, and the majestic wind sculpted, red tinted landscape that surrounds their home in all directions.

In some ways it is wide open terrain, but the massive formations scattered about also gives them a sense of place. Even though they will eventually head southwest, it will be on the other side of Flat Top butte. So, this really is their last look at home for a while.

The desert, depending on where you look, may seem flat from a distance, but that is just an illusion. The Chosen will have many ups and downs to contend with on their journey and for some impassible areas: due to height, drop, or obstacle they will have to take or make a detour.

The desert of the Hohokam is made up of many things: Mountains, mesas, buttes, plateaus, and cacti in all shapes and sizes. What is most abundant though is dirt and rock. Lots and lots of rock. In the desert there are rocks of all sizes. Some of them are small enough to balance on the tip of a finger while others are the size of a mountain, because they are the mountain.

It is a terrain that at first glance looks like it has not changed in thousands of years. The legends say that even with the passage of time, it is more than just the land that has stayed the same. Could the stories of flying ghosts, roaming monsters, and even the land of giants, be true?

While beautiful and vast, the desert is also an extremely unforgiving place. It is where even the smallest mistake can cost a person dearly because it can and probably will lead to certain death.

Since they are all children of the desert, the Chosen take a moment to silently think about those things, and more. Sky Eye, head held high, is the first to speak. With a barely discernable tremor in his voice, he says, "Gumki, I am happy you are our leader. You will keep us safe and all of us will learn many new things."

Some of the others also start offering their words of praise and encouragement. Hugumki smiles, accepts their words, then looks off into the distance at the large mountains that are standing there: massive stony obstructions. He knows that before long they will be heading right at them.

Recalling the real reason for their quest, Hugumki is soon filled beyond full with pure purpose and raw determination. With his eye's gleaming like little suns, Hugumki's calls out, "Eyes ahead, eyes around, let's go!" Then Hugumki, the specially chosen leader of the Chosen, for his first act as leader, starts leading them all in the wrong direction. North.

With their brown face's full of adventure and excitement, not longing, they hang the boto straps from their shoulders and break into a slow trot. They want to warm up their muscles and once again test the various bindings that are tethering the supplies to their bodies.

Once they have settled on an easy pace, the desert is treated to the sound of clacking sandals as they head for the massive Old Man butte, in the distance.

Approaching some large rocks, they are unaware they are being watched by a pair of hidden eyes. Luckily for them, they belong to Horn, who is Bird's father. He is sitting motionless among the rocks, overlooking the trail.

Hugumki and Two Bows are in the lead, "This will show us and them how much they really want to come along." Hugumki looks back to see how the others are doing.

Moving with a curious gait, Sky Eye and Ooha are trying to keep up.

"My sandal straps are rubbing against my foot." Sky Eye starts hopping on one foot so he can inspect one of his new sandals.

"Mine is too."

Just behind them are Ista, Turtle, and Bird. Their young bodies are flowing, rippling along the trail. Their voices sound like they are bursting with more energy than the desert will ever be able to contain, then again.

"My legs are starting to feel tired Bird. I need too slow down so I can drink some more water." Turtle slows down to wipe some crumbs off his chin and sweat off his forehead, then almost gets knocked over.

After dodging Turtle, Ah Ki Wami and Rabbit are side by side, a study in contrasts. Ah Ki Wami is alert and wary, his eyes searching out unseen dangers Will he spot Horn before the others do?

Rabbit's slouch shows how much fun he is having already. Moving his shoulders around, he says, "This poncho feels different than my old one."

"Good or bad?"

"Not sure yet."

Doing his best to keep an eye on everybody, Deerhead knows that before long, his skills will be needed at the front of the line. "Come on Turtle, keep up or you will be left behind. I am not a child watcher," he mumbles while wiping some sweat from his elbow.

A drop of sweat here. A drop of sweat there. Little do any of the Chosen realize that within days, those droplets will turn into a salty torrent.

Even though he is barely off to the side of the trail, Horn is practically invisible because he blends in so well with the rocks he has hidden among. Once they finally spot him, just before they pass him by, he flashes a quick greeting. He feels a flush of pride and a bit of worry for Bird and the rest of his group. Horn knows that once they recross the river to reach Old

Man butte, after they use a semi-secret pass to get there, they will go behind it and set up their camp for the night. Once they leave his sight it will just be the ten of them along with Esan, trying to survive the desert, and everything that is out there eagerly waiting for them, not all with good intentions.

Horn is also thankful that he got to spend some time with Bird, past day. While others may doubt his son, Horn knows that Bird can do what needs to be done once he searches for and finds his inner strength, regardless of what his hovering mother always says.

9

1ˢᵗ day – Early afternoon

The curious crow is so curious that he has left his flock behind. Gliding with the wind, he casts his moving shadow on the red hued landscape below. To his surprise, he hears sounds that he has never heard before. Danger? A meal?

Following his ears, he drops lower and sees a staggered line of encumbered brown bodies. Along with a black furry one, they are noisily working their way through a tight passageway between a mesa and a massive piece that broke off eons ago. *This is not a good place to be a walker,* crow, crows to himself as he skims between the walls that are gleaming with moisture.

One of the smaller bodies vanishes. Does he really? No, there he is. He has wedged himself into a tight dark crevice like an umbra.

It looks like he is waiting in ambush for someone else in his group. Slowly a rounder form comes into view from around a walled edge on the trail that is not much of a trail at all.

Brother crow drifts lower to get a better look at what is about to happen.

The body that is waiting quickly jumps out at the other one. With a startled cry, the rounder one jerks back in surprise then falls onto the pack that is on his back.

A strong, impatient voice rings out, sending its echo booming along the passageway. "That's enough Ista!" Hugumki scolds while trying to decide what to do with his hands other than wringing Ista's or his own neck in frustration. "Are you good Turtle? Do you need help to get back up?"

"I'm all right. I was surprised, that's all. I did not see Ista in time and he scared me." Turtle's rosy cheeks are burning from more than exertion. "My legs are just a little tired and I wasn't ready."

Approaching Turtle from behind, Ah Ki Wami snaps at him. "You were not ready at all, were you? Are you ready for anything? I did not see what happened here but I would have been more ready than you were for Ista getting you back."

Turtle tries to look as innocent as he can.

"You know, after that water trick you played on him earlier. Did you really think you could pretend to spray him with water by mistake and he would not try to get back at you when he could?" Upon rounding the bend, Ah Ki Wami could immediately tell from the look on Ista's face that he was also involved in whatever mischief had caused Turtle to fall over.

Turtle slowly gets up as his pride drops lower. With a stammer, he asks, "Wha, what do you mean?" while trying the best he can to shake some mud off his poncho.

"When you play a childish game, you must expect a childish game in return," Deerhead snap rolls his fingers in unison, sounding like a stern grasshopper rubbing a forewing.

"What we are doing is not for children," Hugumki reminds them. Looking up at the mesa on one side and the sheer wall of the broken off piece on the other, has put an even deeper frown on his face. The walls enclosing them are many men high.

"We will keep moving until we reach a flat open area where we can talk about this. Eyes ahead, eyes around, let's go."

By the tone of his voice and the looks on the younger one's faces, Hugumki is sure that he will not have to warn them again to behave. At least not until they all had a talk together. Realizing some of them are barely more than children, he knows it is a good idea to get his mind on something else. "Hoa, Two Bows, I was thinking about new names again and I don't know who named him Deerhead, but they must have been thinking of that funny looking big-headed deer with the curled horns." Two Bows and Hugumki look ahead at Deerhead and take in his large square head swinging back and forth that is framed by an equally squared off, ragged haircut. Feeling their looks, Deerhead turns so they see his close-set eyes topped by two bushy eyebrows that can transform into a slightly scary one if he furrows them just right.

"I know what you mean," Two Bows says with a laugh. "Before long, we should be out of here and then we will find a place where we can talk about everything."

Two Bows turns to check on Ooha, who is bringing up the rear of the line. Whenever the Chosen walk in a single file there will always be somebody assigned the duty of wiping clear any sign of their having passed through. Like anything, some of them will be better at it than others. Even though this time it is just practice, Two Bows is going to make sure that Ooha is doing this very important job properly and not just singing and thinking about himself, as he is prone to do, as he walks along. Taking turns, it will give each of them the opportunity to identify, read, then obliterate their footprints on the many different, kinds of trails, they will be taking on their quest.

∾

"I do not believe how hot I am right now," Rabbit softly says from his seat on one of the toadstool shaped rocks that are spread around the area they are taking a break in. Gracefully as he can, he tries to fan himself while not flinging his sweat everywhere.

"Why are you being so quiet Rabbit? Are you scared?" Bird asks, taking off his pack.

"I just feel like I am out of place right now. Give me a little time and I will be good."

"Don't anybody get him started or he will never shut up," Ooha jokes under his breath.

Scanning the area, Sky Eye ponders out loud, "It is strange how all of these flat rocks are here, but nowhere else that I can see."

"We are all sweating Rabbit even though it is not hot at all." Two Bows takes off his pack before holding the walking spear out in front of him. "None of us are in hunting shape. I wonder if any of us could run down a deer now?"

Hugumki is starting to realize that watching out for the younger ones might prove to be way harder than he ever imagined. Especially if they did not try to help him help them.

Knowing he needs to burn off some energy, Hugumki takes the spear from Two Bows startled grip. What is even more startling is the imploring look he gives his lifelong friend.

"What," Two Bows looks at the spear in Hugumki's hand and the look in his eyes, then understands. "Ista, Bird, Turtle, you too Sky Eye, sit down by Rabbit. I need to talk to you."

Once he has the spear in hand, back foot set, with his arm and shoulders turned, Hugumki starts feeling better. For some reason, holding the spear has always made him feel more secure.

Ah Ki Wami can't resist the allure of weaponry, so he walks to where Hugumki has found an open area to move around. "Are you going to throw it Gumki?"

"No. Might break the tip."

"If you can't throw it, then what good is it?"

"You can always do this." Hugumki starts to rapidly jab out a larger version of Ah Ki Wami with the spear, turning it into nothing but a deadly blur.

"That was fast Hugumki."

Deerhead walks over with his spear and does the same thing, not as fast but maybe even more deadly the way he is brutally hacking his way through the air.

"Is that how you attack a bear," Ah Ki Wami pretends he is mortally wounded.

"That was more like trying to fight it off," Deerhead scoffs. "I am still trying to learn how to be easy with the spear, not fight with it."

After everything he just saw, Ah Ki Wami knows. "I still have a lot to learn about the spear," he tells anyone listening and his inner self.

Chewing his lips and keeping his head down, Turtle does his best to stay unnoticed because he knows what's coming next, and it does.

"Turtle, instead of playing games, you should try to keep up with us better," Two Bows stares at Turtle who starts putting on his poncho to cover his trembling body.

His pride may still be burning, but Turtle can tell that it has been getting cooler the more the sun has dropped.

"I don't want to keep waiting for you or anybody else. We have just started our test and you and your friends are already acting like children," Two Bows scolds as he glares at Turtle, Ista, Bird, and Sky Eye, who all look like they are barely able to keep their heads up.

Whether their heads and bodies are hanging from exhaustion, shame, or simply trying to hide their anger, it is hard to tell. Their brown bodies are looking so spineless it's as if they are slowly melting into their rocky seats.

"If you are not ready," Two Bows continues around a gulp of water from his boto, "maybe we should send some of you home right now." Reaching down to pet the attentive Esan, he asks, "You don't see Esan playing games, do you?"

A leaderless murder of noisy crow's fly overhead mocking all below.

Once he feels better, Hugumki approaches Two Bows from behind and gives him two quick clicks with his mouth. When Two Bows turns toward Hugumki, is that a smile or the sunlight that flashes in his fiery eyes?"

After squeezing Two Bows arm, Hugumki walks over to stand right in front of the younger ones clustered together. Without even the hint of a smile, he looks at them, once, twice, then starts talking.

"As Two Bows said, we have barely begun this journey. Next day, I will check to see how those that are still with us are doing." After a long pause. "Don't worry, nobody is going to be sent home right now. Next day is a long time away and anything can happen before then. That is why I am talking to you now. Some of you are young, but this is not the kind of journey to act like a child on. What I mean is that some of you must act older than your years. The elders had many talks before we were all chosen, to be the Chosen." Ista looks around, not sure if he should laugh or not. "I will trust in their judgment."

Before anyone can start asking questions, Hugumki continues. "We all like to play. Show me someone that doesn't play games and I will show you someone that is very sad. There is nothing wrong with having fun. How many times have we all seen old Mountain chasing Tre Ne down into their room laughing and grabbing. It does your spirit good to let your inner child keep living. But there is a time and a place for those things. Look around you. Yes, look around." And they do. "Does this look like a place for childish games? What would we do if somebody got hurt, or worse, for something that is so foolish out here? We are on our own now. No one will be out here to help us out if something goes wrong. I know you all can do it or you would not have been picked to come along. Just don't ever forget that everything we do can easily become a reason for life or death out here. Do any of you remember what I said before," Hugumki pauses to look around at everybody noisily sucking from their botos as if their lives depend on it. "We have to start getting used to making our water last longer than we are right now."

"Why Gumki?" Turtle asks, continuing to stare at the ground.

"We will be going places where there will be no water for days. So drink now but start getting ready for that in your heads. Now let's get going. We will not stop again until we are behind Old Man because we have already stopped two times for food, and I can't believe, rest already.

We will wait until we make camp before we eat again. If you are already feeling tired, remember this day is the shortest part of our test. We must always be on guard, so start being quieter than we were in the pass. Eyes ahead, eyes around, let's go."

Warily standing up, Bird whispers to Ista through his clenched jaw, "They had better not talk to us like that during the whole test."

Ista loosens up his small fists, "I know."

"At least Gumki's talk was short," Sky Eye says, rolling his eyes out of sight of any of the older Chosen.

1st day – Nighttime

In a cold, light breeze, a small fire is frantically fighting with itself to stay alive. Around the dancing flames eleven bodies are squeezed in tight. Hardly a sound is heard coming from the small camp near the base of Old Man butte.

There is no laughter, shouting, snoring, or growling. There isn't even any tossing or turning.

Other than the occasional sizzle from little wings that venture to close to the flames, the only sound is the quiet exhalation of breath as the Chosen try to catch up on air and rest.

After a hard day of running and walking through their rugged and colorful desert homeland, even their faces are free of emotion. Only peaceful slumber rests there because they are oblivious to the eye shine from the various animals that stop by now and then to see who or what has the nerve to come into their territory.

Outside the reach of their meager firelight, the desert sounds more than alive. Many of its residents, big or small, are doing their loudest to make their presence known. At the same time, lots of others use mimicry or other tricks so that they do not give their position away.

It all adds up to a cacophony of cries, warbles, clicks, screams, screeches, buzzing, rustling, and caterwauling that all blends together into one living, raucous sound. The warriors in training may be resting, but the desert is awake and waiting with all of its night-time creatures starving for a meal. Some of them may be patient, but most are very, very, desperate.

A falling star burns its way across the sky accompanied by a low growl and the sound of a struggle. So early in their quest, are the Chosen already in danger of becoming a late-night snack?

"Are you awake?" Two Bows, quietly questions the night.

"I think so," Deerhead softly answers back as his eyes pop open to a familiar scene. A brilliant sky overhead. A low fire underneath.

"Do you hear that?"

"Yes, but I can't tell what it is."

"Sounds like something is trying to drag something."

The blood starts flowing through Deerhead's thick head. "Or pulling. Trying to take something away."

"Our packs!" They both shout.

Hearing their excited voices, several exhausted bodies try to stir.

Ooha reaches for his pack. It's not there! He quickly realizes he must get everyone to move a little faster because he knows he is not walking past the edge of the firelight, alone. "Wake up everybody! Make as much noise as you can!"

"Why!" they all yell as loud as they can.

"I think something grabbed one of our packs."

Deerhead tries his best to see past the edge of the firelight.

The Chosen start scrambling to their feet as they all start checking to make sure that their precious packs are still where they left them.

Ooha walks to the edge of the firelight, his eyes searching in vain for his missing pack. The fire is comforting, but not near bright enough to calm his nerves. As he stands there for a precious moment in hesitation, he feels like he is shrinking right in front of everyone. How can he ever admit to them he is afraid of the dark?

No. He must conquer his fear. With no food, no clothes, he would have to head home early in defeat. Somehow finding a lone drop of courage, Ooha steps out of the circle of light.

"I see it," he yells triumphantly.

Hugumki keeps Ooha's shadow in sight. "Don't forget to keep your pack closer to your head than your feet," he tells everyone.

Ooha bends down and runs his finger along the ground. "You are right. It feels like something with long claws was trying to get an easy meal by stealing my pack.

Everybody can hear his deep sigh of relief when he bends over to pick up his pack and head back to the safety of the firelight.

If any of the Chosen had been under the false impression that their test was going to be all fun and games, reality has just shouted at them otherwise. Each of their astonished faces show that those illusions have been dragged out and abandoned in the desert quicker than Ooha's pack was.

Hugumki observes everyone a moment before saying, "Do you understand now what I mean by how one mistake can be one mistake to many. Next day, we will talk again about how careful we must be at all times. From now on, the one whose duty it is to spread the azee must make sure there are no gaps in the circle."

By the looks on their faces, Hugumki knows that all of them, including himself, are going to have a hard time falling back asleep. To his own dismay, he channels his frustration in an unusual direction. "Good job Esan. Can you try to let us know before something happens, not afterwards?"

Ista starts to defend Esan, but remembers that Esan is not really Hugumki's dog, so he keeps quiet.

Esan's sad face looks like he is thinking, *All the running around today has made me tired too. I couldn't help it.* His tail wags as if to say, *Sorry. I will do better from now on.*

The noisy desert carries on and they all lie back down after Deerhead adds more wood to the fire, then nervously listen, and wait for sleep to take them away from their wildly running imaginations, and into its hopefully, secure embrace.

Before long, the fire starts consuming the fresh fuel then bursts forth in a large flame that momentarily sets the night ablaze.

"I am glad that went up or some of us would still be rolling to get out of the way," Hugumki laughs.

Just another danger they must learn to deal with and survive, on their own.

10

2nd day – High sun

After a late start that morning, due to their sleeping in till sunrise, the Chosen have been running to make up for lost time. Their goal is to be by the river before nightfall and they have been heading southwest over uneven terrain to pick it up again.

A bright white Father Sun is beating the shadows straight down across the desert, including those of a group of now resting runners.

Out of all of them, one looks more slumped over and miserable than the others.

After a glance up at the vivid blue cloudless sky and then back at Ooha, Bird tries to comfort their singer. With a face almost as downcast as the one he is commenting on, "Don't be sad Ooha" he says. "You will see Squash Blossom soon and then she can be your mate for the rest of your life."

Ooha's smile is a forlorn one. "I can't help feeling this way because she has become so beautiful and I already miss her so much."

"I wish I had someone to miss like that," Bird admits with more than a hint of loneliness in his voice. "I tried to talk to…, oh, it doesn't…"

Sitting back up before he oozes out of his poncho, Ooha confesses, "I did not think I would miss her so soon."

"At least you have someone that likes you. When we get back and I can take a mate when I am ready, I don't know how far I will have to look or go to find one that likes me."

"Women, aren't really that hard to understand," Ooha says. His black eyes, glinting in the bright sunlight, hold a knowing look.

"Then tell me. How do you make girls like you so much?"

"Unless you are a bad person, you can't make a woman do anything she does not want to do."

Deerhead stands up to stretch his tight muscles, then slowly sticks out his tongue. "Listen to the younger ones, they know all about woman."

"Deerhead, is there a secret I should know about?" Bird asks Deerhead's broad back.

"Like this test Little Bird, you learn by doing."

Bird uses his hands to pretend he has an extra-large head when Deerhead walks toward Hugumki who is making sure Esan is getting his share of water. "Thank you Deerhead, that was a lot of help. I am serious Ooha, the girls of the village barely look at me. All they see is a, I don't know what they see."

"When you look into still water Bird, or your mother's shiny thing where you can see yourself, what do you see?"

"Not much." Bird answers with a shrug of his skinny shoulders. "Just little me."

"That is part of your problem. Girls see you as you see yourself. I know I am a great singer and a friend to all the women I know, so that is how they see me."

Bird stands up on his tiptoes and looks at his small brown arms. "I can already feel my muscles growing. Before long, I will be as big as Gumki."

"Until then, there are some things that you should not do."

"Like what?"

"Do you ever hear girls or woman make the body noises that you and Ista like to make?"

"No."

"Then don't make them around them. We all make body noises. You must learn to control yours, because if you don't, it will tell them that you are still a little boy."

Bird puckers his lips. "I will try," he says, before letting loose a water burp that rumbles across the open desert. "I will try harder when there are girls around."

Ista, quickly answers back from his nearby resting spot with one of his own that he can be proud of.

"It's time to go, here comes Hugumki," Turtle announces as he stands and squeezes out some sweat from his headband.

Before long, the intrepid Chosen continue with their life altering test that will take them to places they never could have thought of and give them experiences that will leave them with either sweet dreams or haunting reoccurring nightmares.

From out of the crystal blue, Hugumki's voice rings out, because he is thinking about that night's rest as he rubs his neck. "Don't forget to grab something soft for your head when you see it, or you can use a rock like past night. Hoa."

Bird spins his head around. "There is nothing soft out here."

"Something dead is," Deerhead says with a smirk.

"Uaah," Ista wrinkles his nose in disgust.

Two Bows shakes his head. "Not an animal. A plant, some brush, even a cactus if you remove the thorns."

"You can then put it under your shirt," Hugumki says. "Or if is too cold for that you can roll it up in your breechcloth."

"Uaah," they all say at once and press on.

2nd day – Sundown

One half of the sky is rippling with purple and fire orange clouds. The other has been slowly gathering the gloom. While everyone else is still eating their last meal of the day in the small camp they have finally set up, Hugumki is taking his turn to rinse off in the cold, albeit, refreshing river. After heading in the wrong direction, for misdirection, the day before, they are once again at their rivers edge.

Emerging with the cold water dripping off all parts of his muscular, brown, goose bump covered body, Hugumki does not appear to be someone who has been running and walking for the past two days. That is, unless you were to misread the look in his piercing black eyes, and on his handsome face. The expression he is wearing is not exhaustion, but caused by having to walk into camp and tell everybody what to do, all over again.

With his skin lightly throbbing where his hot blood runs close to the surface, Hugumki waits a moment before putting his clothes back on. He knows it is a good idea to check for anything hungry or mean that might be hiding in them. Once his breechcloth is declared critter free and is securely in place, with his poncho hanging loosely over his shoulders, Hugumki quickly walks barefoot the short distance back to camp, and the fire that is awaiting him with its warm embrace.

Pausing at the edge of the firelight, Hugumki takes a moment to scan the glowing faces of his charges to see how they are doing.

With their recently cut hair still damp from their turns in the river, they look like they are both refreshed and weary at the same time. "Soon enough, they will get used to this," Hugumki quietly whispers with hope in his voice. The only soreness any of them have complained about is in their tired legs. To his surprise, not one of them mentioned anything about any aches or pains from the, what else can we call it, beating, they had received past day.

They all seem to be in good spirits and Ista is in the middle of his big fish story. Knowing how it ends, Hugumki walks over and grabs another handful of the recently cooked fish.

When he sees Hugumki, Ista realizes he does not have a lot of time left before his leader speaks, so he speeds up his tale.

"Turtle was in the right spot. He had the foot-sized fish blocked off. Bird and I were slowly closing in and moving the fish toward Turtle. A big fish we did not see in the water grass swam right into Turtle's stomach as soon as I started the splash dance. They both jumped, and Turtle came out of the water with this big and good fish held high in his hands."

Ista finishes his story by licking his fingers, after taking one more handful out of the unfortunate fish.

Hugumki smiles at Ista before stepping into the circle of firelight. He remains standing and turns to face the others.

"Past night, Wami, you made a good fire. This time, Sky Eye, you have made a good fire. This, night, unlike past night, we will all help keep the fire going when needed."

Ista glances at the small pile of sticks he has collected and wonders if they will be enough to last through the night.

"I mean anyone can add the wood when needed so the fire does not burn out like before. I will soon go over when we can or can't have a fire. Don't forget, when you are done with them, always give the fire stones back to Deerhead. We must not lose them unless you all want to huddle together in one big pile every time it gets cold."

Hugumki waits a moment while everyone tries to shake that image out of their heads.

Sky Eye can't help that he is curious about things that he is not really all that curious about. "Are the fire stones made out of the same thing as our knives?"

"Yes, but they are much stronger and will not fall apart like the knives will if you rub them together too much."

After a glance at everyone, Hugumki continues. "Each of us hold some of the precious powder-the *azee*-in our medicine pouches. As you know, it is a powerful medicine to protect our camp. Bird, when you can, make sure the line is unbroken, but not too thick. It must last for all the nights of our test."

"It makes me sneeze and burns my eyes," Rabbit whispers into the immensity surrounding him.

Turtle rubs his stomach, but not for good luck. It is due to a memory that is also making his mouth water. "I like the azee when it is cooked in stew much better.

Just not too much," Two Bows says with a grin. "Remember when the Early One put all the azee she had been given after harvest into her pot all at once?"

Rabbit arches his brows, "I remember. I was helping her that day and she did it by mistake. She was rushing like she always does."

Laughing out loud for a change, Ah Ki Wami adds, "Nobody could eat more than a taste."

Don't forget," Hugumki reminds, "Gray Wolf tried two big mouthfuls."

"Oah. He tried so hard to keep acting like nothing was wrong until his face turned bright red, and he could not stop choking and running around with his breechcloth flapping every which way as he kept looking around everywhere for more and more water to drink because he was on fire, and I was surprised he did not end up in the river." Two Bows catches his breath, then starts howling with the memory.

"He had to drink so much water to cool down I thought he was in danger of getting too big," Hugumki jabs his finger like he would have liked to have popped Gray Wolf on the spot.

Turning his mind onto something else, Hugumki makes a face then gets serious. "Even with the azee, always check your bedding and clothes before you put them on. Tell me why?"

As one, they all recite the answers while making hand motions,

"Va li tz."

A raised arm and curled hand.

"Ci ce ci ce."

A low arm with fluttering fingers.

"Susinko."

Outstretched hand with wide open scurrying fingers.

"Chewols"

Stepping in place.

Scorpions.

Centipedes.

Spiders / Tarantulas.

Ants.

"Don't forget about the snake that has a nasty attitude," Deerhead makes winding motions with his hands. "If it gets hotter while we are out here, we will have to watch out for them too."

Ah Ki Wami shakes his hand real fast, "At least he comes with a warning rattle." To make his point he adds, "Zzzzzzz."

"Why do the zizis (rattlesnakes) stick their tongues out all the time?" Turtle wants to know.

Two Bows drops his head in thought, "That is how they smell even though they have a nose like you do."

Turtle and Ista both stick out their tongues to see if that will help them smell any better. It doesn't, as far as they can tell.

"They should still be sleeping now but it is always good to watch out for them," Hugumki says as he nods at Deerhead. "Next day, I want Deerhead, Wami, and Ooha to catch enough fish for our first meal, unless you get another big one. Here is more fish for you Esan."

Hugumki points, at the river. "While they are busy there, Two Bows, I want you to head down river with Rabbit and Bird to shoot some birds. I want to see how long the fresh meat we carry with us will last. Take Esan with you and he can scare them out like he did earlier for fun. Two Bows, make sure that no one loses their arrows, and don't forget, after you clean and prepare the birds to hide all that you leave behind.

"Next day, now pay attention, we will be leaving the safety of our river so we can start following the path of Father Sun when he prepares to go on his night journey this season." Hugumki looks in the direction of the setting sun. "Once we cross the river it will almost seem like we are in a different desert because it will not have as many colors. And to those that have wondered, we are not lost or wandering around for fun. Later, I will explain why we have taken the path we have so far and why we must be so careful with our passing. When we are ready to leave we will go back upstream to that dead tree we saw around the last bend so we can cross back over the river. Yes we could cross here," Hugumki quickly says when he catches a look of surprise flash across a glowing face or two. "We will do it because the river may be boiling with anger and much higher because of the melting snow when we return. When we all return, as men!" Hugumki thumps his forearms together. "I want all of us to have had practice crossing the tree and I want to make sure the tree is strong enough to hold us. No one knows how long it has been there but it has been so long that it almost feels like rock. And don't forget, from now on we must keep all the botos full whenever we have enough water to fill them up."

Lit by a cosmic flame, the sky explodes into all the colors that pink has in its palette. Before their reverent eyes, Father Sun drops further then quickly disappears to end his day.

Ista's eyes are as bright as the sky. "I have never seen it like that before."

Turtle looks up, "What do you mean?"

"Look around. The colors are covering the entire sky."

Bird spins his head, "And most times the clouds all have the same shape."

"You're right," Turtle agrees. "The clouds are all spread out and none of them have the same shape."

Ista smiles, "I see different kinds of bird feathers everywhere."

"I see thin worn blankets here and there," Bird says.

Turtle sees something different. "I see dark holes in the sky."

Deerhead snorts, "I see three boys with their noses in the air."

Ista turns, "Look at Deerhead. He looks pink."

Turtle disagrees, "No, he looks orange."

Bird turns, "His eyes are pink."

When they start laughing, Deerhead realizes that it is going to be a long, trying test. A test of his patience.

Knowing that he stands before a greater power than all of them, Hugumki gives everyone, including himself, some more time to enjoy their Creator's beauty. It also gives them time to offer thanks to Father Sun for the opportunity to share his power every day.

Before everyone starts getting too restless, Hugumki clears his throat to regain their attention, then picks back up where he left off.

"On this test," Hugumki raises his face to the sky, "we must be very careful with our fires. We will make them before first light, and after dark if we have enough cover to keep them hidden. And never forget, it is not just the smoke we have to worry about but also the glow from the flame. We do not want our smoke or firelight to be a signal to anyone that we are there. We may even have to take the remains of our fire with us if we are somewhere that has no hiding place for it. As for other things that could give our position away, we must, and always will find a way to hide our kani, like earlier, so don't worry, we will not have to take it with us."

Hugumki can't help but smile when he sees the looks of relief pass over their faces.

"And when we make water, be careful where the little stream goes. We must not let anyone follow the flowing water back to us." Hugumki's exaggerated stern look quickly tempers the ensuing laughter.

"And never ever be seen up against the sky, be it day or night, or you will stand out like a baby deer and be just as easy to catch.

"Remember what I have said. I do not like to tell you what to do more than one time," he lightly chides, remembering that morning's confusion. "One time should be enough because one mistake out here could be one mistake too many like we almost learned past night. Our test will now get harder, and we will all need to stay straight like an arrow. Not on our path, but in our hearts and spirits."

Hugumki looks around and loudly thumps his chest. "This is not like the old ball games we were told about when we were younger; because, like I said before, this is no game. I want to return home. I want each of you to get back home too. Sometimes we will need to walk or run in two groups, but we are always one group. We journey as one group, and we will return as one group. That means we must all listen to each other. Something that seems very simple could save our lives out here. We will all be needed to complete this test. Right Esan? We need you too. I cannot tell you right now why this is different from the other coming-of-age tests you may have been told about. I also can't say why we need to be so careful with our passing right now, but I can say that this test is a special test, just for us."

"They will always tell our stories," Two Bows whispers to Deerhead.

"We will become real legends," Deerhead whispers back.

Ignoring them, Hugumki keeps on talking.

"Like I said before, the first thing you will notice different about our test is the way we will go after we cross over the river." Hugumki looks up again, then finishes with, "Everyone drink more water and eat more fish, for next day, we will be walking with giants. I know you will need your strength for that."

Hugumki's words fill the camp with excitement and for a couple of the Chosen, a little confusion. Ista and Bird look at each other and in all seriousness ask simultaneously. "What's a tree?"

All they get for an answer is a muted, "Wait and see."

After that, the desert is treated to the sounds of ten youth without any adults around to quiet them down. That is, until they fall victim to the heavy arms of exhaustion that pull harder on them than expected.

With Father Sun now gone for the night, the multitude of other suns overhead take their turns sharing their blazing glory with all below. As the darkness gets deeper, they start resembling a ghostly twinkling bridge stretching from horizon to horizon. Are they the celestial link between the Chosen's youth and adulthood?

11

3rd day – Mid-morning

Not only did the scenery change-less buttes, mesas, and plateaus to avoid-when the Chosen crossed the river, so did the air and temperature. It is as if they had passed through an invisible veil and are now heading toward the burning heart of the desert.

Father Sun is beaming down from a sky that is brighter blue than any turquoise stone Rabbit has seen before. Under his warm gaze, a line of specially chosen, poncho clad walkers steadily work their way toward giant country. They are passing through an area where the remaining mesas and plateaus resemble large islands of rock majestically rising up from the surrounding landscape.

Sky Eye looks at Two Bows who is leading him and the rest of the Chosen. "What is the special object that you carry in your medicine pouch?"

"You know we are not supposed to talk about those things or they lose their power."

"How do you know that? If something has a special power, should it not have that power all the time? My special token is a piece of the sky that fell back to Mother Ground. I have said it. Does that make it any less special?" Sky Eye's face shows the strain of trying to understand the restraints that some people try to put on others and their way of thinking.

Two Bows pulls at the wispy fuzz on his top lip. "I don't know. It is what I have been told. Pay more attention to our spacing. I don't want you to keep bumping into me every time I slow down for something on the trail."

"Sorry Two Bows. I know you have been told things, and I have been told things. What is strange is, they are not always the same things. So how do we know which one is right, and which is wrong?" Sky Eye lifts each hand separately like a scale.

"That, I really don't know." Two Bow's face breaks into a smile. "I know who you can ask, you can ask the giants when we see them."

Sky Eye glances at Bird who is just behind them. Bird is doing his best to stay just close enough, to overhear anything interesting. "Even if we still tell the stories, I know there are no giants living among us."

"Are you sure about that Sky? They will be right in front of us once we clear that higher area ahead."

After a short while.

"Haye Bird, what are Two Bows and Sky Eye talking about?" Ista asks his friend who has slowed down to join him as they meander their way along the winding rock strewn path.

"Something about their medicine pouches and giants."

Wishing that he could have slept in like he normally does in the village, Ista tries to yawn. "We should talk about our pouches too. It will put me back to sleep."

"Do you think one of us has something in our pouches that will get rid of these new bumps on my face?"

Ista reaches up to lightly touch his own face, "I was joking about our pouches Bird, but my face is starting to feel different too."

"Must be all the sweating we are doing. Do you think our test has already begun?"

"Someone said it began as soon as we left the village."

Bird's face takes on a heavy cast, "I almost wish I had stayed home."

"You want to stay a child forever?" Ista asks, bending his legs to make himself look even smaller.

"Would that be so bad? Like MoMo, I could have everything done for me."

Ista's wide open mouth shows how surprised he is that Bird would joke about something so sad. Something that even he would not joke about. "Would you really want to be like him and not be able to do anything for yourself?"

"No, this is just much harder than I thought it would be and I am already tired of it." Bird looks at Ista's face to see if he is ready to share in his misery yet.

"Me too. All I hear now is, don't do this, don't do that. Go here, don't go there." Ista 's upper lip is holding so much disgust it disappears into his mouth.

Glad to have an ally, Bird takes a deep breath and breathes out noisily. "That's right, Ista. We are almost grown up and all the older ones treat us like we are still babies. We should treat them that way and see how it makes them feel."

"You go first so I can see how long you live." Ista holds his arms wide open. "Out here they would have plenty of places to hide your stinky body."

"How can I be smelly already? I washed off in the river earlier."

"That was earlier."

Bird rubs his poncho. "On days like this, I don't know if I should wear my poncho or not. Does it keep me cool or make me hotter?"

"Quiet, here comes Wami, and look, Turtle is trying to keep up with him."

Ista taps Turtle on the shoulder before he can pass them by. "Turtle, walk with us."

Turtle peers at his friend's faces and something hiding in their eyes gives him a sense of unease. "What are you two doing?"

After waiting a moment so Ah Ki Wami can walk on ahead, Ista looks around again to make extra sure that no one else can hear them. "We were talking about this great test of ours."

"Good or bad?"

"Both, we just have not found the good yet. Yes, the big fish we caught was good."

Bird studies his short round friend, "Turtle, is this test extra tough on you?"

"What do you, aah, mean?" Turtle's face instantly starts warming up with the direction the conversation is taking.

With leg's so thin they look like they could snap at any moment, Bird is probably the last person that should comment about someone's legs. "All this running and walking has been hard for me but you have shorter legs than we do."

"So it must be really hard for you, right?" Ista badgers his friend.

"No. Just like you two, or anybody else, one foot follows the other."

Bird squints at Turtle, "You sure sweat more than we do so does that mean that you will have to drink more water than we do?"

"So what if I sweat a lot," Turtle asserts, his body suddenly resembling a small, stout bow when he sticks out his chest and pulls his shoulders back. "It's not my fault my body is like this. My mother told me I may get as tall as my father was. If not, so what?"

"We are talking about…." Ista tries to say.

Turtle ignores him and keeps right on, defending himself. "I do everything you do, just a little slower. I don't eat or drink any more than my share. This is just how I am. I know that some of the others did not want me here but I will show them I can do this, and now, I will show you, too."

Surprised by their friend's reaction, Ista and Bird think about saying sorry or something like that, but Turtle just keeps right on going. "Maybe you two should worry about yourselves more. Sky Eye told me that he thinks this test is going to be longer and harder than we thought it would be. Before it is over, you might need me more than you think you will. Now get out of my way!"

When Turtle abruptly walks away, trying not to cry, Bird looks at Ista. "I think he will be good."

"Your right, Turtle is a turtle after all. I wonder what he meant when he said that this test will be longer and harder than we thought it would be?"

Little do they know that the wary looks they exchange could not even begin to foretell everything that waited to test them, or worse yet, lay in wait for them. Even now, there are unseen eyes watching and biding their time because they know their virtue will be rewarded if one of the overwhelmed teen's eventually falls by the wayside.

3rd day – Mid-afternoon

Thankfully for those who are already feeling worn out and weary, if it doesn't snow or rain, a puffy layer of clouds has drifted in to cover the entire sky.

The Chosen have lived their whole lives surrounded by thorny cacti, the main flora of their desert homeland. Some are small and round while others stand two men high. Some even twist around as if they are waving both hello and goodbye with their thorny arms. From different kinds of cactus, their people get fruit, rope, soap, needles for their cotton, and from some, the elder's strong drink.

Now, just like Hugumki said, they are standing before a dusty desert floor full of cactus so big that they are almost scary, just by their sheer size. Some must be more than five men high and much larger than a man could reach around, that is, if he wanted to try to and hug something that has sharp needles sticking out everywhere. *Touch at your own risk*, they seem to dare.

Upon seeing them, the awestruck group seems to have momentarily lost its voice. The only sound so far has been brother hawk calling out as he glides around enjoying the unseen air currents. After a while, the group's silence is broken by Bird asking, "Do they know they are that big? How about if they fall on us?" which causes everyone to look down at the giant cactus lying right across the path in front of them.

After assuring Esan that he does not have to wear his furry sandals yet, Hugumki jokes, "As long as no one trips on that one there, it looks like it will be easy to get through here. Because they are so big and there is only so much water here, there will be plenty of room for us to walk in between them. If we move through carefully, all will be good. Eyes ahead, eyes around. Let's get ready to go."

Before they get under way, Sky Eye asks Hugumki, " I have heard that we may see even bigger cactus than these, is that right?"

Hugumki exaggerates rubbing his chin, "I guess we will have to wait and see."

Off to the side, Ooha is once again posing for his audience of one. Hips turned, shoulders slightly arched, head held high as if he holds the secret note.

Deerhead looks at all the rugged cacti and then at Ooha. A malicious smile crosses his face, then disappears, leaving behind a mischievous one. "Poor Ooha, I hope all of this sun is not going to mess up your pretty face."

"I am more worried about my voice than what my face looks like." Inside, where his vanity resides, he thinks. *This stupid test had better not mess up my face. I like all the attention I get. My face is perfect. Not too round, not too long, just right. My mouth is made for a song. My nose, not too big, not too small, and my eyes, how they love my eyes. The sun had better not give me those spots Gona has all over her face.*

"Your eyes almost disappeared. What are you thinking about?"

"Nothing. Just a new song. alic uli alic kat ik idi" he sings.

"What does that mean?"

"Something old, something new. I just made it up."

"I was hoping it was something that would help us."

"You never know."

Time slowly passes by, during which, the Chosen cautiously zigzag their way around the standing or resting giants.

After a while, toward the front of the meandering line, Turtle is saying something to Bird about how the giant cactus resemble very large, green people.

Seeing his opportunity, Ista, who has been slowly working his way over to Ooha's side, takes his chance.

"Ooha, can you help me?"

"With what?"

"I heard you talking past day to Bird about."

With a sly grin on his face, "about girls?"

"Yes."

"Did you hear my words?"

"Yes, but I have a different problem," Ista squirms and stammers a little. "I, I can't talk."

"Ista, you talk all the time."

"That is my problem, I can talk to anybody but, but…"

"Who is it?"

"Rain, I can talk to anybody but Rain," Ista blurts out as his fingers start twitching like nervous spiders.

"If you like her, that is a problem."

"I try, I try to say something, but nothing comes out of my mouth," Ista checks to make sure that Deerhead and his sharp tongue, is still ahead of them.

"Watch your step there and let me think for a short time."

"I did not even try when we left because it just feels like my mouth gets stuck. Wait, I thought you could talk to any girl?"

"You're right. I have never had your problem before so I am trying to put myself in your sandals."

"Sky Eye, if you take my sandals, hoa, now I get it."

"Your problem is that you are thinking too hard. You are trying to come up with exactly the right thing to say."

"Don't you do that too?"

"No, I, just be yourself, your real self. If you try too hard your head will fill up with too many things and then your mouth does not know what to say."

"That sounds easy, but what if the same thing happens again?"

"Do you think she likes you?"

"She does smile at me, kind of."

"Then keep it simple. Just say one word when we get back. Walk up to her as a man and say, 'hi.'"

"Do you think that will work?"

"Unless she is real mean inside, it will. Here come your friends. Don't forget about the other things I told Bird about."

"Thank you, Ooha. I can't wait to get back home and try out what you said on her."

Ooha starts to quietly sing his new song in the hope that it will drift its way to Squash Blossom as they all continue heading toward the unimaginable.

3rd day – Before sunset

When Father Sun lays his big round head on some distant fluffy gray edged clouds, preparing to end his day, the desert begins its rapid cool down. Upon closer inspection, it looks like He is not the only one that has rest on his mind.

An exhausted Sky Eye does his best to stay awake. "I can't wait to fall asleep. It has been a long hard day."

"Look, I think Turtle already has," Ista laughs, looking back at Turtle who is starting to wander off the narrow, uneven path they are walking on.

"He does look like he is sleeping and walking at the same time. Gumki," Sky Eye calls out, pointing back at the wandering Turtle.

"Turtle!" Hugumki yells from further behind them. "Pay attention or you will hurt yourself."

Ista stares into Turtles eyes, "He was sleeping."

"I was not. I was thinking." Turtle's empty, drawn up face does not support his words.

"When you think with your eyes closed, that is what we call dreaming," Sky Eye slowly nods his head to laughter.

Fluttering his eyes for a moment, Ista asks, "Turtle, what were you seeing?"

"I said I was not sleeping," Turtle snaps back.

From up ahead, a low voice cut through. "Past night, I had a dream where this woman."

"Deerhead, I don't know if we should hear the rest right now," Hugumki quickly says. With Deerhead's imagination, who knows where a dream about a woman could lead to.

Sky Eye finishes the yawn that he has been trying to hold back. "My dreams are always long and they seem to last all night."

With his eyes twinkling with the memory, "I don't like my scary ones, but I do like the funny ones," Ista says.

"Like what," asks Hugumki, who is glad to veer away from whatever Deerhead was starting to talk about.

"Past night, we all had very short legs so our test was just around our village and it took us many days because our legs were so short."

Trying to act like he is wide awake again, "That is funny Ista. I am glad our dreams are not real, right?" Turtle asks.

"Che Wah says, 'dreams are just our night thoughts trying to see the light of day.' Even he is, not completely sure. Sometimes they seem to have some sort of meaning, and other times, they have none," Sky Eye tries to rub the answer from his long head.

After rejoining the group, "Mine are always adventures," Two Bows says. We don't have much further to go Gumki, then we can all go wherever our dreams take us."

"What kind of adventures do you have Two Bows?" Sky Eye wants to know.

"I have been to places I have never seen before. When I get there, something exciting is happening. I can't seem to remember what, when I wake up. I just know I feel tired like I really did something."

Not being able to resist playing around with someone he thinks is not as smart as himself, Sky Eye looks at him with a straight face. "Maybe your spirit left your body behind, and you really did do something in another land or another time. That is why you don't know where you are."

Rabbit, who has been silent so far during the whole exchange jumps in. "My dreams are special. Past night, they showed me who I really am, I think." With his head in the clouds and his sandals barely touching the ground, Rabbit shows that it is more than his dreams that are special.

Before things can get too serious, Hugumki pretends to rest his head on his hands. "Let's all try to think this night about being home again, then we will see what happens."

"If we all woke up back in the village, would we still pass the test Gumki?" Turtle asks, putting his most sweet and hopeful smile on his wide face.

"If we all wake up in the village, that would mean none of this is real. So, if I hit any of you real hard…., why are you all moving away?" Raising his voice before any of them get too far away. "We will make camp when we reach that rise just ahead."

A rise can mean many things in a flatter part of the desert. In this case, it refers to the edge of a small group of hills in which they can seek safe shelter for the night.

With that, the Chosen continue heading to what should be a very interesting night for all of them. Especially for Esan, who has been trying to dream up a way to get the desert tortoises out of their holes and then get into their impenetrable shells.

12

4th day – Late morning

Thin white clouds are dissolving like a memory, or a dream, in the burgeoning heat of the day. On the rock strewn desert floor, Hugumki signals for a necessary water break. Turtle quickly sits down on one of the smooth, waist high rocks that is still holding onto the shade of the larger boulders scattered around it. His wide, gap-toothed smile of contentment signals that something might be amiss, or even worse, missing.

"Turtle," Rabbit sounds stern, though his eyes are filled with laughter.

"What Rabbit?"

Rabbit makes a face that is a cross between shock and amusement. "Watch your eyes everybody. Turtle is going warrior, and he does not know how to sit properly."

"I like it because it's much cooler this way."

Deerhead leans back and crosses his thick legs. "Hoa. I take my breechcloth off too whenever I get too hot. At least I know how to sit the right way so I don't scare anybody."

"Sorry, I will be more careful from now on." Turtle adjusts his poncho so that his modesty and his friend's delicate sensibilities can remain intact.

"Does going warrior help me become a warrior faster?" he asks, once he is comfortable again.

"Only if you keep sitting like a humble warrior and keep your blessings to yourself." Two Bows can barely finish what he is saying before he starts laughing so hard that he almost falls off the rock he is on.

Glancing at the contorted faces around him, Hugumki takes a deep breath. "I am not trying to be funny, but I want you to remember the look that came over Turtle's face when he first sat down on the rock." With a scowl meant to cut off all interruptions, Hugumki continues. "This is serious. If we are not careful one of us could die out here. On some of the days ahead, it may get very hot. We need to think about all the ways to keep cool and Turtle just showed us one. Cool down the center of your body and it will help cool everything else, right Turtle?"

"Right."

"We also need to talk about what to do in case one of us gets too hot and gets sick, or worse. If one of us gets too hot, what should we do?"

"Give them water, shade, air, blow it or move it, if you have too."

The discussion goes on and on because surviving the rugged dry desert takes real preparation and planning, not wishful thinking.

After staring at his shadow for a couple of days, Sky Eye has something else weighing on his mind. Bored with the water discussion, he asks Ista, "Do I look funny?"

"I don't know if I am the right person to ask a question like that. Do you want a real answer, or a funny one?"

"I know you can make fun of anything, so answer my question anyway."

"No, I mean, your head and face might be a little longer than some people, but that is you. That is who you are and the way you act goes with the way you look or does the way you look go with the way you act? Sorry, I just don't know."

"That's all right Ista, you said more than you will ever know. It is kind of like which came first, the ground or the sky?"

Sky Eye is surprised that it is his funny little friend who has made him feel better about himself.

Once he starts looking up again, Sky Eye notices that part of Little Sun's outline (the moon) has joined Father Sun in the sky. "You are special Little Sun; you can be seen day or night. How many sizes will you be before we get back home?"

With the two celestial bodies observing from on high, the Chosen prepare to continue onward.

4th day – Mid-afternoon

"Is Esan part wolf?" Ooha wants to know, as his nostril's flair, of their own volition.

If possible, Hukumki's eyes get even more intense. "Coyotes look like them too. Yes, I know why you are asking.

Sky Eye asks in a flurry of words. "Do they all have the same blood?"

Two Bows, who is getting tired of Sky Eye just looking at things, says, "You can go back and ask the ones that have been slowly creeping closer and closer."

After a quick look behind him, Hugumki swallows before saying, "I did not see any love in those eyes that just ducked down back there."

Rabbit looks behind him for any cover and quickly wishes he hadn't because all he sees is a small jumble of rock. And it's not very far away.

Hugumki slows down his pace then starts turning his head back and forth before signaling with one quick whistle to get everyone's attention.

Once he has it, Hugumki says loudly, but almost under his breath at the same time. "We have some wolves following or tracking us. We may have some more waiting in front of us. We will keep moving ahead for now, but slow down everybody until we know what we need to do."

Hugumki turns to check the trail ahead again, but finds his view blocked by an overexcited Ista bouncing up and down waving his arms right in front of his face.

"What are you doing Ista, you almost hit me," Hugumki backs away from Ista's little arms slicing through the air like a Hohokam windmill.

"When we stopped for Rabbit's break, Deerhead and Sky Eye kept walking up ahead. I saw them keep going so I came back here to tell you, and I just heard what you were talking about." Fully aware that danger is lurking all around in furry coats, Ista can barely contain himself. "What should we do? They are all alone!"

Hugumki tells Ah Ki Wami, whose eyes are gleaming like eager wet black stones at the bottom of a translucent pool of violence, "Wami, have your spear at the ready. Deerhead has the other one. Two Bows and I have our bows loaded so we will need the quiver to stay near."

Without really needing to, Hugumki says to the closely bunched Chosen. "We will stay together in a group, with Esan in between us. We will move quickly, but not in a rush. Deerhead and Sky Eye should be just ahead. Once we get to them, we will see what we must do. Wami, you lead. Two Bows, cover behind us. Let's go."

The glint of flint and obsidian is suddenly in the air when the Chosen pull out their knives and ready their bows and spear.

Without warning, there is a charge on the trail ahead. Racing towards them, a mass of brown comes roaring out from behind the rocks. It looks like a whirlwind of arms twirling, legs pumping, poncho flapping, sandals clacking, and a pack thumping. Sky Eye's ungainly charge is led by the extreme volume of his exuberant voice. At first, it almost sounds like he is yelling in another tongue.

To the two wolves that were doing nothing more than lazily waiting around for more company to come along, Sky Eye must seem like a raving lunatic, a madman let loose in the desert, not an over excited teen.

Startled out of their resting spots overlooking the small water trail, the yellowish gray wolves quickly disappear into the vastness of the desert. They soon come upon some fellow wanderers and warn them. *It would be smart to avoid the trail ahead for a while. There is a crazy human running around out here and it is in your best interest to leave him alone.*

Glancing behind him to see if Deerhead was in sight yet, Sky Eye starts telling the others what he has seen to get him so excited.

"Deerhead and I were passing a rock that was bigger than I, can reach. Deerhead was looking down like he does, and I was watching the trail ahead, while also looking around. To my surprise, out of the corner of my eye I saw what looked like the bones of something lying flat in the rock. What makes it so different is that it looks like it is inside out, and it is bigger than Esan with a long tail, short legs, long claws, and a different-shaped head with lots of very sharp looking teeth."

Quickly looking behind him, Hugumki squints into the bright light again but does not see anything furry or pointy ducking down or moving around. "Come on Sky, show us what you are talking about."

To himself, he quietly utters, "How did they get out of my sight? I must come up with a better plan."

Hoping the current danger has passed, the excited youth can't wait to see what could have been an even scarier danger from another time. Possibly, long, long, ago.

With some familiar and many new and unidentified scents tickling his nose, Esan realizes that he too is far from home. From now on, he must be extra careful and constantly on guard. It is just him and his ten companions all alone against whatever the desert can and will challenge them with, and he and his four legs might be the only thing that stands between life and death, for all of them.

4th day – Late afternoon

With a hot dry wind blowing up from the south, the Chosen, split up into groups, have been walking and running across the rugged, uneven landscape that is more brown and tan than red now.

When Hugumki splits them into two groups, he tries to put an equal number of older and younger ones in each group.

None of them are wearing much more than their breechcloths, ponchos, and sandals. They have almost crossed a rugged thorn brush covered area that is dissected by dry rivers that went wherever the absent water had originally wanted them to go.

Every time they had come across a dry river going their way, Two Bows hardly had to signal which way to go next. When they did run in the dry rivers, which provided very good cover for them, some of the older one's sang.

"Slow, slow

Or a rock will send you home.

Slow, slow

Or a crack, will send you home."

Once they are out of the dry rivers, and on the sediment packed flat ground, like they are now, they can enjoy their steady pace, or at least try to run through the pain.

Sensing that not everybody is feeling as strong as himself, Hugumki bird whistles to the front group of: Two Bows, Deerhead, Ista, Rabbit, and Bird.

Mimicking the call of a hawk, he tells them to get in the dry river that is not flowing next to them. Since they have been running for two fists of sun time, it is an order that is quickly followed without complaint.

Once they are in the wash, the older ones again sing, but this time in a teasing tone.

"Slow, slow

Or a rock will send you home.

Slow, slow

Or a crack, will send you home."

After a short while, Sky Eye trots up to Hugumki. "When we were in a big dry river earlier this day, why did we suddenly get out for a short time, then get right back in? I did not see a sign of a village or people to avoid; and I know we are not near the old village."

With a bit of sadness in his proud eyes, Hugumki, wipes his brow then turns to Sky Eye who is panting like an old coyote. "Do you have any idea why we separate into two groups when we are in these?" he asks, gesturing around and at the front group.

"Kind of, but not really."

"It is because if there is a lot of rain in the mountains around us, or the snow on the mountains melts early, the water that makes these dry rivers will be back. The mountains, even the mountains with trees, cannot hold all the water. Sometimes the water can come down very fast and we may not see it before it is too late. If it rains somewhere we don't know about, the same thing can happen. That area we went around earlier was where a small hunting group from our village was washed away by a fast wall of water. I did not want us to walk on their spirits and make them angry, even if it happened a long time ago."

Sky Eye, looks around, and takes a deep breath before asking, "Won't we be coming back this way again Hugumki?"

"First, we must reach where we are going." Hugumki answers, while thinking, *Yes, we will pass through this area again, and it will be hotter, and could be much wetter, making it very dangerous for all of us.*

After reaching over and adjusting Sky Eye's pack for him, Hugumki says, "Then we will deal with what we see or can't see on the way back."

Hugumki again signals the front group. This time to let them know that when they reach the shadowy foothills ahead, they will need to start looking for a safe place to spend the night. Hopefully, it will also be protected enough to safely cook the different kinds of lizards they have caught, that day. That is, if you can call digging sleeping lizards out of their holes, caught.

Bird watches Two Bows run for a bit then starts acting as if he is carrying something invisible. "Two Bows makes running with the spear look so easy.

Ista's laughing, panting face gets a little redder. "Wami let me try but I kept hitting things." After a short pause, "With both ends."

Rabbit's eyes light up. "It is like it is part of his body."

"We know. Practice, practice," Ista and Bird recite at the same time.

Before long, they find a good spot for their camp: a small depression enclosed by an outcrop of large rectangular yellow rocks that looks like the perfect place for real monsters to lurk about. As fitting with their surroundings, it soon seems as if some sort of metamorphosis is occurring.

Instead of the Chosen preparing to set up camp, a pack of ravenous beasts is somehow switching places with them.

"Ista, with all the food you are stuffing in your mouth, it looks like you are trying to eat everything in one big bite," Two Bows says as he starts filling up his mouth with whatever food he pulls out of his pack first.

My food is all mixed up again," Sky Eye complains, reaching into his pack.

Deerhead looks up from the small flame he is trying to keep burning. "Don't worry, it all goes to the same place."

With his mouth flapping open with every bite, Ah Ki Wami looks like he is either eating or losing his last meal of the day.

It sounds like you are enjoying yourself, Wami." Rabbit leans away, putting some distance between himself and the food flying out of Ah Ki Wami's mouth.

Turtle burps and wipes a little wayward drool off his chin before taking a sip from his boto that has a recently etched turtle design on it.

Ooha looks at everyone eating as fast as they can, "It is a good thing there are no women around to watch us eat."

What do you mean?" Bird asks, flashing a jerky filled grin.

Always the entertainer, "Watch this," Ista says as he tilts his head back before carefully tossing a dried berry way up in the air.

"You had better catch it or you can eat it off the ground." Hugumki tells him.

Ista sways left. Sways right. He is so focused he does not hear Hugumki's exact words.

Snap. His mouth engulfs the morsel and he takes a small bow for all to see.

"Some of you need to slow down until the lizard's finish cooking," Deerhead declares, "or you won't have any food left." He turns back to the fire he has been patiently stoking while everyone else has been stuffing their mouths with their meager rations.

"That's right," Hugumki says around his own mouth full of food. "We need to get camp set up before it gets any darker anyway."

Each of them then picks a spot around the fire-accompanied by some playful teasing- without too much wrangling going on.

When one picks a resting spot in the desert, there are more than a few things to consider. Is the weather and temperature going to stay the same all night long? Which way is the wind, if any, going to blow the smoke if you can have a fire? If an animal were to pass through for water, which way would it most likely be heading? And that is to name just a few.

Once everyone is happy with their spot, they lay their blankets and some clothes on the hard ground. Then their packs are put in the area where their chests and arms will be.

Since it is his turn, Rabbit reaches into his buckskin medicine pouch and pulls out an even smaller one. Keeping it at arm's length, he starts sprinkling the azee in a circle just big enough to enclose them, while doing his best not to sneeze. Then just like that, camp is pretty much set up for the night thanks to the enclosed area where their camp is set up.

Now, they just need to control their hunger until Deerhead tells them the lizards are cooked and ready to eat.

It is time to relax and enjoy each other's company at the end of a long and trying day.

"Did you hear that?" Two Bows frantically looks around. "It sounded like some sort of angry monster."

The corners of Turtle's mouth turn up. "That was my stomach, Two Bows."

Two Boys eyes disappear in laughter. "I thought maybe it was an attack. I just wanted to be sure."

"Turtle, next day, do you want…" Bird starts to ask.

"No, but we can say we did."

The sky is beautiful, isn't it Sky Eye? Rabbit looks at all the smiling faces around him and is glad that he came along, for now.

Into the night their friendship's grow, and before long, their stomachs and spirits are full, for now.

13

5th day – Early morning

Cutting through the empty black foreboding stillness of an overcast night sky, down, down, comes a wandering spirit without a sound to announce her arrival. Who? Who? she seems to ask, once she has found purchase on a rock safely out of reach from the light of a small dying fire. Patience is her credo as she watches the fire spark and sputter.

One, two, three she counts as tiny bodies hit the starving flames. Soon enough, millions more will join them, on this, one of the best feeding nights of sister owl's entire life.

"Ha ye, ha ye, Gumkiiii! Something is attacking me!" Bird's terror filled shriek pierces the dark and startles the owl into early flight.

Hugumki, who was already starting to scramble to his feet, needs only a moment to realize what is really going on, and about to happen, because of all the bugs flying around.

"Everybody, pull your ponchos and blankets over your heads, cover your mouths and eyes too if you can," he yells to his startled and swatting companions. "Two Bows, cover Esan and keep him calm. Deerhead, put out the fire. All you brave warriors, stay as low as you can."

Another voice screams out, "Are they going to eat us?"

"I can't see anything, they are everywhere," comes Ah Ki Wami's calm voice.

"Stay where you are right now or you might hurt yourself if you keep moving around," Hugumki orders, crouching back down. "I'm not worried about these little bugs flying around. I want us to be ready for what will be coming to eat them."

"What do you mean?" Rabbit screeches from under his blanket.

Gently petting Esan, who is nervous because of all the shrieking going on, "Remember those caves we saw earlier," Two Bows answers back. He readjusts his poncho and blanket to make sure that he and Esan are completely covered and ready for what is coming next.

Using a sound only they can hear: the Chosen's salvation arrives on the loud fluttering wings of an insect's worst nightmare.

Even though he has never experienced this before, Sky Eye is more intrigued than fearful in the rustling, pitch black of the swarming foothills. "It's a wonder the bats don't hit us," he yells. "They are many and not one has hit me. I can't even see my hands. How can they fly around without hitting the rocks or us, and still find the bugs to eat?"

Next to him he hears, "They must have special eyes."

The whirling, rustling, and feeding seems to go on and on, then, just as suddenly as it all started, it stops.

By the faint glow of early morning light, the Chosen, with their relief evident on their faces and in their thankful voices, stand and watch the flowing black cloud of overstuffed bats happily start to wind their way back home.

To cover up his own frightened reaction, which was the loudest scream heard, Ista calmly asks, "Bird, are you going to wait on Father Sun so he can dry out your breechcloth?"

5th day – Late-morning

The whole desert seems to have been put on a steady simmer by the mighty, hot one, causing most of the day animals to stay in their cool shady holes. The only creatures seen moving about on this dry day are Esan, and a ragged line of sweaty brown bodies, walking like they may have lost their way. Though warm, it is still a beautiful day, which the Chosen's body language does not reflect in the least bit. Is it misery, fear, or some other negative emotion that has put them all in such a somber mood?

Pointing ahead at a mountain pass in the distance, Hugumki says, "It's getting too hot for us to keep stopping at every big rock we come across. That just keeps slowing us down. We will keep moving until it is time for the meal break." Hugumki is doing his best not to grind his teeth in frustration about what had occurred earlier, "The shady spots are almost gone anyway."

"I would sing, but my mouth is too dry," Ooha rasps, before taking a sip of warm water. "I don't want to ruin my voice on a day like this."

Feeling his anger starting to get the best of him, Hugumki ignores his singer and asks the question that has been annoying him since that early morning's grave danger. "Wami, tell us what we did wrong when those tiny little scary bugs attacked?"

Slowly rubbing his bare stomach, "We gave away our position," Ah Ki Wami answers, before sending an icy stare at Bird who is sluggishly working his way along the rocky trail. The slow, heavy slap of his little sandals signals the discomfort he suddenly finds himself in.

"That's right Wami, there are other ways to get attention than just crying out," Hugumki somehow exhales loudly through his tightly pressed lips.

"What do you mean?" asks Rabbit, glancing at Bird who looks like he is starting to, or at least wants to, shrink inside his own skin, if possible.

"There is the low warning whistle that some of you need to practice more until you can do it without thinking. Even a quick touch will work at the right time."

Getting in on the verbal assault, Deerhead sarcastically asks, "When the life-threating attack started, did any of you even notice that Gumki was getting up and aware of what was going on?"

"If we had been surrounded by enemies, because of your frightened reactions, they would have known right where we were." Ah Ki Wami shakes his head in disgust. He does not mention that the fire would have done that anyway because he has another point to make.

Trying to kick a small rock out of his way, Hugumki instead stubs his toe, which does not improve his mood any. "Don't forget, we have Esan with us, and he never made a sound."

Bird quietly grouses in Turtles' direction. "It seems like we can't do anything right."

"I know we are being hard on you but think about these things. They could save your life. Our lives." Hugumki heaves a sigh to the sky before he starts walking again, slowly wagging his head.

"Would you rather be mad at us, or dead?" Ah Ki Wami asks.

Mad is apparently the answer because everyone sullenly keeps on walking without uttering as much as another word or bark.

After a while, Sky Eye can't stand the silent tension that his friends are wearing like a blanket of unease. "Let's play a word game," he suggests.

"Like what?" Bird's dimpled smile shows that he is more than ready not to be the center of attention anymore.

"I will say a word, and then someone else will say the first word that comes into their head."

Deerhead scratches an itch on his sweaty neck, "That sounds easy enough."

Rabbit, who is always ready for a fun game, asks, "Can I answer with more than one word, Sky Eye?"

"No. One word for one word, that is what makes it fun. I will start. Is everybody that is playing, ready?"

"Ready," those within hearing range answer back.

"Sky."

"Eye," answers more than one laughing voice.

"That was practice, this will be harder. Home."

"Away," answers Turtle with a small catch in his voice.

"Girls."

"Many," answers Deerhead.

"Test."

"Hard," Bird almost yells.

"Mountains."

"Big," is Rabbit's answer.

"Dancers."

"Tired," Rabbit answers again.

"Esan."

"Aarf" is Esan's answer.

"Snow."

"Cold," Turtle answers with his eyes closed. He is thinking about how wonderful it would be to lay in some snow, right now. Then again, as the saying goes, be careful what you wish for Turtle.

"Thirsty."

"Time for a drink," answers Hugumki, using more than one word. "You can continue after we take a quick break if you want."

By the look's on their sweaty dirty faces it is going to be a long quiet afternoon.

And it was, for a while.

5th day – Mid afternoon

The Sun languidly crosses the sky as the Chosen are passing by the last barren mesa they will see for a while. It is just far enough away to hold back its shade.

Filled with blue sky, a giant eye within the mesa is keeping an eye on them.

"Look at that hole in the white part of the flat mountain over there," Ah Ki Wami says to Ista, who is helping him wipe away any sign of their passing through.

Staring at it for a moment, Ista raises his brows in surprise. "It looks like it does not belong there. It looks like the eye of a real giant. A sleeping giant with a different color of rock. I wonder what is on the other side of it?"

"We can leave you here to find out, and maybe we will find you if we come back this way."

After a short spell of contemplation, or sulking, by all, a sound that was louder than anything any of them has heard so far in their lives cuts through the air with an earsplitting crack. It is louder than the thunder god rumbling in the distance. It is even louder than Mountain when he has an upset stomach. Before they can bat their eyes, they are enveloped by its shocking embrace.

"What was that?" they all ask at once as their heads turn in all directions. Rabbit tries his own version of duck and cover without anything to hide behind, or under.

"I am not sure," Hugumki answers while tapping his head to clear it. "It was so loud I could not really tell where it came from."

"If I had to guess, I would say it came from back there." To reassure his more superstitious companions, Two Bows adds, "Not from the sky, or the ground."

"Maybe your giant is waking up," Ista teases Ah Ki Wami.

Before Ah Ki Wami can respond, Hugumki says. "If he is waking up, that is a good reason for us to pick up our pace a little. We still need to get through the mountains ahead this day. Eyes ahead, eyes around. Let's go."

Looking toward the sky, then down, then skyward again, Sky Eye wishes out loud, "I hope the giant doesn't wake up before we come back this way again, even if it is on the other side."

Stretching out his long legs, Rabbit is eager to put the noisy rock behind him. "I hope he never wakes up," he glances behind him, just to be sure never is not now.

5th day – Late afternoon

It has taken longer than expected for the Chosen to get on the other side of the mountain by way of the boulder filled pass they used to get from one side to the other. The younger ones are gathered around Hugumki and Esan at the lower edge of the foothills.

"Why are you putting furry sandals on Esan?" Ista asks, watching Hugumki tie small pieces of buffalo hide around Esan's paws.

"When some of you asked me before why I was doing this, I never answered because I knew in the village, it would turn into a game. As you can see," Hugumki looks at the desert floor that resembles a fuzz covered green tinted rug spread out in front of them, "We have a whole lot of cactus needles to get by without getting stuck."

With the wind starting to get stronger, the closest cacti were starting to resemble frightened spirit dancers armed with long dangerous looking needles just looking for someone to poke a hole in.

"Letting Esan get used to these back then was more important than playing. Not every thorn stays where it is supposed to be, and I don't want to have to carry Esan the rest of the way. We must all be careful now," Hugumki raises his voice so that they all can hear him. "I don't want to have to carry any of you either because you have holes in your feet. Put on your leggings if needed and wear them lower than usual. Does anyone have sore feet yet?" he remembers to ask.

"No," Rabbit answers. "Walking in the village without my sandals on, like I was told to, made my feet very tough. I can hardly feel my sandals on my feet anymore because they only rubbed for a little while."

To his relief, Hugumki sees the others nodding along in agreement.

Leaning toward Turtle, Rabbit jokes, "If any of those thirsty cactus chase after you, just give them your boto then run away as fast as you can before they know it is empty, like mine is."

"If we quit talking and get walking, we will have enough water to get through here," Ah Ki Wami says as he adjusts his pack.

"Let's go," Hugumki urges as he checks to make sure that everyone is dressed properly in the much cooler air that has dropped down from the mountain top. "Eyes ahead, eyes around."

Being a good leader means more than just leading. It also means understanding who you are leading and where you are leading them. After a short while, with a buffalo shod Esan by his side, Hugumki boldly states, "Stay strong brothers. This night we will have all the cold water we can drink."

14

6th day – Early morning

The desert is alive with the sound of singing, and not just from the birds: like quail, doves, wrens, and cardinals. All the Chosen, including the rough voiced Hugumki, are loudly praising the gods this morning. When Father Sun's light breaks through a heavy cloud cover singeing the edges like a flaming meteor, He gives them one more thing to be thankful for. With their bellies full from their morning meal which consisted of jerky, nuts, berries, some bread, and all the cold water they could drink, they are all, very, very, happy.

They have many things to be thankful for, but they are especially grateful about what happened past day. After they had crossed the cactus filled valley, and waved at the last butte they would see for a while, to their great relief, right in front of them was a small mountain with a light cover of fresh snow glistening like scarlet tinted gold in the evening light.

While everyone else had cried out in joy, Hugumki just smiled even though he was very glad to be right about his prediction, and good eyesight.

After eagerly climbing up to the waiting snow, they had had their fill, both eaten and thrown. They then filled their botos with the most precious thing in the desert. After that, they cautiously made their way back down to an area that was both flatter and warmer to hastily make camp for the night.

In the early morning light of swirling orange, red, and gray Hugumki chuckles quietly. He is recalling when Ista had warned them, once they had climbed up high enough to reach the snow, "Don't eat or throw the sun-colored snow because Esan has been running around up here."

After everyone finishes singing with all their might, Hugumki instructs Rabbit, Sky Eye and Ooha to take every boto that was low or empty and head back up the rocky slope to where the snow line begins. "When you are gone, we will break camp, hide the remains of the fire and everything else, then get ready to go. By then, you should be done so we will meet you when you come back down. Be careful, it looks very slippery up there now."

6th day – High sun

Once again, the sun feels like it is trying to get an early start on a blazing hot summer. After a morning that had begun with everyone feeling refreshed and thankful, the reality of their current situation is slowly starting to bear down on them like a dry, thirsty boulder. If you were to look at their grimacing, strained faces, you would say, most of their boyishness has been lost somewhere in the vast desert. But, as any child of the wilderness knows, Mother Nature is a temperamental lady. One moment she will push you to the very brink of what you can take, if not beyond. The next, she will show you something that will give you a happy memory for the rest of your days.

"Look over there everybody!" Ista yells, breaking the silence that they have been steadily progressing under, whether walking or running. "What is that on top of that cactus over there?"

"Where is what?" Deerhead massages his heavy brows as he looks around. All he can see is the fuzzy silhouettes of the surrounding cactus.

Rabbit and Two Bows, who have eyes like hawks, exclaim at the same time. "I see it."

Two Bows, serious face breaks into a smile. "It looks like that cactus is wearing a furry headdress."

"I wonder how she got up there," Rabbit takes a moment to tuck his wind-blown hair under his headband.

Two Bows, moves his fingers, like they are climbing a ladder. "Only one way: I don't see any wings."

Always assessing the possibilities of fight or flight, Ah Ki Wami wonders, "But how did she" a quick glance at Rabbit, "get up there without getting stuck with all the needles."

"I think very carefully," Hugumki laughs quietly while checking to make sure none of them are getting too far ahead, or behind. And most importantly right now, not sneaking any extra drinks of water.

Lightly clapping his hands with glee, Rabbit's face lights up like the second sunrise of the day. "She sees us now. I just saw her head turn this way."

Trying to relax his tight facial muscles, Hugumki smiles. "I have never seen anything so funny as a cactus wearing a cat for a…."

"I know it is far away, but it does not look very big to me," Rabbit squints and interrupts at the same time.

"Maybe it's a baby," Turtle says.

Watching the cat adjust its position so that it can keep an eye on them, Two Bows muses, "I would say that it is young, but when the light hits it just right, it looks like it has a different coat than I have seen before. It has more circles. So maybe that is as big as its kind gets Rabbit."

Rabbit waves his sweaty hand to say goodbye as they all press on. They are still hot and tired, but in a slightly better mood than they were before.

One other thing about Mother Nature. "She giveth and she taketh away," to not quite quote an old phrase. Before long, the Chosen will be forced to deal with the threatening situation they could have avoided, if only, they had been paying more attention to everything going on around them.

6th day – Late night

The stars are glittering from horizon to horizon, still, it is a very dark night. It's almost as if the sky is enclosing the resting youth in a giant sparkling bowl of nothingness. Into the void, a soft sob is heard, breaking the rhythm of the night.

"Turtle, what is wrong?" Hugumki inquires groggily from his spot next to Turtle, around the equally, worn out fire.

"I, I, don't like being told what to do all the time, but I want to be here with everybody, and I want to show them I can do this." After a choked pause to try and steady his trembling chin, Turtle sticks out his tongue to lick away some of his salty tears. "But I miss home and mother."

Thinking of his own inner turmoil, Hugumki reaches over and gently pats Turtle on the shoulder. "If you weren't told what to do, would you know what to do? I know this test is more than you expected, but you have already done better than some thought you would. You should feel proud of yourself. Don't forget, when we return, we will be seen as men. You too Turtle, even if you are not ready for a mate, or are you, my little Turtle?"

The not so little Turtle cannot help but flash a gap tooth grin into the darkness as he wipes away the last of his tears.

"One more thing," Hugumki whispers before he rolls over in his warm blanket. "I miss my mother too, but that is another reason for this test. We must see how we react to things when we do not have our elders around. Do we have the same spirit, or do we become somebody different when we have no one around to watch us? Now let's get back to sleep before we wake everyone else up. Next day will be another long one, and I will try to be a little more patient. I may be the oldest one here, but I am no elder. Please try not to forget that this is hard on me too."

"Should we add to the fire, or let it be?"

"Let it be. It will be light before too long and we don't want to make too much noise. Sleep well Turtle, and you can take one quick drink if you need to. Now no more crying."

"I could yell right now and I would not make as much noise as Deerhead. He sounds like he is breathing rocks." Turtle rubs his turtle zumi, flashes his grin again after taking a precious sip from his boto, then rolls over to try and get back to sleep before the night is drained of its darkness and mystery.

15

7th day – Mid-morning

The air is still deciding if it wants to get warm or stay cool. The Chosen are taking a break on a low sheltered ridge, and the pockmarked path they used to get there. The view in front of them is so wide open they feel like they can see forever, at least until something cutting into the horizon breaks that illusion. With their rest time almost over, some are using the ridge to scout both the trail ahead and the desert around them as warriors in training should. Others are getting ready in mind and body, in their own way, for the challenging trek that awaits them the rest of the day.

"My turn! My Turn!" Turtle's voice sounds excited and urgent at the same time.

Hearing the laughter behind him that is louder and more focused than usual, Hugumki looks at Two Bows. "Do I want to know what they are doing now?"

Two Bows raises his head and shoulders. "It looks like Turtle is holding his breechcloth in one hand, and himself with the other. At first it looks like he is aiming to put out a fire, but instead, I think he is trying to hit the hole they are staring at. Now Ista looks like he is stepping forward to take his turn."

"Into the same hole?"

"Yes."

Hugumki starts standing up, "This will be fun." Walking toward Ista, who is going through the same motions, Two Bows described, Hugumki stops for a moment, shakes his head, then smiles.

Bird sees him and quickly says, "We saw where Rabbit went, so we…" and points with a chin that is holding up one of the most pathetic looks ever seen.

Rabbit turns away, "Don't blame me, I didn't do anything," and does not try to hide his snigger.

Hugumki peers at the hole up against the ridge bank that they have been using for target practice. Keeping a safe distance, he motions to the younger ones involved to gather around him. "I am going to tell you a story so pay attention. Before there were people on Mother Ground, Spirit People lived here."

"Why?"

Because Mother Ground was not ready for man yet."

"Why?"

"Just listen to the story. After a long time one of them was walking along the empty parts of the ground when water suddenly started dripping everywhere. Right away the ground spirit could tell that something was different. This water was not clear and cold like rainwater. No, this water was warm and…not good for life at all. To the Spirit People, that was their first sign that man had arrived. To say it another way. Watch where you make water. We are not trying to avoid Spirit People but real people. If you all go in the same place, the little stream, might turn into a raging river."

Once the laughter stops. "Water will always find the easiest path. So, it might go into the hole there, but it might come out down there," Hugumki points down below them. "Someone we can't see might notice a yellow stream that is more than one animal can make."

Deerhead can't resist. "Have you ever seen any other animals doing what you were doing all together? No, because they know better."

"Just remember that water will always find a way to keep going like we should right now." Hugumki bends down and reaches for his pack. "Eyes ahead, eyes around. Let's go."

"Doesn't that look like the rest of the giants body?" Sky Eye points at the undulating horizon in front of them.

"Look over there. Doesn't that look like the claws of the giant poking up from the ground?" Two bows, starts his first step toward the horizon and whatever waits beyond: Real or imagined.

7th day – Early afternoon

Some of the small mountains the Chosen have already passed by looked like they were made of crumbled gray rocks of various sizes. The ones that stand tauntingly before them now are tall imposing walls of solid rock that jut up here and there, turning the horizon into an imposing sawtooth barrier.

Turtle, running the best he can on his short legs, can't hold back his tongue any longer. "Two Bows, why are we heading straight for those very tall mountains?" he asks, pointing and panting. "I can keep running but I don't think I can climb over them," he adds, a very serious look on his round weary face. A face that is redder than everybody else's due to the extra effort he must expend to keep up with them.

Two Bows, who is carrying the spear for his group of five, asks Turtle, between his own deep breaths. "Do you think we would have come all this way if there was not a way for us to get through there?"

"We will find a way without having to put on wings," Ah Ki Wami's glistening thin face passes by their conversation and position. They are trailing Bird and his group that is led by Hugumki on this hot and sunny day as they run through the scrub brush, heading toward the more than thousand-man tall mountains.

After three fists of sun movement, Hugumki, face shining brightly, but still the strongest after a long run, raises his dripping hand. When Two

Bows catches the movement, he sees it is the signal for all of them to stop. After a moment, he sees a brush forward motion to signal everyone to approach cautiously.

The area they are in has so many boulders stacked on top of each other in piles, it looks like the landscape has grown giant brown warts in various shades and sizes.

Once everyone is around him, using the rocks for cover, Hugumki observes the panting group, including Esan, whose tongue is sticking out so far it looks like he could trip on it. "Sometimes, you even have too, sneak up on a mountain. Anyone could be up in those mountains watching our approach," Hugumki gestures ahead.

When they all turn to look, they realize that the mountains are so big and close now that the only way to see the top of them is to tip their heads way back.

While everyone takes advantage of the break and starts to greedily drink from their botos, Deerhead looks back and forth at all of them with a very stern look on his face. "Don't forget about our water problem," he reminds. "As you know, first, we approached this area straight like an arrow, then like the sideways zizis to bring us here. Gumki, Two Bows, Wami, and I have been watching all along, and so far, the way ahead looks safe and clear.

"Two Bows, why do we always have to be so careful. I thought only our people lived out here?" Sky Eye quietly asks.

Two Bows lifts his nose into the air as if he is sniffing for danger, because he is. "Like Gumki has said, for our test, we are not supposed to be seen by anybody no matter who they are. For me, the real reason to be careful is because, like us, there could be other people out here that don't belong here. I have heard too many stories about hunting and raiding parties from roaming tribes to think that that could not happen to us, wherever we are. So always be alert and on guard, not just thinking about the things you can see."

After making sure Esan can drink his small share of water from a little mud turtle shell that has been split in half without tipping it over,

Hugumki says, "When we top this foothill, I will have a question for you. For now, once we leave the cover of these rocks, we will stay low and use the brush and rocks ahead for our cover as we approach."

When they reach the top of the foothill after a long hard leg sapping climb, Hugumki throws his hands in the air, stretches out his back, then asks his question. "Which way do we go now?"

"That way," everyone answers and points at once.

"That looks like a crack in the lower part of the mountain there," Sky Eye rubs his perplexed face.

"Because it is a split in the mountain," answers Hugumki. "When we get up there, I have been told that we will also see some very large rocks that have been cracked right down the middle on each side of what is supposed to be a very tight trail, if you can call it that. I don't know what caused it, but thank the Gods. If the crack was not there, we would have to go around the edge of these mountains and that would add another day or two to our journey this way."

"I wish they would tell us where we are going," Bird very quietly whispers to Rabbit as they hover off to the side. Bird's face has taken on a weary quality that is almost unnerving on a face so young.

"I think I know. Be patient. It will be worth the wait if I am right. Now be quiet, you are being tested my little man."

Sky Eye looks high and low at the mountain. "Maybe the split happened when Mother Ground got angry and shook, real hard."

Hugumki continues unabated. "I am sure we will have to climb over and around some very big rocks that may be blocking our path. We will all keep an eye on Esan in case he needs help."

"Too bad he is not part coyote," Ah Ki Wami says louder than he intended.

"And if needed," Hugumki says more firmly to stop the interruptions, "we will help each other. When we reach the other side of the pass, we will enter a valley that would be full of furry rabbits if it was warmer right now. I have been told that they are smaller and taste much better than the tough, big eared rabbits of the desert. And guess what? Whoever was asking earlier, you will finally get to see what a real tree looks like, not a shrub or cactus.

"Now is not the time of year for people to be up there and we have not seen any smoke, but you never know. We will approach quietly and when we enter the valley, we will move in very slowly to see if anyone or anything is hiding there. Be ready Wami for whatever danger could be lurking there. Would you rather have a spear or bow?"

Ah Ki Wami casually shrugs his shoulders because he doesn't care. His narrow face looking back and forth shows that he is ready and waiting. Eager for any kind of encounter, regardless of what weapon he is carrying since he has been practicing hard with both during his alone time.

Hugumki looks around again, "Then we will all walk to the other side of the small valley to make sure that path is clear too. When we can see that we are safe, we will make camp, a little way off the side of the path. Esan will be the only one that gets to eat rabbit- if he can wake one up- because we will not make a fire this night until we are ready for sleep.

"Before first light, Esan, Two Bows and Wami will dig out some sleeping rabbits while Turtle will get the fire ready to cook them on. Two Bows, you might want to mark a hole or two before it gets dark." Seeing a look or two of disappointment, he adds. "I can't wait to eat them either. After first meal and Ooha sings blessing to the new day, we will head out again."

"Hugumki," Rabbit lowers his voice. "After dark, can anyone see us up there if we are in a valley?"

Deerhead answers instead, "If they can't see us, that means we can't see them."

"Too bad we can't have a fire right away and not just for cooking," Ah Ki Wami slowly says so his words have their desired effect.

"Why?" Turtle looks at him, a little fear and worry in his eyes.

"With all the rabbits around, even if they are still sleeping, do you think we will be the only creatures up there?"

Bird's disquiet takes flight in his sputtered words, "Ccreatures upp tthere?"

"It will be cold, this night so later put on everything you brought if you feel like you need to. We will all stay in a very tight group and we all should sleep with one eye open, if you know what I mean." Realizing not all of them do, Hugumki explains. "What I mean is if any of you hear anything, react quick, don't wait, and even asleep, be alert. And that means you too Esan. Now I wonder who Esan, my best, best friend, will choose to sleep with to keep warm this night?" Hugumki reaches down and gives Esan his favorite scratch, just behind his ears, in the hope that Esan gets his hint and chooses him over all the others to sleep with and keep warm. "This night, we will put the azee a little further around camp," Hugumki looks around one more time before pointing up ahead. "Let's go. Eyes ahead, eyes around."

Through the pass comes a strong gust of wind. At first it resembles a child's whimper. Then it sounds like a ghost is whistling an eerie song. To the Chosen, it is nothing more than the winds of change blowing their way. For good or bad? That is still to be determined.

7th day – Evening

The first thing Ista does when they enter the cool mountain valley that has some aspen, cottonwood, and maples scattered about, is, hug a tree. "I just have to see what it feels like," he tells the others who are starting to reach for one themselves. "It stands tall like some of those big cactus we saw but without all those thorns. I have never seen a plant so big and tall."

"I thought they would be a little bit softer." Bird pinches a cottonwood without leaving a mark. "It's, what do you call it? it's bark is very hard."

Even though some of them had seen its bark before, as art, they are surprised to see the trunks of the aspen trees covered in white.

"These trees look like they are wrapped in dirty snow." Ooha rubs one as if he is trying to clean it.

After his initial encounter, "Why do all of the trees look half dead?" Ista asks.

Hugumki turns to look up at the sunlight cutting through the trees. It is a sight most of them have never seen before because they have never stood among a copse before. "They aren't dead Ista. They are just resting for the season. Just before they fell off their leaves would have turned many different colors. More than one pair of eyes close while they try to imagine what that must have looked like. A couple of them also try to imagine what leaves of any color look like, without ever having seen them before.

Hugumki points out a thick branch they should not walk under, "That looks like it could fall at any time. When it gets a little bit warmer, all these trees will have green leaves popping out everywhere on their branches."

Sky Eye is slowly walking around his companions in a lazy circle while being mesmerized by the intertwining shapes and shadows being cast on the ground by the branches. To himself he observes, "It looks like the small parts of the tree has the same shadow as the big parts do." Louder, he says, "I would love to see that. Everything coming to life here at the same time like our crops do."

"Probably the only place around here, other than behind a rock, where you can find shade during the hot time."

Soon enough, exhaustion starts rearing its ever present, head, so Turtle, Ista, Bird, and Sky Eye are instructed to take a short break.

The others start walking around to check all the entrances and exits of the valley-some more visible than others-to make sure they are safe and secure.

"I wonder what they talk about when they are away from us?" Ista asks, eagerly taking off his pack in preparation for that night's rest.

"Probably you," Sky Eye teases. "Doesn't the air smell cleaner up here than down there? It is so nice to get away from dust for a while."

Ista sticks out his tongue to sample the air of the valley. "I hope they keep doing that so we can talk all alone too." He starts taking off his poncho to put on his deerskin shirt in the chilly evening air. "Do any of you remember any of our secret words?" The empty looks he gets gives him his answer.

When the older ones walked away, Turtle was comparing size differences. "I don't think I will ever get as tall as Hugumki, Rabbit or Two Bows," he says to no one in particular. "When I am next to them, I feel so short."

"Would you rather be like Two Bows or Deerhead?" Bird asks.

"I would like to look like Hugumki, but I am probably going to be more like Deerhead," Turtle answers.

"I would rather be like Two Bows than Deerhead," Bird straightens his shoulders and back as his eyes seem to drift away in flight. "I remember when Cloudi was taller than me."

Ista bursts out laughing. "Hoa. She was when we left home."

"I know when we get back, I will be bigger than Cloud ever will be."

"Are you sure?" Sky Eye laughs. "She will still be your cute ah older sister."

Bird starts to hold his hand up, then drops what he can't hold up any longer. "I am tired."

Turtle pats his, padded stomach. "I hope I get as hard as Deerhead is someday."

Sky Eye moves his neck around. "I know what you mean. I bumped into Deerhead not to long ago and he is like a rock with two tree legs."

"That's funny Sky Eye," Ista says as he goes to sit on a log next to the one Bird just sat down on. It does not go according to plan. "Haye, Bird, that looks good to sit on. I will try this one because it is old and strong looking."

"It's soft," Bird warns too late.

"Ooowuh!" First, Ista's rear end sinks into the log. Then his eyes and mouth pop open wider than one would have thought possible as his legs fly up so fast everyone is ducking for cover when his sandals go hurtling through the air.

"Watch out!" Turtle yells, seeking shelter behind a tree.

Ista is stunned for a moment. "What happened?"

Wiping tears of laughter from his eyes, "You fell through," Bird says.

Ista slowly gets up then reaches for the sturdy log Bird is sitting on. "I did not know that they could get soft like that."

Sky Eye walks over. "Are you alright? Sorry for laughing but that was funny."

Through his own laughter, Ista says, "That's what I am here for."

After taking a sip of water, Bird stands up, looks around, then leans forward like he is starting a conspiracy. "I would never wonder this in front of Gumki or the others, but do you think we are lost Sky Eye?"

"I don't know where we are, where we are really going or even what we are doing, but I do know this, we have already gone further, and in a different direction than the last group did on their coming-of-age test."

Ista rubs his neck, "How do you know that?"

"Because Shadow told me all about his test. I like to ask questions, that is how I learn new things."

"We are not lost because I heard Gumki and Two Bows talking about how much further we still have to go." Turtle stares into the distance and sees a beautiful cloud speckled sky.

"Did you hear where we are going?" Sky Eye raises one eyebrow then the other to laughter.

"No."

Ista cups his ears, "They must have known what you were up to Turtle."

Sky Eye squeezes his boto before reminding his thirsty friends. "Don't forget what they said about our water."

Sky Eye looks them all in the eye. "We are in a valley in the middle of nowhere. We don't know where we are going or even what we are doing. This must also be a test to test our trust, in each other."

"Time to get busy," Turtle whispers sullenly, "Here they come and I sure hope they know what they are doing."

"Turtle, can you help me? My neck is still sore from turning it real fast when we heard that loud noise." Bird slowly starts turning his whole body to look around instead of just his head.

"Hoa, now you say that. Your neck has been working, good all day."

"Let's hurry up and finish before it gets even colder." Sky Eye rubs his hands together before getting busy with what he has been assigned to do that evening. "The quicker we are all done with everything, the sooner we can get close to keep warm until we can build the fire."

Ista's voice is muffled by his poncho and blanket. "If it wasn't getting so cold already, I might take a long time so I don't have to huddle with any of you before the fire is ready."

Slowly the light retreats, fades, then eventually falls to the bitter cold darkness, just like the Chosen's inhibitions do.

16

8th day – High sun

With the breathtaking mountains peaks behind them and one of the tastiest meals any of them can remember giving them more energy than they have felt in days, the warriors in training have been on the move since daybreak. Their morning had started out very cold, but like frozen tundra warming to spring, their muscles have been loosening up as the sun climbed higher and higher. Too bad their attitudes have been heading in the opposite direction. There have been some recent looks of doubt and disgust aimed Hugumki's way, not to mention a whisper or two of distrust troubling the air. Without even trying, Hugumki sees and hears it all, and it bothers him more than he expected, especially the looks of doubt.

On his break earlier, Hugumki had his own questions, but they were of a different sort. They are not full of doubt but curiosity. "Why me? Why am I the only one that knows where we are going and why? How will everyone react when they finally find out?"

When they reach a wide-open area of crumbled regolith, Hugumki knows the time has come because the weight he carries has grown beyond a burden, it has become an irritant. Like tiny claws digging into his body, it is not a feeling he can simply squirm out of. It is a responsibility that needs to be shared. The thing bothering him now is that once he says what needs to be said, he is going to end everything with a lie.

When they stop to watch a fledgling hawk try to chase a smaller bird across the infinite sky, Hugumki tells everyone to gather around him. "I have something very important to say. I know we are out in the open so we will sit down, form a circle, then pull our ponchos or blankets over our heads."

"Good idea Gumki," Two Bows does his best to joke. "Our blankets are the same color as this area so we will only look like rocks having a counsel.

"Hoa, I will put the black rock called Esan under mine," Hugumki's laugh rings as hollow as his eyes.

"Don't sit down yet," Ah Ki Wami does a quick check for anything that would like to take a piece out of them. Not seeing anything, he starts sitting down.

Once everyone is around him in a tight circle with their ponchos or blankets over their heads and bodies, Hugumki thrusts his chin out and raises his voice. "Don't forget, rocks don't laugh and move," which causes a couple of the smaller rocks to jiggle about.

Once they are all as settled as the land around them, Hugumki begins.

"As I said before, this coming-of-age test is special. In fact, it is extra special." Seeing their looks of impatience, he gets to the point. "In case some of you can't tell yet, we are heading to the great waters at the end of our people's land."

"I knew it," Sky Eye says, the pride in his dark intelligent eyes lights up the rest of his face.

"So did I," Rabbit boasts quietly.

Hugumki pets Esan to calm himself down. "When we get there, that is where and when our real test will begin."

"What do you mean?" Two Bows asks quickly, and sharply.

"The elders told you before we left that this test was going to be different. Each of you said you were ready."

Turtle looks down at his short legs, "I never thought I would make it to the great waters."

"I hope none of you thought that we are carrying all of these supplies to last less than half a cycle of Little Sun," Hugumki says.

As mother hawk screams forlornly for her wayward youngster as only a torn hearted mother can, Hugumki presses on.

"I can't say what we will do once we get there," he pauses to take a small sip of water, "because I don't really know yet. What I do know is that it will get harder. What I know even more is that it can be done because it must be done. Any questions?"

Deerhead, with a head shake, is the first. "If you don't know what we are going to do, how will we know?"

"It will be revealed to us when the time is right."

"Why us?" asks Rabbit, stretching his tired feet and legs out from under his poncho. Rabbit likes to be special, in the ways he chooses, not according to someone else's plan.

"Because of the number of us needed to complete this unusual test. That is one reason some of us had to wait to have our test. That way, all of us would be old enough to come along." Hugumki looks at Ista and Bird.

Two Bows leans in Deerheads direction to quietly ask, "Are Ista and Bird really old enough?"

"Sky Eye, how many people did Shadow say went on his test?" asks Deerhead.

"Three."

Hugumki tries to explain without giving anything away. "Even if they were seasoned warriors, three could not do and finish, I mean, pass this test the right way. They just would not be able too."

"We can, can't we?" comes Turtles proud muffled voice.

"Yes we can and we will Turtle."

"Yes we can and we will," they all repeat as one.

For a brief, moment in time, human voices resound in an area of the desert where they will not be heard again for many, many years, if ever.

"Let's get moving before we get stuck in this spot like real rocks," Ah Ki Wami starts getting to his feet.

"I think my leg fell asleep," Two Bows thumps his dead feeling leg on the ground.

Watching Two Bows shake his leg, Hugumki says, "We can talk more about this later. Right now, my throat is getting very dry, as I am sure yours is too. We will have one quick drink before we get going again."

Reunited again, mother and fledgling watch the strangest sight start to unfold below them. A tight cluster of rounded rocks slowly starts shaking and moving. Then the rocks each grow a head, two arms, and finally, two legs. Unexpectedly, out of one of them darts a furry black spirit. What magic is this in this mysterious land?

Rabbit has a feeling he is not alone. Once everyone starts walking ahead, he cautiously turns over the flat rock that has gotten his attention and is immediately outnumbered. In legs that is.

"I knew you were there ci ce ci ce, I thought I heard your legs, but you still surprised me. You are the biggest one I have ever seen and look at all those legs. Do you ever trip on them?

Rabbit is looking down at a large brown centipede with at least forty legs. "I must go now. Have a good life," he says as he carefully puts the rock and shelter back in place for his new friend then quickly scurries to catch up with the others while also making sure he is not leaving signs of a trail behind him.

8th day – Evening

The Chosen can see gray empty clouds twirling in front of them that look like wispy whispers of darkness, or a dry foreshadowing of things still to come. The past two days were supposed to have been one of the easier parts of their test as they worked their way gradually downhill to the great waters. Instead, it has turned into a lesson in water conservation for them in a desert that could, and would, quickly dry them out like pieces of Hohokam jerky. In very dry air it is not just the heat that will steal your moisture, as you would expect. Cold weather, like they experienced earlier, can also have the same effect on your body.

Their education stated two days ago when Ooha, Sky Eye, and Rabbit had caught up with everyone else after filling all the empty botos with snow. After they did, no one had noticed how much lighter the snow-filled ones were. Whether it was the joy of singing and feeling blessed or the excitement of a new day's journey, no one could say for sure.

It was not until they had had a break and Ah Ki Wami went to have a drink of water then started checking his boto for a leak, did they realize that many of their botos were barely half-full. Ignoring everyone's suggestion to go back and refill their botos, Hugumki simply said, "We must all learn from our mistakes."

It also seems like they drink less water when they are running than when they are walking, like earlier this afternoon when they slowly passed through a wide field of cactus that everyone agreed looked like Che Wah's feathered headdress. The whole time they cautiously walked through, Two Bows and Deerhead had to keep reminding everyone, including themselves, to take very small sips from their botos.

Hugumki, even quieter than usual after his earlier talk, had just said, "As I already said, this is a good lesson for us to learn from. On our return journey home, we will be moving even slower so we will need to make sure our water lasts even longer then."

"Why will we be moving slower?" Bird quietly asked Ista. "Will we eat too much fish?"

With the day's trek almost over, the Chosen have fallen into an easy, though brisk pace of walking. Passing through what can only be called paradise's rugged landscape, there is hardly any talking to be heard. Even though they are surrounded by cacti standing proud, majestic mountains on guard, and the clearest, purist air you cannot see, other than a little dust here and there, each of them seems to be deep in thought. Maybe they are just a little more worried about running out of water than any of them are ready to admit out loud, yet.

Esan, who has been getting his share of water, but not as much as he wants, does not look overly happy either.

Just when things are beginning to feel dire for all of them, Esan, walking in the middle of his silent group of friends suddenly takes off the best he can in his buffalo hide sandals. It looks like the small animal trail he is hobbling along leads up to a rocky bluff. Two Bows, remembering what Hugumki had told him about a surprise, yells when some of the others call after him or try to catch him as he passes by. "Let him go. I think I know where he is going."

When they eventually catch up with Esan after climbing the hard scrabble, rock covered bluff, they stare in disbelief at what caused him to take off on them. It is a pool of crystal-clear water. The water is slowly bubbling out of the rocks, which has formed the small pool where Esan is waiting with fresh cold water dripping from his happy black face. It's an oasis in the middle of the vast and arid desert floor.

"So, this is the surprise the elders were talking about," Hugumki quietly says to Two Bows. "They must have wanted us to feel like we were in trouble without enough water. Thank the gods it is not too hot yet. You and Rabbit have a drink then go do a quick check."

"It looks like the water goes back into the ground over there," Sky Eye declares, before he starts to splash Bird and Turtle. "This must be how the cactus around here, get their water. Underground rivers maybe?"

After drinking and splashing more than their share of cold, refreshing water, they are waiting to hear what Hugumki has to say. While they stand around in various stages of undress, Ista looks at their bellies, swollen due to all the water they just drank. "You all look like you will have babies before harvest time."

"So do you," Ah Ki Wami pats Ista on his round, brown belly, like he is checking for twins.

That causes everyone to laugh, including Hugumki, who decides not to caution everyone about drinking too much water. He is keeping a close eye on them though.

While giving out the assignments for later, Hugumki also explains why camp cannot be next to or near the water that night, which quickly stifles any discontent. "If there is something out here bigger than us that is also thirsty, I don't want us to be between it and the water. Do you?"

It is so quiet for a moment you can hear a cactus needle drop before Bird and Ista's nervous laughter breaks the silence.

Before long, Two Bows and Rabbit return. After another drink and splash, they let Hugumki know that they found a good spot for the night and that the small range of funny looking hills that he had told them held another surprise for them, were still there and waiting in the distance. They also tell him that they would probably reach them by high sun next day, if they are not delayed. And then, everyone tries to get into the small cold pool of water, at once.

17

9th day – First light

Dawn breaks along with Hugumki's voice when he starts shouting. "Get uup. Waaaake up eeeverybody. Now."

Ista reluctantly opens his eyes. "What is happening?"

His answer is a slash motion from Hugumki and a hissed, "Be quiet."

Ista's eyes get even bigger when he realizes there is no one lying on either side of him like there was earlier. In fact, all he sees is Turtle, Bird, Ooha, and Sky Eye still in bed, thrashing around in confusion.

Once out of bed and crouching down like Hugumki is. "What happened? Where are they?" he whispers to Hugumki.

"They are hiding and now you must find them," Hugumki answers to rippling groans of laziness.

Once their brown, bewildered faces are all in front of him, Hugumki explains what is going on.

"I have seen that some of you still need to work on your trail skills. I am now going to test your tracking skills. I am surprised none of you heard the others get up early, and I think Esan even licked one of you."

Ooha smiles, remembering a strange dream and kiss he had.

Hugumki points at the desert spread out in front of them. "They are hiding out there in different spots. The first one to follow their trail and find someone wins.

Turtle grinds some dirt underneath his sandal. "What about first meal?"

"If this was real, you must be ready at all times so leave everything for now and get ready to move."

"Even when hungry," Ista mimics an elder's voice.

"Get going. One of them could be in danger and needs your help, so knives out."

Feeling his patience drain out of him as he watches them bump into each other, luckily without stabbing each other, then slowly start wandering aimlessly around while destroying every clue that was in front of them, Hugumki gives a pitiful shake of his head and with one loud whistle, calls everyone back in.

"We will try this another time," Hugumki says in a voice devoid of all emotion.

Turtle stands on his toes to see better. "Where are they at?"

Hugumki's face breaks into a smile as the desert comes alive.

A dark green cactus off to the side suddenly has two brown arms.

The resting rock not far in front of them is sneezing.

What looked like an undulating shadow now has Esan's nose.

Hugumki covers his eyes. "They were right in front of you all along. You just don't have the right eyes to see them yet. Keep practicing your eyes ahead and your eyes around. Let us eat quickly and then get ready to leave.

Once under way, Hugumki notices that some of the looks he is receiving once again have his greatest enemy hiding within them. Doubt.

∽

A hot dry wind slowly picks up and starts blowing across the brownish gray arid landscape. A perfect excuse to take a longer water and food break. After everyone is sheltered and comfortable, Hugumki tells the others that he is taking Esan for his walk. Once he is alone with Esan in a small, sheltered ravine, Hugumki starts to berate himself, causing a covey of quail to scatter at the intrusion.

After he is finished, Esan looks up at his friend and this is what he sees and hears: A clenched jaw holding gritting teeth, followed by, "My mistake, my mistake. I should have been paying more attention to the snow-filled botto's. Will this cost me my chance at becoming chief when the others talk about it, and I know they will? Kani! It's not their fault, it is mine. I must pay attention all the time, just like I always tell the others. We were never in too much danger of running out of water, still, I seem unprepared and not in charge. Am I meant to do this? Of course, I am. I was made for this. I will lead us to the great waters and back. How about you Esan, do you feel better? I don't really but don't tell anyone about this," Hugumki almost chokes on his own strangled laugh. "You have nothing to worry about, I am ready again. I am Hugumki and I will be the greatest chief ever. Do you need help, out of here my furry friend?"

The short walk back feels both lonely and satisfying, to his surprise.

Hugumki can hear rising voices as he approaches their resting spot and the walls of rock scattered around them. "What now?" he asks as he heads toward the latest commotion.

The first thing he notices is that Ooha's face is so red it looks like he is going to burst open with more than a song. "You did too. You did it on purpose." Ooha gingerly touches his head.

Sky Eye sneers, "We did not."

"You did it to yourself. We weren't even next to you," Turtle adds defiantly.

"You tried to kill me," Ooha says as pathetically as he can.

"He is so…." someone starts to comment before Hugumki interrupts.

"What happened?"

"One of them," Ooha points at Turtle, Bird, Ista and Sky Eye, "dropped a rock on my head."

Deerhead wants to get involved too. "Show us where each of you were when it happened."

Once they are all standing in place, everyone can see that Ooha was not even in the same area as the others.

Hugumki tries to be as patient as he can. "Ooha, do you think that maybe your climbing made a piece come loose, and that is what hit you?"

While Ooha tries to come up with an answer, some of the others have plenty to whisper about.

"What a baby."

"He is so special that nothing will ever happen to him unless we do it."

"We are only with him. He is not with us."

Ooha does not say another word, but he does grumble a bit as they prepare to continue onward.

Just before he takes his first step, Hugumki glances toward Ista, who has been much quieter than he usually is. Is that a wicked grin tugging at the corners of his mouth?

9th day – High sun

With the sun burning overhead, the Chosen continue onward, with their goal steadily getting closer but not yet in sight.

Without warning, the dust is stirred up in an unexpected and unnecessary way. It is a dust up that has not gone unnoticed by the large group of vultures that have been patiently circling and soaring overhead in the cornflower blue, desert sky.

Below them are two fools starting to roll around in combat. They resemble flailing dusty tumbleweeds as they try to pummel each other into submission over nothing but ego and attitude.

The vultures are hoping and waiting to see if their next meal is going to be delivered to them, or not. Their hope is that if one of the fighters should die in battle: they can swoop down to start picking away at the carcass for a tasty lunch.

Gracefully clutching his hands together, Rabbit observes the scene. "Thank the gods that Two Bows and Deerhead are fighting without weapons."

After a long moment or two, maybe even three, "Enough!" commands Hugumki. "Save your energy, you will need it. You are both important, just like the rest of us on this que.., test." After delivering a couple of not so gentle kicks to the brown fighting ball still rolling around in front of him, Hugumki takes a sip from his boto to clear his throat. "There could be a path to the god's right over there," which causes a couple of heads to turn in the direction that Hugumki is pointing, followed by sheepish laughter. "But if you don't stay alert and take the time to find it or follow it, what good would it do you?"

Slowly unwinding like a very thick snake, the two dusty bodies still cling tightly to each other.

"I could have taken you if Gumki had not saved you," Deerhead snarls. His eyes are bugged out and his mouth is foaming as he cautiously starts to let Two Bows go.

Standing in only his breechcloth, which to everyone's alarm has been turned sideways, Two Bows loosens his grip on the stockier Deerhead. "That must be why your life is leaking from your mouth and nose."

Not yet finished with his lecture, Hugumki slowly turns his head as if dealing with two oversized babies. "Now both of you will spend the rest of this day dusty and dirty. You both know that you can't spare enough water to rinse off unless you would rather be thirsty for a while."

Ista like always, sees the funny side of things. "It made me laugh when Two Bows made a loud noise after Deerhead grabbed him and squeezed the smelly air out of him."

"What a waste of time and energy," Rabbit raises his face to the sky, then sighs. "They are already friends again." He fakes a sob, glancing at the now hugging fighters.

When he releases Two Bows, Deerhead's wane smile drips blood. "Sorry Two Bows. We are brothers and we will more than likely fight now and then our whole lives."

"Thank you Deerhead. Now I have something to look forward to in my life." Two Bows grimaces, trying in vain to dust himself off.

Hearing Two Bows words, Bird looks at Hugumki. "I didn't know they are blood brothers."

"Most likely we all are Bird, even if we do not have the same mother's."

Sky Eye adds, "I know a lot of us in the village are blood related Bird."

"You're right Sky Eye. Those of us born in our village are more than likely blood related one way or another," Hugumki nods. "Even if we are from different clans."

Still not sure if he is ready for a mate or not, Sky Eye says, "That is why it is a good idea for some of us to take mates from the large village, not only from our village."

"Why?" Bird asks.

"Some of the girls in the large village come from other tribes and have different blood so that we don't all look the same or act the same, and that is a good thing."

"Look what happened to Momo," Deerhead is referring to the fact that Momo's parents, were probably brother and sister. Whatever truth there was left the village when they abandoned Momo.

"That must be why Wami, and I do not look the same as everyone else. We were not born in the village." Rabbit looks at Ah Ki Wami with a sad, proud smile.

"I always wondered why my face looks different than everyone else's." Ah Ki Wami closes his eyes so that he can try and see into his past. "Maybe someday I will learn how I got this scar: mother won't tell me."

Ah Ki Wami's scar, in the right light, glistens like the knife blade that probably made it. The only problem it has caused for Ah Ki Wami is that he has a slight paralysis in his face which causes everyone to think that he has no emotions, except anger.

Hugumki starts putting his pack back on. "Like I said before, on this test, we are all one. It does not matter when or where you came from, but where we are going, and that is nowhere right now."

"Fun is over everyone. Sorry to tease you vultures." Two Bows wipes a slightly cleaner streak across his dirty sweaty face as he glances at the sky, then the path in front of them. "Let's get ready to continue our journey. The great waters await."

The vultures slowly circle around once more, disgusted at wasting their time. They then soar up and away: slowly turning into black rotating dots with wings, patiently waiting for something else to die.

"I bet nobody even knows what the fight was about," Rabbit whispers to Esan. "Oh them worked up boys, men, hoa."

"Eyes ahead, eyes around," utter a couple of voices without any real enthusiasm, which is surprising, considering they are steadily drawing closer to something they can't even begin to imagine.

'I know I should be excited," Turtle says to Sky Eye, once they are underway again. "I just feel like, instead of losing weight, I am getting heavier."

Sky Eye takes a deep breath. "I know what you mean. I can breathe easier now, but I feel heavier too."

Before long, whether they realize it or not, their backs start getting straighter and their strides start getting longer because there is a new force drawing them ever closer to the great water and they are reacting to it like little brown desert fish. Excited and driven.

9th day – Mid-afternoon

Each eager teen cautiously creeps forward without the slightest inkling of what truly awaits him.

Ooha looks around when they reach the top of a small rocky hill, "I still don't see….oh."

As one, they gasp: For in front of them are large mounds of white sand filled with sparkles.

Even though Hugumki had described the area to them, just as he had been told, he along with everyone else is still surprised to see the large piles of sand that Bear had talked about.

"Could we be looking in the wrong direction?" Turtle shields his face because the sunlight, reflecting off the sand, is hurting his eyes. He too is surprised by all the sand, but he knows that Hugumki was also referring to something even more special earlier.

Hugumki lightly smacks his palm against his temple. "Not everything in life is going to hit you on top of your head. A warrior does not see with just his eyes," he patiently says. "Close them, tip your head back, and take a deep breath through your nose."

Once they do that, realization slowly registers on their faces. "Wet life. We can smell wet life! We have made it! We are almost at the great waters!" they exclaim with their arms waving in the air which they quickly put back down when they realize what they are doing.

"The air smells so different here, it is alive." With his heart pounding in his chest, Two Bows takes another gulp of air to enjoy the experience he never thought he would have.

Rabbit is trying to decide if that is good or bad. "I would not say it stinks, but it does smell different than I thought it would."

"Does it taste even better than the water of the desert?" Turtle licks his dry lips in anticipation of all the water he could ever drink.

Hugumki smiles before he breaks Turtle's heart. "Turtle, even though we will see more water than any of us could ever imagine, we can't drink any of it without getting very, very sick.

"Is it poisoned, or worse, is it cursed?" Bird almost demands, the worry lines he should not have on his face already, get slightly deeper.

Hugumki points in front of them at the sand that look like large piles of misplaced snow. "The water is full of that kind of sand. I have been told that it makes the water very strong and thick."

Wondering how that can be, Two Bows takes another deep breath, "So nothing can live in the water? Even from here, it smells so alive."

"Once we get there, the biggest surprise and mystery will be that the great waters will be full of all kinds of life."

Two Bows looks at the horizon. "Hugumki, have you ever seen clouds look like that?"

"No."

In the distance, they see what looks like a solid line of low clouds hovering in the direction of the great waters.

When Hugumki prepares to utter his motivating words, Sky Eye, in his excitement, beats him to it. "Eyes ahead, eyes around. Let's go."

Filled with the energy that only the excitement of a new discovery can bring, the Chosen all scramble down the other side of the hill. They want and need to finish the day's journey a short distance away from the great waters.

Once on flatter ground, barely able to control the excitement that is surging through his body, Ista asks, "Turtle, how great do you think the great waters will be?"

"After what I just learned, don't know, don't care anymore. I am just glad I get to see them."

"When we get there, Turtle, do you?"

"No Ista, but we can say we did."

"How about you Bird, what do you think?" Ista asks.

"I hope the great waters are bigger than I think they can be. I can't wait to see something that I never thought I would see my whole life."

"I remember one of the stories I heard said they had waves. Does that mean that the creatures that can live in that water will wave at us?"

Sky Eye, who has been ambling along with them, lost in thought, lets out a laugh. "No, Turtle, what that means is that…"

Hugumki, walking back to check on the younger ones, because, as you would expect, those with the longer legs are letting their excitement carry them a little further ahead, says, "Just wait and see. I know we will all be surprised. Great job everyone, you have almost made it to the great waters."

From up ahead, Esan looks back at them as if to say, *if you don't hurry up, we will never get there.* Too bad Esan will soon be disappointed.

Hugumki slows down to wait on Deerhead who is sweeping away their dusty footprints with his blanket. He can barely contain his own excitement and pride at leading the boys this far. "I am Hugumki, we are the Chosen," escapes his lips and into the salt-tinged air.

9th day – Evening

On a gentle breeze blowing in from the great waters, the sea fog has slowly come ashore to obscure the setting sun.

Sharing a ride with the moist wind is the aroma of salt and life from a place the Chosen have never been before, either in their wildest imaginations, or dreams. It is so close now that they can almost reach out and touch it, if only they were allowed.

"We will be getting up very early, next day, even before Father Sun starts lighting the sky," Hugumki tells everyone huddled around him. "We will have no fire, this night, because we cannot risk anyone seeing or smelling us. This close to the river we must be extra careful, and I do think this is a different river than ours."

They turn toward the river which looks like a shimmering glistening rope in the light mist.

Hugumki continues, "When it gets darker, we will go to the river for more water and to wash, which two of you need to do very much." Seeing a stir or two, "No fishing."

Hugumki can't help but notice that everyone, including himself, are filled with an energy they have never felt before. Not even earlier that day.

It is the primal pull of the sea, and even though they had felt its light tug before, now it feels as if it is reaching out and grasping every fiber of their being.

"I know we all want to see the great water right now, but we must all wait."

Once the groans of disappointment die away, "So no sneaking away to have a look. Take this time before dark to rest and think about what you have learned so far. I know I will."

"I know what I think," Rabbit softly exclaims, abruptly picking Bird up in the air. "We made it, Bird! We made it!"

Birds skinny flailing legs look like he is trying to run on air so that he can reach the great waters before anybody else does.

Taking off his poncho, Turtle asks, "Why does the air look like that Sky Eye?"

"Don't worry Turtle, it is just extra water in the air, like fog. It might be a little harder to breath, but it won't bother you."

Two Bows smiles. "It is what we saw earlier in the distance."

From off to the side, Hugumki watches with a mixture of pride and unease.

The pride comes from the mere fact that they have all made it this far without any big mishaps.

His unease comes from thinking, *How long is it going to take them to fall asleep? Are we going to find what we came all this way for?*

Hearing his own answer echo around in his head, Hugumki knows that he can do nothing, but wait and see.

18

10th day – Before Daybreak

Oha softly singing a morning song, meant for babies, lets everyone know it is time to get up and start one of the most exciting days any of them will ever have.

While groaning, stretching, and yawning Ista jokingly complains, "I thought I was supposed to be the funny one."

The Chosen's life changing day has arrived as quietly as the fog it rode in on. Visibility, so far, is a heavy moist ground covering gray, topped off by a layer of swirling white that is felt more than seen in the early gloom.

"Funny or not, it does not make this getting up before Father Sun all the time, any easier," grumbles Deerhead, standing up and removing the buckskin shirt he slept in.

Rabbit, like usual in the morning, is almost invisible, and when he does start moving, he looks as slow and wispy as the mist that covers their camp.

Wiping the beaded moisture from his face Two Bows walks over to where Hugumki is standing. "Are we still going to do this? I just walked around a little bit. I could barely see my feet when they moved the air, and the fog seems to be everywhere."

"It is what we are meant to do. In some ways, the fog will be good. It will give us cover. I just hope it is not so much that we can't see the water."

"That would be very bad, wouldn't it?"

"Yes, it would."

Knowing that the new day's revealing light will soon be coming, Hugumki reminds everyone to hurry up, and still, be very careful with their footing on the damp slippery ground.

Their sluggish movements are heralded by rising pillars of mist.

Cutting through like a blade, Ah Ki Wami starts circling everybody while softly clapping his hands and stomping his feet. It is excitement not nervousness that has him so worked up, and ready to go before everyone else. "Come on, hurry up everybody. I had a dream about the great waters. Let's get going so I can see if it is true or not."

After quickly eating some jerky, nuts, and dried fruit washed down with water retrieved from the river, past night, the Chosen are soon on their way. What part of the great waters are they going to, and why? Hugumki is still the only one that knows.

In just their sandals, breechcloths, and cotton shirts, the teens are barely able to control their excitement, even after Hugumki told them again that they needed to be both cautious and quiet. Besides the knives tucked into their leggings, they are each carrying the small empty bag that is loosely filled with cotton cloth inside. Turtle is also carrying Hugumki's extra bag, the bag that is filled with the rope that will soon be needed. For what? Hugumki has not said anything about that either.

Everything else, including an upset Esan, have been safely hidden until they are retrieved on the way back. They have even left their zumis and medicine pouches behind, without too much disagreement between them.

After a short walk filled with growing anticipation.

"I hope we can see through the fog what I am starting to hear and feel." Deerhead cocks his head like his namesake as a low rumble of unimaginable power starts to fill the shrouded air and send vibrations through the ground.

In silent prayer, ten damp raised heads reverently send their wishes to the sky. In response, the fog slowly starts drifting away. It is as if the great body of water has taken a deep breath, then exhaled because it wanted to get a good look at the Chosen to see why they are approaching so quietly, and cautiously?

Soon enough, they are in the right position, according to Hugumki's directions. Warily, they approach the edge of what Hugumki was told was going to be a high cliff face. Turns out, it is more like an angled double layered slope above the raging water that is eight man high. The only sound they are making is the shuffle of their sandals because each of them seems to be holding his breath in awe as massive waves slam not too far below them while sending tingling vibrations racing throughout their bodies.

Finally catching his breath, "Here comes another one," Turtle announces as he leans back.

"A big one," Two Bows says, his eyes getting wider.

When Bird leans forward to get a better look, he gets what is coming to him.

"Look at how wet you got," Ista points and laughs.

Bird cries out in pain. "My eyes, my eyes. It's burning my eyes."

After rubbing his face with his damp hand, Bird tries to open his eyes again. "I can't see. I'm going blind. It hurts."

Hugumki wipes some mist from his own eyes. "Stop it, Bird. It is just salty water." He reaches out his hand as another wave sends up its spray. After a quick lick of his hand. "See. Just salty water, like it smells. After your tears wash out your eyes, you will be good."

Besides the waves and their immense power, the first of many things that surprises the Chosen is the foaming dark water that stretches out farther than any of them can see and the rock face they are on that seems to want to embrace it.

The squawking and coordinated chaos of the hungry seabirds-whose numbers almost cover the horizon-as they fly, and dive, over and over again into the raging tumultuous water below is even more chaotic than the largest festival any of them have ever been to, or heard about. The ions of the churning gulf are also taking their turn, affecting them all the way too their very core. It is almost more than they can take at once, leaving them once again momentarily speechless.

Hugumki smiles as he watches them enjoy and be mesmerized by the amazing spectacle from the top of the rock face they are crouched on. After warning everyone to watch out for any water floater below (*a canoe),* Hugumki takes another moment to be amazed by all the new sensations he is experiencing.

Feeling the skin on his cheeks grow taut when his jaw almost drops off his face, Ah Ki Wami can do nothing but stand there and let the majesty of the sea wash over him in sight, sound, and energy. As amazing as his dream was, it is nothing compared to what he is seeing and feeling right now.

"I did not think there could be this much water in one place, anywhere," Ooha is stunned to see something even greater than himself.

Shaking his head with a rueful smile, Bird can't believe his itchy eyes. "All this water, and we can't drink any of it."

"That is strange, Bird," Ah Ki Wami peers through the lingering strands of fog. "With all the fish those birds are catching, the water looks very much alive."

Two Bows, notices what looks like a waterline below. "Hugumki, it looks like sometimes the water gets even higher than it is now. I would say we are almost ten men high above the water right here. Good thing we don't have to go down there." Seeing a strange look flash across Hugumki's face, he asks hesitantly, "Do we?"

Ista is disappointed he cannot see where the river flows into the great waters.

Turtle is surprised to see that the cactus grows right up to the edge of the water in some places.

Looking over at a noisy gray and white bird that is pecking away at a dead crab, Rabbit proclaims with a stifled yawn, "That bird looks the same as some I have seen back home."

After giving everyone, including himself, another moment to take it all in, Hugumki reluctantly chirps to get their attention as he leans toward Turtle and pulls out the rope. "We will all climb down there," he starts explaining, pointing out a small flat area that is just below where they are crouched. "Underneath that overhanging part is a cave that you can't see from here. In that cave is where our real test begins. When we are all on the ledge, I will climb down to the cave, once the four strongest on top are hanging onto this. It is not very far, but because of this fog, it is going to be very slippery. That is why we must all tie the rope here around our waists before we go down. It's in case any of us slips and loses their grip on the holes that are in the rock."

"This will be so easy," Two Bows puffs out his chest and raises his head. "Unlike some of you, I climb the rocks back home all the time."

"Now pay close attention," Hugumki looks at them sternly. "I don't want any of us to slip and fall on those down there." He pauses a moment so that they can all see how sharp the encrusted rocks below are. "Once I am in the cave, I will fill Two Bows' bag with singing stones. When I am done, I will signal by tugging on this rope three times that it is time to pull the rope back up so someone keep hanging onto it the whole time, all right. Bird, when Two Bows and I each go down, watch what we do. I have been told that you, Ista, and Turtle may have to reach around the mouth of the cave with your feet, just a little bit. There should be a ledge that starts just inside the cave that you will need to reach. If any of you need help, let me know before you let go of the rope because you will not like what happens then. After that, I will let you feel the weight of the bag I have filled for you. Then, I will strap it onto your body. When we signal that we are ready, once again, three tugs on the rope, the four strongest that are on top need to be ready again. It's just in case Two Bows or whoever is next loses his grip when he climbs back up. After Two Bows, we will go from the youngest to oldest so I will know how much to put in each pack. Sky Eye, you're younger than Ooha, right?"

Ooha nods yes.

"I will take two bags with me and everybody else make sure you bring down one with you, and don't forget to be careful. Hugumki bends down, wipes the ground, then shows the others the moisture his simple gesture has collected. "Be prepared, because each one of you will be heavier coming back up than when you went down."

Seeing the looks of puzzlement on their faces, he quickly adds. "None of us will be given more weight than a large one hand sized rock, weighs. That is why all of us are here to share the load. Does anybody care if Two Bows goes first since he is the best at climbing around on rocks?

The waves crash. The wind cries. The birds scream. Not one voice of protest is heard.

"Wami or Deerhead will tie the rope on whoever goes next until we all have our bags filled, and everyone is back on the ledge. Remember, be careful and keep watch below, and around."

Hugumki starts getting in position to carefully ease himself down to the ledge. He stops and looks back with a big smile on his moist brown face. "Yes, I did say singing stones."

"Gumki, when did you find out what we were going to do?" hangs unanswered in the misty air that is starting to glow like an impatient ember just waiting to burst into flame.

Once everyone has gotten down and is safely on the lower, wide sloping ledge, Hugumki ties the rope around himself. After double checking to make sure that Deerhead, Ah Ki Wami, Turtle, and Rabbit have a good grip on the rope, he slowly and very carefully starts climbing down using the natural handholds that are in the porous rock face. Since his muscles are not yet warmed up, Hugumki can feel more than just the tension of the moment coursing through his body. Before he knows it, he is staring into a moist black hole that looks like it could be the beginning, or end, of everything.

To his surprise, the entrance to the cave he had heard about in his elder's stories is not much higher than a very tall man, or wider than three men can reach. Then he notices that the floor of the cave, if you can call it that, is full of small sharp edged holes.

Hugumki can't help but find the foreboding cave, fascinating.

This cave is different from the ones he has seen back home because this cave and its walls are filled with wet life. Even though he still can't see very well yet in the soft glow of the early morning light, he can smell the salt water, seaweed, and sea life all blended into one pungent aroma.

This is not the time to explore. I hope I can come back this way again, he thinks to himself. *I must be careful now, and I am glad getting down here was easy. The elders made it sound like we were all going to have a very hard time.*

Using the skills that he has also learned back home, Hugumki easily enters the cave. He is thankful though that his friends are holding onto the other end of the rope, just in case.

I am glad I took my sandals off. He reaches out to touch a slimy wall. *I hope Two Bows does too.*

Once inside, but not as high above the raging water below as he would like, Hugumki wedges his end of the rope into a small crevice so that it will stay secure until needed.

Hugumki closes his eyes in the hope that they will quickly adjust to the semi-darkness of the cave. Then, in what can only be called perfect cosmic timing, Father Sun breaks above the far shore of the cove. Like a guiding light he starts cutting through the mist with his mighty beam. Opening his eyes in surprise, Hugumki now must wait for his eyes to adjust to, too much light. While waiting, Hugumki thinks about how the cave and its hidden treasure had been found in the first place.

One story is that Coyote and his brother Lizard were on an expedition to search for a different trade route to reach the legendary people of the hot green land. The other is that they were really following rumors, of flashing, shiny rocks. They had somehow gotten lost, so once they had arrived at the great waters, they simply followed the curved coastline in the hope of finding the trail that would help them continue their journey. After some hard travel, they had made camp at the water's edge. Like now, Father Sun had broken across the horizon with a flash of His brilliant glory. Much to their surprise, there had been an answering flash coming from a small cave they could barely see in the distant cliff face.

Using the skills honed while stealing bird eggs from the many nests on the sides of the cliffs, Coyote had stood in the exact same spot that Hugumki is standing in now.

Knowing that they would someday return better prepared, they took only a few singing stones back home with them. They eventually arrived back in the village, more dead than alive. No one believed the incredible story told by two raving mad men at the time. That is, until they showed Che Wah a singing stone. Then one night, they just disappeared, never to be seen again. Some thought they had believed their own crazy stories, and went after the rest of the treasure, alone. Others, including Che Wah and Hunter, who had listened to their story when they were clearer of mind, knew better. They never would have left the village without telling anyone or being properly prepared for another trek into the desert.

With that in mind, Hugumki hesitates just inside the gaping, pungent maw again because he has just realized that he could be starting a whole new way of life for his people by what he is about to uncover.

Nervousness and excitement surges throughout his body.

Upon closer inspection, Hugumki realizes the cave floor has partially eroded away, leaving what appears to be flat columns of rock going every which way.

To his dismay, each column or pathway has too much empty space between them for his liking.

To his surprise, what he originally thought were jagged edged holes are small lumps sprouting here and there out of the cave floor.

Hugumki steps in further and rubs his barefoot back and forth. With his head tipped back in relief. "Thank you, thank you, for being rough and not slippery. If I am careful, I should be all right," he says out loud to keep himself company.

Leading up to this moment of discovery, Hugumki has built up so much anticipation, unwittingly, it has turned into apprehension.

Looking towards the back of the cave, fifteen footsteps away or so, Hugumki can barely make out a white flowing shape, or shadow.

"If that comes after me, I won't even need the rope to get out of here."

The salty air and moment, feels thick enough to chew on, or at least crawl on Hugumki's skin.

"Rabbit is not going to like this very much," he says, a clammy shiver passing through him.

The cave's strong aroma, and its enclosed space is also causing Hugumki to think of things that go bump in the day, or night.

Splash!

Is something climbing up to attack, or dropping down to escape?

Hugumki peers through a gap and sees what appears to be something slithering sideways.

It is on the rocky shelf below with a pair of giant claws leading the way.

Besides giving the crabs and other sea life something to grow, or crawl around on, the semi-submerged shelf also keeps Hugumki from getting soaked every time a rumbling wave crashes under him.

Hugumki looks at the greenish brown, glistening walls that surround him. Some parts look like they have green fuzz growing on them.

"This is not a deep dark hole to the underworld. It is just another cave. Only wetter and much, much, smellier." The voice he hears in the cave does not sound overly confident, even to him.

Nor is it a hidden lair for an unknown monster. It's dark, rank, moist walls only feel to Hugumki as if they could harbor terrors, yet to be realized.

Hugumki reaches out a damp hand to brace himself. "This feels like someone spit all over it," his tense voice reverberates.

Beneath his feet, the orange-tinged fog floats like little wings of curiosity.

Every time they try to fly high enough to see what is going on inside the cave, a surging wave comes along and breaks them up. Then the whole process starts all over again.

Hugumki spies what he had seen before. This time it looks like a thin white translucent waterfall.

Like mother's milk, frozen in place.

"Oh, the gods! That would make the most incredible zumis."

His face drops. "Too bad we don't have any carving tools with us."

Hugumki also spots what looks like long rocks growing down from the ceilings. Some of them are even crying at their precarious predicament.

Just moments earlier, it felt like the cave was starting to close in on Hugumki.

Now it feels as if it has turned into a massive black hole.

Cavernous feeling, but definitely not empty.

For there it is.

No longer part of a story.

It has become something solid.

Something tangible.

Something real.

Something unbelievable.

Something that is right in front of him.

"I thought I could feel you." Upon entering the cave, Hugumki could sense its presence.

Tentatively he walks toward the angled form protruding from the murkiness.

"What can this be?" Hugumki touches it as he looks it over. "You're in better shape than I was told you would be, except for that hole."

Hugumki tries to walk around what looks both familiar and strange to him. For some reason, the rear cave wall keeps getting in his way.

"I have not seen many in my life, but I have never seen one that looks like this before." Hugumki gives it a light thump, then drops his head deep in thought.

"This water floater is amazing, but that is not why I am really here, is it?"

Hugumki blows out air like he too is trying to part the fog.

"Am I ready? Ready to finally see them?"

He tries to take a deep calming breath.

Slowly, so slowly, Hugumki reaches out and flips back the tattered blanket Coyote left behind to cover up what will hopefully never be found by strangers.

"What is that?"

His eyes are almost as big as the rusty oarlock he is staring at.

"What does it do? What is it for?

Hugumki picks it up. Feels the cold indifference of the metal for the first time in his life.

Puts it back like it's hot.

"That feels so hard and empty," he wipes his rusty hand on his breechcloth.

After a careful step back, Hugumki can tell that the unusual craft is tipped slightly forward, as if in the hope that someday it will slide right out of its resting spot.

"Why would they? Why is this made, out of such thick wood, and so wide I can't reach the other side?"

Hugumki tries to turn his troubling questions aside: The who's? The what's? The why's?

Right now, there are more important things for him to deal with.

Hugumki studies it some more. "I am surprised you have not started falling apart yet. How long have you been here?"

He pats it feeling a sudden affection for the resilient thing.

To his discomfort, Hugumki is starting to get a little chilly in the moist cave.

The cooler air is coming from behind the wooden mystery, and it is dry. That is perplexing to Hugumki because it feels like the air back home.

"This must be stuck in a longer cave that goes back into the desert. That's why the air is dry and why I could not get behind it."

Hugumki taps the slimy wall. "You were in my way sneaky one."

When the next wave crushes, Hugumki can only imagine how big the one must have been that wedged the water floater up where it is now.

He also thinks about how miraculous it was for Father Sun to have caught, then lit up the singing stones for one brief instant. What if that had not happened? Coyote and Lizard never would have seen their answering flash.

"Everything would be so different." Hugumki can't help but laugh. "I would probably still be in bed right now. All of us would."

A slight creaking sounds more like a loud crack in the cave.

"I have never seen this kind of wood before. It sounds like it is breathing." Hugumki reaches out and feels a splinter try to enter his tough skin.

"What kind of trees does this come from? Would it make good firewood because it is so hard? Would it burn right?" he wonders out loud.

Hugumki is also becoming more aware of the air pressure as it changes every time a surging wall of water slams the shelf below. Especially the larger ones.

He is astounded to realize that the waves dance to their own rhythm, like a giant watery heartbeat.

The rhythm of a life that is starting to throw his own a little off balance. It also feels as if the cave is breathing, and he is having a hard time adjusting to that strange thought and sensation.

Hugumki strokes his headband and hair. Closes his eyes. Takes another deep, breath. Opens his eyes, then leans in.

When Coyote first saw them, the singing stones were in three jumbled piles. It was as if whatever they were originally in had fallen apart just to reveal their treasure.

Right now, the remnants of that are on top of the stones where Coyote had spread them for camouflage.

Still, how can something so extraordinary not give itself away?

In the early distorted light, the singing stones make themselves known without even having to sing their song.

Though partially hidden, they seem to possess an inner flame.

From outside the cave, agitated squawking cuts through Hugumki's curiosity.

An awakening?

Hugumki answers the call of the wild.

After checking his clearance: he stands erect, sticks out his chest, throws his shoulders back, and holds his head high.

If the thud from his heart gets any louder, it will sound like he has company in the cave.

"I am Hugumki.

I will be the leader of my people.

I will show the way."

He can feel his ancestors hot blood pounding within him, urging him on Hugumki wipes his hands on his breechcloth again then bends over and cautiously picks up one singing stone. It almost slips out of his hand. Gripping it tighter, feeling its weight, Hugumki squeezes it like he is trying to get something out of it.

"It feels like that other thing did, but different, too."

He puts it in front of his face. Holds it there. There is not enough light for it to truly sparkle. But more than enough for it to momentarily mesmerize Hugumki.

"It is special, I can see that now."

Hugumki keeps staring at it as his finger starts rubbing the rough edges of the stone. After studying and thinking about it some more, "Why is it so flat?" he asks himself. "These would be good stones to throw."

Try as he might, Hugumki just can't see very well anymore because that small window of opportunity had quickly angled away with the rising sun.

After brushing the top layer of wood aside, Hugumki grips Two Bows' bag in one hand, with the other, he quickly figures out how to separate the stones without letting them sing their song.

After staring at one of the piles of shimmering stones long enough to lose track of time and place, Hugumki jerks his head to snap himself out of what was beginning to feel like a trance.

He makes a halfhearted vow to himself. "Before we get home, I must see them in the light."

Hugumki shakes his head again. Gets to work.

When one taps against another in his hand, he stops. "That sounds like a lot of other stones I have heard. Maybe they are not so special after all."

If Hugumki looks up, he will see that reflection is making the cave ceiling appear as if dapples of sunlight are embedded within, while others are dancing happily about.

Once Two Bows' bag is ready, Hugumki carefully places a stone on top of the one already in his palm. Then he bounces them together. "Special or not?"

The instant one stone, hits against another, the result is otherworldly.

A magical singing.

A tinkling crescendo.

The sweet sound of the Chosen's success.

When he closes his hand, Hugumki's face is aglow.

He can hear his future generation singing along with the stones.

Hugumki cries with joy at what he just heard as their ringing echoes into the dampness of the cave.

But.

Like anything special. Precious.

It always needs more attention.

"What would it sound like if I brought a bunch of them together." Hugumki can feel the cave encircling him with its glowing temptation. His eyes suddenly light up with the mischief that is hiding there. "Why can't I do both? I can hear them sing, and still, keep the secret. If I don't look at them in the light now, I have done nothing wrong."

Hugumki glances over at the waiting, dangling rope that the others will soon be using.

"Two Bows can't come down until he pulls the rope back up. The sound won't leave the cave, so what do I have to worry about?"

Hugumki gets startled. What was that? Did a giant shadow just pass through the rocks below to go along with the shadow of guilt he is trying to deny himself?

Hugumki tests the weight of Two Bows' small bag. It feels heavy. Like his thoughts

"What are they and what can they really do. How can they ever be a god?"

Flexes his fingers. "Will all this make sense someday?"

Not caring to resist anymore, Hugumki secures the full bag and slowly reaches for a glimmering handful of singing stones.

∽

Two Bows impatience has gotten the better of him. "I think it has been too long so I'm going to check on Hugumki," he says to the others, a strong bravado in his voice.

That is, until he looks around at all the dangers surrounding him as he hangs by his feet and hands from the rugged cliff face.

"See you soon," is barely heard coming from his constricted throat, and dry lips.

With a flash of black and brown, he drops from sight.

Suspended in the misty morning air, Two Bows is now part of the living chaos going on around him.

There's the crashing, roaring waves and their drifting spray.

The floating, dancing fog gives more than leaves an impression of the surrounding land and seascape.

And all the birds.

Two Bows does not want to think about all the hurtling shapes he keeps catching out of the corners of his eyes. The ones that are darting every which way behind his back. All of them screaming at him, each other, and everything else at the same time.

Feeling a brush of wing or its air, Two Bows knows if he leans back at all, one of the birds will fly right into him and possibly knock him off his perch.

That was one thing he did not want to experience right now because even though he may feel like a free bird himself, he has no wings.

Two Bows, looks left.

Two Bows, looks right.

"How far does this wall go? Maybe someplace no one has ever been before."

Two Bows, tries to shift his weight. "This isn't easy. I must be careful."

Glancing up, he expects to see an excited face or two, watching, waiting to see if he makes it. Sky Eye? or at least Bird who was told to watch.

Instead, the only movement he catches is the ledge rising, up and away from him. At least that's how it feels to the dangling Two Bows.

"Maybe I should hurry up," he says, because he is beginning to feel like he is floating in time and space.

His time: The opportunity to be doing things that he never, ever, could have dreamed of.

His space: Being suspended over the churning water and rocks by hands and feet that are starting to feel tender.

"If I fell in, I would never get out in time, would I?" he asks the wild world around him.

"Would the fish eat me like I have eaten them?" A nervous laugh cuts off any thoughts about that answer.

Without even trying, Two Bows has been absorbing the energy of the world he is hanging around in.

"This is amazing! I am Two Bows of the Bitter Water and Salty clans, and I am here above the great waters," he calls out, under his breath.

He knows he should check on Hugumki, but he has just heard something unusual that he can't even begin to identify. "Who is down there?" he asks a large, noisy, hazy silhouette on the rocks below.

His answer sounds like squeaky barks of irritation.

The barking is rudely interrupted by a loud whoosh of air from somewhere behind Two Bows' prickling back.

Not yet feeling confident enough to spin his head around, Two Bows can only hope that whatever it is, it passes him by. It does, and at their next encounter, Two Bows will not only hear the air, but see it.

To his astonishment, from out of the mist, like a beautiful song meant for the afterlife-cutting through the seals admonishments and everything else-rises a wonderful musical melody of hope and a dream.

Haunting and pleasant at the same time, one tinkling note after another sings, rings, and rides along on the damp air.

They are mystical waves of sound that will reverberate within Two Bows for the rest of his days. "Unbelievable!"

Two Bows looks up as if he expects the sky to open before him, right then and there. "I am alive to hear the joyful spirits singing," he shushes himself.

"So unbelievable," he whispers.

Two Bows' face beams with pride at being able to hear something that sounds as if it comes from another time and place.

He tries to turn his ears like Turtle can, to follow the ringing tones.

His next thought causes his fingers and toes to tighten even more. "Is it coming from the cave?"

Two Bows looks to his right and quickly tries to figure how far the cave is, in relation to how loud the singing, ringing is. Was.

The magical sound is already starting to fade away on a strong gust of wind.

"That was like a dream. Real, but already gone. I wish I could hear it one more time."

He turns his head. "If it was the stones, I know how they got their name now."

He pauses for a moment. "Should I tell Hugumki what I have heard?"

Carefully stretching his neck back, Two Bows can feel his tight muscles get even tighter with his conflicting thoughts.

Under his breath, he asks, "What if it was Hugumki? What would I do then? Probably nothing out here," he snickers as he looks around, "It would not matter anyway, would it?"

Two Bows frowns, then makes up his mind. "I got to hear them singing. Now I just want to start heading back home."

Two Bows, like some of the others, is torn between a strong sense of longing and a desire to keep experiencing new and exciting things.

Shaking his head he says, "This fog is making me sleepy. Must have been a dream, right Gumki?"

When a strong shiver rocks his body, Two Bows can feel his grips slip the slightest bit.

"I hope the cave is drier than it is out here. Should I…"

Looking over, he sees the rope start to twitch.

Hugumki tugs on the rope three times before releasing it, fully expecting it to be pulled away.

But before he can even think of any good excuses, if needed, Two Bows' excited, quivering face appears.

He easily enters the cave on his own.

"It feels cold…"

"How are they doing?" Hugumki motions over his head, while looking around to make sure he has left nothing incriminating in sight.

"Just looking around. Not really doing or saying much."

Hugumki can feel Two Bows' eyes trying to bore a hole right through him.

He gives him an equally intense stare in return.

"I thought I heard something, Two Bows. Did you hear anything different or unusual?"

Since he can't see into his eyes very well, Two Bows studies Hugumki's face.

A twitch of the nose?

A flick of the ear?

A shift of the eyes?

"No," he eventually answers.

A tacit agreement passes between lifelong friends.

No words are necessary. Their exchanged looks say it all.

We can never talk about what we have heard because we never heard anything.

To break the silent tension of the moment and return things back to the way they were between them, Hugumki starts to instruct him on what he must not do.

Before he can get out more than a few words, Two Bows gushes, "This is unbelievable Gumki! To be inside a wet cave!" His eyes are wide with excitement as he looks slowly around, and then, out the mouth of the cave. "The smell in here is very strong. The air is heavy and wet with the life that lives here."

"I know Two Bows but look down. Be very careful with your feet. Maybe we can come back here when we have more time. Right now, Father Sun is telling me that we must stay busy and finish before the fog is completely gone. If that happens, we could easily be seen by anyone."

"It sure is beautiful the way the light is cutting through the mist: a fire stick through the fog."

"Turn around Two Bows so I can take off the empty pack and put this one on your back." When Two Bows feels the weight of the burden that he, along with everyone else, will come to despise more than they can imagine, Hugumki starts giving him the same instructions he will give everyone else. "Part of this test is that you never look in the bag and you never take your eyes off it, even when sleeping. If anyone approaches us on the way back, you will guard it like it is your own child. The reason they are called singing stones is because if they bump together, they will make a singing sound. I have wrapped each stone in cloth so that on the way home, if they make any noise, we will all know that you have opened your bag and looked inside. I am sure you do not want to stay a child forever," Hugumki makes baby noises before laughing. "So, do as I say, and we will return, all of us, as men."

Before Two Bows can ask him why he is talking to him like a child, Hugumki adds, "I am going to say the same thing to everybody, so I am just practicing on you my friend."

By this time, Hugumki has securely strapped the bag of singing stones onto Two Bows damp muscular back. "Don't forget to tell the others to take their sandals off," Hugumki reminds, before releasing, handing, then tugging on the rope three times, sending Two Bows on his way.

One by one the boys appear so that they can take the place of the last one. Out of all of them, only Turtle needs Hugumki's help entering the cave. His legs are just too short to reach the inner ledge on his own. While strapping on their bags, Hugumki gives each of them the same instructions that he gave to Two Bows until only his bag remains to be filled.

Taking a moment to reflect on what this could mean for his people, Hugumki thinks about everything he knows so far about the singing stones as he fills his bag. Realizing it is not much, Hugumki glances around one last time before starting to strap his pack on.

All over again, he has too, resist the urge to get a better look at the singing stones.

After his pack is securely strapped on, he recovers the stones that are left, then walks along the cave floor to the rope that Deerhead left behind for him. He pulls it free from the small crevice, looks around one last time while tying it on then signals that he is ready to start climbing back up.

After a bit of a struggle, because the extra weight they are carrying has thrown off their center of gravity, the Chosen are safely back on top of the slopping cliff.

With his shoulders heavy from more than the weight on his back, Hugumki tells them to look at the great waters one more time because they may never be this way again. And, sad to say, there is no time for fishing. Besides, any fish they caught might be too big for them to handle.

"Gumki, Gumki, you won't believe what we saw!" eight excited voices exclaim at once. Knowing that Two Bows is the least likely to over stretch the truth about whatever they had all seen to get them so excited, Hugumki looks at him, and nods.

Two Bows, takes a breath as large as the tale he is about to tell. "When you and Deerhead were in the cave, we were all just watching the big waves smash onto the rocks. Out of nowhere, a giant fish came out of the water right there." Two Bows points just offshore from where they are standing.

"It was so big Gumki that it's head would not have fit in the cave," Sky Eye excitedly adds.

Hearing Deerhead's snort of doubt, Two Bows, defends Sky Eye's honor. "He speaks the truth. It was huge. It was bigger than you could ever imagine. But to me, that is not the most amazing thing about it. Hugumki, it blew water right out of the top of its head. That's right. Right out of the top of its head, and it was loud enough to hear it."

Hugumki studies all of them fully expecting them to start laughing at the joke they are trying to play on him, and Deerhead. Instead, all he sees are dancing, glistening eyes and wild gestures of agreement.

"Then it went back under water, and when we saw it again, it was further away, but it did the same thing. It came out of the water, and then it blew water right out of the top of its head, and this time, I could tell that the water went way up in the air. It was like rain going the wrong way." Two Bows is more than happy that no one has brought up the idea of going for a swim. "It was so big that it could swallow any of us whole if we were in the water."

Hugumki scratches his head. "Maybe that was the sound you told me about."

Two Bows' eyes grow big. "You're right. I am glad I didn't fall in."

Turtle starts to say something, thinks better of it, then adjusts the small pack on his back.

Hugumki turns to scan the water one last time in the hope that he would see what they had seen. "I wish we had more time to explore. Let's go. Eyes ahead, eyes around. Don't forget, from now on, we must all be extra careful."

Once they are on their way, Hugumki takes a moment to give silent thanks to his Creator. He is thankful for all the wondrous things he has seen and experienced, so far. He is also thankful that no one got hurt while retrieving the singing stones. Another reason he is thankful is that none of the others acted overly curious about where the singing stones came from or about the strange shape in the cave. Their only interest seems to be the task at hand and returning home as quickly as possible. Maybe they just aren't awake enough yet.

Trudging the short distance back to where they had hidden their supplies, was easy enough. It was finding the exact spot that was a little bit tougher. The wet darkness earlier had made everything look the same. Now, the fog that was still lingering around was trying to do the same thing. It was not until a very relieved, red-faced Esan let them know that they were getting close, were they able to find their own hiding spot. Esan's face is bloody from whatever he had caught for his breakfast earlier.

Packing up, all the Chosen know that their journey back home will be much harder now. Especially, if Bear was right when he told Hugumki that the first part back home would feel like they were walking up a very, very, long mountain. Another thing they have noticed is that the air, being both wetter and heavier by the great water, is making it harder for them to breathe than they are used to. To their discomfort, it was starting to make them feel damp and limp, inside and out.

Almost from the beginning, none of the Chosen like the way the thin yucca straps of the heavy singing stone bags are digging into their bodies.

"My bag does not feel that heavy, it is just very uncomfortable the way it hangs there." Turtle tugs on his ears as if that could help balance him out.

Deerhead has the perfect way to describe it. "It's like the weight of the dead."

"Haye everybody," Ah Ki Wami calls out. "I know what to do about this. Why don't we put the small one inside our larger pack, that way, the weight will feel like it is spread out more, and they will be better hidden."

With the Chosen, agreement means action. In a flash, everyone is rearranging their supplies to make room for the special packs that hold the singing stones, while still, keeping their food at the ready.

Once they are all fully loaded, Esan too, who has a couple of things strapped to his furry black body, the Chosen start the slow walk back to the sandy hills from the day before.

As soon as they turn to start heading home, you can see a different look in each of their eyes than they had before. They all have a slightly dazed glaze about them now.

First, they had come straight from the middle of the desert, hot and tired. Then, almost in a flash, they were standing before more water and life than they knew their Creator had ever created. Add to that everything else they have just experienced, and it is very easy to understand the looks of awe still on their faces.

Sky Eye tries to add his narrative. "I don't know what to say."

"Then don't," Deerhead sharply responds with a smile on his face.

"How do you put into words what we have just seen?"

Two Bows, adjusts his load. "I can't Sky."

Ista looks in the direction of the great waters one last time. "Let's try to remember everything the best we can. There are already so many great stories to tell."

During a quick detour by the river for more water, Hugumki tells them that it is very important for them to leave the area as soon as possible. Because of that, they are going to be eating and drinking their second meal while on the move.

"Stay alert everybody," Hugumki pops a piece of jerky in his mouth. "It is harder to eat and walk than you would think it is."

At long last, after a bit of effort and aggravation, and a couple of extra breaks, the Chosen arrive at the hills where they will set up camp for the night. Right away, Hugumki can tell by the growing grumbles, what is about to erupt. He raises his hand, for silence. "I have not given anyone any more weight than I know you can carry. If you do not believe that, just pick up Two Bows', Deerhead's, or my pack. Like I said before, none of these bags are heavier than a regular sized stone weighs. They just feel heavy because all the weight is in one spot, and not spread out. Go ahead now, take your load off. Somebody help Esan with his. Don't forget, we are the first people, and we live in a land of…"

Knowing Hugumki's love of words, Sky Eye lets his mind wander and wonder about the journey back home. *I wish I could disappear from here for a while. I was not made to carry heavy things. How much longer will it take to get home since we can't run now? The night sky looks almost the same here as back home. On and on he goes, and he did say large the first time….*

Before his leader can see into his mind, Sky Eye starts paying attention again.

"…if anyone needs help on our way back home, just ask, and together we will all help you." Raising his voice for emphasis, Hugumki says again "We are the people of this land, and we are strong. Now let's set up camp. Tonight, we can have a big fire because we are surrounded by these big piles of sand. That is why I asked all of you to grab any firewood you saw, big or small. And thank you Esan for doing your part."

"Gumki, may I?" Ooha poses with a song on his lips.
"Of course, you can sing."

"Through light and shadow, I walk.
Through light and shadow, we walk.
At night, I rest under the sacred lights.
At night, we rest under the sacred lights.
With a task, we are found.
My friends and I, are homeward bound."

Hugumki knows how long and hard the journey home could turn out to be, so he too tries a song. As soon as he opens his mouth, the others start on their tasks making all the noise they can, or they just blatantly, cover their ears.

"In the land of our ancestors.
On this quest, we are bound.
Esan, guide us home.
Keep us safe.
Until we are home.
Until we are home."

Hugumki starts laughing because he knows, yes, he knows how bad he sounds, as do the rest of the laughing sweaty faces surrounding him.

When a nearby sand dune starts glowing pink in the evening sun, everyone comments on how pretty it is. When that same sand dune starts emitting a sound that is eerie and beautiful at the same time, Sky Eye is intrigued. Even though he is as exhausted as everyone else, the mysterious sound is calling out to him. "Hugumki, I am going to walk over there, and try to figure out what is causing that sound, so I am going to leave my pack here."

"Take Esan with you. Don't be long," is all Hugumki says in return.

"I hope you are still not mad at us because you did not get to see the great waters?"

Before Esan can answer, Sky Eye realizes he has some company. Ah Ki Wami and Two Bows have decided to tag along for the opportunity to see something new.

To their surprise, the bigger mounds of sand are even higher than they had looked like from a distance. Once they are standing at the bottom of the glowing sand dune, they realize that it isn't really glowing. It is just reflecting the colorful light of the setting sun.

Sky Eye is the first to stick his foot into the large mound of sand. "It's very soft, almost too soft. I think it just ate my sandal." After thrusting his arm into the sand, over, and over again, Sky Eye finally feels his missing sandal, to his great relief. "While you two try to climb it, I am going to figure out where that noise is coming from."

As soon as Two Bows and Ah Ki Wami start climbing the dune, they quickly realize it is a mistake.

"Let's stop Wami, the sand is trying to do to us what it did to Sky Eye's sandal." Pulling their bare feet free of the shifting sand, they sit down, and slide the short distance to the bottom.

"Now this would be fun if we did not have to worry about the sand having us for its last meal," Two Bows says.

Once at the bottom, "Look at us two Bows, we did not get dirty like everyone thought we would." Ah Ki Wami easily starts brushing the sand off.

"Did you figure out what was making that sound," Two Bows asks Sky Eye when he sees him walking around with his eyes half closed.

"The sand makes the sound when one layer moves on top of the other."

Ah Ki Wami agrees. "When we slid down, the falling sand kind of made that same sound."

Two Bows waves his hand in front of his face. "We should get back before it gets too dark. Come on Esan, where are you, time to head back."

Once he reunites with his companions, Esan gives the closest dune a final look that pretty much says it all. *I am a dog, all that sand is not for me. Let's get out of here.*

On their way back to camp, Sky Eye looks at both his companions, "Take your headbands off, it looks like both of you have some sand still stuck in your hair."

After a vigorous shake, Ah Ki Wami and Two Bows once again declare themselves sand free. They are about to learn that sand is easy to brush off a fairly, dry surface, but it loves to stick and grate upon any area that is moist and damp.

"Why are you two walking so funny?" Sky Eye asks after he notices that Two Bows and Ah Ki Wami are walking like they have chewols in their breechcloths.

Two Bows looks like he is in pain, "The sand is sticking to parts of my body you don't want to know about."

Ah Ki Wami is sharing the same discomfort. "When we get back, we will have to use some of our precious water to rinse off because I can't take this much longer."

Both of them continue walking like Canasake, but without the humor attached, that is, until Sky Eye tries to practice walking in their footsteps, creating three wobbly looking shadows.

When you are carrying a heavy, uncomfortable load on your back while trying to remain unseen in a wide-open rugged land, the journey home becomes not much more than one cautious step after the other.

Eat and drink in between when you can, make camp, fall asleep, wake up and do it all over again, and again, and again…

Fortunately, the Chosen's desert homeland holds many more surprises and things they can talk about and experience.

19

2nd day – Homeward Bound – Early morning

Father Sun reflecting off the white fluffy clouds scattered across the sky is making it a bright, shiny day. It's as if He is personally touching each one to check and see if they are going to provide any shade for the scantily clad youth below on what is already feeling like a warm day that will only get hotter.

After breaking camp at first light, the Chosen are still trying to deal with the new, awkward load on their backs.

"I know what you mean now Gumki. I can tell that we are slowly climbing up, or at least my legs can," Sky Eye says, neck throbbing along with his effort.

Through half-closed eye lids, Bird quietly asks Rabbit, "Do you see Deerhead in front of us? It looks like this part of the trail goes down."

"Deerhead might disappear right in front of our eyes." Hugumki is watching Deerhead start to walk into a fog filled depression ahead of them. He makes a single bird call to tell Deerhead to wait for everyone else to catch up with him before he continues onward.

Hugumki wants to make sure that no one in the group will get lost or separated in what appears to be a lone cloud that has settled onto the uneven ground ahead of them.

Once they are all together, Hugumki says just loud enough for everyone to hear. "All right Deerhead, lead on. Everyone else, stay right behind the person in front of you. Don't forget to be quiet and watch where you put your feet."

"It looks like some parts of the fog, is much thicker than other parts," Sky Eye whispers.

"Just stick together until we are on the other side." Hugumki says.

Slowly, and carefully, the Chosen start walking down into the thick, wet white murkiness.

After a short period of time, Hugumki asks Ah Ki Wami, who is in front of him wiping his face, "Are we starting to climb up the other side now."

"I feel all wet and sticky," Ah Ki Wami whispers.

Without warning, Deerhead stops mid stride. Ah Ki Wami instantly knows something is wrong so he raises the walking spear he is carrying into the ready position, without stabbing Deerhead. "Did you see something?" he quietly checks.

"I did not see anything," Deerhead softly answers, tilting his head into the light breeze blowing their way. "Can you smell that?"

"Yes I can and it stinks. Must be something dead. Nothing alive could smell that bad."

"I don't know Wami. I hear something heading our way."

"I do to." Ah Ki Wami quickly gives the double flutter alert signal.

"What is…," Hugumki starts to ask, then he too can hear what is noisily approaching.

"Something is coming, and it smells like living death," Ah Ki Wami hisses quickly and quietly.

"I think there is a small crossing path just ahead." Deerhead scratches his head as he tries to remember exactly where the side path is.

Who has the quiver, Two Bows motions dramatically with his hands. He knows one arrow is not going to do him or anybody else much good if the situation turns deadly.

"Get off," Hugumki whispers, "now!"

Whatever is coming is almost on top of them. They can all hear its noisy approach as they scramble to quickly get off the barely visible, main trail.

Out of the swirling mist a snotty snout appears, then two large tusks and two beady eyes attached to a large head. The thick head is followed by a small course gray haired body with short legs on four hooves.

First there is one, then another, and another until there are eight in all. They are of various sizes making weird high-pitched squeaking sounds. What are they? Where did they come from? All the Chosen's wide-open eyes are filled with life-and-death questions.

"Will they attack?" Ah Ki Wami asks under his breath.

"They don't seem to have noticed us," Deerhead whispers back.

"Quiet." Hugumki mouths.

Thankfully for them, the smelly creatures stay on the side trail and never seem to pay them the least bit of attention.

After the ugly, mysterious, foul-smelling animals have disappeared back into the mist, and can no longer be heard, everyone starts relaxing.

With his wide eyes cutting through, "What were they," Sky Eye asks.

"Do you think they will come back?" Bird stammers. "I did not like the way they looked, and their teeth were huge."

Two Bows points. "I think they are headed in the direction of the river."

"I hope it is to take a bath so they can get rid of their rotten smell," Ista jokes to laughter that sounds as nervous as him.

Thankfully, Esan has also gone unnoticed.

Turtle shakes his damp head. "I wish it would be clear one day then like this the next."

"Why?" asks Rabbit.

"That way I don't get to hot or too wet inside."

Rabbit wipes his chin. "That would be good."

Because they were so smelly, not one of the hungry warriors in training mentions anything about whether the funny looking javelina's are edible or not. One by one they get back on the trail to resume their long journey home.

2nd day – Homeward Bound – High sun

A hot wind is starting to stir. The sun is high in a pale blue sky, and the Chosen's energy level is quite low as they amble along. When his hunger finally starts getting the best of him, Deerhead brings up what he has been thinking about ever since he saw them.

Looking around at the rise and fall of the desert with a hint of mountains in the distance, he asks, "Two Bows, do you think those ugly things would have tasted good?"

"I don't know, but they might have been tough to kill."

Deerhead reaches down trying to recall their size. "I guess it depends upon how fast they could run. They could come at you from a low angle, and with those teeth, it could be dangerous."

"If I ever see them again, I will make sure I have the high ground, and have my bow ready so we can see what they taste like. I will just have to guess where its heart is at."

When the wind gets stronger, it starts pulling the dirt up into the air in a twisting, twirling column. Staring into the sky as if he is seeing it for the first time, "Look how big it is getting," Sky Eye excitedly shouts.

"You can see where it goes into the clouds," Turtle points straight up.

"We have the same dancing wind back home," Ah Ki Wami's eyeroll shows how impressed he is.

Hugumki spreads his hands apart, to see if he is right about the size of the dancing dirt. "Not that big."

"Part of the sky is turning brown," Turtle says, pointing up again.

"Your right Turtle," Sky Eye says. "It looks like the twisting air is trying to push up the sky and create another desert above, to go with the one we are on."

While some remain standing to watch it cross the desert floor right in front of them, most of the others start sitting down on their damp ponchos. They then decide to take the opportunity to have a quick drink and meal to rest their tired feet and bodies.

After sitting down and picking out what he wants to eat, Two Bows puts some food in his mouth with one hand, and drinks from one of his boto's with the other. "Seeds are much more fun to eat than plant."

Nodding his head, Sky Eye agrees. "You are right." He is thinking about how much he hates the bending over for planting the seed properly, straightening up, then making another hole in the ground, over and over again.

Bird takes such a small bite of jerky it is like watching a child eat. Or in this case, a little bird pecking away.

"Bird, how do you eat so much eating like that," Ooha asks.

"I just don't like the rabbit jerky as much." Bird scrunches up his face, "Turtle has more food than me.

"You're just eating more on each break," Turtle taps his head, while grinning at Sky Eye.

"I wonder if that could lift me off the ground?" Bird asks no one in particular, squeezing his small arms that have not grown as fast as he feels like they should: no matter how much he tries to get away with eating.

Ista, with a hopeful look on his weary face, studies the twirling brown column of dirt and grit. "If we got in its way, I wonder if it could take us straight home?"

"I would never, ever, get clean," Rabbit shivers with the horror of it all.

Slowly the dusty swirling brown wind continues its journey across the warm desert floor, heading for a distant landing, or just the opportunity to fall apart.

After taking a moment to compose himself, "Don't forget," Hugumki reminds the others when they slowly start getting ready to move on again. "Even if you are tired, do not drag your sandals. Yes, you may feel heavy, but you do not want to wear them out before we get back home. Just as important, you are making the job of whoever is last in line even harder. Remember, we do not want to be seen, and if you are leaving a path, kani, just don't do it, all right?"

Unseen, Sky Eye leaves a piece of food, not much larger than a crumb really, behind a crystalline rock. Is it an offering to the fickle desert gods? No, it is a gift to any hungry animal coming along that will be thrilled to have a savory piece of jerky to eat, instead of just another bug. More than likely though, the lucky one will be an ant, soon to be the hero of the colony. At least for the next couple of days.

Before Hugumki can add his usual words-which lately have become more cautious than motivational-Ista starts twirling his large black eyes around to show his leader, and the others, that he knows what to do next.

With the way now clear, Esan, with his thirst quenched, is the only one to show any real excitement at continuing the day's hot journey.

Poor Rabbit is crestfallen and feels like crying, or at least crying out, when he sees the endless energy draining desert that waits in front of him.

Licking his dry lips in the hope that they will not crack, he puts a mint leaf under his tongue. "I hope this will make me feel better," he quietly hopes.

Suddenly he feels very sad, but not alone, just far, far away from the comforts of home.

2nd day – Homeward Bound – Early evening

Like obedient puffy children, the clouds get in line to follow the setting sun. As the shadows on the desert floor get longer and longer, the strides of the worn out, spread out Chosen, are getting shorter and shorter.

Trying to straighten up his own weary shoulders, "Bird, you look like an elder that can barely walk," Turtle says through parched lips.

"That is how I feel."

From off to their side, "I feel that way too," Ista agrees, clenching and unclenching his jaw. "The way my back feels right now, I may never stand up straight again."

"I am glad that we are almost done this day." Bird is fighting the forces trying to make his day even longer. Gravity, and extreme weariness.

"This is not so bad," Turtle takes a couple of quick steps to show what he means.

"How can you say that Turtle, all of this walking doesn't bother you?" Ista's voice cracks again from dryness, puberty?

"What bothers me more is these things on my face. When one breaks, my sweat burns, see," Turtle points at his bumpy face. "And now my lips are starting to hurt too." After a quick glance around them to make sure that they are all alone with their burdens, Turtle challenges his friends. "Gumki told us we can all do this. Are you going to stop trying?"

Bird leans forward and sighs. "I know I am never giving up. I will feel better next day."

"What do you think the secret is in our packs?" Ista inquires, before he trips over his weary feet. "That was close. If Sky Eye was not up ahead, I would ask him."

"Rocks, just rocks, or some heavy shells," Bird grimaces at the sun that is not dropping quickly enough for their exhausted bodies.

Turtle raises his voice in defense of his leader. "Why would Gumki call them singing stones if they are not special?"

Bird's reply is an unhappy moan. "Hoa, they are only a test, just like he said."

"I know I am not going to look and see. I don't want to be the oldest child in the village," Ista says, trying to put on his crooked smile that has turned into a mere shadow of the grin that he always wore so proudly back in their village.

"Let's not talk about our secret packs anymore. I don't want to stay a child either," Bird says, looking at Father Sun again with hope in his eyes, and a prayer in his heart. "My head is starting to hurt inside."

"Don't forget," Turtle goads his exhausted friends. "We are all the Chosen."

At long last, they hear the signal that they have been waiting to hear all day. It was time to stop and shed their loads for the night, then eat and drink all Hugumki will allow them to while wondering to themselves if what they are just starting to go through will be worth it in the end. If they make it that far.

20

3rd day – Homeward Bound – Mid-morning

As Father Sun heats up during his passage across the wide open sky, you can almost hear his sizzling crackle from on high. Even the resilient cacti look like they are trying to lean away from his onslaught. On a hot day like this, a distraction is needed for the Chosen as they continue on their quest across the lower part of the desert.

Rabbit squeezes Deerhead's thick arm, then squeezes it again. "Come on Deerhead, why won't you play along. Everyone has some secrets," he prods, faking a sniff of disappointment.

"I have no secrets, I uh, I have no secrets. I need to check on Two Bows at the front of the line."

"He is always so much fun," Rabbit exclaims, listening to Deerhead's sandals sounding like heavy drumbeats as he stomps away. "Who wants to go next?"

"One time I was away from the village practicing my singing when I heard these loud, I will call them noises coming from behind some rocks. It sounded like a hurt animal, but instead, I saw two people without their real mates, and they were touching their lips together like they were running out of air." Ooha sheepishly glances at the attentive younger ones nearby.

"Who was it, who was it?" they want to know.

"We said one secret. Who is next?" Rabbit asks, even though he can't wait until the next time he is alone with Ooha.

"Sometimes I wish I could turn off my head."

Rabbit's sarcasm slices through the air. "Thank you for that exciting secret, Sky Eye."

Looking as proud as any guilty person ever has, Ista confesses, "Sorry you got blamed Turtle, but I was the one that broke the Early One's water pot." There is no remorse evident in his voice or on his grinning face.

"I knew it! My mother was the only one that believed me when I said I didn't do it."

"I did not mean to break it. I was just trying to have fun and I got scared. That's why I did not say anything."

"This is more like it," Rabbit laughs with glee as Turtle and Ista glare at each other before their faces break into smiles.

"I have one for you Rabbit," Hugumki surprises them when he joins the small group. "Not too long ago, I snuck some of the elder's strong drink."

Sky Eye stares at him intently, "Did you like it?"

"No. It tasted bad and part of me felt like I wanted to be happy, but all I kept having were bad thoughts. It makes things seem different than they really are. The girls don't look the same, and it makes you weaker, but you feel stronger inside."

"Is that why people always get in fights when they have been drinking it?" Bird asks.

"Yes, then the next day my head hurt, and I felt like kani. Since then, I have never had it or want to have it again."

"I want to try it," Ooha quietly says to himself.

"Anyone else?" Rabbit looks at the backs that are mysteriously moving away. "My turn then. I know who all the girls in the village really like."

"So do we," comes a confident voice.

"I said, really like."

"Oh ah," comes a not so confident voice.

"Just playing," his face breaks into a big smile. "You still have a lot to learn about life. I have an even better secret that I will tell another day."

Turtle shakes his head slowly, as if he can't believe what he just heard. "I think that pink lizard back there just laughed at me."

"He did sound that way, but I think he was just warning you to stay away," the lovesick Ooha points toward home. "I do miss…"

Onward they trudge, slowly making progress while higher and higher the blazing sun climbs, raising their discomfort and aggravation to new heights.

3rd day – Homeward Bound – Early afternoon

Another sweaty head droop's, another exhausted body starts to wander off the path. Hugumki, wiping at the thick sweat clinging to his headband gives the signal for a meal, and water break. Too tired to travel any further, the Chosen all just stop where they are and sit down on and among the surrounding brown speckled rocks.

After everyone feels a little more refreshed and alert, Hugumki softly whistles to get their attention. "Last hot time, I was sent into the nothing lands with no food or water for three or four days. The reason was so that I would understand what happens to our bodies when we do not eat enough food or drink enough water when it gets real hot. First, you start feeling tired, then your body has trouble staying in balance. After a while, your head does not think right. Two Bows, Deerhead, do you remember when I came back, you told me later that I got you mixed up because I was not thinking right?"

They both nod.

"I think some of those things are already happening to some of you. Make sure that when I call our breaks you drink water and eat something even if you don't feel like it. I don't think this hot time will last much longer. One thing you can do until then is to put a small rock in your mouth. It will keep your mouth wet. When it starts getting cold again, remember this time then, it will help you keep warm inside. Like I already said, I know we can all do this. Keep an eye on each other just to be safe. Are you ready to continue our journey? Eyes ahead, eyes around, let's go."

Slowly, ever so slowly, the exhausted teen's, along with a dusty Esan, start onward, mere youth, but thrust into the role of village saviors, whether they know it or not.

As Deerhead's heavy foot passes overhead, a hairy scorpion raises his stinger of a tail in salute. "Be strong big brothers. It can be done. It must be done."

3rd day – Homeward Bound – Twilight

After their last meal of the day, and with their thirst partially quenched, most of the Chosen do their best to relax around their small fire.

In front of them, Father Sun drops into the waiting clouds then briefly reappears as a fiery red dot before disappearing for the night.

"Did you see that?" Rabbit's face looks as uncomfortable as his body feels.

Yes, and it was just Father Sun keeping his eye on us," Two Bows says as he quickly looks around, "not an evil eye."

Hugumki has taken a moment by himself to gather his courage. When he was picked to be leader, he knew that he might have to make some tough decisions. He might even have to fend off one of his friends, for leadership. But he never thought or dreamed that he would have to bring up what he now must say.

Once he has found the necessary strength, Hugumki heads back to the fire and the rest of his group.

Hugumki enters the edge of the firelight, closely observing his noisy companions. Rabbit is the first to sense that Hugumki has something very serious to discuss with them. Without prompting, he gently shushes everybody before Hugumki has to do it.

Trying not to look anybody in the eyes, Hugumki stands very still and erect for a moment. He then begins talking in his most serious voice. "I don't know how you have the strength or energy, but one of you is taking this time to get to know yourself better, in that special way. Yes, that is something a lot of people do, but they do it all alone. You are doing it while being surrounded by friends. If you keep needlessly wasting part of your life's energy..."

"You will always feel tired and sometimes sick. That is what I have learned," Deerhead finishes for him.

Hugunki nods, "So, learn to control yourself now, and we will all be better off until we get back home." He gives them his best scowl which immediately turns into a big grin. Everybody else starts laughing until tears are streaming from their eyes, and down one very warm set of rosy, brown cheeks.

"That's why it's called alone time," is loudly whispered, to more laughter.

21

4th day – Homeward Bound – High sun

It all started with ominous sandy whispers riding on the warm desert wind.

Because he is the last in line and tasked with wiping clean any sign of their passing through on the trail, Rabbit is the first to sense that something is bearing down on them with bad intent.

When he checks behind him, he sees what looks like a giant billowing brown poncho approaching in the distance. When he stops and watches, the poncho quickly turns into what looks like a rolling line of giant brown waves that keep getting bigger and darker the closer they get.

Realizing that they are all in imminent danger, he calls out a warning as loud as he can. "Look behind you!"

When the others turn at the sound of his voice, they can't believe what is approaching faster than any man could walk or run.

It has turned into a monstrous brown wall roiling upon itself that seems as high as any mountain they have ever seen, and it is almost upon them.

"Form a circle and cover your heads with your ponchos or blankets and cover your face with whatever you have." Hugumki yells.

Doing its best to fight through the menace, the sunlight starts taking on a sickly yellowish, brown tint.

Quickly doing a body count, Hugumki shouts over the approaching danger that is getting louder and louder the closer it gets, "Where is Deerhead?"

Pulling his cotton blanket from his pack, Ah Ki Wami answers. "He should be just up ahead behind those large rocks."

"Esan, we will be ok, just a little dirtier than we already are," Hugumki tells his nervous furry friend. "First get under my poncho with me then I will cover us up with my blanket."

Realizing he did not have time to warn Deerhead about the impending danger, Hugumki can only hope that for once, Deerhead takes his eyes off the trail and scans the darkening skies behind him.

What is taking everybody so long, Deerhead thinks as he watches a small hungry lizard with horns try to drag a large beetle back to its lair. *They should have caught up with me by now.*

Caw-caw-caw, his uneasy reverie is broken by a conspiracy of ravens that look like they are flying for their lives, even though, fleeing would probably be a better way of putting it.

Finally noticing that the wind is blowing in reverse and that the sunlight has taken on an eerie glow, Deerhead suddenly has an uneasy feeling about what is going on.

Moving as quickly as his sturdy legs can carry him, he goes to the bend in the trail and looks back the way he had come mere moments before. His mouth drops open like Ooha's when he is in full voice, then just as quickly, he shuts it when blowing sand not only stings his face and eyes, but the back of his throat as well.

After taking another peek, Deerhead feels like he is standing in judgement before a brown wall of justice just before it says guilty and sweeps him away forever.

When he tries to pull out his poncho or blanket-he does not care which comes first-he inadvertently steps off the barely visible trail. Realizing he can easily become disoriented or hurt if he moves in the wrong direction, he shouts as loud as he can for the others.

Nothing. Nothing but the howling wind answers back.

Then yes.

A bark that does not seem very far away. Keeping his head down while only using his ears before they too fill with sand, Deerhead makes his way in the direction from where the familiar sound came from.

As the sand and pebbles start hitting them, Hugumki talks with Esan under their cover. "Your bark sounds loud under here, and yes, I hope Deerhead is safe too."

Bark, bark, Essan replies.

Knowing Essan's different barks, Hugumki peeks out from under his poncho and blanket to see what can only be described as a flying Deerhead approaching.

With his poncho flapping every which way, Deerhead looks like he is in midflight even though his feet are still on the ground.

When Deerhead plops down next to them, his first shouts are filled with relief and praise. "Thank you Essan. I could not see any longer and until you spoke, I could only hear the howling wind."

Then it got darker still until all light was lost to the brown, then black darkness of the massive desert sandstorm that soon covers everything and everyone in desert grit, dirt, and sand.

4th day – Homeward Bound – Mid-afternoon

After their recent sandblasting, you might expect everyone to have slumped, heavy shoulders. Instead, excitement is in the air. It is because they can practically smell and feel the cold refreshing water that awaits them, just ahead.

The Chosen cautiously approach the bluff and spring from a slightly different direction than they had left it. Wearing the desert for camouflage, the creeping warriors in training resemble the legendary ghost warriors. Even Esan's coat has turned from black to pale brown and he has been told that he can't run ahead this time.

If anyone was watching from the top of the small bluff, he or she would have seen them coming from far away. It is a good thing the approach they are using is not for any human but for any other animal that might be resting after quenching its thirst.

Feeling dirtier than he ever thought he would, or should, "What was that?" Rabbit suddenly asks.

Scanning the bluff, "I only saw the movement," Two Bows answers.

"Maybe it was a deer. I don't care right now. I will take anything. I can almost smell it cooking," Turtle whispers between smacks of his lips.

"We will split up into two groups," Hugumki quickly orders. "Two Bows take Wami, Ista, Rabbit, Bird, and Esan. The rest of you, stay with me. Two Bows take your group to the other side. Use the quiet signal when you get in position. Then we will all work our way up without making any noise. Once we are all at the top, we will squeeze whatever is up there, and the water, between us. Two Bows, I see you waving your arms. Yes, you get the first shot, if you have it."

Taking their time, the dusty warriors in training soon make it to the top edge of the bluff with still no sighting of what will hopefully be a big meal later. With the spring in the middle of the two groups, they take a moment to ready their spears, bows, arrows, and knives. With their hearts pounding from exertion and excitement, the two groups cautiously approach the pool that is using the rocks for cover. Within twenty paces of each other now–nothing; fifteen paces–nothing; ten paces–still nothing.

Turtle, whose legs seems to be getting stronger the longer the quest goes on, loses track of his group's line and is staring toward the pool with his wide-open mouth frozen in a silent scream. Why? Because staring back at Turtle from the other side of the pool is a mountain cat the size of a small bear, with its mouth also wide open.

Turtle is so petrified he looks like he has been carved out of dusty brown stone and left there for just this moment.

The cat is still too but does not look like it will stay that way for long. They can all feel its coiled-up energy. It is hard to tell if it is preparing to attack or jump to safety.

In less than a heartbeat of time, Deerhead, in one fluid motion has his walking spear in position to protect Turtle without startling the large cat.

Two Bows, who is approaching from behind quickly raises his loaded bow into the firing position.

Hugumki, instead of a bow, raises a hand for a hold, then makes a soft flutter sound. Like a thunderous roar, Esan's ferocious bark rings out across the whole bluff.

Acting as if he has been shot out of a giant bow himself, the startled, big gray, brown cat, in one mighty leap, clears the pool and the ducking Bird who is at the edge of his group. Almost as fast as they can blink, the cat is gone in a flash of streaking fur.

All the Chosen, who have been sweating in more ways than one, simultaneously let out a cry of relief. "Hi eee!"

"I am glad you followed my signal," Hugumki tells Two Bows and his group that are still on the other side of the small pool of crystal-clear water. "We are only killing to eat and if anyone had shot in fear, we may have hit each other."

Ah Ki Wami shakes his head in amazement, "That cat was big."

What no one has noticed yet is that Turtle's breathing has turned into rapid shallow breaths that don't seem to be getting him any air.

Noticing at last his rapid chest movement, and the panicked look still on his face, Deerhead realizes he must give Turtle something else to think about. Smack, he hits Turtle on the back with his open hand and just like that, Turtle takes a few deep breaths and seems as good as new. He does look a little bit paler, and shakier, than he did before though.

"How did he get away so fast," Bird looks around without seeing any trace of the rabid cat that will revisit him now and then in his dreams and thoughts.

"He knew he was in big trouble with Esan around. Right Esan? Even with the madness in his eyes, I still would like to have seen if I could have taken him down with one shot. Oh, well," Two Bows says, disappointment written all over his face.

Hugumki looks at Bird, "He probably has a way through the rocks that we cannot see, then he just blends into everything else down there." He starts taking off his packs along with his sandals, shirt, and breech cloth. "When Deerhead showed me some large kani near the rabbit valley some days ago, I knew we might see a large cat. I just did not think it would be so big. That is, if it was the same one as before."

Bird can't believe it. "Why didn't you say anything?"

After another large exhale of relief, "Would you have had a good night's rest until now," Hugumki answers. "Thank the gods it wasn't bear kani."

Sky Eye tries to remember something he learned about desert life. "Shouldn't he still be asleep?"

"Like Two Bows meant, it has the snow color around his mouth" answers Deerhead.

"He is not well, so he does not act like a regular animal," Hugumki says while scanning the area again before putting a black foot in the cold pool of water.

Preparing to join Hugumki, Two Bows warns, "Maybe it is too warm now for them to still be sleeping."

"If that is true, we will have to watch out for the zizi's, and keep Esan away from them," Deerhead replies.

With a pained expression appearing on his face, Rabbit asks, "Does that mean we will have to wear our leggings even when it is hot?"

Deerhead waves a muscular arm back and forth, "You decide. Hot or dead." He is always willing to give anyone a choice about how long they live.

"We are not staying here this night, are we?" Ista's teeth clack together. "And I am glad we are not going up to the rabbit valley this time."

"Those rabbit's would be good, but we have many steps to go before dark." Hugumki looks in the direction that the dust storm took. "Before we leave, make sure all the botos are full and I am happy that the dust did not get in the water."

Rabbit pleads with everything he has. "Since we are all so dirty, let's drink before we all get in."

Cupping his hand, "Drink this Rabbit," Ah Ki Wami says, sending a small wall of water Rabbit's way.

In a flash, the drinking, splashing, and bathing, all commences at once.

4th day – Homeward Bound – Late night

Mother Earth keeps on turning. New stars rise into the already stellar sky.

Spin, spin, then they too move on.

In the middle of a warm night, deep in the heart of desert starkness, one bright, out of place light looks like it is slowly, aimlessly drifting across the desert floor.

Or is it?

While most of the happily quenched Chosen lie sleeping around their crackling, concealed fire, one stands apart, watching, waiting. As his warm breath rises into the night, he is joined by two more.

"How long have you been looking at that strange light in the distance, Gumki?" Rabbit asks, a nervous tremor coloring his soft voice.

Looking like the leader he is, Hugumki stands in the dancing shadows pondering another one of life's mysteries. "Long enough to wonder what it is."

Staring at the mysterious light, Two Bows tries to stretch his tight body. "What do you think it is?"

"I just said I don't know yet."

"I would say it is a fire, but how would a fire move around like that Hugumki?"

"You're right Two Bows. It does look like the light is moving around, but if it is, it does not seem to go very far."

"Has it made any noise?"

"Not that I can hear."

"Did the noise wake you up, or do you know what it is?" Rabbit is more nervous than paying attention to what has already been said.

"No, Esan woke me up. Once he had my attention," Hugumki starts to laugh, "he went right back to sleep as only he can."

Looking up, Two Bows feels a little uneasy. "Did it come from above like some of the stories we have heard or pictures we have seen on the rocks."

"It was already there when Esan nudged me," Hugumki utters around a yawn.

"Do you think he heard it, or only saw it?" Rabbit asks. "Should we be afraid?"

"Only if it heads this way."

Two Bows quietly wonders, "If Sky Eye was here, what would he say about this?"

"They need their rest," Hugumki looks toward the campfire.

Reaching down to flap his breechcloth, Rabbit softly groans to show his disappointment. "I was hoping it would get cooler this night."

"When you stand here without moving, the desert comes back to life," Two Bows whispers, trying to see what is noisily scurrying by in the darkness.

Taking the desert's hint, Hugumki turns around. "We should head back to the fire and try to go back to sleep."

As they take one last look at the distant mystery, Two Bows, tries to reassure himself. "It does look a little bigger now. It must be a fire, even if it started in the sky."

"When next day comes, don't say anything to the others unless we know or discover what it is," Hugumki suggests, before he starts heading back to camp and his noisy, snoring companions.

Overhead, the twinkling lights slowly continue their incalculable journeys.

22

5th day – Homeward Bound – Mid-morning

Break time has just been called, though not soon enough for Ista and his exhausted body. He feels like all the humor has been wrung right out of him, leaving nothing but thirst.

Under an empty cerulean sky, he looks for a place to sit down and starts heading toward Bird, and the empty volcanic rock next to him.

When Bird's voice, complaining about something, reaches his ear's, he decides he is not in the mood, and heads in the direction of Sky Eye and Ooha instead.

Sky Eye beckons Ista to come over and join them. "Ista, I was just wondering what my father would think about all of this."

Ista holds both his arms out wide. "About being in the middle of the desert, or about our test?"

"Knowing him, he wouldn't like anything we are doing that keeps me away from home longer than he thinks I should. At least, once I become a man, he can't tell me what to do anymore, I hope."

After taking off his pack and sitting down, Ista asks, "I don't understand. Isn't he proud of you?"

"I know my parents are proud of me," Ooha says in the way, that makes it sound like he is bragging, again.

Sky Eye shrugs. "He doesn't like it that I spend so much time learning with Cansake, and he would feel that this is just part of that. He would rather have me working in the village, preparing the crops, or even learning more about hunting. He just doesn't understand that I find those things so boring. I would much rather learn about the mysteries of our life."

The thin smile on Sky Eye's face looks sad and defiant at the same time.

Ista makes the funniest face he can come up with, face scrunched, tongue out, "My father doesn't like me being funny. He believes I should be serious all the time or else nothing will get done. I don't think he thought I can and will pass our test, or what we are really doing."

With his perfect nose turned to the sky, Ooha boasts, "My parents are proud of me because ever since I was a baby, they knew I was special."

"Why, because you had an extra nose or something?" Sky Eye barely shakes his head.

"Hoa, no. When they first heard my cry, they knew I was special."

Deerhead's low voice reaches their ears. "I think some of the elders still talk about the baby that used to cry all the time because he liked to hear his own wailing."

"What about you Deerhead? What do you think your mother…, do you think she is missing you?" Ista asks.

"I just hope she has not found someone to hug as good as she hugs me and Little Bean."

Not sure whether he should laugh or not, Ista is glad to see Hugumki stand and start looking around. It is time to put all thoughts of home and family back in their hearts, safe from the blistering sun as they prepare to continue what was starting to feel more and more like a trial by fire.

5th day – Homeward Bound – Mid-day

Where some people only see emptiness, others can see, what is really, there. When some people feel nothing, others can feel more than those will ever know.

As tired as everyone else as they slowly trudge along under the effulgent sun, Two Bows closes his eyes to draw power from an unseen source. "It's amazing."

Feeling absolutely no strength, drawn or otherwise Rabbit mumbles, "What is?"

"Even out here in the middle of nowhere, you can still feel life everywhere."

"You must be joking. There is nothing out here."

"Can't you feel it Rabbit."

"Feel what?"

Two Bows sadly shakes his head. "The life that is in everything you see. It's in the sky, the clouds, the ground, the rocks in all their shapes and sizes. Even you and me."

"I don't know about all that."

"Look at Gumki and Wami over there. You can tell they feel it too. It's almost like everything has little happy parts moving around inside."

"Do you mean like a spirit Two Bows?"

"I don't really know, but I can feel it though. Something may not be moving, but if you try, you can still feel the power that it is giving off. That is why I think everything is made up of little pieces that we can't see. They make up the whole. And if you can feel their power, they must be alive, even if we cannot see them."

Sky Eye must prove again he is as smart as he thinks he is. "I just heard what you said Two Bows, if only it was true."

Two Bows can only ruefully smile to himself as the Chosen keep on walking, some of them more in tune with their surroundings than others.

Bird, who was off to the side listening to everything that has been said, makes a vow to himself. From now on and whenever he takes his alone time, he will try to start feeling the life that is around him-not just in him-in the hope that that will give him more strength and energy because he does not know how much more he can take before he has had enough, of everything.

5th day – Homeward Bound – Early afternoon

In the desert, on a dry hot day, it is very easy to see things that are not really there.

"Wami, Wami. Look over there! Do you see them?" Ooha squints, looks again, sees nothing but desert.

Hearing the urgency in Ooha's voice, Ah Ki Wami has immediately, gone into warrior mode. Hand on knife, no movement but getting low.

When he looks in the direction Ooha is pointing, he does not see anything out of place, or menacing either.

"I don't see anything Ooha."

By now, everyone else is also on alert.

Flowing like water, Hugumki appears at their side. "What's going on?"

Ah Ki Wami only moves his mouth. "Ooha thought he saw…."

"What did you see Ooha?"

"I saw a line of strange looking warriors surrounded by water, waiting for us to pass. They were right there, but now they are gone."

Seeing a line of worn rocks that might vaguely resemble people, if he closed his eyes, Hugumki still does his due diligence and scans the entire area. Once he is sure that they are all alone, he starts laughing. "The hot sun is making you see things. I should have said that that could happen before now."

"If anybody else sees water, could you grab some before it disappears." Deerhead doesn't even try to laugh at his own joke because his throat is starting to feel too dry. "Do you want me to keep the same pace Hugumki?"

Without waiting for an answer, Deerhead keeps on walking, and wishing with everything he has.

5th day – Homeward Bound – Evening

"How did those rocks get up there?" a sweaty red faced Turtle asks Ooha.

The Chosen are passing by what can best be described as a group of tall, skinny, windblown rock sculptures that could resemble people, if they had big giant rocky heads.

They are not mirages this time.

Scratching away at his tired red eyes, "I don't know, but some people might think they are resting gods," Ooha answers.

"I have heard that water made them that way," Sky Eye reaches out to touch one as if that would give him the answer.

"How can that be?" inquires Two Bows. "It would have to rain for many, many seasons. I don't think it rains here at all."

Sky Eye looks for a water line, while thinking about the stars and their slow movement across the sky. "Maybe before our time, it was different."

Holding his head in his hands, Rabbit says, "I think they are women from long ago that are missing their men. Their heads are so big because they are full of dry tears,"

"I know a woman who is not missing her man as much as she should," Deerhead aims a grin at Hugumki.

Rabbit waves his hand with dismissive twist, "I think the chief's wife is missing much more than that."

"I think I know what you are talking about Deerhead, and it is not even worth talking about," Hugumki snorts. "Unless you want to talk about that woman you have waiting back home, whether you want her to or not."

Deerhead brushes the few scraggly whiskers on his chin. "I wish it was only one woman. Just before we left the village, I had three after me."

"Must be the extra hair you have," Ista rubs his own smooth face.

"How old do you think Hunter's wife is?" asks Sky Eye, wobbling a bit on the path. "With her, I just can't tell."

"If she was here, she could tell Rabbit the names of her big-headed rocky friends," Ista says to cackles of laughter that sound raw with the effort.

Sky Eye answers his own question, "I think she is many seasons old."

"Every woman is precious, regardless of her age, even her," Ooha proudly states.

Continuing past the odd rock formations, the lonely among the Chosen try their best not to think too hard about, anyone.

Deerhead just can't help himself so he interrupts everyone's quiet interlude by starting to sing his favorite song in what can only be called a naughty manner, accompanied by the occasional thrust of his poncho.

Ista and Bird scrunch up their noses as their bodies lean inside their ponchos like curious saplings in a gusty wind as they try to get a better look at whatever Deerhead is doing as he sings at the top of his lungs. Though they are trying their best they can't quite make out his words.

"What does that mean Deerhead?" Ista asks.

"What do you mean?" Deerhead looks surprisingly nervous all of a sudden.

"The words to that song. What are they about?" Bird asks in eager anticipation.

"Hoa. Nothing."

"Are they bad?" Ista and Bird ask at once.

"Kind of."

Ooha is now curious. "Come on Deerhead. Sing your song. I want to hear it too."

Deerhead takes time to carefully study all the eager young faces in front of him. He wants so badly to shock their little ears right off their heads. All right, he wants to do it to all of them. Then he feels those eyes on him.

"I will sing it for a family." Deerhead starts to sing in a low, and to some shocked ears after all, sweet voice.

"Soft of heart. I miss her.

Soft of body. I I miss her again. Hoa.

Strong of spirit, she is with me.
Strong of body, she aah is still with me.
A good woman, she is.
A wild woman, she ah is.
Where are you?
Where am I?"
Everyone joins in.
"Wait my love.
Wait for me."
Two Bows can take no more. "Let's think about something else."

23

6th day – Homeward Bound – Early morning

The sky is awash with burnt orange, red, and purple streaks shooting through a deep azure field. The quail, cardinals and other birds are all singing and talking to each other.

The Chosen are once again on the move, talking, but not singing to each other. They are all wearing as little as they feel comfortable in on what already feels like will turn into another long, hot day.

Rabbit stops for a moment on the trail, rotates his shoulders, then shakes his head to wake up. "Did anyone else feel the ground shake last night?"

"It woke me up for a little while, or maybe it was Esan's cold nose." Two Bows lifts his head into the morning light that is just beginning to color the cacti, thorn brush, and small rock outcroppings, in crimson glory. "I saw a flash of Sky Fire in the distance there," he points in the direction that they are just starting to head in. "So, I quietly sang to myself, `rain, rain, go away, stay away,' then I calmed Esan down and went back to sleep."

"It must have happened on the other side of the mountains," Hugumki scans the desert ahead for any indication that rain fell from the sky. "When we clear the high pass next day, we should see some signs."

To get everyone's attention so that he can remind them of what happens when water meets very dry ground, Two Bows throws his arm in the air, waves it around then quickly drops it back toward the ground with a loud grunt. "If it does rain, the ground can get very slippery, and when it dries, the new cracks can get bigger than you would think they could."

"And don't forget, if we have to walk on the shiny rocks that are the color of night, be extra careful because they can be as sharp as a knife," Deerhead warns everyone. "I sometimes wish we made our knives out of them."

Thinking about the time he fell on them when he was much younger, "That is why we avoided them before," Hugumki says, touching the scar on his chin.

"What will we do about Esan then?" Rabbit asks.

"When it is time, I will think of something," Hugumki jokes as he bends over and holds out his arms in preparation for an extra, furry load.

Rabbit tentatively reaches into his medicine pouch and pulls out the small piece of obsidian that he has. "I have only seen small pieces of the shiny black rock, but you are right, when the pieces break off, they can be very sharp." He holds up his small piece, which has a very sharp edge, "But as you can see, it is also very pretty because it is so shiny."

"We know it is sharp Rabbit. That is why we use it for our arrow heads and spears," Two Bows smiles at the obvious.

"Oha."

On into the sweeping expanse they go, one heavy step after the other, ever so slowly drawing closer to the imposing barren mountain barrier waiting in front of them.

6th day – Homeward Bound – Still rising sun

The sky is so blue that even the air has its tint. Before the Chosen lies what, to the untrained eye, is an empty brown landscape of various shades. As the sun continues its relentless assault, it rises up again in endless shimmering waves that, as we have found out, can make things look different than they really are. As the seasonal temperature of the lower desert continues to climb, it also causes certain sleeping creatures to awaken from their winter hibernation.

"Kani, it is hot here," Ah Ki Wami grouses through chapped lips while using both hands to wipe away at his face. "Even my scar is sweating now."

Hugumki tries to pant around a tongue that feels like it is getting thicker with every step. "I thought our hot time back home was bad. I would not want to be here then."

From behind them in their spread out line, Rabbit raises his soft voice in praise while massaging the bridge of his nose. "I am glad that we got to have all the cold water we could drink. Too bad we could not bring it with us."

"Other than my sweat, I already feel as dried out as those bones we see scattered around," Ah Ki Wami pants. "I am surprised I am not rattling right now."

With a look of both puzzlement and concentration on his long face, Sky Eye tries to coax an answer from somewhere. "If only there was a way to keep our water cold," he quietly wonders about the still unknown.

Hugumki lets out a hoarse laugh. "I know what Deerhead's dreams will be about this night."

"A pretty woman made of snow," Ah Ki Wami adds with his own dry laughter.

With a voice that sounds like it could rupture at any moment, Sky Eye wishes out loud. "When Two Bows reports back, maybe he will tell us he found a shorter way back home."

Hugumki, upon realizing that he has let his attention wander, peers back around Sky Eye to see that Ista is starting to fall further behind than he should. He then glances up the winding trail, "Here comes Two Bows now."

Turning his attention back to Ista, he prepares to call out and tell him to try and hurry up with his trail wiping. Hugumki knows with the ground being so hard and dry, they are hardly leaving any sign of their passing through.

Before he can, Sky Eye says under his breath, "Poor Esan, his black coat is…."

Looking around, "Where is…," Hugumki begins to ask.

Ista's scream pierces their ears. "Esan. No!"

Quickly turning, they see Esan dancing and Ista's bulging eyes and body resembling a frightened praying mantis. Ista's mouth is silently opening and closing, but his body looks like it is stuck in place.

In a brown flash, Hugumki heads over to help his friends. When he gets closer, he can see that a zizi is still trying to decide who to strike for his first meal since awakening.

The starving snake slithers into a better position to attack, looking just like what he is. One big long colorful muscle of bad intent, and his darting tongue is telling him that whichever warm body he chooses, will do just fine.

When Ista's droplets of sweat start hitting the dry parched ground, to the snake, it must sound like the beat of a thousand war drums.

With his decision made, the yellow, gray, and pink snake slithers toward Ista, only to be cut off by the courageous Esan.

Hugumki's last thought is a wishful one. "If only I had…"

Time seems to stop for everyone who can see what is about to happen, but one.

As the snake coils and starts his strike, Ista turns away in dread as a woosh cuts through the air.

Then he hears it.

Thump.

"No," Ista begins to scream.

From behind his trembling back, he hears a loud cry.

To his astonishment, it is not a voice filled with pain or sorrow, but a shout filled with joy.

"I did it! Did you see that?" Two Bows yells in triumph, his black eyes flashing with the thrill of the kill.

Ista turns around and sees what Two Bows is so excited about.

To his great relief, Esan is cautiously circling his vanquished foe.

When Hugumki starts pulling Esan away from the dead snake, he brags to the whole desert, "Two Bows, that is the best shot ever made."

"I did not think I could, but I had to try to protect my friends," Two Bows shouts.

Due to his walking, sprinting, and adrenaline, Two Bow's rich brown skin is shining so much that one might think he has smeared bear fat all over himself when he trots up and reaches down to pull out his arrow from the poisonous snake's side.

He then proudly lifts it high while saying, "This night skinny one, you are part of our last meal, if you last that long. Hoa."

Ista, who is slowly starting to realize what really happened, starts dancing around shouting, "Two Bows, Two Bows! And from so far away. How?"

"Practice, my young friend," Two Bows replies with an elder's grin on his face. "That is what my alone time is for. Practice, practice. I know if I miss the cactus I am aiming at, I could break my arrow and our good ones are not easy to make. To be good at anything, you must practice at it over, and over again."

"I heard the movement of the air as it went by, still, I thought it's too late, the first shot will miss," Hugumki shakes his head in amazement. "I should have known better, even if you did not have the clearest shot."

By then everyone else is patting Two Bows wherever they can except around the area of his still full hands.

Hugumki, always the leader and teacher, asks, "Esan, did you learn your lesson?"

"Arf! Arf," he answers.

"Good boy. Leave them alone, we don't want to go through that again, do we?"

And the mighty sun keeps beating down, one oppressive sunbeam after another which is starting to make the Chosen's blood simmer if not outright boil. Undaunted, so far, they continue onward while keeping a constant eye out for the loose dirt, rocks, and holes that want to trip them up. There's also the cactus, spiders, venomous snakes, and everything else that just wants to have a piece of them. And of course, we can't forget about the coyotes, wolves, cats, and even bears that just want to eat them. What an exciting time and place to be alive.

6th day – Homeward Bound – Mid-afternoon

The extremely dangerous and ravenous zizi's are awake, and it appears some of the Chosen would rather be anywhere than where they are right now.

Even in early spring, the sun in the lower desert can get quite hot, especially if it is the first heatwave of the season, and you are not used to it yet as they are learning more and more to their discomfort.

They are sluggishly heading for the last thing their already exhausted leg's need, the higher ground of the upcoming foothills that lead up to the mountain pass, without any breeze to help push them on their way.

Some people say that home is where the heart is. But what if home is not where your heart is right now? You would probably look for something to keep you preoccupied, even if it deals with a homeowner of a different sort.

"Look at that pretty bird, Ista," Bird says, pointing out a tall thick cactus off to their side that looks like it had a new resident moving in. The bird, moving in and out of a small hole is making its home right in the side of the prickly cactus.

"I don't care how small I was. I would never live inside a cactus." Ista starts moving around like something is jabbing him.

"You would never get any visitors to hear your stories." Bird tries to laugh when he thinks about Ista with nobody to talk to. What comes out of his mouth instead is a sound as dry as the desert they are passing through.

"Are we ever going to make it home?" Ooha asks around the small stone that does not seem to be doing anything to keep his mouth moist. "My throat hurts, I may never sing as good as I used to…" his voice trails off.

Distracted or not, with his little brown exhausted body barely able to walk in a straight line, Bird whispers to Ista in a raspy, nasty voice. "Ooha is right, this test feels like it just keeps going on and on. Now my legs feel so heavy I can barely lift them, so what do we have to do next? We have to start climbing again."

Turtle has not forgotten when his friends made him feel bad.

"Don't forget, it's just one foot after the other. It's easy, right?" he taunts, looking at the upcoming foothills they are steadily approaching.

"If only Hugumki or one of the older one's would tell us why this has to be so hard," Ista practically demands, his black eyes, hollow.

Through bared teeth, Turtle wonders, "Do they even know?" While he has held back his tongue the longest, he joins along with his friends in their bad mood and complaints. "I am starting to feel like another piece of dried out meat"

The fire of anger in his eyes makes Turtle look like a mad brown cherub, with an uneven haircut.

Bird moves his arms around as if he can conjure up some cool air, "A test, a test, that is all Hugumki says." Bird tries to yell but instead it comes out like a squeaky croak. "I wish they would all just go away and leave us alone until this test, this test is over and we are back home again."

Hugumki, who has waited on Bird and the others, overhears their complaints and is trying his best to control himself. Still though, he can feel his anger starting to build up as their whining goes on and on, making more than just his ears burn.

Even Rabbit starts in when he slows down his long legs so that the struggling ones can catch up with him.

"How do you think I feel?" he asks sullenly. Defiantly looking Hugumki in the eyes, he throws his head back in disgust.

When he finally takes a good look at his young companions, he sees weary faces and lips that are starting to flake and crack. "Look at you poor boys. It looks like you have fish scales on your lips," he pulls his medicine pouch out from under his dusty poncho.

Rabbit cups his pouch in one hand and carefully reaches into it with the other one. "Try some of this," he starts handing out small pieces of a special cactus that he collected earlier for such an emergency as this.

"Take it and squeeze the juice on your lips, it will help a little bit. Later when it is cooler, I will show you what to look for and you can get some more because I know we are all going to need more of it."

Even when his lips start feeling a little better, Bird's attitude does not improve. "I am surprised Sky Eye did not know about Rabbit's cactus. He is supposed to know so much."

"This heat has probably burned everything he has ever learned right out of his head," Ista raises his lips to go along with his mean snicker.

"I know my mother would not like what I am doing right now for that reason." Bird tries to remember how easy life was back at home, but all he can think of is heat and pain.

Ista agrees, "I don't think mine would either."

Bird grips his face in his hands, "My head does not feel right, like Gumki said."

Not thinking about anything but the present, Ista tells Bird to drink more water if he needs to. "Don't listen to what they say," he adds, after Bird worries about getting in trouble.

Just ahead of them in the staggered and ragged line, Ooha tries to talk to Sky Eye while thinking once again that he may never sing the same way he used to. "If this is ever over, ah kani, it doesn't feel like this test will ever be over."

"Maybe we all got bit by zizi's, and we are in another time and place, stuck here forever."

"Don't say that Sky. The only thing keeping me going is the memory of Squash Blossom's pretty face, and how I can't wait to see it again." Ooha can still feel the soft thud of her heart, in his heart, when he had pulled her close to say, "See you soon."

At the front of the line, Deerhead and Two Bows are also beginning to succumb to the toll that dry heat can take on your body when you do not drink enough water to replenish the water you are losing, whether by sweat or evaporation.

Dry mouth, confusion, followed by blurred vision, headaches, cramps, eventually no sweat, then worse. Another thing they are about to learn is that it can also loosen a thick heavy tongue.

"I can't believe it has gotten this hot so early in the season." Deerhead's large head looks like it is trying to pull him to the ground.

"Was it you or me that said that none of us were in shape to run down a deer when we began this test? I don't think I could catch that turtle over there if he decided to run for it," Two Bows says with dry course laughter, while looking at a large gray tortoise lumbering by in the distance.

Deerhead lumbers a few steps of his own, "I don't know if I am ready to be a man yet."

"Why not?"

"I already feel like I have been."

"We do have to grow up fast around here. When we get back Deerhead, we should live on each side of the village."

"Front or back or on the sides?"

"Just so we are not on top of each other."

"Your right, wild men need room."

"Do you miss your mother?"

"I miss a woman."

"Star was after you, but now I think she likes me."

"I am glad I am a man. Women are so different."

"How do they have babies?'

"I thought you knew all that Two Bows."

"I mean have," Two Bows cups his hands in front of his flat stomach. "What does it feel like to have a life come out of you? They have a harder time than we do in many ways and.."

Deerhead's rough face tries out different looks of puzzlement.

"I can't believe I even miss my…." Two Bows, begins to feel like he may have revealed too much of himself. "You know I was only joking."

"It's the heat," they mumble as one.

Time drags by.

More endless desert.

More endless steps.

Finally, Bird, worn to his very core, can take no more.

Deep into despair, his red eyes sink soon followed by the rest of his glowering face. After taking a hot sip from his boto, he starts yelling then crying over, and over again. "I am so tired of this test. I want to go home!" until big thick gummy tears are leaving streaks halfway down his thin dirty face.

Learning that being a leader means that you must lead in both good and bad times, Hugumki walks over and tries to encourage him.

"Leave me alone, I am tired of all of you. Two Bows, Deerhead and…, we don't need you. Go away!" Bird swings away at nothing.

"That's right," Turtle and Ista join in. "Go away. We want to be left alone. Just leave us alone!"

Hugumki bites his tongue, literally, then quickly walks away before he says or does something that they all might regret for a very long time.

Following Hugumki's lead, they are soon on their way again.

Besides their glum faces, the sound of their sandals really gives their moods away. There is the loud smack of disgust, the subtle dragging sounds of the fed up and weary, a stomp or two of anger, and a slight pitter patter from the ones that feel like they may have pushed Hugumki too far.

To make it feel even harder, in order to keep their weary legs underneath them as they begin their climb, the Chosen must bend their backs and legs. They are almost doubled over with their effort.

As if making fun of them, the ramrod straight cacti look like they are slowly creeping their way up the mountainside too, all while pointing up at the searing sky that may someday hold some rain for them if they wait long enough.

After many heavy and noisy steps, at long last, the Chosen, now walking in two distinct groups, are up in the rocky foothills. With a quick search, they see a couple of good flat spots on which to make their small camp. Without any discussion at all, the closest spot is hastily picked.

One pack is laid on the ground, then another, still, not a word is heard.

Esan does not make a sound either. He just looks back and forth at all the silent, miserable, glum, and surprisingly, smug face or two.

The uncomfortable silence, is broken by Hugumki's tense voice.

"Starting right now, Bird, Turtle, and Ista you are in charge, of each other. You don't need us or want our help, so do whatever you want to do or feel is needed to be done. Two Bows, Deerhead, Wami and I are going to stay out of your way just like you want us to. Sky Eye, Rabbit, and Ooha do what they tell you to do or whatever you want to do. It's up to you."

Under his breath he hisses like a disgruntled snake. "I don't really care right now."

Hugumki walks over to join Two bows, Deerhead, and Ah Ki Wami who are leaning on some large rocks in the shadows waiting to see what would or would not unfold. Unlike some of the others, they have not taken off their packs yet.

Stunned silence follows Hugumki's shocking declaration.

A new leader quickly tries to fill the void. Standing as tall as he can, Bird commands, "Turtle, start looking for some wood because it is getting dark."

Acting like he has just been slapped in the face, "You're not in charge," Turtle shouts back, sending pieces of spit flying everywhere.

"There is not much firewood up here anyway." Sky Eye realizes their mistake when he starts looking around at the barren rocky ground." We should have been gathering it already,"

Wishing he had eyes like an owl, Ista asks, "Is it even safe to have a fire up here this night?" He turns his head toward the setting sun, eyes searching for whatever danger is lurking on the desert floor in front of them.

What he sees looks like a curtain of flame being pulled rapidly across the desert floor. Even some of the cacti look like they are aglow.

"If we…, does anyone have the fire stones?" Turtle looks where he can't see.

Bird pulls out his flint knife with a flourish, "You know who has them. We can try rubbing our knives together, can't we?"

With a voice too haughty, and proud for the situation, "You can't use mine, you might break it," Ooha starts backing away into the shadows.

Even though he is not sure where he is at, Bird asks, "Rabbit, can you help us out?"

"I am not doing anything right now," Rabbit's voice seems to fade away on a pout.

"Let's hurry up and do something," Turtle urges when a shiver, filled with dread, races up his spine. "It's starting to get cold."

Impatiently rubbing his hands together, "If we weren't so stinky, we could get closer to stay warm," Ista offers.

Once again, trying to appear taller than he is, Bird asks, "Sky Eye, do you have any ideas?"

"Not about this."

"It's starting to get dark fast, should we just get ready to eat?" Turtle looks around, "I can barely see."

"We will be good. Together we have nothing to worry about," Ista insists, his false bravado caresses his words, but not his wavering voice.

"That's ri….," Turtle loses all his air as a tortured scream rips through the air.

It sounds like a child's wail, a woman's cry, and pure pain all rolled into one blood curdling sound.

It also cuts through every bit of confidence any of them had, or pretended to have.

Bird whimpers, "What was that?" His eyes have gotten so big that they can easily be seen.

Turtle reaches up, to pat his chest. His heart is beating so fast that it feels like it is a trapped animal trying to beat its way out, either to flee, or fight.

Wishing that he was safely back home, Sky Eye answers as calmly as he can, "I think it was something that just became another animal's first, or last meal. If only we had a fire."

"Haye, smell that? Look up there. I think it's a fire!" Turtle yells.

"So that's why Wami kept bending over when he was behind us," Bird says. "He must have been picking up wood."

Ista's tired voice drifts toward the smoke, "I thought he was trying to act like Deerhead."

"Two Bows was doing that too for a while," Turtle exclaims as he remembers wondering at the time why Two Bows kept checking the trail behind him even though he was not the last person in a line that was more spread out than straight.

Another scream pierces their ears, their blood, the night.

With every hair on his body reaching for the sky, Bird sheepishly asks in a trembling voice. "Do you think they will let us join them?

"Maybe if you, I mean, if we admit we need them after all," Sky Eye's murmurs uncomfortably into the darkness. "We should tell them that we now know that it is harder to lead than we thought it was. I know I did not complain much, but I was feeling the same way you all were."

"We should say we are sorry, too," Turtle's meek voice barely reaches their ears.

"Only one way to find out." Sky Eye feels around with his foot, picks up a pack, a couple of botto's, then starts heading for the flickering light of promise. "If any of you want to stay here…."

Following his lead, the other's grab their things and walk with drooping heads and even lower pride in the direction of what they can now hear and see are happy chattering silhouettes.

"Look, Rabbit is already over there," Turtle whispers. I thought he got real quiet. What a friend he is."

"So is Ooha. Gods forbid that he does anything but sing," Sky Eye sticks his nose in the air like Ooha does.

Esan, being no fool, knew what group to stay with.

"There's Esan looking quite proud of himself too," Ista says quietly.

"Does that mean that he is smarter than us?" Turtle taps his head.

"Ask him," Sky Eye answers before taking a deep breath.

One by one, they walk into the firelight.

Was the lesson about teamwork learned?

Oh silent night, but only around the fire. The desert below and around them slowly fills up with lonesome cries and eerie sounds of conquest, or defeat.

24

7th day – Homeward Bound – Mid-morning

After a very awkward and tense night for all of them, the Chosen slowly worked their way along the mountain pass. To their surprise they discovered that some of the porous rocks held a little bit of rainwater. It was not enough to refill their bottos, but enough to quinch their thirst, one blessed handful at a time. After the nearby rocks were drained dry, they continued through the pass.

Once through, they are simply amazed at the colorful sight that lies before them.

From their vantage point in the foothills, it looks like a part of Father Sun has been taken from the sky and spread out in front of them almost as far as they can see.

Even from a distance, they are all in awe of the pretty yellow flowers that have bloomed overnight on what was a green, cactus filled desert floor. With the sun shining through them from behind, some of the flowers are so bright that they appear to be in flames.

"What would this dry land look like if it rained here more often?" Rabbit asks, trying to hold his hair in place.

Sky Eye raises his arms in thanks for such an incredible sight to behold. "I did not see any of them on the other side past day, so all these flowers must have just woken up."

"I don't know, but with those gray angry looking clouds in the distance, we may get more rain on the way home then we need," Hugumki answers, the caution unmistakable in his voice as he stares at what looks like a large slab of black granite with long twisting arms slamming into the ground in front of them. "Does anybody remember what Two Bows said about what happens to the dry ground when it rains?"

"Slippery cracks," a voice or two answers back, not realizing they are wrong.

"Let's enjoy this beautiful sight given by the Creator before we get going again."

"Hugumki, when we reach them, should we try to step between the flowers so that we don't leave an easy path showing the way back home?"

"Oh, Rabbit," Hugumki sighs, making a sad face. "The flowers aren't growing by themselves, they are on the cactus. Did you already forget what was here when we came through this area the first time?"

"Some parts we are taking are not the same way as before," Sky Eye comments quietly. "I can tell that much."

Hugumki, with his face aglow, says, "They may look like they go on forever, but they are probably not spread out as far as it looks. O haye, don't forget about the zizi's, I know Esan won't."

Hugumki goes to see how the wandering Esan is managing among the rocks.

Declaring his buffalo zumi before Father Sun, Rabbit exclaims, "Look at our zumis!"

"They look like they have the spirit of Father Sun burning in them," Ooha says, turning his coiled snake zumi into the light. "Even its eyes look like they are on fire. Just like the flowers were."

Pulling out his eagle zumi, Bird tries to look through it. "Can you feel it's power Ooha?"

"Yes, but I can already feel the heat from Father Sun even more."

Heading back to the group, Hugumki's face fills with alarm when he sees what they are doing.

"Put your zumis away!" he yells. "They're flashing in the light! If anybody is out there," Hugumki gestures at the desert in front of them, "we will look like a line of brown shiny stars moving around. That would not be very good, would it? Get ready to move!"

"Gumki, why do we always have to hurry?" Bird bravely asks, then nervously awaits his leader's reaction.

Before Hugumki can answer, Sky Eye asks. "How far do you think we can see from up here?"

"Two day's easy running. Four or five walking," Two Bows answers from behind him.

Sky Eye squints his eyes in the light. "I think it is special to be in a high place and see what a bird sees. That part over there without the flowers looks like cracked eggshells."

"If you can see like a bird, are you only going to eat mice and bugs now?" Deerhead questions seriously, before his tough looking face breaks into a big smile.

"Only if I am hungry enough."

"Haye, don't you dare look at me like that. I know I would not taste good," Deerhead begins to laugh until his whole body starts shaking.

Looking over at Bird, "I know I could let this go on and on, but if I did not keep hurrying us along, we would not get home before our supplies ran out," Hugumki says.

"Then we would all be eating mice, and before long, we would start to squeeze each other's tender spots to see who has the most meat left," Two Bows pinches his fingers together while laughing.

Before long, everybody, including Turtle, who is looking less meaty by the day starts laughing as hard as Deerhead.

Once they are all ready to continue, after a song of praise. "Let's go," Hugumki calls out. "Remember, keep those hungry eyes ahead and around, just not on me."

After doing a head count, Two Bows realizes someone is missing. "Where is Wami?"

"He was over there throwing rocks," Ista answers.

Rabbit turns, his sharp eyes searching for someone out of place. "There he is. He is starting to climb that big rock over there."

Hugumki sees a peculiar sight, which quickly turns into a perplexing one.

"What is he doing?" Bird wonders out loud.

"I hope he is just going to stand on it," Hugumki answers quietly.

Ah Ki Wami is just a little way off the trail: he is standing on a jagged precipice jutting out into the barren sky hundreds of feet above the rocky cactus-filled desert floor below.

Rabbit's soft voice gets even higher, "It almost looks like he is going to jump. See how he's bending his legs."

Turning toward the unexpected life and death drama, they all can feel the tension of Ah Ki Wami's life hanging in the balance. Just as quickly, they all realize the same thing.

They could yell, cry, or scream. It would all be for naught. Fly. Dive. Live. Die. It is going to be Ah Ki Wami's choice because they are too far away to do anything but watch and wait to see what happens.

"Has he been upset lately?" Hugumki softly asks.

"No different than usual," Two Bows answers.

What will Ah Ki Wami decide? Yes. No.

Thank the gods, it is no.

When Ah Ki Wami starts to turn for safety, his sandal slips on the ever present, grit. Trying to regain his balance before summersaulting off the rock his other sandal catches in a crack, and he starts to trip.

As everyone prepares to help their friend, they can see by the look on Ah Ki Wami's face that he has no intention of giving up on life.

Heads down, they all charge to the rescue.

With his poncho acting like an air brake, Ah Ki Wami flings his body backwards as hard as he can.

By the time they reach him, Ah Ki Wami is sitting down on the boulder with his feet jutting out over the abyss.

To everyone's surprise, his sandals have stayed on his feet, stuck together by dirt, fear, and sweat.

The questions come fast. "What were you doing? What were you thinking? Why would you do that?"

"I don't know. I only wanted to see what it looks like from up here overlooking the flat part."

In order, to lighten the heavy mood, Turtle lowers his voice, "Wami, does this look like a place to play childish games."

"No, it does not," their answer echoes through the foothills.

Other than that, Hugumki never says a word about what almost happened.

Like almost anyone he can think of, he too has faced tough and trying times in his life. He also understands that a little bit of fear can sometimes help a person understand how precious life really is.

Reacting to the heat of the sun, Hugumki starts downhill to let everyone know that it is time to get going again.

Trying to hide his smile, Ista looks at Bird. "Bird, I have a new, secret way of talking."

Ista toots as loud as he can.

"Mine has more words," Bird answers back, twice in a row.

"I have a deep thought for both of you," Deerhead starts tensing up his face, causing everyone to playfully run for cover.

With laughter ringing in the foothills, the Chosen are once again on their way as if Ah Ki Wami's misadventure and the past day's problems had never happened.

The lesson about teamwork, leadership, and strength must have been learned after all.

7th day – Homeward Bound – Early evening

The concealed body patiently waits in the cover of the thick thorn bush.

When it finally moves, it is only a slight turn of the head to make eye contact with another nearly invisible form.

They then cautiously rise from the surrounding cover as one, their eyes searching for what they did not see. After taking ten quick sideways steps, they once again meld back down into the hardscrabble desert landscape.

Neither of them is one of the Chosen.

The way Hugumki's eyes are darting about it is hard to tell if he is the hunter or prey. "Do you think we have been seen," Hugumki quietly asks Two Bows who is lying next to him in the small dusty wash they have taken cover in.

Two Bows answers cautiously, "If I saw him or them, they could have seen me."

"Spread this word," Hugumki whispers to Sky Eye who is on the other side of him. "Make no noise, keep low, and we will stay here as long as it takes to see what is going on. Keep the bows taunt and ready and ask Wami to come over when he can."

After thinking for a moment, Hugumki asks Two Bows, "How did you see him or them?"

"Father Sun showed me. I saw something small and shiny over there," Two Bow's points east. "Then it moved up and down like a man."

Keeping as low as he can: Hugumki starts taking off his pack. "How many and who do you think they are?"

"Not many. Could be our people from the old village, you never know."

"I think they are our people too. Still, we are not supposed to be seen by anyone. We will wait and see what happens."

Hearing a barely perceptible rustle heading his way, Hugumki tells Two Bows, "Leave your pack with me, then very carefully, work your way back the way we came and tell me what you see. Don't use any sound signals when you get back."

When Two Bows cautiously creeps away clutching a walking spear, Hugumki turns to look at Ah Ki Wami who is now at his side.

In the low light of the wash, Ah Ki Wami looks more reptilian than human. By the look in his eyes, a very eager, hungry, and dangerous reptile.

"Just tell me what you want me to do," Ah Ki Wami pants with excitement.

"I know what you want to hear, but I now think they are just scouts from the old village that is over there somewhere," Hugumki also points east.

"Still, I could sneak up and pretend to mark them with my knife," Ah Ki Wami pleads.

"I am sure they would find that real funny Wami, but then, they would know we are here. We don't need or want that. We will just wait them out unless Two Bows tells us something different when he reports back."

"Will we make camp here?"

"No, I think we will be able to move out before dark."

Hugumki starts to cautiously scan the area again.

"Check on the others, and I know you need your fun, so yes, you can sneak up on them," Hugumki answers Ah Ki Wami's unasked question. "Just make sure they don't cry out in surprise."

When he turns back toward Ah Ki Wami, who is no longer there, Hugumki starts thinking of the things he left unsaid. It had not surprised him when Two Bows had warned that he had seen someone at a distance. Though they were not quite at the boundaries of the old, abandoned village, if the elders had arranged an avoidance test, or surprise for them, it would probably be in this area. No doubt whoever had been sent to scare them was careless in wearing a zumi that had reflected the light-like they were earlier-a real enemy would not be so foolish. For now, though, Hugumki will let everyone feel the fear of being watched or even attacked flow through them. It will show them what it feels like and will also keep them more alert and on guard for the rest of the quest.

More than anything, he is proud of the way they had all reacted when Two Bows had signaled danger, danger, unlike the time they had been attacked by the terrifying bugs. No one had cried out, the younger ones had immediately stopped moving except for dropping down for cover. Even Esan had reacted as he should, quiet, with his nose in the air.

While waiting on Two Bows to return and confirm that the scout or scouts were heading back in the direction of their village for the night, emanating from his heart, Hugumki feels a warm wave of energy race through his body. His eyes open wider, his grin gets even bigger. He can't help it because he is just so happy and proud to be the leader of his special group.

After a short spell of contemplation.

"Admit it Hugumki, they aren't warriors yet," he laughs. "But they were much better than before."

25

8th day – Homeward Bound – First light

Day has arrived but the darkness seems reluctant to leave so it has left some lingering shadows behind to keep an eye on things. But that doesn't matter, because in the desert, morning comes very early and noisy, whether you are ready for it or not. It could be the soft lament of the mourning dove, the screech of the early hunters, or the trilling whistle of the unseen. All seem to be calling out, time to wake up, time to get up.

Still keeping his own heavy eyes closed, "Bird is mad at the birds," Ista laughs.

"Why can't they sleep late just one time?" Bird pulls his blanket tighter over his sleepy head.

From under his blanket, Deerhead scoffs. "That's right Little Bird, they should all change their ways just for you."

"Hoa, I know you don't like getting up early any more than I do."

"The first thing I will do when we get home is nothing. I will sleep for many days."

"I think that is what we will all do," Rabbit's mouth agrees, even though his body has yet to move.

After Two Bows starts stretching in his bed-a blanket and some clothes laid out on the hard ground-he says, "At least we did not have to get up before first light this day,"

"Be quiet everybody, I want to go back to sleep," Turtle rolls over on his side.

"Sorry, the new day has already started," Hugumki announces, standing up to face the brightening sky with his poncho draped over his broad shoulders. "This day, we will not build the fire back up because it's already too late."

Deerhead stands up and flexes his tight muscles, "Will this day be hot or hotter?"

Hugumki tries to prod his singer into action. "Ooha, time to get up and sing the morning song."

"I dnt wnt tu," is Ooha's muffled reply.

"Why is everybody moving so slow this day?" Two Bows joins Hugumki who is watching the horizon take on ever changing shades of fractured light.

"I think the past day's danger made them more tired than ever," Hugumki looks back down at the still unmoving bodies. "All of us had trouble going to asleep because we were so excited."

"Has Wami even moved yet?"

Pointing at a small bundle of bedding under which Bird is trying to remain unnoticed, Hugumki laughs. "Look, Bird is trying to sneak back to sleep."

Before their watchful eyes, the sky is starting to turn a flint gray with bright orange streaks shooting through it.

After another moment of reverently staring at the morning sky as it steadily grows brighter and brighter, Hugumki turns around and looks down at all his dawdling companions. Holding back a laugh, he loudly challenges, "I am going to eat, get ready, then leave. If any of you want to head towards home with me, get up or you can stay here and take your chances."

Glancing skyward, where the first shafts of sunlight are starting to look like flaming lines tearing across the sky, Two Bows offers mock encouragement. "If you need help climbing out of bed, reach for those fiery ladders and pull yourself up."

Slowly, ever so slowly, the exhausted two-legged creatures, along with a four legged one, start to stir.

Oblivious to their trials and tribulations, the birds keep on singing their noisy morning songs of joy and celebration.

8th day – Homeward Bound – High sun

The sun overhead is so hot and bright, everything seems caught in a white glare of warning. Is it going to be another miserable day for the Chosen to deal with, or are there finally signs that the weather might be changing?

In the north-western sky, moisture is being pulled together in the form of towering columns of darkness. They are reminiscent of the Pillars of Creation, until they are slowly coalesced, into one massive black cloud.

Above it, a layer of luminescent pink slowly forms a feathered curtain of downy feathers.

"I can't believe it!" Hugumki skin feels shocked into relief.

With his eyes closed, Two Bows stops to enjoy what is flowing over his body. "I have not felt a cool breeze in too many days."

One by one, everyone stops moving so they can enjoy the refreshing sensation that is washing over them and immediately energizing their spirits.

"This feels so good." Sky Eye jabs his hands like he is stabbing westward. He is not sure if he sees danger or relief hovering there. "That sky looks different. Do you think it holds rain or snow Hugumki because I can't tell if those clouds are running into each other or running away together?"

"It looks like it could be both. I mean, it depends where we are when it comes, if it is even heading this way. If we stay low, it will probably rain.

If we climb a little higher, it might snow. Either way, we will not be as thirsty again as we have been and…"

With energy surging through his body again, Ista interrupts. "I know Hugumki, we will just have to wait and see what happens."

Feeling cooler and calmer than he has in days, Hugumki smiles. "I could not have said it better myself."

A projectile, soars through the air, quickly followed by another. Sky Eye raises his arms in triumph. "Mine went further."

"Look at this one." Ah Ki Wami throws a rock so far, it almost disappears.

"Watch this one," Bird says with pride, before his rock skitters sideways.

"Like Two Bows says, just keep practicing," Sky Eye reminds him.

For some reason, Ista and Turtle turn around and start walking backwards.

"What are you two doing?" Two Bows grills them with a smile.

They both answer while giggling. "We want to see if Ooha back there gets all mixed up when he sees our backwards path."

At long last the weary teens are starting to feel young again, for now.

8th day – Homeward Bound – Late afternoon

The sky has turned a heavy whiteish gray and dropped down to coat the mountains in front of the Chosen, with snow.

Ista, Ah Ki Wami, and Esan are leading the small procession up dirt and cactus encrusted hills toward what they all know will be a very cold night, even if they can somehow build a fire to try and stay warm around.

They are moving a little slower on the large animal trail right now because Rabbit has recently hurt his foot. He is bravely limping along doing his best to keep up with everyone else. Turtle is doing his part to help by carrying Rabbit's heavier pack as Deerhead and Hugumki take turns carrying his, while still toting their own.

Seeing the pain in Rabbit's watery eyes, Turtle looks down at his swollen ankle. "How did you hurt your foot?"

Looking more fragile, but not as graceful as he usually does, "I was not paying enough attention to where I put it."

"Why, are you only used to walking in the village?"

With his thin chest puffed out from either pain or some other hidden emotion, Rabbit tries to explain. "I was looking at uh one, something else when I should have been paying more attention to where I was going."

"Oh," then what Rabbit almost said works its way into Turtle's head. "Were you looking at one of us?"

"Not at any of you, younger ones. I am me, but I am not sick like, I won't mention his name that was thrown out for hurting Willow."

"Then tell me, tell me."

"Come on-keep up-you can talk and limp at the same time," Deerhead's impatient voice booms out from in front of them.

Rabbit shakes his head. "I can't say. Can I lean on you as we walk around these rocks?"

"Yes, and I won't say anything."

"I know Turtle, you have always been nice to me."

"Like you have always been to me."

"I was just not paying enough attention, that's all,"

Deerhead yells back at them again.

"I think I know anyway."

"Don't make up things now. Let's talk about something else." Rabbit looks behind them at Bird, "Bird has ears like Esan, and we don't want to distract him from clearing our trail.

Meanwhile, at the front of the line-in his deerskin clothes and poncho-Ista is almost feeling warm as he walks along with Ah Ki Wami, and Esan, who is wearing his buffalo hide sandals again.

"Ista, the way you keep looking at me gives me the feeling you want to ask something. You do know that if you don't ask your question, you will not hear my answer," Ah Ki Wami says through his usual stern expression.

Ista, who has traded his happy face for one of unease, hesitates for a moment, then responds. "It is not a regular question.

"Well, ask Ista."

"I know we can have a fire this night because it will be very cold. What I want to know is did it bother you when we had to be close before we could have a fire in the rabbit valley?"

"I hope you have not spent the whole journey wondering about that. The hard part will be just to get a fire started this night. To answer you, only a fool would freeze to death without trying to stay alive. What is more important, staying alive, or how you stayed alive?"

"It's just, you're right, being alive is best."

"Go back and ask Gumki how much further he wants to go before we stop for the night. Haye, leave Esan with me. Now get going my funny friend, or I might knuckle your head to keep it warm."

Looking off to his side, Ah KI Wami sees something interesting. "Look at that mountain Esan. The snow blowing off the top of it looks like your furry tail."

Just in front of them, the gray heavy clouds have come down and started to kiss the ground with their icy breath. Another unmistakable sign that a cold white greeting awaits them. It is also a gift of life, of sorts, if you can survive its bite. A cold mouthful of snow is a cold mouthful of water, and soon, it is going to be everywhere.

26

9th day – Homeward Bound – Early morning

Like an icicle knife, a piercing wet cold is cutting through everything in sight.

A glistening layer of snow only adds to the bone-biting chill.

Father Sun is hidden away behind some thick, heavy snow clouds, though he is trying his best, in vain, to come out.

In the middle of all the icy whiteness, a small campfire is doing what it can to stay alive on such a miserable morning. Around its meager, lifesaving heat, a group of quivering bundled up brown snowmen huddle around it trying to stay warm.

The darkest one has his spot too, but he is not clapping his paws or stomping his feet like some of the others are doing.

As another snow shower begins, the sounds of chattering teeth and moving limbs is joined by the crunch, crunch sound of sandals in the snow as first one, then another snow-covered figure cautiously or carelessly leaves the warmth and safety of the fire.

After realizing he is being followed, the first figure pauses to wait on, this latest intrusion.

Staring intently into the falling snow, Hugumki can feel the ghosts of past and future responsibilities hovering about him in the frigid air.

Ah Ki Wami is the first to speak, "Gumki, with your cold face, I can't tell what is wrong."

"Then don't try." Hugumki tries to snuggle deeper into his blanket, poncho, deerskin shirt, cotton shirt, and breechcloth.

Blowing on his hands to try and bring some warmth into his thin cold body, Ah Ki Wami says, "Something is. I don't know if I feel the cold more on the outside or on the inside where it feels like it wants to make me cold all the way through."

"When it is this cold Wami, you must use your head to overcome what your body is telling you."

"Right now, my head is telling me that I can't feel my back side anymore."

"Then why did you leave the fire to follow me?"

At a loss for words, Ah KI Wami shrugs his shoulders.

"I must say, one of the biggest surprises on this quest has been you."

With a flicker of negative emotion flaring through his eyes, Ah KI Wami tries his best to calmly ask, "What do you mean?"

"What I mean is, thank you. Thank you for your help dealing with everyone and for your leadership, too. Just being here right now shows me that you care about more than just yourself. Sorry I have not said anything sooner, but I did not know how you were going to keep acting. You can be a little unpredictable, you know?"

"I know."

"As for what is bothering me. I knew it would be hard keeping us together and safe. Now Rabbit is hurt, and it is very cold. How were we so hot not long ago?"

"Hugumki, I don't think you have to worry about us staying as one. We are together in body and spirit around the fire. Or are you more worried that we would be easy to catch if someone tried?"

"I don't know. I just feel like running to nowhere to warm up right now.

"The easy part is we will stay together. If seen, we will do what needs to be done. Even, if we have, to fight."

"Right now, I want to be alone for days by a big fire. All the constant questions are going to make me start acting like the chief's wife soon. I can't though, can I? I am the leader, I must lead. I know it is what I wanted and was made to do. To be truthful, I kind of thought that leading meant to lead people somewhere or through things. I did not understand that on this test I would have to be a mother, a father, and everything in between. And it never stops."

"When we make camp for the night, Two Bows and I will watch over everybody so that you can take a break."

"Will you answer everyone's questions? Will you take away the questions in my head? You can't, because before the elders, I am the one responsible."

"For what?"

"For everything. For everybody. Even you. Someone is standing up now, probably wanting something else."

"Do you want me to move him away?"

"No. We can and will do this. But I also must prepare for the bad things that could happen. And when you think of bad things."

"You can have bad thoughts," they both say.

Before they are interrupted, Hugumki must have the answer to what has been troubling him. "You weren't really going to jump, were you?"

"If your head thinks of something, that doesn't mean that you really have to do it, right?"

"Right. We need to, we all need to talk about that and more when we get back home."

"Why."

"Because we all get sad. Let's get back to the fire before we can't move anymore."

Hugumki and Ah Ki Wami join the others and either pray or wait for the snow shower to end. When it does, it is once again a stark motionless in white world, except for the quivering bundled up snowmen, that is.

9th day – Homeward Bound – Mid-day

In a land that seems to stay the same forever, it can also change quicker than you would ever think possible. That is something the Chosen are still learning to deal with as they carefully walk through lightly falling snow.

Wearing practically everything he has with him, "Two Bows, you were right," Bird says before loudly clapping his hands. "I am not as cold. My spirit and body have gotten warmer."

Even though everything is covered in a thin layer of icy whiteness now, they all remember what the fuzzy cactus needles looked like. Since none of them want holes in their feet, they are taking their time.

With his blanket tucked underneath his poncho, Deerhead is carefully weaving a path in between the snow encrusted cactus while everyone else is following right behind him.

Ista, in the middle of the group asks Two Bows who is in front of him, "Why does Wami have to slow us down even more by dragging his blanket behind him? There is nobody out here and won't the falling snow cover up our passing?" He quickly sticks his tongue out to try and catch a snowflake. "And we are walking in each other's steps."

Two Bows quietly answers him as his eyes continue to watch all around. "Do you know for sure that we are all alone? Do you know that the snow will keep coming down? It could stop snowing, as fast as it started. To be careful means to be careful all the time, not just when you want to. Have you already forgotten that we were almost seen not too long ago?"

"Woooossooooah."

Two Bows looks down at Ista.

"That is what the wind sounds like Two Bows."

In front of them Rabbit whispers, "It sounds like evil screeching."

Two Bows raises his voice. "It is just the air in the sky moving very fast and making the same sounds it would if it was down here."

Ista waves his arms overhead, "I wonder how fast the clouds are moving?"

"Faster than a slow bird can fly on a good day." Two Bows stops to wait on Ah Ki Wami to make sure that he is wiping the path so clean that even Deerhead wouldn't be able find it.

Further up the trail.

"Bird, is this test and journey still going the way you thought it would?" Turtle asks.

Esan, who looks like he is turning a frosty gray, carefully works his way around them with a little totter in his steps.

"Yes, and no. I know this is a special test, but to be so hot I could not think right, and now I am so cold I can't think right either, does not seem right. I just hope that I will warm up some day before I get too old." When Bird stops to huff and puff, he is quickly engulfed, by his own foggy breath.

"Quit complaining," Rabbit scolds. "It does not solve anything, remember. Look around and see how beautiful it is. I just love how the white of the snow, and the dark parts of the land look together."

Turtle studies his limping friend, "How is your foot feeling now?"

"It is feeling much better, unless it freezes off. Hoa, now you have me complaining. What I would really love right now is Che Wah's buffalo blanket. It would feel so warm and good on my body."

When Rabbit reaches up to brush some snow from his hair, he has a chilling thought. *My hair feels so cold and stiff. What would I do if it all broke off and I was left with nothing but, ah...?*

Hearing a small grunt of agony escape Rabbit's lips, Turtle checks on him. "Did you hurt yourself again."

"No. It's nothing."

"That looks like Deerhead coming. "We had better keep moving," Bird grumbles without any joy or appreciation of the incredible beauty that is around him perceptible in his voice.

The snow keeps drifting down, one icy flake after another upon the Chosen and the shrouded picturesque landscape they are passing through as the whistling wind mocks their slow, but steady, progress.

9th day – Homeward Bound – Evening

For a while, the sky had turned as clear as blue ice. To the Chosen's dismay, it has once again darkened, gotten heavy, and dropped down before them.

This time, in a way that they least expected it to.

From out of a heavy mist that resembles a wall of empty whiteness, a ghostly form emerges that looks like it is dripping with tears.

"We should stop, Gumki. Up ahead it is even harder to see through than the snow was. I could hardly see anything in front of me," Two Bows warns while wiping away at his face. "Like I said, up ahead, it gets even harder to see through than the snow was," he repeats. "Let's all pray that it does not get cold enough for the fog to freeze," Two Bows lifts his face to the sky.

"We will make camp now," Hugumki calls out. "Everybody spread out and quickly gather as much wood or kindling as you can find. Don't go far, just spread out. We need to make the fire before everything gets too wet, so put the wood in your pack if you have room. Let's be thankful that it has not snowed, here yet. Deerhead has the fire stones, so, Deerhead, you are in charge, of preparing the fire. Let's get busy."

When Rabbit picks up a twig, something he knows should not be in the fog, catches his dark, suspicious eyes. "Did you see that Two Bows?"

"See what."

"The fog looks like it is hiding shapeshifters."

"Don't say that. The last thing we need is shapeshifters about."

"What are shapeshifters?" Bird's narrowed eyes show his apprehension.

"Right now, we have other things to worry about," Two Bows spins his hands. "Let's hurry up."

Before he bends down again, Two Bows takes a moment to cautiously peer into the white mist to make sure that a malevolent spirit or two has not decided to join them.

While the wet white wall tries to decide which way to drift next, all the Chosen quickly and quietly set about their tasks, including Esan, who is trying to help Deerhead decide where to build their fire by marking a spot or two himself.

27

10th day – Homeward Bound – Mid-afternoon

On a day that is as clear as it is cold, Esan wishes he was resting around a cozy fire. Instead, even with his thick furry coat, he is getting a little chilled while waiting for his poncho, deerskin, and blanket covered friends to get moving again.

But what are they standing around waiting on in the middle of the desert?

"There he goes again." Waving his blanket around as if it were a shield, Rabbit scowls before looking away from poor Ah Ki Wami who is bent over and flapping his blanket like broken bird wings as he wretches over, and over again.

Ah Ki Wami's unwashed face has taken on a greenish cast: like a dirty piece of peridot.

Deerhead callously says to the unfortunate Ah Ki Wami. "Until you're done Wami, you could walk a little further away before you get sick again."

Ah Ki Wami groans between spasms. "I'm the one feeling like kani."

"Sure, we will move the many for one," Hugumki responds, pulling his blanket tighter around himself before turning away from Ah Ki Wami's noisy pain.

"I am done, my body just does not know it yet," Ah Ki Wami says with a pale faced grimace.

Hugumki not so gently chides him. "Next meal, don't eat so much if it is something that you are not used to eating."

"I told you we should have cooked that large lizard better," Deerhead reminds anyone listening. "I have never seen a green one like that before."

"We don't even know what made him sick. The rest of us are good." Sky Eye moves away just to be sure.

"Don't talk about food right now," Ah Ki Wami moans, resuming his bent over position.

Hugumki tilts his covered head. "I knew this might happen to one of us sooner or later. I did not think it would be Wami."

"He must be tougher on the outside than he is on the inside." Rabbit raises his covered arms gracefully to the sky because he is overjoyed that it is not him in Ah Ki Wami's position.

"I wonder if we will always eat the same foods?" Sky Eye asks himself as much as anybody else.

"Of course, we will," answers Deerhead. "It is what the gods have given to us. Why would we ever want anything different?"

"I was just thinking."

"Maybe you think too much Sky Eye." Deerhead starts bobbing his large head back and forth, causing Turtle and Ista to start laughing.

"How can someone overuse what the Creator has given them? That could be the funniest thing I have ever heard Deerhead."

"Wami, do you feel like you are strong enough to continue our journey," Hugunki takes a step back just in case. "We still have a long way to go before dark."

Surprisingly, it is Ista that comes up with an answer for Deerhead and Sky Eye. "Maybe the best thing to do is have a strong body, and a smart way of thinking."

"Like me?" Bird asks more seriously than the size of his blanketed body should allow.

"Yes. Just like you Bird, and Turtle, and Ista. Just like all of us. We should all try, for that," answers Hugumki.

Turtle, whose face is barely visible under his blanket asks his leader, "What do you mean Gumki?"

"We should all try to be strong of body and head," he answers, before glancing at the weak-legged Ah Ki Wami again, who has yet to respond. "I know some will do that better than others. It must be sad to not even try."

Hugumki looks up at their tall scout who has come back to join them.

"Two Bows, does the way look clear so that we can continue?"

"Yes it does. Did I miss anything? Why does Wami look so bad?"

"You don't want to know," answers a snickering voice or two.

"Ooha, did you want to sing something?" asks Hugumki.

"No. I was just thinking about the last time I had a big meal. Sorry Wami."

"Oh no, not more thinking," Deerhead exclaims to laughter.

Ah Ki Wami stands as proudly as he can, in the condition he is in. "I, I can continue now."

"Let's get going everybody." Hugumki calls out. "Eyes ahead, eyes around."

Onward they trudge. All of them wishing, thinking, and praying about something extra good to eat, even Ah Ki Wami and his upset stomach. Will the desert hear them in time?

10th day – Homeward Bound – Night-time

It is so blustery and cold that not even the nocturnal creatures of the desert are scurrying about their tasks. Up above, a pale waxing moon is hanging with the stars. Below, a fire burns away the chill. Partially sheltered from the wind among some large boulders, the fire does more than burn warm and bright. With the wind still managing to whip it around, it looks like a tethered serpent in orange and red thrashing its heads about, pent upon escape. What a perfect setting for the Chosen to share fun, friendship, and scary stories.

Esan takes a breath as his tail taps out a steady beat of happiness. He is glad to be warm again among his friends. Exhale. Another breath of contentment, exhale.

Looking even thicker than he usually does, due to everything he is wearing, "I know what Esan's breath looks like," Turtle says from his cozy spot around the fire.

"Like mine," Two Bows blows a long thin smoky looking trail into the frigid air.

"No. It reminds me of a story, something I heard," replies Turtle.

"Was it a story or something you were listening in on?" Hugumki looks at him like he already knows the answer.

Ista, with the face of an accomplice, asks, "Is it listening in if your ears are where someone else is talking, even if they don't know you are already there."

"What I heard was Che Wah talking to someone I could not see," Turtle confesses.

Two Bows leans back with his hands behind his head. "So, you were listening in."

"What I heard was Che Wah talking about spirit stuff, and worse," Turtle slowly looks at each eerily glowing face around the fire. The firelight is making them look like evil versions of themselves with elongated faces, dancing chins, and glowing eyes.

In a low rumbling voice, Ah Ki Wami, feeling a little better, says, "Being around a fire like this is a good time to scare each other."

"What do you see in the fire?" Sky Eye asks everybody.

Quickly the words: "Spirits, ghosts, flaming wings," even, "fiery bats," fly, through the air, and drift up and away with the smoke.

"Sorry Turtle," Sky Eye nods.

"Well, go on then," Deerhead urges.

"It all started one…," Turtle begins.

"Please get to the story," Rabbit shakes his head impatiently.

Turtle gets to the story. "I was passing by the holy room where I knew that Monapa was waiting to go on her next journey. I was almost around the corner when Che Wah walked outside and started shaking his death rattle to the four directions. I knew then that Monapa was on her last journey, so I turned to get away. I took a couple of steps, then I heard Che Wah starting to speak to someone I could not see."

With an uncertain look clouding his face, "Maybe he was talking to himself, or a spirit," Rabbit whispers hoarsely.

"What I heard him say," Turtle continues, "was when Monapa moved on, he could see her spirit come out of her mouth, then circle the room, before leaving. Seeing Esan's breath made me think of that. We are not living and dying with every breath are we?"

Instead of answering, Two Bows has his own question. "I sometimes wonder what happens to us after we die. When we kill an animal, we say the spirit goes on. Does it really?"

With his face starting to freeze from more than the cold, "I don't know if we should be talking about these things Two Bows," Rabbit starts reaching for his zumi. "My brother says some things should not be talked about."

"Just because he wants to be the next medicine healer does not mean Chu Eh Oh Se knows everything or anything." Deerhead sticks out his lips to show how he really feels.

"Maybe we are entering a time when knowing things will be good for us, for everybody." Hugumki stares into the fire. "I don't know if I can believe someone just because they say that I am supposed too. How would they explain this?" Hugumki spreads his hands dramatically. "Remember Two Bows when the smoke from that fire was following me to whatever side of the fire I stood on? It was strange. There was no wind, no breeze, yet wherever I went, the smoke went. After a while, I had trouble breathing. What was also strange, it happened the day I was chosen to lead us."

"Ooooooh, oooooh" Bird timidly laughs, nervously clutching his face.

"Look at us now. We are all different. We do things differently, but we are all on the same journey right now. Maybe life after death is like that. We all come from different places, but we all go to the same place to keep working together." Two Bows' own words of wisdom have put a surprised look on his face.

"Maybe that place is where all the night lights are," ventures Sky Eye. "Sometimes it seems like there are more lights than other times. Sometimes they are brighter than other times, and sometimes, they move around like a wandering spirit. This I would like to know before my end time comes. Where do we really go?"

While everybody thinks about that for a moment, Bird innocently asks. "What are shapeshifters?"

As if a veil of darkness has suddenly been pulled over them, the camp immediately gets very still and quiet.

After a quick glance at Two Bows, and the barely perceptible nod of his head, Hugumki answers, "Now is not the right time to talk about that. They are very evil people, and we will leave it at that."

The hopeless romantic can take no more. "Can we just go back to talking about girls now?" asks Ooha, making a female's outline with his hands.

And they do.

Two Bows talks about a woman in their village, and how her, and her mate are always so happy. Then he brings up her younger sister, and how if she is anything like her sister, she would probably make a good mate once she gets a little older.

Ooha goes on and on talking about Squash Blossom.

Unfortunately, Rabbit does not have anyone to talk about yet, so he doesn't.

Sky Eye mentions that he would like a smart mate, just not too smart.

Deerhead and Ooha almost get in a fight, because, once again, Deerhead is dismissive of woman, and Ooha just can't understand why he has that attitude.

As the firelight keeps on dancing around-and time passes-it starts illuminating ten, maybe eleven, agitated, aggravated, potentially aggressive faces with bodies to match. Deerhead's face is still flushed, and his thighs keep smacking against each other. Bird is bouncing in place so much that it looks like he is ready to run anywhere, if only his legs could carry him. Ah Ki Wami's dark looks are starting to look dangerous, for everybody.

You can't really blame any of the Chosen for their sudden change of attitude? Like all developing teens, they are dealing with growing levels of testosterone, one of the most powerful forces ever known. While needed and necessary, left unchecked, testosterone can also lead to lots of bad behavior such as anger, hostility, and sexual aggression. All, which explains the sudden change of mood of everyone around the fire. In fact, the Chosen have become so loaded up on testosterone, their cups runneth over.

The Chosen don't really have a word for what they are going through, just a lot of bad jokes. And I do mean bad, so we will leave those alone.

When a couple of shoulders start banging to hard against each other, Hugumki knows he needs to divert their attention. "I still remember the first time I saw her." He starts talking about a pretty girl he has seen in the large village the two times he has been there. He has watched her get older, and well, let's just say he can't wait until he can go back as a man, and a successful leader. His only hope is that the shy smiles she has given him means that she feels the same way he does and will wait for him until they see each other again.

Out of their respect for Hugumki, and his leadership, nobody asks him the most obvious question. "Do you know her name?"

Bird, Turtle, and Ista don't have much to add, but they are doing what they are supposed to be doing. They are learning about life, and all the wound-up boys are learning about self-control, whether they realize it or not.

As the tension filled night slowly crawls on, an uneasy, not so peaceful mood has filled the Chosen's camp.

From out of the distance comes a roar that speeds, spreads, and then resounds across the desert. sounding just like what it is, a low rumbling wave of ferocious sound.

What roars in the desert? Bears? Yes. Large cats? Yes. But a low rumbling roar?

"What was that?" Two Bows does not try to hide his nervousness.

Hugumki stands up and spins his head around. "I have never heard that before."

"Hoa. Look at how big our eyes are. Is this what you meant by being scared around the fire, Wami?" Deerhead snorts.

Ah Ki Wami's face looks even more serious than usual. "That sounded big whatever it was."

"Did not sound like any animal I have ever heard before," Hugumki says, still standing. "Makes all our disagreements seem less important, doesn't it? If we don't hear it again, we should, we will be all right."

Before long, sleep begins her gentle, but firm tug. Time to head to the uneasy land of dreams where all wishes can be realized. Or can they?

As the night moves on, one flame is in danger of burning out while another is just being lit.

Her clothes are real, beautiful.

Her hair, a light.

Her upturned throat is bare.

Her lips, apart.

Her eyes are dreamy, focused on another time and place.

She reaches out with the gentle touch of thought.

To pull him near?

To take him away?

A feathered breath behind whispered words.

A sweet caress of impatience. Does she have someplace better to be?

"My dream. My dream. I can feel her drifting away. Just a dream," is mumbled, then the snoring restarts.

28

11th day – Homeward Bound – Early afternoon

Father Sun is warm and the breeze is cool, but not cold. In two groups of five, the Chosen slowly work their way through a wide strewn out field of large rocks in only their shirts, ponchos, sandals, and breechcloths. The packs on their backs have become such a part of them that they are hardly worth mentioning, that is, except for the secret hidden inside their small one.

When the rear group of five approaches the tightest part of the trail that meanders among boulders of various sizes, they are given a hint of what awaits them just ahead. It has taken flight in a dark kettle of vultures.

"What is that horrible smell? Did one of you forget to clean up after you were finished?" Rabbit teases both Ista and Bird, who are in front of him in their winding line.

"Even you know that only one thing smells like that, Rabbit," Deerhead mocks.

"Whew," adds Ah Ki Wami from behind Deerhead.

"To fad we are ott in a apen orea," Bird seems to say through the hand covering his nose and mouth.

Deerhead points in front of them. "Whatever it was must have fallen between those large rocks over there and broke its leg, or something, then got itself stuck until it died."

"Deerhead, why is it still so smelly when it has been so cold around here," Ista asks, turning his nose away from what could be anything.

"I am sure it was hotter in this area before we got here."

"Let's hurry and catch up with Hugumki's group. The smell is starting to get to me," Ah Ki Wami grunts while half-heartedly checking the trail behind him.

"I think it is sad even for an animal to die all alone," Rabbit says with all the flourish he can muster in such a smelly situation.

Deerhead pretends to kick Rabbit's backside, "That's how we all go."

From up ahead, Bird exclaims, "I can't take much more of this or I am going to get sick like Wami did past day."

Ah Ki Wami answers with an edge, "You're so funny for talking about that now, Bird."

Ista abruptly raises his voice, "Look ahead at Two Bows. Doesn't it look like he is taking deep breaths? Let's hurry up."

"Sure looks like they are all laughing at us." Bird can't quite believe his eyes, "Esan looks like he is making a face at us too."

Rabbit fumes softly as only he can, "They could have at least warned us."

"I guess they did not want to ruin our surprise," Deerhead gives Rabbit a not so gentle shove in the back. "Hurry up will you. Let's get out of here."

As they hurry by, the buzz from all the happy flies sounds more like a swarm of angry bees.

11th day – Homeward Bound – Late afternoon

The clouds look like a churning mass of gray and white indecision. It's as if they are trying to decide whether to stay together and cause more trouble or fall apart and disappear into oblivion.

Even after a long day of walking, the Chosen are feeling quite good in both body and spirit, unaware that they are about to witness that something destructive can also create something new.

Lost in thought, Hugumki is thinking about how long it will be until they get home. "What is wrong Esan?" he asks, catching the sudden change in Esan's posture.

Esan's answer is a soft whine before he stops and stares at the mesa, they are about to work their way around.

Instantly wary and alert, "Do you see somebody or something up there Esan?" Two Bows scans the top of the flat mountain the best he can.

"Look, look!" Bird shouts. "Part of that looks like it is starting to dance the snow off!"

"Stop here everybody," Hugumki orders to the others who have already stopped in place. "I think we are about to see something unbelievable."

Sky Eye smiles because his wish has been answered.

Moving his ears around, Turtle asks, "Isn't this near the area where we heard that loud noise before?"

Only Esan answers with his agitated whine.

Then the vibration that has been bothering Esan gets loud enough for everyone else to hear. It is the signal of what is about to happen right in front of their astonished eyes.

The whole front end of the mesa starts moving with a slow shimmer that quickly turns into a shake turning what was the giant's cold stare into an eternal blink.

As the dust of destruction starts to rise into the air, the shake creates a tumbling landslide of large rocks that sounds like the gods are once again ruling the old ball courts.

With fear and indecision filling his eyes, Ista stammers, "Is the giant waking up?"

"He is not waking up, he is falling down, and it looks like he is going to bring the whole end down with him!" Sky Eye exclaims, waving his arms and jumping up and down.

At first, the small, then larger rocks start tumbling upon themselves. Then the large white part that is bigger than their village slowly starts falling apart then quickly drops down the slope of the mesa sending smaller rocks and more dust and snow flying everywhere.

Trying to match the tone with his voice, "It almost sounds like a noisy river," Ooha says.

"It is a river of rock after all," Sky Eye replies.

While watching the rumbling rock show, they all try to guess which ones will roll further down the slope toward them than the others.

A round chunk of torn off rock starts hurtling downward. The massive piece and its bumping companions are twice the size of Hugumki's room. Other pieces that are more sheared off are doing their best, but their awkward tumbling is starting to slow them down.

It looks like the winners are going to be the bear sized rocks that have flown with gravity to the bottom where they are now crashing, banging, and jostling against everything else.

Eventually, it all comes to rest among the rocky debris that was already there from previous rockslides.

When it is over and the dust has cleared enough to see again, Ah Ki Wami says, "The part that is left up there is all brown again."

Some of the fallen rocks are starting to sparkle like pure quartz. A couple of fingers point, but they know that now is not the time to turn into rock collectors.

"Those rocks have not settled yet," Hugumki says. "But we may have to send a harvest party this way someday."

"I hope that never happens to Flat Top or our entire village along with us could disappear forever," Rabbit's face looks as worried as his voice sounds.

Sky Eye thinks for a moment. "I would guess that is why it was built a little way away from the bottom of Flat Top. But then again, you never know."

"Well, let's get going then, or we will never get back home to check on it," Hugumki says. "Let's go. Eyes ahead, eyes around. Hup, hup," he adds, just to see if they are paying attention.

11th day – Homeward Bound – Early dark

Flash, flash, at the speed of light, streaks of fire burn across the sky.

The Chosen nervously watch the dazzling show from their sleeping spots encircling the campfire. In a light breeze, the fire looks like it has flapping wings that can't take it anywhere. Not even to join the flaming light show above.

An amazed and nervous Turtle looks at Sky Eye. "Are those falling gods or what we talked about before?"

They both watch as another light streaks its way across the starry filled sky until it disappears in a flash of flame.

"In my lessons, we are still trying to decide if those fast lights were once part of the lights that stay in the sky" Sky Eye replies. "I don't really know because they don't seem to last long enough to drop down to the ground like the special stone, I have in my pouch."

Watching another light burn its way across the celestial curtain, Rabbit quietly comments, "To me, they are our ancestors moving to a new home."

Bird peers at Rabbit from across their own flame. "Where do you think their new home is at?"

"I do not know, and I do not want to find out too soon."

"I don't know either," Hugumki says with a reverent tone in his voice as two more burning lights dance across the sky. "But I have heard, if you head on the other side of our village for many days journey, you will see a giant hole made by one of those lights when it came down. I was told it happened long ago. Maybe they are gods coming back to us, Turtle."

"Am I bad if I hope they stay up there?" wonders a drowsy Ista.

Rabbit snuggles deeper into his blanket, "I have the same wish since we don't know what they really are."

"If Little Sun was not up already behind those clouds over there, the flames would look even brighter. I wonder if a man will ever go up there before he dies," Sky Eye wonders as he continues to solemnly gaze overhead from his sleeping spot.

When he reaches over to turn their small fire and add more wood, Deerhead asks, "What would he do up there if he was still a man, and not a god?"

Then all is quiet in camp as the Chosen watch the flaming lights burn the sky for many heartbeats until all their eyes are closed for the night, including Esan's, who did not care or understand what all the fuss was about since he could not smell or eat it.

29

12th day – Homeward Bound – Late morning

On a day that is warmer than the Chosen have felt in a while, a large cloud carrying the promise of shade lazily drifts into view. Wearing the coat of an extra shaggy sacred white buffalo, it looks like it is grazing as it slowly works its way across the forever-blue field of sky.

Just when it seems like all is clear, a smoky blemish is seen slowly rising to the firmament above.

A signal? Danger?

Trying to stand as tall as he is proud, "I am the greatest hunter ever," Ista proclaims. He then bends down to tear himself off another piece of savory meat from the deer thigh that is still cooking on the fire the Chosen are loosely gathered around.

Acting as if he is eating his last meal, "Luckiest walker ever is more like it," grunts Deerhead, between bites of the roasted meat that they are all ravenously gobbling down as fast as they can.

From off to the side of their small fire, Hugumki looks at Esan who is happy to have something warm and tasty to gnaw on. "See how fast we can work together when we want to."

Feeling hungry, rather than caring about how he looks in front of his companions, for a change, "You're right," agrees Rabbit, making satisfied grunts of his own, they're just not as loud as Deerhead's. "I don't think I have ever seen a spit and fire put together so fast."

Cautiously scanning the tight drawn in horizon that surrounds them, "Speaking of fast things, we should put out the fire, finish eating, then get moving again," Ah Ki Wami insists.

"I know, I know Wami." Hugumki draws his words out slowly as if it takes a lot of effort. "I know you aren't as hungry as the rest of us yet, but if I had told everybody that we were going to let the whole deer go to waste, I may have been cooked too. Look at us. We were all getting thin, and hungry, trying to make our supplies last this long. And I don't know about you, but I was getting very tired of eating just lizard, tough rabbits, or whatever else we could easily catch then get rid of."

Between licks of his fingers, Rabbit looks at his leader, "Do you think we have been seen Gumki?"

"Don't tell them this," Hugumki answers quietly, studying the wolfish eaters spread around him. "If we had not been in an area surrounded by nearby mountains, we would not be doing this. When we entered this area this day, there was no signs that there was anyone around."

Looking as if he is ready to take on anything, "But that was then," counters Ah Ki Wami, scanning the horizon again.

"With the cold we have had, I thought it was safe," Hugumki says, trying to keep the tension out of his voice. Taking a deep breath, he looks at everyone in their buckskin shirts, leggings, and ponchos. "We needed the spirit and meat of the deer to give us the energy to make it home. It is a blessing."

To break the tension in the air, he asks, "What do you think Esan?"

Esan, like only a hungry eater can, ignores his friend because he has reached his prize, the bone marrow.

Knowing when to keep his mouth shut and deal with other people is something that Ista is still learning about. "I am a hunter," Ista brags again, this time, directly to Deerhead from across their small fire. After he takes a few more bites of the first tasty meal he has had in a long time, he adds, "I am the one that killed, blessed, and prepared the deer. With some help."

Two Bows gives him mock encouragement, "At least you did not trip over it as it lay there," causing Ista to defend himself again.

"Was it my fault he had just fallen on those rocks over there and broke his leg? The gods knew that you were letting me lead this day so they gave me this gift to share."

Feeling energy pour back into his body, Turtle is thankful. "Ooha, your prayers for a real meal must have been heard, thank you,"

Turtle pats him on the back with a shiny hand.

Ooha silently takes another bite. He does not care right now who gets the credit for his answered prayers, he is just thankful to have something good to fill up on and something greasy for his throat.

"Too bad we will have to give most of the deer back to the desert before we can use all of it," Deerhead complains, starting to pick between his teeth.

"Should we cut out the, you know, to make another boto when we get back home?" Sky Eye asks.

His answer comes back from everyone who doesn't have their mouths full. "No, it will start to stink bad."

Hugumki lightly pats his stomach. "It is a good thing Deerhead because if some of you ate everything you wanted, you might get sick just like someone else we know did."

"Why are these animals hurting themselves Two Bows?" Turtle asks. "Aren't they used to living out here?"

With a meaty finger poised in the air, Two Bows answers. "Because it is beginning to warm up, some of the animals are starting to get more active. They might not have had enough to eat during the winter, so they are a little weak, and as we all know right now, the rocks can be very slippery with all the melting snow around. So, as we all saw, it did not take a great hunter to bring this deer to us."

Finally feeling like he has accomplished something useful in his life, Ista does not understand why everyone else does not feel the same way.

"Two Bows, you are jealous because I am the only one with a big kill on this journey," Ista looks proudly at the remains of the dangerous beast.

Deerhead glances at Two Bows and tries not to laugh. "Keep talking like that Ista and when we get back, I will drag you with us when we go on a real hunt," he dares the young Ista rather sharply.

Two Bows turns and glowers at him too. "Then you will see what it is really like to be out there waiting and waiting for something that may or may not come along. Sometimes it can take days."

Deerhead continues in a voice that is starting to make Ista nervous. "And if we don't catch anything, we can always cook you. Then we will all say, this meat tastes…."

Everybody else stops eating and joins in on the last word, "Funny," which makes Ista realize that Deerhead and Two Bows have been teasing him all along, but in a serious way this time.

Once his stomach is full, Hugumki can feel the chilly air take his alertness back up a notch. "When we are done here, everybody cut and take as much meat as you can eat while we travel, but not as much as you want," he says. Standing up and heading over to put out the fire, Hukumki concedes, "You are right Wami. We do not know for sure that we are all alone out here." Hugumki looks at his friends who are still enjoying their bounty. "We are out here and on the move, but there could be other people out here on the move for their own reasons. Our people live in villages, but there are other people that still follow the game, look for other food and water or whatever else they need. I still think it is too cold for other people to be out here, yet here we are. Let's finish up, including hiding the rest of the deer we aren't taking with us. We must hide it good because it is easy to tell that we have cut meat from it. After that we will be ready to go."

Once they are under way, that invisible force called home, along with a very good meal, gives them the extra bit of energy they all need right now.

After one fist of sun movement the warriors in training are dutifully working their way across the desert with nothing left of their delicious meal but greasy smiles which Two Bows decides to take advantage of.

"Bird, do you know that some animals may sleep during the winter but on warmer days, like now, they wake up to see if there is something good to eat walking by."

Bird spins his head around in mild alarm, "That's not funny."

"It's true, so instead of just looking around, make sure you are really seeing, what is all around you."

Hugumki walks over and whispers in Two Bows ear, "What made you think of that?"

"How warm it has become this day and the area we are in. You know who gets hungry on warmer days."

"I thought so, but I won't say his name.

The Chosen continue onward, but with a little more caution in their steps.

Until.

They are almost through what can be called an enclosed valley. The mountains that surrounded them on their break earlier have slowly eroded in size until they are just rocky hills that lead to another expanse of desert that only looks flat from a distance.

After a short passage of time, some of the Chosen have already forgotten Two Bows' coy warning. Turtle for instance has his head down as he quietly repeats to keep his rhythm going, "One step after another."

"Ohaw," He is abruptly halted by his pack straps because Deerhead has grabbed them to keep him from running into Two Bows.

Just in front of him, Two Bows has raised a slightly trembling fist and frozen in place. When he opens his hand and feels for the wind, you can hear everyone's collective gasp. They all know what he is doing but not yet why.

Hugumki motions for a hold and for someone to hold Esan and keep him quiet. Now they must wait, every moment feeling longer than the last, until Two Bows points the way.

He slowly does, across his left shoulder and up to what appears to be a flat outcropping in the distance. An occupied outcropping, occupied by something dark and very big.

The Chosen, caught unaware, are immediately shocked to attention and the source of that surge is a real eye opener that has them astonished, confounded, flabbergasted, and stunned, all at once. What is registering on their faces is simply alarm, panic, and fear. In other words, sheer terror.

"Oh, my gods," Rabbit says without moving his lips.

In the not so far distance, is a dark fuzzy form sluggishly moving around in front of what could be a hole or cave.

"Bear,' is quickly and urgently relayed up and down the line.

"How is the wind,' Hugumki asks.

He gets back a terse, "Not good,' from Two Bows.

When the black form stops moving, turns their way, raises his nose, and obviously sniffs, all the Chosen drop down without thinking.

Rabbit slowly lifts his head back up, "Where did it go? There's nothing there now."

In a whisper filled with dread, Ista proclaims, "It smelled us."

Quicker than a hungry bear can swipe, they once again share looks of alarm, panic, shock, and fear, mixed with, so what do we do now?

After a quick exchange between Hugumki and Two Bows.

"How far? How long?" Hugumki asks.

"A little time walking. Not too long if running,"

Two Bows takes charge.

"Get in a circle facing each other's backs. Then cut a small piece out of the poncho in front of you. Hurry up now, we may not have a lot of time. After that grab a little bit of food out of the pack in front of you."

From off to the side, it looks like the Chosen have been called to perform a strange ritual of stabbing each other in the back before stealing each other's food, all while in a circle.

"Ista, you had better be cutting only a small piece of my poncho or I will cut."

"Save it for the bear, Ooha," Hugumki cuts in.

"Two Bows, can you bend your legs. I can't reach your pack."

"Sorry Turtle."

After a little confusion they all wait on Two Bows' next words. "Sprinkle the food around and let the cloth fall where it may. Let's spread out a little and if you have to make water, do it now. Leave some jerky behind. We want to make sure the bear stays here a long time and forgets all about us,"

Once they are all done. "Let's get out of here, now," Two Bows says.

"I will watch behind us," Deerhead volunteers.

Hugumki starts to say something, but instead checks to see if he has Rabbit's attention. He then uses two fingers to point at his eyes while saying, "Rabbit, can you check behind us now and then while Deerhead is watching out for the bear?"

Rabbit starts to protest but smiles instead. "When I need to, I can still run faster than you," he softly sings to himself.

The joker must have some fun too. "He was looking at you Turtle,' Ista makes his version of a scary face.

"A turtle has a shell. You Bird have no wings and I can walk faster than you."

"No, you can't."

Turtle's eyes suddenly get huge. "Here he comes. Let's find out."

"Hey ah, get back here," Ista starts laughing as he picks up his pace.

The Chosen start walking as fast as they can without worrying about a trail left behind because they know that the bear will not be using his eyes to follow them. For that reason, Two Bows starts leading them at a slight angle to their original trail. That way, once they find an overlook of any sort, they will check to see if they are being followed or not before they start heading in the right direction again.

Once there.

"Do you see anything" Hugumki asks his scout.

"No."

"I don't either," Rabbit says.

"I don't think it will follow us because it does not want to give up its warm cave yet because there is still too much snow around this area," Two Bows says as he checks around again.

Hugumki looks at their sweating, pleading faces, but he knows that the danger is not over yet. "Take a fast drink of water then let's get going again to be sure."

After a few deep but not so relaxing breaths the Chosen's sandals are once again pounding their way across the desert.

12th day – Homeward Bound – Nighttime

With their bellies and spirits full, the boys are enjoying each other's company and resting the best they can after that day's earlier excitement, around their fire. They are brothers of the trials, and trails of the desert. Rabbit looks like he is already nodding off; even though, he seems to be laughing at all the right times. Two Bows is quietly lying there with a serene expression on his face. Bird is on his side looking over the desert, without really seeing anything. Everyone else is busy talking and joking about whatever pops into their tired heads. At the end of another long and eventful day, each of the Chosen seems to be filled with the last of that day's energy just before they fall into a deep sleep. To their surprise, this night is not only going to be different, but also much, much noisier.

The only face that does not look happy or content, is Esan's.

Under their watchful eyes, at least the ones that are watching, what had started as a warm glow along the eastern horizon has slowly gotten brighter and brighter until it looks like it might set everything ablaze.

"Is that a fire over there?" Ista asks loud enough to silence the small creatures just out of the reach of their firelight.

"If that is a fire on those distant mountains, it must be the biggest fire anyone has ever seen," Two Bows answers while thinking of the strange fire or light he had seen before. He is still not sure what it was that had puzzled Hugumki, Rabbit, and himself on that night. The next morning, they had surreptitiously looked around for evidence of what they had seen the night before. They didn't see anything that would help explain that mystery.

"What do you think it is?" Ista asks Hugumki, who looks quite comfortable wrapped up in his poncho and blanket as he enjoys the shielded fire they have built on a small rocky hill.

"Wait and see," was all Ista got as a reply from his leader.

Happy that his foot is feeling much better than it has in days, "Maybe we fell asleep, and it is Father Sun ready to start a new day," Rabbit says, snuggling a little deeper into his blanket.

From his spot, Ah Ki Wami whispers, "I know I have not fallen asleep yet."

Hearing those words, Hugumki smiles proudly. He knows that they are almost ready to pass into adulthood and become men. He has watched them steadily grow into themselves the longer their quest has gone on. One difference, about them, is that they do not need to sleep quite as much as they used to before. Before long, he will test them on that so they can see how challenging it is to travel in the desert, at night.

"Maybe we should ask Esan," Turtle jokes. "He sure acts like he knows."

"I know what it is too," Sky Eye points. "See!"

Little Sun slowly pokes the top of its bright fiery looking head above the mountains like it really does want to set everything ablaze.

It is so big and bright that the shapes and silhouettes on the distant rim disappear in a blinding white flash of light.

As the larger than usual moon starts showing more of itself, Bird holds his fist in front of himself for comparison. "I have never seen Little Sun look so big".

"The coyotes and wolves will be howling like crazy tonight," Ooha manages to say before a couple of lone singers start yipping, which will lead to their mournful songs of praise, or lament. It is sometimes hard to tell which is which.

"I am glad we are up here, and not down there," Turtle says when more four-legged singers join the now, not so distant chorus.

Bird studies the full moon then the rest of the slightly dimmed sky. "Ever since we started this journey, Little Sun has been changing sizes. I wonder how that happens, Sky Eye? Is there more to the sky than we think we know?"

Sky Eye tells him that it is all due to movement and shadows. Realizing that nobody knows what he is talking about, he asks for help. Using three fists, he rotates them around like a mini planetarium to show how the earth casts its shadow on the moon.

Two Bows asks, "Is that why, sometimes if you look quickly at Little Sun, you only see a small part of it, but if look at it longer, you can see the whole thing?"

"That's right."

"That same thing happens in the daytime," Ah KI Wami reminds them.

Bird's face is full of anguish when he asks, pointing up, "Sky Eye, does that mean that Mother Ground might be like Little Sun and is up in the air somewhere?"

"And round?" someone asks.

Sky Eyes anxious face shows that he is not sure how to answer those questions. Does he tell them what he is starting to believe under Canaske's guidance. Their ground, their land might be part of something much bigger and it may-he still can't quite believe or understand it himself-be moving through the sky just like Father Sun and Little Sun do. That is why the stars move across the sky and the timing of their crops is so important. How do you tell someone that everything they have been taught and believe might not be true or real.

"I don't know."

Rabbit's countenance looks like it is withering on the vine. "I don't want to hear any more of that talk."

"I have heard that Little Sun can make Father Sun disappear and," Hugumki is rudely interrupted.

"I said."

Before anyone one else can say anything, Ooha starts to sing in a soothing peaceful tone.

By the light.
In the night.
Do all the singers sing.
Brother coyote.
Brother wolf and owl.
They may be near.
We are far.
By the light of Little Sun.
Do we all long for home.

Before sleep can begin to claim them, Hugumki cautions loud enough to be heard by everyone. "If you want to sleep all night, cover your eyes because Little Sun will be as bright as her name. If Esan stays excited, we may have to cover his eyes too. As for his ears and ours, it may be a long noisy night for all of us."

Hugumki looks at Esan who looks excited, but not overly happy about what is taking place. "Now, now, Esan. Don't even start whining. You know why I had to tie you up again. You will get all excited and then you will just happen to wander away from the fire and that is when the trouble will start. We may not get as lucky this time in scaring off your wild brothers. Sleep well everybody, or at least the best you can."

Brighter and brighter the sky grew. Louder and louder did the night too.

30

13th day – Homeward Bound – Mid-morning

In the desert, like any wilderness, the hunters come in all shapes and sizes. Those that are the best have become masters of stealth. In other words, they have honed their ability to sneak up on their prey without being seen or sensed by their unfortunate victim's.

Circling high above in the clear wide open sky, riding the warm currents of opportunity, a large raptor patiently watches, waits.

Fluttering above the desert floor, a small bird aimlessly goes about its day.

Rabbit is moving along the trail like a hunter, but acting more like a bird watcher. "Look at you pretty bird. What have you been eating?" he calls out to a plump looking black bird with a bright yellow head flying by.

Being a hunter, more than a bird watcher, "He should be aware of more than just what he is eating," Two Bow cautions.

"What do you mean?"

"Like you, it has not noticed the danger that has been flying on the wind above us."

"Do you mean?"

"Yes, and there goes your little bird without a worry."

Both turn and watch the pretty bird skim over the rugged landscape of thorn brush interspaced with scraggly looking cacti.

Two Bows looks toward the sky again in time to see the mighty hawk tuck its wings in. It is the signal that the aerial attack has begun.

Grabbing his face with both hands in awe of one of the greatest hunters alive, Two Bows whistles like a falling bird, then yells. "Watch out everybody. Here it comes."

A streak of brown and white cuts through the sky almost faster than their eyes can track it. "It might catch it right in front of us," Sky Eye quietly says.

Whether it was out of insight, foreboding, or just plain survival, the little bird starts trying to use evasive maneuvers to get away. Unfortunately, even before the attack began, it was already too late for the little one to have any chance at all.

"Watch how it slows down and adjusts its body just before it catches the other bird," Two Bows whispers.

With an audible or imagined thud, the hunter envelopes the much smaller bird in its mighty talons and body.

Since the mid-air collision took both birds out of sight, the Chosen carry on, once again bearing witness to another story of survival in the desert, besides their own.

If only they can find somewhere to stop for a while so that they can try to catch up on the sleep that they are sorely lacking from the noisy night before. Now where could that be, in the middle of a warm day? In the middle of the desert?

13th day – Homeward Bound – Early evening

A blinding flash, followed by a terrifying crash. The whole desert seems to reverberate when Thunder God's roar follows his swift, flashy brother. Within a few heartbeats, a brilliant blaze rips through the sky when Sky Fire makes his presence known, again.

With his eyes blinking faster than he can think, "Hugumki!" Bird cries out. "They are getting closer. Too close!"

Taking a quick survey of the small, narrow, reddish brown sandstone passageway they are cutting through, Two Bows spots the only shelter around.

Noting where his scout is looking, Hugumki points shoulder high at a concave, smooth walled area that is just in front of them. "Look there. Quickly climb the rock and get under the overhang. It will give us some protection."

He watches them all start scrambling up to the ledge as a huge bolt of lightning tears its way toward the ground. "Hurry!"

Using the extra energy that only fear can provide, all the Chosen, including a trembling Esan, quickly get up the small incline.

Just as they are all side by side underneath the narrowest of coverbacks and packs firmly pressed up against the rocky wall-with a sizzle and boom, another volley splits the air.

His soft eye's bigger, and voice louder than usual, Rabbit yells, "Why did we leave that cave we were sleeping in earlier?"

"This is still better than being out there in the open," Deerhead leans out from under the narrow cover of the overhanging rock, then quickly pulls his head back in, just in time.

Flash, boom. The twin Sky Gods show they are steadily drawing nearer.

Still unsure of his place in the world, Bird cries out in irrational fear. "What have we done wrong that the gods would be so angry?"

"This is not about being right or wrong," Ah Ki Wami answers back. "This is simply being in the wrong place at the worst of times."

Rabbit tries his best not to show fear in front of the younger ones even though it feels as if his insides are being twisted and bounced around every time the walls shake around him. He is shivering so hard he knows the only thing holding him together is the tautness of his goose bump covered skin. "I want to get out of here," his voice manages to tremble.

Realizing he is about to have a full-blown panic on his hands, Hugumki quickly comes up with a plan. "One by one, each of you tell me your biggest fear," he suggests, looking up and down the line of tightly pressed bodies. "Not a real one, just a funny one. I will go first."

After a few strokes of Esan's standing fur, Hugumki begins.

"My biggest fear is that I lose my voice, and nobody can hear me and all the important things I still have to say, and as you all know, that is a lot. After everything I have learned so far, wouldn't that be a bad thing?"

No one responds. A few roll their eyes. Turtle swallows his laughter.

Hugumki laughs when he realizes that they are acting like they can't hear him.

Wearing a smile as thin as his nerves, Ooha begins. "My biggest fear is that I can be heard by everyone." After a short pause, "And I sing as bad as Gumki!"

Just as their forced laughter spreads up and down the shuffling line, another flash, crack, and crash rattles their bones and nerves.

Not caring if it is his turn or not, Rabbit raises his voice to disguise his fear. "I would not want to be short, fat, or ugly. Sorry Turtle, you're not ugly, and you are still growing. Even worse than that would be for me to have a low, scratchy voice." Rabbit finishes his turn using his high soft voice which quickly flies away on the cool wind starting to tear its way through the pass.

Since his name has just been mentioned, Turtle goes next. "My biggest fear is that when I return a man, all the women of all the villages of our people come after me to be their mate. What would I do if that happened to me?"

Deerhead begins to answer, only to have his unhelpful reply drowned out by the thunderous clash of the Sky Gods.

Once their echo starts rumbling away, Sky Eye snorts, "My fear is that my head keeps getting longer and longer as I get older. It then gets so heavy that I cannot hold it up anymore, and my name gets changed to, Ground Eye." While the ensuing timid laughter barely makes a sound, the mighty drum of the Sky Gods sounds like it is beating directly overhead in the over charged air. In fact, the air is almost sizzling.

"That was close, look at our hair!" Sky Eye yells.

"I felt a strong shiver start on my back through my poncho," Two Bows loudly gasps, looking around at the bodies of his friends which are all, unexpectedly, instantaneously, twitching in place. "Should we take off our packs?"

"Yes. Now. Pass them and we will stack them," Hugumki orders, pointing off to their left side. "We will sort them out later. Pass the botos, too."

Once the packs and botos are in two hastily made piles, Ah Ki Wami is encouraged to go next so he can continue the distraction they need more than anything right now. "When you have lived the life I have, you have no fear. If I tried I, uh-aah, I can't even think of a funny one. I don't fear anything.

With a rumble, almost as low as the thunder Deerhead says, "Everybody is afraid of something, like falling off a high rock."

Feeling their eyes upon him, Ah Ki Wami relents a little bit. "You're right. My biggest fear is that I become full of fear."

With his fear quite evident on his face, Ista begins his turn. "I would hate it if I could not laugh and tell stories about life. It would be so sad to never be happy and have fun. I would also hate to forget about everything that has happened on this journey so far, except maybe, what is, you know, right now."

Before he can finish, another roar crushes the air out of the air. When it slowly reverberates away, Deerhead goes next. "I hope you were finished Ista?" Without waiting for a reply, Deerhead continues, "I would not want to wake up and discover that I have become as small as Little Bean, but my head is still the same size as it is now."

"You would look like a funny doll," Bird jokes from Deerhead's side. Seizing his opportunity, the usually timid Bird presses on. "I would be afraid if one of those giant birds we saw by the great waters picked me up." Bird pauses as once again the darkened landscape is smeared with

Sky Fire's light, and the high sandstone walls shudder under Thunder Gods might.

With the rumble slowly dying away, Hugumki urges him to continue. "Go on Bird."

"If, if one of those huge birds picked me up and then took me to its nest just because of my name."

"That is funny Bird," Ista manages to sputter.

Hugumki points, "Two Bows, you're next."

"Hugumki, that last one did not quite feel like it was right on top of us. My funny fear is that I move my arms around and like a Sky God, I suddenly start flying and I can't stop. I just keep going and going. Where would I go? What would I see? Would I be able to find my way back home?"

"Look, look!" Turtle cuts in. "I can see clear sky over there."

While the others bend down and lean out from under the overhang to look, Rabbit reaches over to pat the top of Turtle's head. "Being short is not always so bad."

The sky starts to light up again, causing everyone to quickly pull their heads back in, just like turtles.

Tracking the ensuing thunder, Hugumki says, "I think the Gods are moving away or at least going somewhere to hide until the next time they make their appearance. We will wait here a little longer, then I will climb down and check and see that everything is safe for the rest of you."

"It did not even rain," Ista whines, looking down in disappointment.

Deerhead looks at him with feigned disgust. "You just want to go back to sleep. If it had rained, we might be stuck up here for a long time."

"Don't forget when you climb down Gumki, look and listen for any signs that it rained anywhere," Two Bows reminds his leader. He wants to be sure, just in case Hugumki forgets in his haste, to do the most important thing in their situation.

Bending down to look at the sky again, Sky Eye says, "That storm came and went so fast, it may have just been one big angry cloud."

"Do you and your head need help to stand back up?" Ista, now feeling much braver, teases.

With the thunder and lightning slowly drifting away, a sense of surreal calm settles over the brown and red hued swirling, sweeping walls of the narrow slot canyon the Chosen have found themselves trapped in.

Just before Hugumki hops down from his restricted perch to take a first cautious look around, a pathetic whimper slices through everyone's still taut nerves. The forlorn tone of Esan's cry immediately sets everyone more on edge than they already are.

Hugumki quickly realizes that once again it is an inaudible sound that is bothering the usually brave Essan. Slowly, but oh too surely, they all start to hear it too.

Some of the more experienced Chosen know immediately what the rapidly approaching roar is. They know that no creature with four legs rages quite like this angry beast when it tears its way through a narrow, restricted area.

"Everybody set your feet and hold your position," Hugumki yells as loud as he can over the approaching danger. "Here it comes!"

It is a massive surge of debris, filled, water. If it had a head, it would resemble a dark angry churning foam filled monster bent on washing away anything in its path. With a watery rumble, it starts tearing through the narrow canyon just under the precarious feet of the Chosen.

Seeing the shock on everyone's faces, Hugumki knows that once again he has too, come up with some way to keep everyone calm until the latest danger passes. While he struggles to come up with another plan, Sky Eye's voice rings out. "Look, our fast flood is just that. The water level is starting to drop already."

Feeling as thankful as he ever has, Hugumki says, "We will wait here for a bit longer until we are sure that it is safe to climb down. I will go first and then I will signal whether you can climb down or not once everyone has the right packs and bottos. I think, when we can, we should all take our sandals off before we climb down, or we will probably lose them in the mud. Don't forget to be careful where you put your feet because there will be lots of sticks and stones in the way now." Hugumki looks around to make sure everybody has a good foothold, like Esan does with his extra two.

"So, Sky Eye, is sounding like me really your biggest fear?" With those simple words, Hugumki breaks the nervous tension that is keeping everyone so quiet. The chatter continues until Hugumki looks up and signals that it is safe for them to climb down and continue their quest as the darkness slowly gathers itself together to create another obstacle for the Chosen to conquer, or at least, learn to deal with, if they can.

13th day – Homeward Bound – Later that night

Under the brightest light of the night sky, the Chosen are slowly walking along inside a dry wash. They are being extra careful because they remember variations of Deerhead's warning about extremely dry ground meeting unexpected water. Even with Little Sun being big and bright, they know its light is not able to illuminate the deeper cracks in the ground. As they are quickly learning, the desert night has a habit of eating the light, be it star, or moon light.

"I know we came this way before, but it looks so different now," Bird comments quietly as he tries to wipe the sleep out of his heavy eyes. "Doesn't the light from Little Sun make the mountains look like they are covered in ice, and everything around here looks like it could be hiding something."

"Everything is hiding something." Ah KI Wami"s sharp tone cuts right through Bird's jittery nerves. "You do hear all the different sounds they are making, right?"

"Yes" Bird's head nods in silhouette.

"Do you see anything?"

"No," the silhouette shakes this time.

"That means they are hiding so that they can watch you, without you seeing them."

"Why?" Bird's voice sounds more like a tremble than the confident sound of a warrior who is ready to survive in the desert at night.

"You already know the answer, Bird. They want to see if they can eat you, or not."

"That's enough Wami," Hugumki admonishes jokingly. "If Bird's eyes get any bigger, he will be able to lead because his eyes will be as bright as Little Sun."

"Is somebody keeping an eye on Turtle? You know how he likes to walk and sleep at the same time," Rabbit's teasing voice teases.

"Hoa, that is so funny Rabbit," Turtle responds loudly. "I am so glad I helped you when you could barely walk."

Rabbit laughs, "If you could see my face, you would know I was just playing with you."

"Why are we traveling at night again?" Ista asks from nearby.

"Because we did not sleep good past night. Then when we found shelter in the cave earlier, we rested up. With Little Sun being so bright now, we can easily see after dark." Ah Ki Wami moves closer to his target. " Who would expect us to be traveling at night," Ah Ki Wami whispers menacingly in his ear. "You did not even know I was right next to you, did you? You weren't looking."

"The nights are getting shorter now," Sky Eye starts to say, stretching out his neck. "Never mind, I can't think right. Even though I slept good today, my head feels like it should be sleeping right now."

"How much time did we lose because of that storm?" Ooha asks the gray shadowy darkness.

"Not too much," a voice, answers back. "Good thing we found that water to rinse our feet off in or else we would be walking much slower than we are now."

Peering into the darkness but seeing only silhouetted shapes that are starting to play more and more with his imagination, Ooha asks anyway. "What do you mean?"

"If the mud had dried on our feet, we would all feel like we are walking with pots on our feet or paws right now."

There is a laugh or two at the thought of all of them thumping along.

From out of a shadow comes Hugumki's voice, "To be able to move quickly and quietly, from place to place at night, is also a good skill for a hunter to have. Many of the things that can be eaten are more active in the dark than in the light, as you know. Don't worry, this is only practice, we will not be hunting this night. We don't want anyone to kill any cactus that looks like it is attacking us. Now be careful and watch where you put your feet. We are almost home, let's not make the journey any longer than it already is. And remember, if you hear or even think you hear Deerhead's or Two Bow's call or that roar we heard earlier, get out of this dry river as fast as you can. Like that storm did earlier, it may rain somewhere without us knowing about it. If a fast flood does come, I will be the one to make sure Esan gets out."

From out of the darkness an attack begins. "Can you see this?" Ista asks, tapping Turtle on the head.

"Hoa, can you." Turtle starts to raise his hand.

"Stop it!" Hugumki squeezes his head. "What did I just say about being careful. Wouldn't it be stupid to get hurt now and hold us up from getting home? Even if you can't see very well, eyes ahead, eyes around. Hup hup, let's keep going.

Onward they walk, slowly fading from sight like desert apparitions.

31

14th day – Homeward Bound – Nighttime again

When the falling sun touches the dark jagged horizon, the cloudy sky responds in colorful joy. First orange, then red bands started churning their way across the sky. Pink also shoots out to have its time in the waning light.

Soon enough, the colors turn lavender and gray, then purple and black, changing a bright day into a cloak of darkness that hides everything within its encompassing embrace.

The daily change from light to dark accomplishes many things. One of them is letting the day creatures know that it is time for their rest. Another is, it tells their counterparts that it is time to arise and start their night. Just don't say that to the blanket covered Chosen who are traveling under the stars once again. With one look at their heavy shoulders and drooping eyes, you can tell they would rather be in a warm bed than just starting a long, slow, chilly, boring night walk. Then again, boring is all relative in the desert, especially at night.

"Slow down everybody," Hugumki turns and calls out from just behind Deerhead at the front of their line. "This is not much of a trail, is it Deerhead?"

"Even with the light from Little Sun helping, it is very hard to see. There are so many kinds of cactus, and they all want to grab us or cut us."

Deerhead bends his thick torso out of the way of a long spiny arm, just in time.

Once he has also escaped its grasp, Hugumki looks behind him at Bird, who, even though he looks like he is sleepwalking, deftly dodges the tentacle like obstacle.

After a quick tap to let Deerhead know what he is doing, Hugumki stops, then turns, and whistles everybody forward. Once Two Bows catches up and does a quick count, then gives a nod to his leader, Hugumki begins talking about what he was too tired to go over with them the night before.

"Safely passing through the desert at night involves two things. One is knowing where you are going, even if you can't see very good. The other one is just as important. Always be aware of what is going on around you."

"Even if I can't see anything?" Turtles asks, waving his nearly invisible hand in front of his face.

"That is what we are going to talk about Turtle," Hugumki answers patiently. "Even though we can't see very good in the dark, everything else out here can because that is what they are made for."

"I can feel many eyes watching me," Deerhead's low voice sounds scarier than usual.

"They are all watching us, and that is why we must learn to become brothers with the creatures of the night."

Rabbit's shaky voice lets it be known that he is no friend or brother of the night. "I am not touching anything I can't see."

Wishing they could see the dirty looks he was giving them, Hugumki continues. "I am talking about the wolf, coyote, deer, cats, owls, and other birds. And don't forget our friends that are always around, the noisy bugs. Did any of you see the stripped smelly one that was just back there?"

Deerhead nods his head.

Ah Ki Wami grunts yes.

Two Bows shrugs his shoulders, as if to say, *I can't see everything.*

The rest act like they don't know what is going on because they don't.

"If any of you had gotten sprayed, you would be paying a lot more attention right now," Hugumki laughs at the thought. "Then, we would all keep walking away from you, hoa. What I am trying to say is, be alert to what the animals are doing. Even if you can't see them, you sure can hear them."

Hugumki stops talking and lets the noisy night wash over each one of them.

First thing they hear is what sounds like strange laughter: the ever present coyotes. Then they hear the buzzing, clicking, and grating noises of the myriad insects that survive on the desert's bounty. Blending, or competing with it all is the assorted whistles of the different night birds. There are innumerable species of owls and their various calls. The loud killdeer and mockingbirds make their presence known. From down below, comes the light thump of a busy little kangaroo rat and the surprising sound of a small mouse howling in triumph. After adding the barking of the foxes, a wail from a cat, the howl of a wolf, along with everything else, it all sounds like a living wall of distraction meant to keep the Chosen or anything else, off guard.

"You must get used to the different sounds and what makes them. If something changes suddenly, what caused the change? If something starts moving, real fast, is something chasing it?"

Hugumki pauses again to let his words sink in.

"Look at Little Sun, it looks like she is going to lay down on a bed of cotton clouds," Rabbit says, wistfully thinking about how wonderful that would feel.

Deerhead complains, "It will get even harder to see now."

Esan's eyes, filled with moonlight, look like two small spectral orbs scanning the trail as he searches for what the others can't see. When darkness that feels so powerful it seems to gather even more, suddenly grips the night, Esan disappears right in front of them. It is as if everything has been wiped clean with a pitch-black cloth.

To Ooha, it suddenly feels empty, lonely, and scary, even with all the rapid breathing going on around him.

Imitating a scorpion strike, Ista reaches out and hits Ooha's arm. "Eaahh!"

"Did I scare you?" Ista's laugh bounces around in the dark.

"That wasn't funny." Ooha swings deep into the night. Hits nothing. Ista's laughing, bobbing head, has saved him once again.

"I was just playing. I did not mean to make you mad." Ista had felt a stiff breeze pass just over his head and knew instantly what that meant.

Ooha's fear makes his body look like it is deflating, if they could see him. "I don't like it when it gets to dark. All right."

Deerhead's voice cuts the gloom. "I thought you looked a little scared sometimes. Too bad I can't see your face right now."

"Gumkiiii!" Rabbit's voice sounds like it is whimpering and trying to be brave at the same time.

"Yes."

"Remember the sounds we are supposed to listen to."

"Yes." Hugumki closes his eyes and lets his mind and spirit fly.

"I can't hear anything right now. All the noises have stopped."

"Quiet everybody. Somethings not right."

Not a sound can be heard, except for more rabid breathing.

Bird somehow skitters about without hitting anyone. "I don't like this."

"I will watch behind us," Two Bows turns around, spear in hand.

Ah Ki Wami, who is holding one of the bows, says, "Whoever has the quiver, keep it close."

Hugumki keeps cocking his head, expecting the desert to tell him what has happened. What has caused everything to go quiet, all at once?

Into dark, deathly silence, runs imagination. The cacti turn into ghostly marauders. The shrubs and rocks become veiled monsters. The surrounding mountainous shapes appear as if they too are creeping closer.

"I'm scared," Turtle is shaking so much it is a wonder the singing stones he is carrying have not started singing their song.

"Something must have just been killed around here and now everything else is being extra quiet," Deerhead whispers. "That way they are not next."

Ah Ki Wami offers his kind of encouragement. "At night, every hunter is also the hunted."

"If we aren't hunting, does that still mean us," Ista asks almost imperceptibly.

"Looks like Little Sun is starting to come back out again." The hope for more light fills Sky Eye's voice.

Hugumki stretches for a moment then listens again for what he can't hear. "As soon as it does, we will move out at a steady pace."

"Gumki, does every hunter being hunted include us." Ista waits again for the answer he knows he does not want to hear.

"Yes, now stay alert." By the size of Ista's eyes, Hugumki knows that he will not have to worry about him staying awake for a while.

"I did not hear anything get killed, did you?" Two Bows quietly asks Ah Ki Wami.

"As you know, not everything screams before it dies."

The Chosen cautiously walk on. Some of them not sure if they will ever feel at one with the night-time desert, and its many nocturnal residents.

14th day – Homeward Bound – Later that night

As we have learned, the desert is a noisy and busy place after dark that can also be quite intimidating and scary. With a bright moon angled low on the western horizon, the silhouettes of the cacti on the nearby hills are once again looking foreboding. This time, they look like they are twisted up in bad dreams while waiting for any of the Chosen to get too close so that they can reach out and grab them with their nightmarish intent.

"How did you find that cave we slept in earlier this day?" Bird asks Deerhead, who is in front of him and Turtle as they carefully walk single file through a shallow, cacti filled valley.

"The better question is, why didn't you see it?" Deerhead answers over his shoulder. "This land gives us everything we need or want. You just have to look for it."

"Deerhead, we all know you are our best tracker. You can see a trail that most people don't even know is there," Turtle's toes start to nervously dance in the moon light making his feet look like black chubby spiders in sandals. "But why can't you see things that are far away? I mean, that time when we were all looking at that cat that was on top of the cactus, I could tell you kept looking the wrong way and…."

"Maybe," Deerhead takes a long pause, trying to keep the anger and frustration out of his voice, "I have near sight to be a good tracker, but not far sight so I don't lose my trail. Now keep paying attention to where you are going. I can almost smell our home fires burning."

Further up the trail, Hugumki checks on Ah Ki Wami. "How are you friend?" Hugumki asks.

"I feel good and almost happy for a change, if I know what happy feels like. This journey away from home has made me thankful for home and my mother more than I ever thought I would. Even I don't understand why I get so mad sometimes. That is just how I feel then. I don't really know why I feel that way, but from now on, I will try to control myself better. Now I wonder, am I supposed to be nice all the time except for when I am needed to be fierce?"

"That seems to be the way life will always be for some of us. We must learn when to be a warrior, and when to be a happy villager. That is another reason for this test. We will learn about ourselves and our place in life better."

"What does a person do if their place in life is to never stay in one place?"

"That Wami, I just don't know. I like living in one place but being able to move around when needed. Wouldn't it be bad to be stuck in one place all the time?"

"Maybe my people were one of the wondering tribes and that is why I always feel so restless. Like I said before, mother won't tell me anything about my past."

"Take your time and you will find your way Wami."

And new friend or not, Hugumki also knows that it would be a good idea, if, at the very least, he and Ah Ki Wami talked privately sometime about what almost happened in the foothills. Better to know sooner than later if he has the sadness sickness. Sometimes, the best thing that can be done for a person if they can't help themselves, be happy, or stay happy, is to have a healing ceremony for them.

There are others also talking about and doing important things, in the desert night.

"Look down at your shadow, Ista. Why are you wearing Che Wah's headdress?"

"I am not, haye, what! How did you do that?" As he spins his head quickly around, Ista barely catches Rabbit putting his long arms back down by his side. "Do it to me again. Do it again!"

"This time I will make it look like you have zizi's on your head."

"You're right, that is what it looks like. Rabbit, they even look like they are moving around and might get me."

At night, the desert can be a scary place indeed.

32

15ᵗʰ day – Homeward Bound – Mid-afternoon

The Chosen-clad in whatever they are comfortable in-have been on the move since high sun. They are just now beginning to feel fully awake and alert. The walking pace they have set so far on this sunny though brisk day, is slow and steady.

After one fist of sun movement, Rabbit is the first to spot what looks like a dry shallow river cutting right across their path. When they get closer, they realize that its banks do not look natural. These run as straight as an arrow. Usually, both banks would kind of wind their way across the dry desert floor like water normally does when it has been flowing freely.

Before the questions, if any, start, Hugumki calls everyone toward the edge of what, upon closer inspection, looks like a dug out and long forgotten, dead river.

With pride in his eyes through a youthful mask of sadness, Hugumki tells them, "This dry river was dug out by our people to help them grow crops on this flat area a long time ago when they lived near here. Back then, when the rains were better around here, this dug out river would take water from our real river when it was bigger and closer to here. With that water, they grew their crops over there," Hugumki points to an area that is nothing but barren empty wasteland. "Things changed and our river got smaller and moved away, keeping the two rivers apart forever.

That is another reason we have made our journey. It is to see if we can each change when things change around us."

Once they cross what was once an irrigation canal, most of them think that Hugumki was talking about making superficial changes.

Peering around as if he has suddenly become an inspector, Ista asks, "Have you made any changes Rabbit?"

Rabbit, not sure if Ista is trying to be funny or not, does not answer right away.

"I know now that I can't always be funny," Ista says in response to his own question. "I must be serious sometimes, but only sometimes. Too bad, but that is the way it seems it must be."

After another pause and deep breath, Rabbit smiles to himself before saying, "My problem Ista is that I have not been able to change enough."

"What do you mean?"

"I have not been able to change every time I am dirty. Out here that seems to be every day. Even if I could, these are not my favorite clothes to wear."

"I know. Why do you like to wear different clothes than us?"

"I know you have never tried them on, or have you?" Rabbit jokes. "They are just more pretty, and comfortable to me and they keep my body a secret and protect me better. Look at all these scratches I have now."

"A secr… Oh ah, all right" Ista manages to sputter, as a red flush races across his brown face. To make him feel even more foolish, that is followed by the laughter of some of the others who have been listening to their exchange. Knowing Rabbit was barely tolerating the clothes he was wearing, they knew his response was going to be interesting when they heard Ista's question, and the beginning of Rabbit's reply.

Bird, listening in like he usually does did not laugh or say anything. He is still trying to figure out if the changes he is making within himself will ever make themselves known. At least before he gets home.

15th day – Homeward Bound – Sunset.

A cool evening breeze has stirred in time to help blow the remains of the warm day, away. Father Sun is a piercing bright yellow, and he has no apparent clouds to kiss goodbye before dropping from the bluest of blue sky.

At the end of another long, beautiful day, the Chosen are at one with their surroundings.

Or are they?

"Good work everybody," Hugumki brings his strong hands together with a smack. "I'm glad we are finally good and fast at setting up camp for the night. Remember when we first started out, we would not always be ready before dark? Ooha, will you sing a song to end the day while we watch Father Sun begin to go on his night journey."

All but one prepare to watch the setting sun.

Rabbit looks the other way, then exclaims, "That must be one of the most beautiful, and special things I have ever seen!"

Still upset that his eyesight has been questioned, "We have seen prettier," Deerhead shrugs his thick shoulders.

"You are all looking the wrong way." Rabbit stands tall and spreads his long arms out like a poncho-clad, guardian of the desert.

They all turn. First one pair of eyes opens wide, then another, until everyone is taking in the incredible, colorful sight, shimmering in front of them.

While thinking only about their stomachs and rest, they did not realize that the best artist in the universe has been hard at work using the giant palette of empty blue sky.

During the short time that it took for them to set up camp while they tracked the setting sun, a stormy darkness had formed in the east. When Father Sun shot out his longest rays of light into the passing storm, the unwatched part of the sky lit up in all the colors of an iridescent rainbow.

After more than a moment's time of standing there in awe looking at it, Hugumki pats Rabbit on the shoulder. "You're right Rabbit, this is a special gift."

Sky Eye lightly spanks his bare thigh in fake admonishment. "I can't believe we almost missed it."

"Right now, I won't mention what we should learn from this," Hugumki wags his smiling head.

Looking back and forth across the colorful sky, Bird asks, "It is so pretty, how does it happen?"

"It is water and light," Two Bows answers, thinking back to the few times he has seen smaller ones.

"They can't do that. It is too big and bright," Deerhead looks at each end of the rainbow, "I think the go…."

"It looks like it is on fire," Ista blurts out.

"It is definitely the biggest and brightest one I have ever seen," Two Bows says.

"It could be the colorful belt of the storm Gods," Rabbit is thinking about how pretty the colors would look on a belt or anything else he can imagine.

"Have any of you ever watched the rainwater fall off of Flat Top?" Hugumki asks. "It does not happen often, but when the light hits it just right, the same thing happens. It's just not as big, or as bright as this one."

Sky Eye, who would normally have something to say just stands there in his poncho trying to count the different shades of light. After a while he softly says, "Five, seven. Now what do we call them all?"

"I think I can see both sides of it where it touches the ground!" Rabbit is bursting with more excitement than he usually has for such things. "I wish I had a necklace that looked like that. What do you think Turtle?"

Before Turtle can come up with the right words, Deerhead playfully orders, "Quick Rabbit, run and grab it."

"It does look like it is close, but the storm is falling apart and that is good for us." Hugumki takes his own unspoken advice and checks the other way. "Father Sun's light is almost gone too."

"You're right, it is disappearing," Rabbit waves goodbye. "Does it go into the ground?"

"Is anybody hungry yet?" Hugumki asks, as almost everyone's attention quickly goes back to their stomachs, and tired bodies.

Turtle playfully nibbles on his own finger, "Do we have to wait on Ooha to sing?"

"After what we have just seen, there is no need to sing," Ooha shrugs. "Let's just thank the gods for their special gift."

Ista beams up at his tall slender friend, "And don't forget Rabbit's eyes."

"Could be the same thing," Rabbit flips his still short hair with pride.

33

16th day – Homeward Bound – Early afternoon

With some dark clouds looming in front of them, the Chosen continue on their trek. They are traversing another broad open area that is filled with nothing but cactus, and scrub brush, to the unseeing eye.

Ooha hears a slight rustle off to his side.

A streak of gray breaks cover, then just as quickly, is gone.

Turning a head that is full of wishful thinking, Turtle says, "If we could run that fast, we would be home already." He kicks out one thick leg from under his poncho to point the way.

"Would you rather fly, or run like that?" Ooha asks?"

"Poor bird, to be able to run that fast, and not fly," Rabbit makes little fluttering hand motions.

"I would be happy to do either one right now," Turtle answers.

Rabbit looks around for any sign of the swift running bird. "That bird is the one that Che Wah used to bless us, isn't it?"

"Yes, and most people think that bird can't fly, but it does. I have seen it," Hugumki says.

Bird feels a little left out of his favorite subject. "How far have we not flown, so far, Hugumki?" Bird starts laughing at what he just said.

Hugumki pauses to look at the potential danger ahead, "This is not about how far we have come or gone. It is about how we have traveled so far together."

"I can tell one thing about our journey up to now," Sky Eye rubs his long forehead, leaving behind a streak of slightly cleaner skin.

Hugumki knew it was going to come up sooner or later, "What is that Sky Eye?"

"I can tell that the way we took to the great waters was longer than the way we are coming back."

"Did your stars tell you?" Turtle wants to know.

"No, my feet and eyes told me. Am I right Gumki?"

"You are right. We have been taking a straighter way home in most of the places we have passed through."

Rabbit's face looks worn and befuddled as he looks around in all directions. "So many of these places look alike to me."

Deerhead, walking just ahead of them, can't let that one go, unanswered. "It only looks that way because you are not looking with the right eyes."

"Are you trying to be mean Deerhead?" Rabbit stares at Deerhead with a look that says, *I am in no mood to be messed with.*

"Not everything I say is like that." Deerhead looks back at Rabbit with such intensity that Rabbit can feel it. "If you would look at everything very close Rabbit, you would see that even the rocks look different from place to place."

"If everything we walk on is all Mother Ground, why should it change from place to place?" Ista asks, picking up two completely different looking rocks. He is not sure if he wants to add either one to the small collection he has started to put together. Now that he is feeling stronger, Ista does not mind adding a little more weight-if it is beautiful- to his pack, which has been feeling lighter to him the longer their journey home has gone on.

Sky Eye squeezes his eyes tight in thought before answering. "For us, this journey is long, and we have seen many changes in the land. But we have all heard stories of even longer journeys, and even more different looking lands. Teacher says the land changes because…"

"Maybe our Creator did not want to make the same thing, over and over again," Bird says.

"Don't ever forget," Hugumki raises his voice. "To go the same way two times makes a path that is very easy to follow."

Ah Ki Wami, who is bringing up the rear grins because he is glad that he hardly has any path to wipe clean, if the bad weather stays away. Even though he still enjoys being left alone now and then, Ah Ki Wami has come to like being part of something bigger than himself, and that makes him happy, if he knows what happy feels like.

16th day – Homeward Bound – Evening

More than proud to be one of the Chosen, but not so happy to be chosen to go next, Turtle ponders his fate. "I know I already did this Hugumki, but the river was not as angry then, he tells his leader over the loud sound of rushing white water that is moving below him way faster than he can run.

After one look down at the raging torrent of runoff that is churning its way through the narrow area they are using to get from one riverbank to the other, it is very easy to understand his fear. A fear that is making his chest so tight that he feels like he is wearing a real turtle shell on his chest. He then takes another moment to contemplate his turn to cross the log connecting the two banks of desert, landscape. One side, almost drab looking, the other is starting to show the red tint of their homeland. To all the Chosen's relief, the log has stayed firmly in place since their first crossing.

Looking at his dried out, dirty companions, Hugumki tells Turtle, who is still getting in position, along with everyone else clustered around, what he already told Two Bows, who is waiting on the other side. "The river just looks too cold and dangerous to go swimming right now, so don't wander off until we are all on the other side. Once over there, we will fill our botos, and drink all the water we want. With the low clouds everywhere, we can't tell if it is raining upstream or not. If it is, it will make the river even more dangerous."

"Just trust your balance Turtle and do it one step at a time," Two Bows shouts. "If you fall in, we will find your body when the waters calm down," he quietly says to himself. He knows that all the younger ones are more than a little afraid, as they should be. He also knows that learning to deal with and conquering your fears, your real fears that is, is one of the most important lessons to learn in life.

"Even with the extra weight you are carrying, you are not heavier now than when you crossed the first time," Hugumki tells him with all the encouragement he can muster.

"I think your legs are longer too, I know your hair is," Ista calls out when Turtle steps onto the log with Hugumki's help.

Slowly Turtle starts to make his way across. Sideways. Barefoot.

One step – "I am stronger than before."

Two steps – "We are almost home."

Three steps – "I have seen and done things some people in the village will never see or do."

Four steps – "What was that sound!"

Five steps – "Am I still too young for a mate? Do I even want a mate yet?"

Six steps – "I am glad it has not rained here.. This log would be very slippery then."

Seven steps – "Will Esan walk? No, Hugumki will carry him."

Eight steps – "Two Bows is grabbing my hand."

Nine steps – "I made it!"

One by one, the others make their way cautiously across. Rabbit practically dances because his foot feels as good as it ever has, and he is more than happy to be eight steps closer to all the beautiful things he has waiting at home.

Before long, only Esan and Hugumki remain on the other side.

Getting Esan ready, Hugumki takes a moment to quietly reflect with his furry friend on what he has learned and accomplished so far.

"Esan, when we cross over, I have done it. We have all done it. We have made it back. You know they could not have done it without me. I am the leader. I led the way. I would have got all the kani, bad words, and thoughts, if I had not held us all together and kept everybody safe. This should show everyone I deserve to have a chance to be chief when the time is right? Hold Esan. This cover over your eyes is not for long. I am so glad we made it back safe. Ready, I am going to pick you up now. Here we go."

After Hugumki carries a blindfolded, trembling Esan to the other side, all the Chosen simultaneously let out a loud cry of joy and relief. "Hieeee, hieeee yaheee."

They are on the village side of the river. They are almost home.

If only there was a way to safely enjoy the swollen, dangerous river from one of the many side pools along its banks.

Is that someone at the river's edge? It doesn't look like he is playing, yet. It looks like he is drinking with one hand and dipping a very stiff breechcloth into the water with the other.

Rabbit is soon surrounded by his companions who all eagerly start drinking and dipping some of their dirty clothes into the freezing water. They are going to be clean, clean at last, or at least their clothes are going to be cleaner than they have been for quite some time.

After joining everyone at the river's edge, Hugumki takes a moment to look around. "I know what I said, and it's true. We must be very careful but there is no way after everything we have gone through that we are not going swimming right now. Like Wami said, there were times my bones felt so dry that I am sure I sounded just like Che Wah's rattle. Just keep your packs near you."

To anyone who has been out wandering in the desert for days on end, the flowing water looks exactly like what it is. The answer to many a wet dream, and most important of all, it is liquid life. It is also a great place to swim and have fun.

"I saw a place over there," Hugumki turns to point down river, then realizes he is talking to an audience of one. Following his own finger point, Hugumki starts laughing. Everyone is already getting in or preparing to get in the water, but him. Should he make a fire first and possibly miss out on swimming? Or should he go swimming and freeze later? The burden of leadership can sometimes be a heavy one.

Based on an experience he had earlier at the water's edge, Esan has decided to stay dry and watch the packs, along with everything else going on around hm. When he had had a drink, some of the lapping water hit his nose, chilled his nose, froze his nose. After that, he didn't even bother to stick a dusty paw in.

Hugumki heads over as he watches Two Bows and Ah Ki Wami leap into the water.

Ista, Turtle, and Bird pause at the water's edge, then they all jump in with a yell worthy of seasoned warriors.

"The water is freezing," Two Bows yells just before Deerhead tucks in his legs and hits the water like a falling boulder, sending his splash everywhere.

When Bird's head pops out of the water, he sounds like a baby taking his first breath. "It's, it's too cold," he sputters.

Ah Ki Wami, his muscles rippling like the water he is submerged in, says, "Just stay in and you will get used to it sooner or later.

Once Ooha is in, he immediately starts humming to warm up, then accidently swallows some water.

"If you are going to drown Ooha, you should at least get in deeper water." Hugumki swims right by him like a fish.

Out of the water rises a round, hairy rock, followed by broad shoulders, torso, and thighs. It is Deerhead again, yelling and shivering before he plunges back into the water.

After a while, it seems like they are staying in the water just so they don't have to get back out.

To everyone's surprise, Sky Eye gets out of the water, immediately wishing he had pulled out his blanket. "I will go start the fire," he yells over his shoulder as he grabs his pack, and the fire stones then runs to where camp will be set up for the night.

"I wonder how much weight we all lost?" Turtle looks at his companions who all look as lean as they ever have in their lives.

Ista notices something else most of them have in common. "Which one of us has the most scars?"

Bird starts looking around. "Wami has scars on his face and elbow. Hugumki's are on his chin and knee. Deerhead's are on his stomach and leg."

Two Bows swims over and shows his scared ribs. "I thought the deer was dead, until it kicked me. That is a lesson I will never forget. Always make sure that dead, is really, dead."

"Don't forget those strange marks Rabbit has on his knees and elbows."

"Are they really scars Turtle?" Bird asks.

"Maybe he got them like I got mine, from playing and trying to climb the rocks."

Rabbit swims over. "Even when I was younger, I never played in the dirt," with a toss of his head, he drifts away.

Watching him, puzzles Bird. "Rabbit looks just like a man, but he acts so different."

Two Bows floats over. "Anyone should be allowed to act any way they want as long as they don't try and change me into something I am not."

Hugumki swims around them, "I don't know how, but Rabbit has always been in good shape, and fast. He usually never does anything but look good, but on this test, he has gotten in even better shape."

Having forgotten that Rabbit can hear every word that they are saying because the water is carrying their words right into his ears, they are surprised when Rabbit resurfaces right next to them. "What am I supposed to do? Outside I look like this, but inside I feel very different. So, what am I supposed to do? I must be who I am, who I was meant to be. Don't you agree?"

"Yes Rabbit," Bird nods.

"Just because we don't understand everything about you does not mean that we don't love you," Hugumki pauses to let his words sink in. "You are and will always be one of us."

A drop of water, a tear? How touched Rabbit was by those kind words is evident by the warm glow radiating from his bright shiny eyes, and big open smile. With a lump in his throat, he simply says, "Thank you. That means a lot to me."

To be accepted is one thing. To be loved is much more special.

"I smell smoke," Ah Ki Wami starts climbing out of the water, moving faster the more his trembling, goose bumped covered body, is exposed to the chilly air. "Last one around the fire has to hang the wet clothes," he challenges over his shoulder.

Like an unscheduled salmon run, there are suddenly wet shiny brown squirming bodies everywhere splashing and climbing out of the river as quick as they can as the freezing water pours off their bare quivering skin. They all race noisily toward the welcoming fire, practically dragging their packs behind them.

Up above, the sky still holds a blush of color as if it is embarrassed about what it is witnessing below.

34

17th day – Homeward Bound – High sun

When the Chosen broke camp this morning, they finally felt at long last, their ultimate goal was within reach. In the distance-with nary a cloud in the sky-they could see the multicolored hues of home starting to appear more and more. Once they saw the red top of the tall sandstone spire called, "Needle Point" they knew in their hearts and feet, they were almost there.

They had left the river's edge once they had started out, after another quick chilly swim, and first meal. It was not to take a short cut, but to travel in a straight line while the river took off on its own meandering journey through the desert. Once the wayward river had returned, back to where they were, they walked its banks toward a small umber colored pass that the river had cut through the bluff ahead over many thousands of years.

At first glance, the pass looks less like an opening than a fissure in the large bluff that appears to be blocking their way. It is so small that if you did not know it was there, you would probably walk right by without seeing it. That is, unless you were following the churning water, or felt the cool breeze that whips its way through like it has somewhere important to go.

Once they get closer to the narrow gap, the rush of air starts sounding like a whistle, if it was made by a real giant. "I am glad my hair dried out," Rabbit says when he hears, and feels the first blast of cooler air."

After they are in the pass and surrounded by its shear rocky walls, one of the Chosen tries to imagine what it must be like to be at the top looking down on them.

"If someone was up there, do you think they could see us, or would we just look like bugs," Bird asks Ah Ki Wami.

Ah Ki Wami stops and looks up. "Bird, I am thankful that those walls can never be climbed. They are just too high for a man to climb them. The only way to pass through here is the way we are going now."

Before long, the bright welcoming light ahead signals that they are just about through the narrow gap.

Once through, they are treated to one of the most beautiful sights they have ever seen. Their homeland in all its natural glory.

It is like being reborn into a new, colorful world.

"Finally, I can say. We have made it. We are home." Hugumki declares to the reddish landscapes of plateaus, mesas, buttes, and giant rock formations that are spread out in front of them: massive guardians that have been chiseled into various angular shapes through the passage of time.

From behind him, Hugumki hears one loud shout of "We are the Chosen, we have returned as men."

So what if a voice or two still has a high-pitched squeak.

"I know we are not at the village yet, but I can say without a doubt, this area is much prettier than the desert we have been passing through." Sky Eye closes his eyes for a moment then opens them so he can enjoy the beauty of where he lives, all over again.

"I know what you mean. Just look at all the different colors you can see from here," Ooha twirls his hand around.

Two Bows scans the area with his sharp, intense eyes. "I see lots of red, blues, blacks, and orange. All kinds of colors."

Turtle gives input from his perspective. "Don't forget all the different shapes that are out there too."

Some of the others are just taking it in. By the expressions on their faces, you might think that they have never been here before. That is one of the true wonders of their native land. Its beauty is mesmerizing, regardless of when you look at it or how many times.

Scanning the area, Sky Eye tilts his head up, "One thing I never noticed or paid much attention too is the long streaks of color that are almost everywhere.

Bird flashes his crooked grin, "I always thought they were…"

"I still think they were left by some gods when they climbed up into the sky," Rabbit remarks.

"I never noticed how shiny some parts of this area are too. It is as if someone took a giant blanket and rubbed them real hard to polish them." Two Bows scans the area again. "The places we have been traveling through, and here, look like they are all made up of different kinds and colors of rock and dirt."

Sky Eye's ears perk up with interest. "Two Bows, I have closely studied some of those things around our village with Cansake."

"You mean, like Flat Top."

"Yes, and more. When you look at them closely, you can tell that the different layers of rock and dirt were put on top of each other, one part at a time."

"Not all at once?"

"Look over there Two Bows. You can see what I mean." Sky Eye points out some massive shapes that have many layers of color.

"When do you think that happened? It does not sound like any of the stories I have been told about the beginning of this land."

"As slow as things change around here, we have also seen how fast things can change too. So I really don't know."

"I have seen some layers of rock that look like they were poured in place like thick stew, before they got hard," Ah Ki Wami says.

Sky Eye closes his eyes again. "That is one of the things we are trying to figure out. If it did happen that way, imagine how hot it must have been here then."

Two Bows quickly shakes his head, "I don't even want to think about being hot again. At least, not for a time."

Rabbit's mind drifts to the village and all the special things he has waiting there for him. "I am glad we have made it this far, but are we ever going to really get back home."

Esan seems to be getting impatient too. He barks a couple of times then cocks his furry head as if the echo will tell him how much further they still have, to go.

Having been mesmerized himself, Hugumki expects to see joy in everyone's eyes when he turns back around. Instead, looks of, will this ever end? When will we get back home? Greets him.

Upon seeing and feeling their impatience, he knows it is up to him to calm their homesick, agitated spirits.

"When camp is made, next night, I will get the camp ready. I will do everything. Catch last meal if needed, cook, clean, whatever needs to be done."

Realizing his words have had little impact, Hugumki then says. "I wonder what new names we will be given around our first counsel fire."

That gets the attention of everyone.

Rabbit is the first to respond. "I would like to be called Sunflower, after the flowers we saw. What kind of name is Rabbit anyway for someone special like me?"

A weird sounding voice asks, "Don't you mean Father Sunflower."

"Hoa. So Funny."

"I like my name," Sky Eye raises his eyes up to the clear sky. "After we tell our stories, I may be called something I don't like.

"It is not up to us," Hugumki presses his lips together while nodding. He is glad to see everyone more alert and energized. "But don't forget, not all of us will get new names."

"I know my new name could not be any worse. Have you ever seen a deer that looks like me?" Deerhead asks, the ensuing laughter wipes the fake scowl off his face.

"I think Ista will still be my name, but I wonder what I will be called after that?"

"There is no second name. It will be a new name if you have earned it," Hugumki's tone suggests that he too is ready to get home.

"It will probably be Funny Man, or Too Many Stories," jokes Ah Ki Wami."

Striking a fierce pose, "Don't forget, Greatest Hunter Ever," Ista proudly suggests to playful groans.

Puffing out his muscular chest, Two Bows boasts. "Maybe mine will be Two Bows with Two Mates."

Rabbit tries to remember who was available before he asks. "Are you going to find mates as soon as you get to the village, so you can earn your name?"

Taking a moment to stretch, Two Bows says, "Maybe I will earn that name after I have slept for many days."

Ista looks up at Two Bows. "Did you get your name the way I heard you did?"

Deerhead laughs before he says, "They say he carried two bows when he was young because he thought he could kill more that way."

Two Bows says nothing as he calmly looks around because he knows the quickest way to stop someone's teasing is to not react at all. That takes all the fun out of it.

Well, there is another way, but not among friends, of course.

"I like my name too. Maybe they will only change…"

Before Bird can finish, "To Bigger Bird," Ista teases loudly, causing more laughter.

"No more Little Bird," Deerhead mutters under his breath.

"How about you Gumki?" asks Turtle.

"I don't really like the way my tattoo looks so I hope I am not called, kani man."

Studying Hugumki's and Ah KI Wami's shoulders, Ista asks, "Wami, do you like the tattoo you got before we left?"

"Aah, once it stopped itching, it's alright," he turns to show the small black tattoo of a turtle on his right shoulder. The turtle is to show that he is someone on a journey, and the design on the shell tells where he comes from. In other words, the tattoos are for village identification in case something catastrophic happens to the Chosen that leaves their faces unrecognizable.

With a design already in mind, "When we get back, we can get real ones, right Gumki?" asks Ooha.

"Yes, these tattoos were only for, they are in case something happens to us."

Wearing an expression like he is being tortured, Ah Ki Wami reveals what it really felt like. "What I remember most was that when it was burnt into my skin, I felt like I was on fire."

"Yes, it did." Hugumki makes his own face of agony. "If any of you want a real one, be ready for the pain."

Clutching his aching heart, Ooha asks. "Gumki, would we get in trouble if we went straight home from here?"

"What do you think?" answers Hugumki, sharply tapping Ooha on the arm. "Do you want me to give you another pain to think about? We will get to the village when we are supposed to, not before." Hugumki does not mention that their arrival with the singing stones must remain a secret and had been planned out way ahead of time.

With that, everyone continues their slow trudge home, the long way, as more new names are tossed in air, even for Esan. The Brave, Wonderful, Courageous Esan.

17th day – Homeward Bound – Early evening

On a day when it seems like you can see forever, some of the Chosen just might be trying to look too far.

Watching his furry friend's expressive black face, "I wonder what Esan is thinking right now?" Ista asks as they casually walk along.

"More than I am," Two Bow's wipes a drop of sweat from his forehead.

"Do animals really think?" Sky Eye picks up where Ista left off. "Do they have the same thoughts we do?"

"You don't see Esan walking into things like you did earlier, do you?" Two Bow brings up Sky Eye's earlier mishap. "That was funny when you said that big rock must have jumped in front of you for you to have hit it; not because you weren't paying enough attention to where you were going."

Ignoring what he has already been teased about, "I mean, do they think about the things we do?"

"Food-yes, sleep-yes, fun-yes, family-yes, friends-yes. Esan already looks more eager than he has in days." Two Bows heads to the rear, of the dawdling line of poncho clad walkers.

"Will animals ever speak again like the stories say they did in the early times?" asks the hovering Bird.

"Esan does speak," Hugumki answers, emphasizing the words Esan and speak.

Arf, arf.

"See."

Between snorts, Ista manages, "That was funny Gumki."

"Just a little further and we will stop early for the night. Is that alright with everyone?" Hugumki glances about, not really expecting any one to complain.

"Thank you so much," Rabbit cries out. "My feet feel good, but I am so tired. This part has been easy, but I am still tired from before."

"Even better, we get to play longer in the river this time," Hugumki announces around a gulp of water. "Just remember, even if we have a flatter area to swim in, we must all be very careful."

Soon, shouts of joy are ringing across the land that is starting to glow a coppery red in the angled sunlight.

"Don't forget, we will have time to catch fish too," Ah Ki Wami pretends he is grabbing invisible fish. "Unless they are swimming by too fast or deep."

"Good, my food is almost gone," Ooha says, pinching his stomach.

"We are all about out of food," Hugumki says, shrugging his shoulders. "Let's be quiet and enjoy this," he respectfully nods at Father Sun who has started coloring the sky in a blend of colors so vibrant and bright there is no way to describe them, in any language.

Looking at the skyline, from the lit up jagged monoliths of the east, to the hazy silhouetted mountains towering in the west, the Chosen are proud to be alive and able to enjoy what life has given them.

With a catch in his throat, "I am glad this is almost over, but sad that we will never be like this again," Sky Eye reveals.

Trying to take off his shirt with his packs still on, "Oohew hoo," Deerhead starts to mock, but says instead, "You're right, the eleven of us will never be like this again."

After that, all is quiet, except for the quickening slap of their sandals as they each think their private thoughts of life, and how they all fit into it.

Then again, they might just be thinking about how good fresh fish will taste after another chilly swim, but not before they have built a fire this time.

35

18th day – Homeward Bound – Mid-morning

Under Ooha's guidance, the Chosen are once again talking about his favorite subject. The difference this time is that they are no longer talking about girls, but woman, as they walk along together. Under the warm glare of the mighty sun, none of them are wearing much. They are slowly crossing one of the few areas of their mesa and butte filled homeland that can be called, flat.

"Rabbit, what kind of mate do you want?" asks Sky Eye, causing a groan or two to escape from lips that are suddenly pressed firmly together.

Rabbit looks at him, then says, "Do you really want to know that right now, Sky Eye?"

Always happy to join a conversation already in progress, Bird boldly states, "My mate will do it all."

"Like what?" Sky Eye knows that is one thing he must learn more about.

"Helping with the crops, going on the hunt, and then, you know."

"No, we don't. Tell us," prods Ah Ki Wami.

Before Bird can fake an answer, Deerhead wags his tongue at him. "You don't even know yet, do you?"

Wearing a false smile that shows his own state of mind, "Be nice," Hugumki reminds everyone. He knows they are all wound up tighter than a drying reed basket.

"The mate I pick will be the most beautiful in the village," Deerhead looks in the direction of the large village to the west, after a quick glance at Hugumki.

"She may already have a mate," teases Sky Eye.

Rotating his tight shoulders around, "Then the next one then," Deerhead says.

Baring his sharp teeth, "She already has a mate," Ah Ki Wami snorts, "me."

"Maybe you should start with your last pick first," Hugumki laughs.

Without a doubt in his voice, Ooha proclaims, "As you know, mine will be the prettiest."

"Is she even ready for a mate yet?" Deerhead questions.

"How do you know when a girl is ready to become a woman?" asks Turtle, his innocence obvious from the expression on his face.

"That, we are not going to talk about right now," Hugumki quickly vows. "When we get back, talk to your maternal elder, and then you can learn all about those kinds of things and more, if you want. That goes for all of you, even if you think you know everything already."

Ista decides to pose a tough question, just for the fun of it. "What do we do if we all want the same mate?"

"We will just have to fight for her!" Ah Ki Wami quickly responds with eagerness in his voice.

Rabbit quietly snickers, then whispers to Esan who is once again by his side. "Mating, eating, fighting. That is all some of them think about."

"Out of all of us, who would win in a fight?" Bird flexes his still small, but much firmer arms.

"That is easy to answer," Ah Ki Wami slyly looks sideways at Hugumki.

Deerhead lifts his chin in the air. "Of course, I would." He has apparently forgotten his scuffle with Two Bows, or has he?

Bird panders to his leader, and hopefully, future chief. "I think Gumki would win."

Before things can completely get out of hand, Hugumki announces, "I think it is time for us to have a race."

"Yes, yes!" They all yell at once, instantly forgetting about their tired or sore legs.

"For fun or a prize?" asks Hugumki.

"Winner gets the first choice of mate," answers Deerhead, stretching out his muscles which have not seemed quite as tight lately thanks to all the river water he has been able to drink.

Noticing a head or two turn in his direction. "Don't even think about her," bellows the suddenly ferocious Ooha.

"I meant from the big village," Deerhead looks like he is ready to fight anybody, for anything.

From off to the side, Rabbit, Hugumki, and the resting Esan, watch the runners shed everything except their breechcloths. They have even taken off the packs containing the secret that they have each been guarding as if it was their own child, for many days. Like Hugumki said, they are almost home, and should be quite safe in an open area.

One by one, wearing serious looks of intent, they start getting in line.

There's Deerhead, still the biggest, but even his bulging muscles look much leaner.

Bird, who was soft and thin before now has sinewy strips of muscle he has earned from enduring a long hard quest.

Ah Ki Wami, whose smooth and shiny body is so wiry now that it looks as sharp as a flint blade that will easily slice through the air.

When the light catches Two Bows and Ooha, their eyes are shining like eager obsidian.

"This race will be over fast." Rabbit waves his hand with a flourish at the now ready group of runners. "Standing here without my load on, I feel as light as a bird feather."

"Sandals on or off?" Hugumki notices some of the runners have taken theirs off while others are still wearing theirs.

Off, is the final decision.

"How far do we go?" inquires the short-legged Turtle.

"This is for speed, not distance," the much longer legged Two Bows responds.

Ista sneers his distraction from the far end of the line of racers, "Poor Turtle, you don't even stand a chance."

"It will be from here to that large rock over there," answers Hugumki. "It looks like it is the flattest area around here."

"This will be funny," Rabbit spins around while giggling.

"First one there will turn around so I can see who it is," Hugumki says loud enough for everyone to hear. Their expressions are a mixture of aggression, desire, and hope.

The runners tense up, Hugumki raises his hand, then quickly drops it.

Off he goes with a burst-of-speed. Suddenly Turtle, short legs, and all, realizes that he is the first one off the line. Looking back in astonishment, Turtle sees his leader prepare to drop his hand again.

Even though they had all caught Hugumki's subtle signal to let Turtle have a head start, there was one thing they all missed. They did not notice that someone else had slipped off his sandals.

Hugumki drops his hand again.

Bird, as light and quick as a jack rabbit has the early lead. Then Deerhead's thick powerful legs put him in front, giving hope to the similarly built Turtle who knows his dreams of glory are soon to be dashed. Sky Eye and Ooha are doing their best, but soon they see Two Bows long muscular back slowly pulling ahead of them. Ah Ki Wami sees Two Bows off to his side, and knows he still has a chance.

Suddenly, all the runners, and not just Turtle, feel like they are running in place. Woosh comes the breeze, the breeze of a poncho clad runner as he passes those much slower than himself. Even Two Bows who had the late lead feels it as he is passed just before the finish line.

Then it's over. As the victorious runner turns around to face the others, Deerhead crosses the finish line. "I can't believe that even though he runs like a woman, Rabbit is still the fastest out of all of us."

"And he didn't even take off his poncho" adds Two Bows.

Smiling at the victor in front of him, Sky Eye asks, "What does that say about us?"

"Rabbit, who will you choose?" Turtle asks when he catches up with everyone else.

"Don't start that again," rings out more than one voice, including Rabbit's.

18th day – Homeward Bound – Nighttime

The stars are mesmerizing with their vastness, sheer number, and brilliant twinkle.

The Chosen are relaxing in the small camp that Hugumki set up all by himself to show his appreciation for the teamwork they have all displayed.

After telling Hugumki how well he gathered the wood, made the fire, put out the azee, caught then prepared their meal, they plan their next day. They are hoping that it will be an easy one, at least until they are once again gathered around a fire.

All they have, to do then, is sleep in until sunrise, if they can, break camp, then circle a little closer to the village. At some point, they will set up camp again, then prepare to be tested on what they have each learned while they were away on their quest.

What they don't know yet is that Hugumki has one more test for them. One that will take them to heights they may not want to reach.

Once their planning is finished, they eagerly start talking about the memories and impressions of their journey.

As it turns out, Turtle may still be the slowest runner of the group, but put some weight on his back, and he can go and go. "I never thought I would see a Turtle, beat a Rabbit," Ista jokes, recalling how Turtle had carried Rabbit's pack, when his foot was sore. "What do you get if you mix up a turtle and a rabbit?"

"You get a slow rabbit or a fast turtle," is everyone's answer.

Sky Eye talks about how the stars overhead seem to be almost identical, yet a little different from the ones by the great waters, and the other wonders he has seen in the sky. "Remember that night the fire flew across the sky?" Sky Eye closes his eyes so he can see the amazing spectacle again in his memory.

Hugumki gives Sky Eye an odd look because he knows that Sky Eye has kept a secret, and he is curious as to whether Sky Eye will reveal it or not.

For Bird, the strongest memory was of the giant birds they saw by the great waters. Birds that were so big that at first, they thought they were Sky God's. That is until Hugumki got hit by falling bird kani. Everyone, including Hugumki, laughs, recalling how seriously he had tried to keep acting, even after his shoulder had caught the last sticky stinky remnants falling from the sky.

"Remember how their shadows looked so big it looked like we could fly on them if we could have caught one," Sky Eye puts both arms out like a soaring condor.

Two Bows remembers something else they saw that was very large. "Don't forget about that huge fish we saw. I know I won't. I still can't believe how it blew the water right out of the top of its head."

A pall falls over the Chosen, like a foggy memory. Enough voices spread around the fire say "The cave" at once, that for a moment, it sounds like they are once again back in the dark treasure filled cavern at the great waters.

"The smell, little light, all the wet life, the raging water right under out feet." When someone says, "The strange sounds," Hugumki and Two Bows do their best not to look at each other.

Sky Eye closes his eyes, "I want to see a cave like that again even if it is not the same one."

Hugumki breaks out in laughter. "Rabbit, I have never seen anyone make so many funny faces as you did in the cave. I knew you weren't going to like it."

"Sorry Hugumki, but a wet stinky cave is not for me."

Two Bows puts his arms out and squeezes his hands, "I will always remember hanging onto the rock above the water that seemed to go on forever."

"I wonder how far it really goes," Bird wonders.

Ista starts moving his fingers around like he has two squirming tusks. "Don't forget about those stinky animals with the big teeth."

"I am glad we never saw them again," Rabbit says with satisfaction.

Once it came up, all the Chosen recall the awe they felt when they saw the massive rockslide.

Deerhead gets his well-deserved praise from everyone for making sure that based on Hugumki's and Two Bows' directions, they had not gotten lost, and had even found the wet cave through the fog, on their first try.

Of course, they all took credit for finding their way back home.

Ooha, always the lover, is trying to look into the future. "I hope Squash Blossom has an etched shell for me when I get back."

"When she gives it to you, are you going to give her the big flat one I saw you put in your pack, so she can start on another one for you?" Hugumki asks, raising his eyebrows playfully at Ooha.

"As for me," Rabbit turns his face away from the firelight, pulling his blanket tighter in the evening chill. "I will take one day to get clean and stay clean. Next day, I will wear all my jewelry at once so I can see what they look like on me again."

A couple voices say, "All the animals we saw."

Turtle thinks about, "The deer that stayed just out of reach."

Ah Ki Wami holds his fingers close together. "Don't forget the little ones like the squirrels, rabbits, mice…"

Rabbit laughs before saying, "Don't forget the birds and their pretty songs. Even the early ones, hoa."

"I will say this one time. One bear is one bear too many," Ooha's face still looks uneasy.

"Like this?" Ista stands up, raises both his arms, holds up his hands like claws, then lets out a ferocious growl to everyone's laughter.

Esan gets thanked for being a good guard and friend, and for scaring the big cat that Turtle and Bird still see in their dreams some nights.

Esan then takes the opportunity, sounding a lot more like Ista than himself, to thank Two Bows for being such a good shot and saving his life from the attacking zizi.

Two Bows, recalling some bigger game he had to let get away, cannot wait for the next hunter's moon when some of the men and women of the village would go in search of deer and antelope, and if life was good, maybe even bigger bear or buffalo.

Turtle scans his face. "Will you take one of your wives with you?"

"I can always catch one on the way back," Two Bows replies in such a way that the others aren't sure if he is joking or not.

"That reminds me of something I have really been missing." Turtle waits for them to guess what that is. Since no one says anything, he continues. "I have been missing a lady's voice. It doesn't even have to be my mother's.

"You mean mine doesn't count?" Rabbit asks in his high-pitched voice.

Turtle looks at him, unsure of what to say.

"How about this then?" Everyone has forgotten how much lower Rabbit's real voice is compared to the one he normally speaks in.

Once his shock wore off, and seeing the grin on Rabbit's face, Turtle starts laughing along with everyone else.

"What I can't believe happened," Hugumki keeps chuckling, "is that funny Ista and mean Ah Ki Wami have become friends." Those words immediately earn him two scowls, followed by more laughter.

Suddenly bashful, Turtle quietly chimes in. "I think I saw a monster at the great waters."

"You mean in the water like that big fish we saw," asks Ah Ki Wami. "Or more like the one that had that bone we found in the cave?"

"It was not in the water, but it was on the rocks at the great waters. It looked like it was resting on arms only a monster can have."

Hugumki looks at him protectively, "Why didn't you say anything before?"

"I was not sure, and I did not want to be teased all the way home. But it was very big and had a very dark color."

"Was it before or after you went into the cave?" Ooha asks.

"After."

"I think I was looking at you when you saw it," admits Ooha. "When you were looking at the great waters, your face changed like you had seen a night spirit. I looked around but I did not see anything."

"Thank you Turtle. Now we can all wonder if monsters are still alive and can you tease the truth right out of somebody's mouth." Hugumki dips his head while thinking, *This is another thing I must learn.*

Two Bows leans toward Turtle and whispers, "I saw the same thing when I was climbing down to the cave. I think. It was hard to see then."

Turtle's face almost cracks his smile gets so big.

"I wasn't sure before, but now I am. Thank you."

Two Bow peers around at what he can't see. "I am thankful I got to see the great waters and the low desert was different, but our home is much prettier. We have our river, and not as many cactus."

"That's right," Deerhead agrees, leaning back. "The other place is all gray and way too dry, even if you look closely," he grins at Rabbit. "Here, it can be the color of Father Sun before he goes to sleep. Both places have mountains, but here we also have flat mountains to hunt or play on. We also have giant rocks of all shapes and sizes. I just like it better here. This is my home."

"That made me think of the old village for some reason." Sky Eye says. "Does anybody know how the old village got its name?"

"It's old," Ista beats everyone else to it.

"I don't know how old it is, but it is much older than ours is," Hugumki raises his head in Ista's direction and smiles. "The old village's real name is, I can't remember right now. We, just call it the old village, because that is what it has become.

"How old is ours," Turtle asks.

"Not real old," Sky Eye answers. "Our people used to move from one village to another. At some time, they made ours, and that is where we live now."

"I heard the village was made on the ruins of an even older village, which is bad medicine," Ah KI Wami points out through his frown. "It even smells strange sometimes."

Hugumki thinks about what he has also heard, "I am sure those are just stories."

"How many people live in the old village now?" Two Bows, asks.

"The people that used to live there disappeared a long time ago. The people that live there now just moved in when they needed a home."

Giving Hugumki a curious look, Ah Ki Wami interrogates, "How do you know so much about them?"

Hugumki is barely able to keep from laughing at his wary friend. "Because some of the people that live there now used to live in our village."

"The scouts we avoided were more than likely from here," Two Bows slowly wags two fingers in the air. "I have heard they have gotten lazy like lizards down there. Those two did not seem to try very hard to find us."

"So, they knew that we were going to be coming along sometime?" Ah Ki Wami almost implores.

"I think it was still good for all of us to know what it feels like to be hunted by a man," Hugumki's eyes fill with sadness. "In case it ever happens for real."

Sky Eye then takes such a deep breath of air his eyes almost pop out. "Thank you for taking care of us, and I know all of us tried as hard as we could." Sky Eye cocks his head. "At least most of the time." When he meets Hugumki's gaze, he sees the same odd expression he glimpsed earlier. Then it finally dawns on him. Hugumki knows. After clearing his throat, "I need to say something else. I was supposed to help guide us by using the stars, but I did not pay enough attention when Canasake went over them with me. From the beginning of our test, I was not sure which ones I should point out, so I thought I should not say anything. Sorry."

Wearing a smile full of warmth and kindness, Hugumki says, "You were smart not to say anything wrong, and thanks to all of you for helping us and each other out. I know a lot of our early problems came from our age difference."

"And our different sizes," Bird looks up.

"That is true," Hugumki agrees. "It is not like any of us are your true elders, even though some of us kind of had to act that way at times. It was easy for me to remember how I felt at your age, and guess what? It is just about the same way I feel now. You wonder about the same things. You worry about the same things. The only real change is experience, and now, we have all shared an experience to last our whole lives."

As their eyes start getting heavy, Ooha breaks into the night song.

Oh ani Oh ani.

Nye nye nye nye.

Wawis a hy.

Wawis a Hy.

Shu shu shu.

Shu shu shu.

The unpredictable Ah Ki Wami does the unpredicted. He jumps up and starts dancing around the fire. "Happy. Happy. I am so happy we are almost home." After another quick turn around the fire, he practically falls into his spot.

Soon enough, they settle down for the night and are quickly asleep.

One dream of any kind, closer to home.

36

19ᵗʰ day – Homeward Bound – High sun

The clouds are aimlessly drifting bye, but the air is so still it feels as if the desert has stopped breathing in anticipation of what may happen, next day.

Almost finished with their second meal are a small group of resting youth-soon to be men-enjoying the warm sunshine.

The night before had gotten so cold it felt like winter had reached out with its icy breath for one last dying grasp at them. It was as if it wanted to take one more bite out of them so there would be no doubt that they were going to be different men.

After eating some dried berries, nuts, leftover fish, pieces of their remaining jerky, and breadcrumbs, their conversation eventually takes up an intriguing mystery.

"Do you think that huge bone we found in one of our sleeping caves belonged to a different monster than the one Turtle saw?" Sky Eye asks the whole group that is scattered around him on the ground.

"I can't think of it as a monster," Deerhead answers first.

"Why."

Deerhead reaches around to scratch his itchy back. "Can a monster be killed? "When I looked at the bone, I could tell that people cut meat from the bone."

"If it was not a monster, then what could it have been?" asks Ista.

Sky Eye is curious about all parts of the mystery. "What I would like to know is. When did it happen? When did that creature, and those people live?"

The scout and tracker are only thinking of the beast. "That was only one bone we saw. If it had many bones like most creatures do, it must have been very big." Two Bows, looks up, trying to imagine how big the creature must have been if it was all in one piece.

Turtle, dreaming of the day he gets bigger and faster asks, "Would that make it fast?"

"Not fast enough," answers Two Bows before chuckling. "Not fast enough."

"Even on the hard ground of that area, because of its size, it would have been easy to track down," Deerhead bends his head down like he is looking for signs of a trail to follow. "Too big might mean too slow. I wish we had found what they used to kill it."

"What if it flew?" Sky Eye tries to hide a small smile.

"Don't say that." Rabbit scans the sky just in case.

"Did it eat people?" asks Ista. "Is that why they killed it?"

"To kill in hunger is greater than anger," the lean Ah Ki Wami licks his lips to prove his point.

"That's right Wami. The cave told us that those people made fire to cook the meat on," Hugumki says.

"Someday, I must come back out here and look around some more," Sky Eye promises himself out loud. "There is so much more to learn about, from here all the way back to the great waters."

"What do you mean?" asks Bird, who, like many of the others, is mainly thinking of home.

"Well, one thing is those pictures we could barely see in the first cave we slept in. Were they made by our people, or by other people, even longer ago? And don't forget about those strange bones we saw in the rock." Upon seeing Bird's disinterest along with everyone else's, Sky Eye stops talking, and keeps right on thinking about the mysterious and wondrous world they all live in.

Without warning Deerhead's body tenses up, his face scrunches, and his ears start tingling. Like a roar of thunder, his sneeze startles his friends and anything close by as it echoes off the desert. "I have needed that for days," he says, a warm glow coloring his face.

Lowering his voice to try and prove his point, "I cannot believe I am almost a man," Ista says, his pride evident in his posture.

"When you have a couple of hairs to pluck from your chin, let me know," Two Bows teases by gently pinching Ista's smooth, hairless chin. He then brushes the fuzz on his own upper lip.

After a shake to clear his head, Deerhead reminisces, "I was already a man when I was born."

Those closest, give him a solemn look, before bursting into laughter at the thought of a little, baby man Deerhead.

"We have all earned the right of passage once we are back home," Hugumki holds his chin high.

"I know I have earned it," Turtle proudly states. His voice sounds like it might get as deep as Deerheads, someday.

"Yes, you have, Turtle. We all have. Once I knew where we were really going, I was not sure if all of us would make it all the way to the great waters and back." Sky Eye tries not to look anybody in the eye while saying that.

"Are you talking about me?" Rabbit glares at him anyway.

"Oh, Rabbit, I was talking about any of us," Sky Eye quickly corrects. "Look at us. All of us look different now than we did when we first left the village."

"We're all a lot darker now," Ista laughs.

Esan turns to look at him as if to say. *Really?*

"I am glad my night skin never burned," Sky Eye smiles. "Now I am as healthy looking, as the rest of you."

Hugumki, who has been keeping an eye on the trail ahead stands and stretches. "There is Bird and Wami waving us forward. Let's get ready to go."

"Aren't we safe this close to home? Why do we still need to keep scouting the trail Hugumki?" Ista asks.

"The real danger now, if it ever came, would probably come from in front of us, and it could come quickly. Eyes ahead, eyes around. Don't ever forget that. Let's go. Hup, hup."

"Hugumki, I think I will hear that in my head until I join the stars," Ooha taps his head like he is trying to knock the words right out through his ears. "That didn't work, they are still in there like they want to become a song."

"No," is everyone else's response as a cool breeze starts stirring to help guide them in the direction of Old Man butte.

"What does hup, hup mean?" Deerhead quietly asks himself.

19th day – Homeward bound – Mid-afternoon

Cloud shadows are racing across the land. It looks like they are eager to get home before the Chosen who are casually walking along enjoying the beautiful day. When they approach the small flat mountain that they will camp behind for the night, Deerhead continues walking on the path that will take them around it.

You can usually tell how big a mesa is on top by how big it is at its base. Of course, that depends upon how much of the top has been eroded away. Most mesas are flat and rocky with a little vegetation, while others are barren on top. Much like a butte, a mesa can hold many guises. Sometimes it can look like it is merely touching the sky, and other times, holding it up or disappearing into it. It all depends on the weather.

The one they think they are passing is not really that high but is more than high enough to accomplish what Hugumki wants.

Two Bows is walking next to Hugumki. "Gumki, why do you keep looking up there? Do you see something that doesn't belong there?"

"Our quest is almost over, but the test is not," Hugumki answers, still looking up.

Following his gaze, Two Bow's sees what Hugumki has been searching for. It is a narrow, treacherous looking trail that winds its way up the side of the mesa. "No. Don't tell me."

Hugumki calls everyone to gather around him. "I have one more test for you. It is a test of your courage, and your fear of heights. We are going to walk up the side there, then down the other side."

"On what," Ah Ki Wami can't help but ask.

"Don't worry, there is a trail, even if you can't see it yet."

"A trail for what? A mountain deer?" Deerhead is hoping it is wide enough for his two big feet.

"This is even smaller and steeper than it looked like from the ground." Two Bows is not afraid of heights, but he does have a fear of falling hundreds of feet, straight down.

Hugumki looks behind him. "Spread out a little more everybody. That will give you the time needed to see any rocks one of us might send down your way."

Feeling his sandal slide reminds Ah Ki Wami of what can easily happen. "Be extra careful everybody. This trail is very slippery too."

"And steep," Rabbit looks to his side and sees only air.

"I already said that" Two Bows keeps his eyes on the trail.

"It is."

Turtle keeps climbing with slow steady purpose. "After what we have been through, this feels pretty easy."

Ista's smile has a bit of a quiver to it. "I am glad it is not hot. That would make this a lot harder than it is."

"My legs sure feel stronger," Turtle glances at Deerhead down below him who has stopped on the trail for some reason.

"Mine too. They may not be any bigger, but they sure are stronger than they were before we started." Bird lightly taps his face to steady his nerves. Height does not bother him either, but like Two Bows, he has no desire to go flying into the abyss next to him.

Rabbit can't believe his eyes. "Look at that bird! We are looking at the top of that flying bird!"

"Look out below!" Hugumki suddenly warns.

A single rock, about the size of the lump of singing stones they have in their packs is bouncing and careening its way downhill on the narrow trail.

"Jump everybody!" Two Bows yells after he has cleared the latest obstacle to face them.

Hugumki turns to watch what happens and is pleased by what he sees. One by one, the next one to face the rolling rock, waits, then easily avoids it by either jumping or deftly getting out of its way, without tumbling over the side. Not one of them seems scared or intimidated by their precarious position. Looking back up the trail, Hugumki asks the sky, "Who or what sent that rock our way?"

When they reach the top of the mesa, they don't find anything that can answer Hugumki's question.

Once everyone catches their breath, they all walk in the direction of a pile of rocks that even from a distance, looks out of place on the opposite rim of the mesa.

Once there, Esan stays clear so he can keep chasing some flying bugs, while Ooha looks over the edge and immediately wishes he hadn't." The darkness, now heights," he moans to himself.

The strong wind on top starts blowing everyone's hair around and chilling their skin. "I hope my hair doesn't get all tangled just before I get home," Rabbit tries to hold his hair in place, but soon gives up when his headband pops off.

Ista waves his trail worn blanket over his head. The wind billows his blanket so quickly that it is almost pulled out of his hands. Gripping harder, Ista's can feel the strength of the wind when he starts getting pulled toward the looming edge. "Oh no blanket, you must fly free."

Twisting around, the blanket furls and unfurls.

"If it goes over, at least you can get a new one soon," Hugumki laughs.

After a few more twists and turns of freedom, the wayward blanket lands meekly at Turtle's feet where it is quickly scooped up and stowed away.

"How far down is it?" Ooha quietly asks, stepping backwards.

"To far to fall, so everyone be careful up here, and when we start climbing back down," Hugumki calls out.

While looking around, Two Bows has an idea. "Gumki, should we practice our watching from up here and our trail tracking when we head back down?"

"We have been all along. Rabbit, look at me, but tell me what you have seen over there," Hugumki gestures in front of him.

Rabbit closes his eyes. "In front of us is Old Man, then over there is…"

"See what I mean Two Bows. I also know that they have all gotten much better at following a trail. Just watch their eyes when we get back down, you will see what I mean.

"I guess that saying of yours worked."

They both laugh without saying it.

Turtle feels like he can touch the sky. "This is my first time, and now I know why being up here is so much fun."

"I know what you mean," Ah Ki Wami's eyes hold the fiery light of excitement.

"Everything looks so different from up here."

"Sometimes there is small game up here, but I think we have scared them all away."

"I just like looking and walking around."

Bird and Rabbit are studying the different formations in front of them. "From up here it looks like the land of the gods," Bird picks up a rock.

"Should not do that from up here," Rabbit exaggerates shaking his head back and forth.

"Your right," Bird turns and throws it behind him instead.

Once they are all alone. "Did you ever think that we weren't going to make it?" Hugumki asks Two Bows.

Two Bows' memories make his brow furrow. "Not really, but it did get very hard sometimes."

"Turtle really showed how tough, they all did, didn't they?"

Two Bows turns his face to the sun. "We all did."

Hugumki doesn't say anything but his body and posture, speaks for him. It carries the pride and self-assurance of someone who has earned it. "I wonder how the village is doing?" Hugumki finally asks.

"Still the same, I hope. Even after past night I can tell all our cold days are gone."

"For now. Cover your ears. I have been wanting to do this for some time."

After some of the cracks and crevices of the mesa have been explored. After enough laughing and yelling to keep the birds away, a shrill piercing whistle cuts through the air.

Bird can barely make out Hugumki with his head back and his arms in the air. Slowly his arms drop and point.

Ista looks at the others, "Will he say, 'eyes around or eyes below' this time?"

Time to start heading back down, and before they reach the bottom, they will rearrange the trail like Deerhead did earlier so not just anybody, can come along and climb the mesa, for any reason.

19th day – Homeward Bound – Early dark

With the stars shimmering impatiently, the Chosen are clustered in a tight circle around their fire. They are wearing their breechcloths, ponchos, or whatever else they feel comfortable in with their blankets draped loosely over their shoulders.

By the intense look in their eyes, and the stiffness of their spines, you can tell that the testing of what they have each learned on their test has already begun. Even Esan looks like he is paying extra close attention in case he is asked a question.

"Ista, your turn again. What made that call and why is it wrong?" asks Hugumki, as a singing bird call fades away into the night.

"Horn made the call," answers Ista to laughter. "It is wrong because it is the song of a day bird, and that bird only calls in the light of day."

"Sky Eye, when we left home, we crossed the river three times. Now we are near the village, but we have only crossed the river one-time. Why is that?" questions Deerhead.

"When we left the village," answers Sky Eye, "we were showing the wrong path. When we headed to Old Man, we crossed the river again. Now we are out of sight of the village, and our fire is low. We will get home before first light, so we do not have to show the same longer wrong path. That is the same reason we only passed through high cliff pass, one time. We went a different way."

"Very good Sky Eye," praises Hugumki. "Wami, what is the easiest way to have a bad journey?"

"Not be patient, lose control of your feelings. If you do not control them, you will not see what you need to see," answers a calmer than usual Ah Ki Wami.

"Rabbit, what is that sound?" asks Deerhead, as Horn, having switched positions in the dark, makes another call.

"I have not heard it before, it does not sound like a night creature," Rabbit answers confidently.

"You're right, Rabbit," Deerhead says, nodding his head. "Horn made that one up."

Seeing Bird's ears perk up again when his father is mentioned, Hugumki looks at him and softly says. "Don't forget what we talked about earlier."

Hugumki had tried to explain to Bird that it would not be fair to the others if he was able to spend time with Horn before any of the others got to see their families. To his surprise, Bird had agreed without complaint.

Even Hugumki gets tested. Out of all the questions they could have asked him, he had anticipated, and was prepared for the one they did.

"If we had really, really, run out of water Hugumki," asks Turtle. "What would we have done?"

"Most important out here is to know what season it is. There are times, even if you could carry a river with you, that still might not be enough water to drink. For this journey," Hugumki takes a cold sip from his boto, "if we had run out of water, first I would check to see what kind of cactus was around. Many of them hold water as you know, right? If there was no cactus around, I would have gone up to a big rock that had ground around it, went around to the cool side, dug into the moist dirt there, put that dirt in my shirt and squeezed. It may not be a lot, but there will usually be some water there. And if needed, I would follow a dry river and check the rocks to see if any of them still held any water, above or below. Like when we found the water just before we saw the yellow flowers. Am I right Turtle? Do you remember the things we have practiced?"

"Yes," answers Turtle, stretching the truth just a little bit.

"We should be thankful. Once we left the lower desert and with all the snow still around, I was never real thirsty again." Sky Eye takes a sip of cold water to prove his point.

"That is what I meant by knowing what season it is," Hugumki says while nodding.

"And don't ever forget to check your boto's two times if you fill them with snow," Ah Ki Wami reminds everyone.

Ooha, who is thankful he still has his singing voice softly says, "Don't forget about the small rock in your mouth, it helped me even though I did not know it then."

"Two Bows, what animals are best to stay away from and how can you tell?" asks Hugumki, giving his friend an easy question.

"An animal that is not well. He may have the snow color on his mouth. He may be too thin and he will not act normal," answers Two Bows, thinking of all the rabid animals he has seen in his life.

"Ooha, where did that night sound come from?" quizzes Hugumki, as the hidden Horn, well out of reach of the firelight makes another sound after moving to a different spot.

"At first it sounds like it came from over there, but if you listened carefully, you could hear it start over there," answers Ooha, pointing in opposite directions. "Then the sound goes over there and then comes here. It is like when I sing in the rocks, it can sound like there is more that one of me."

"That is something an enemy might try to use against us," Two Bows warily points out.

"Turtle, why do we have to be very careful in the dry rivers?" Hugumki asks.

"I have been told, and as we found out," Turtle lifts his feet up, "that the water that made the rivers, big or small, could come back at any time, and it could come back faster than even Rabbit can run."

"Deerhead," asks a confident Bird, "What are the signs to look for?"

"Storm clouds in the distance, what season it is, and if you hear or feel the sound of the Thunder God coming, get out as fast as you can."

"Esan," asks Ista "How long until we get home?"

One bark, answers Esan, who seems as anxious as everyone else to tell family and friends about his journey.

"Bird, what is the easiest way to hunt a bird?" asks Two Bows, barely holding back his laughter.

"Pick a hiding spot by the birds and wait until they are calm. Then have Esan come from the other direction, and scare the birds right into your waiting bow," answers Bird, trying to control his own laughter.

"We need to get up early, and I am sure Horn wants to get back to his fire." Hugumki pauses for a moment as he tries to clear a lump from his throat. "I want to say I am proud of all of you. I know this was very hard, but we all made it back. You are the best group that could have been picked to go on this test and quest. We listened to each other and did what needed to be done, for all of us. To those that did not keep acting like children, thank you so much. I know at times it was a struggle for all of us, but we did it. Most important. Remember this. For the rest of your life you will know that you can do anything you want to do. Anything you put your heart to. Your spirit has been tested and all of you have passed. In my eye's you are already warriors, and men of our village.

Two Bows just has to bring up what has been weighing him down. "Are we going to keep doing it?"

"Doing what," Deerhead asks.

"I mean not doing it."

Deerhead motions impatiently with his hands.

"Not talking about you know," Two Bows reaches behind him and makes a humpback motion.

With his eyes blazing like a god and a snort to get every one's attention, Hugumki looks them all in the eye one by one, so they know how serious he is.

"We will finish this test as men. We do not have to talk about what we already know.

"How heavy.

"How Hard.

"How long.

"Just know that what we have done is for our village and for our people. There is no reason to talk about it any further," Hugumki makes a humpback motion with a smile on his face, "Agreed?"

In this case agreement means no reaction at all as the Chosen quickly turn their attention to other things.

Let's tell Horn we are ready."

"Hi ah ee."

"Hi ah ee."

They all sing with the joy of knowing that even before Father Sun comes up, at long last, they will be back home, as men.

Without warning they feel more than hear a disturbance of air heading right toward them. First one head turns, then two, then eleven, all spin like gyroscopes to get their bearings. Not a single voice yells out in surprise or fear but all hands reach for and quickly grip the handles of their knives in preparation for what is rapidly approaching.

Wheeew, a giant shadow passes overhead, and in the next breath, it has blended back into the darkness from which it came.

"Very good everybody." Hugumki's satisfaction is written all over his face. It is almost as if he is the father and he has watched his nine boys grow up right in front of his eyes. Not only have they grown up and become men, but they have also grown closer together.

They are not merely the band of one hand, but two, intertwined together into one mighty fist. Sure, there will still be teasing, disagreements, and misunderstandings, but the look they are giving each other now can be described with one single word: Respect.

Their confident mood of camaraderie is ruined by a simple observation from Two Bows. "I thought at first we were being attacked by a shapeshifter who wanted to know what we have brought back from the great waters."

"What are shapeshifters?" Bird asks again. "No one ever told me before."

Realizing they are treading on dangerous ground, Hugumki stands up to face everybody, and does not mince words. "Shapeshifters are very evil people, and they must be avoided. Because of their evil, they can take over the spirit of different animals. Usually something sneaky like a coyote, snake, or vulture."

"Are there any in our village," Ista asks.

After a quick glance between them, Hugumki, Deerhead, and Two Bows all answer firmly. "No."

"If they can change their shape, how would we know?" Sky Eye asks. "Could that have been Horn flying back to the village?"

Bird looks insulted but does not say anything because he is also a little curious. How much does he really know about his father after all.

"That's enough everybody," Hugumki stretches before sitting back down in his spot. "If we don't get to sleep, we won't be able to get up, and if we don't get up, we won't be able to get home. At least not when we are supposed to."

Soon enough, everyone is eagerly getting ready for bed, more than aware of, but ignoring the occasional eye shine from a curious creature or two.

37

20th day – Homeward Bound – Before first light

On the last night of their quest, you would think that all the Chosen would be having sweet, peaceful dreams, regardless of whether shapeshifters are on their minds or not.

Dreams of home, goals met, a task accomplished, of family and friends, even of future mates.

Instead, restlessly tossing and turning, they are once again out in the middle of the desert, dealing with the dust, the endless glaring light, the thirst that seems to have no end. Some legs are even twitching under their blankets with worries of another day of endless walking.

What a joy, what a relief it is to wake up and see Old Man's distant silhouette behind them.

"Aaaahhhh," pierces that morning quiet anticipation. "Thank the gods we are finally here," After a stir and a shake, Ah Ki Wami says, "We are so close now I could crawl home if I had too."

With his sleepy eye's fluttering, Bird thinks he can see their village already. "I can too Turtle. See. It's right there," he points from his bed.

"You just know where it is. Our test has not made your eyes so good that you can see right through rock," Turtle shakes his head.

"Who cares right now," Two Bows stands up. "We are here, we made it everybody. We did it men, we did it," he singsongs.

With shouts of happiness starting to ring out all around him, a worn out Hugumki awakens with a start. Next to him, Rabbit gently checks on him from his spot around the fire that is patiently waiting for something odorous to burn. "Is there something wrong? That is not the first time heading home that I have seen you wake up like that."

"There's nothing wrong. I'm just having bad dreams, that's all."

"I just heard him so I thought maybe you had forgotten how sad Short Nose sounds."

"Not really. He does sound bad though, doesn't he, poor thing?" Hugumki listens as Short Nose cries goodnight to the night again from somewhere out of the darkness.

"Bad singer, good hunter though," Two Bows says.

Hugumki laughs quietly. "He has to make up for his bad voice."

Short Nose got his name because of his damaged snout which some say was caused by a wolf. His injury has also caused him to be the worst singer around, which is saying something, considering Hugumki's well-earned reputation.

"What are your bad thoughts about?"

"They are of a great snow colored wave that is coming toward the village. I can't tell if it is trying to swallow us up or move us along. That thought must come from seeing the great waters, or maybe..." Hugumki doesn't finish the thought that has been on his mind for many days.

"Maybe," ventures Rabbit, "it is because of the stories that those good-looking visitors told us a handful of seasons ago. Do you remember their stories about the long, big wave that changed their homeland along another great water?"

"I don't know. Time is passing by fast. We need to get going, I need to get going. I can't believe I am the last one awake, this last time."

Turning his head to scan the eastern horizon for the telltale signs of a new day, Hugumki wonders to himself. *Will these singing stones make the god that Hunter thinks will help us?*

Out of all the chore's the Chosen have done on their quest, their last one is their favorite. They all enjoy burning their tattered and extremely smelly sandals.

"Should we have a ceremony?" Ista laughs.

"Yes" Rabbit starts singing in the voice of an old woman, "Oh sandal, you have given so much."

"That's so funny," Ista will remember that one for his stories later.

Esan looks a little disappointed that his paw covers are not burned also, but then again, who knows what the future holds for Esan, and his specially made sandals.

Once they are done with that, their faces are practically glowing. They are alive, awash with glory. Their voices are proud. They have passed their test. They have made it back as men. Soon they will be on their way back to their village with a very eager Esan leading the way.

Taking a moment for himself, Bird walks away from the others. It is something he has done more and more lately, and it has paid off. All alone, he can feel the strength of the universe settling in his bones and soothing his fears.

Two Bows and Deerhead look in each other's direction.

"I think I have run out of things to say," Two Bow says.

"Me too."

"I think we have said it all, done at all."

They each shrug at how quickly things can change, then quietly wait on Hugumki.

Once Hugumki is finished putting out and hiding the remains of their fire, "Men. It is time to go home."

Before too long.

Jutting out of the darkness the shear angular walls of their village are made to repel or welcome. The Chosen have made it. They are back home.

Silently entering the perimeter of their village, barefoot, they all easily pick out a human form squatting against the northern wall. Seeing how quickly they spotted him, the shape stands up in his poncho so that they can see that he is a friend, not a foe. It is Bear, still the acting chief.

Realizing that Horn must have returned to the village on foot, or otherwise, to tell Bear about their impending arrival, Hugumki makes sure that everyone stays very quiet while they wait for Bear's instructions.

A thin form-moving like a shadow distilled in liquid-walks over to the wall, reaches out a darkened hand and touches it, while also clutching his zumi in thanks. Soon he is joined by everyone else doing the same thing. To say you are home is one thing, to touch it is quite another. The Chosen are back. They have all made it safely back home, including Esan, who has been told that he must sit and wait on everyone else before he can announce his arrival.

Under the cover of the fleeing darkness, a shoulder slams into another, then silently moves away. It is hard to tell who has the sore shoulder because as soon as it was received, the blow was returned in kind.

Apparently, there are still some things that need to be resolved.

Bear and Hugumki heard the smack, but could not tell who was involved, so Hugumki looks at Bear, "Could you hear us coming?"

"Hardly a sound. I could hear the river better than I could hear you approaching. I did not see any of you either until you were almost on top of me. Very good everyone. Each of you have gotten so dark that once you got close enough all I could see was your eyes and teeth coming, just like Esan." Bear reaches down to pet Esan who is overjoyed to have someone different to scratch and sniff.

With the eager men jostling around him, Bear glances at the eastern horizon. He sees a thin ragged, jagged orange tear that is beginning to separate night from day.

"Father Sun will be making his appearance soon. I want each of you to follow me around the corner to the old storage room, one by one. Stay here until it is your turn. We must all be very quiet, especially about what you have brought back. I trust all of you not to tell anybody about what we are doing now because it must remain a secret. And yes, you can consider that part of your test. I will climb up the ladder, enter the room and then wait at the top. Each of you will climb the ladder when it is your turn, then walk over to the opening and hand me your bag of singing stones. The next person must wait until the last one is done before you climb up. It does not matter what order you go in but wait until everyone else is finished. After that, you will walk into the village just like you passed your test. You passed your test as a group. You will enter the village as a group of new men. As your first reward, I have put some ladders in place for you."

The exuberant men are barely able to control the energy coursing through their bodies, prompting Bear to throw his thick arms in the air for complete silence.

"Except for you Hugumki," Bear says firmly. "When you are the last one left, I will leave you alone so that you can see where the singing stones go."

As Bear turns away, Rabbit, who has suddenly turned helpless, trips and starts to fall. When Bear grabs him, he feels the feathers that are laced through Rabbit's tangled botos, and remembers something else he still has to say.

"Keep your botos with you. Someone will collect them later. If you want to keep your things, take them off when you can.

Even in the twilight, their botos look different than they did at the beginning of their quest. Some have designs drawn or scraped on them. Others have dried flowers, strips of cactus, or other remnants of the desert interwoven into the straps. Two Bows' has some mysterious teeth dangling from his.

With his hungry eyes aglow, Turtle leans toward Bird and whispers, "I smell something good."

"Turtle, later on do you want...?"

"Yes, I do."

Bear recalls one last important instruction he still must give. Glancing around, he says "Oh, and leave the bows, arrows, quiver, and spears for Hugumki to take to the holy, weapons room. Hugumki, that will give you the excuse you may need as to why you are slower than everyone else."

After that, Bear walks around the corner, climbs the ladder, then quickly drops down into the opening using another ladder that is already in place inside the mid-sized storage room.

One by one, the Chosen easily climb the sturdy wooden ladder, walk along the roof to the opening then hand their small, loaded pack to Bear. Bear waits a moment to make sure each of them has started back down. Once assured, Bear climbs down and slides back the false floor in the pitch-black storage room that leads down into a narrow hole that could have once been part of an old pit house. Bear is working by feel more than sight as he carefully places the packs where hopefully, they will be safe until needed.

When he is finished, he slides the false floor partially back in place, climbs back up the ladder, then waits for the next pack to be placed in his hands.

Hugumki is and is not surprised that they are all patiently waiting for their turn to climb the ladder.

He is surprised because he can tell by their eyes and furtive motions that they are all bursting with excitement at being home. With just enough light, he can see all the different ideas of what they plan to do first racing across their faces. Watching them, Hugumki can barely contain his own turbulent emotions and a plan that keeps trying to rear its shiny head.

The reason he is not surprised is because of how much they have all changed on their quest: There's Turtle, who started out as a big child, but proved how tough he was through sheer determination. He is a true testament to the fact that the physical body is one thing, and the spirit is another altogether. Even Two Bows has shown there is more to him than just hunting and killing things. As for Rabbit, new name or not, he is always going to be who he is meant to be. "Besides", Hugumki whispers to himself. "What would life be like without a little color in it, a rainbow in the desert."

When everyone, except for Hugumki, have given Bear their packs, he climbs down from the top of the old storage room. After spreading his arms to let them know that the village is theirs, Bear shuffles over to

Hugumki and gives him a proud smile and a hearty hug along with these words of instruction and praise. "I have left the special floor open for you. When you are done, put it back together the right way. When I check it, I want it to look like we were never there. You will easily figure out what to do. Just be very careful because it is still very dark in there. Take five steps from the ladder and you will find it. I must say Hugumki, they all look and act good. You have done a good job and proven yourself to be a good leader." Bear's face breaks into a smile, "I do have one question Hugumki. Why do you all have the same holes in your ponchos?"

"Bear," is all that needs to be said.

As the human Bear starts heading around the corner, he issues a quiet warning. "Beware fellow villagers, the Chosen are back and they have returned as men, hoa." Hearing the growing commotion in front of him, he fights the urge to just go back to bed and his own family.

Little does he know how fast events are unfolding: A maiden or two has had their ladders rattled. Some parents are being appreciated and hugged tightly. Rock is still trying to recover from a surprise sniff. A warming pot has had its contents tested already. A life altering decision is being made. A Little Bean is flying through the air and down a ladder. The Chosen are safely home at last, and the village has ten-new-men.

Hugumki is so lost in thought as he climbs the ladder that he does not notice any of the raucous jubilation caused by the new men, or their awakening families.

He pauses at the top of the ladder, looks around, part of him already feeling like he is the next chief. All alone, again. Will he be able to live like that? Will it be worth it?

Knowing it is almost time for Father Sun to show his majestic might to a new day, Hugumki cuts those thoughts short and walks over to the second ladder.

Even though time is rapidly passing by, he takes a quick moment to look around after climbing down into the opening until just his head is showing. The roof is open on three sides with a higher wall on the back side of it giving him cover from the rest of the village.

Looking at the small yucca strapped bag he is holding in his strong hands; his thoughts turn to what is hidden inside. *With all the early struggles we had carrying these, how big of a God will all of this make? Will all of this go into making the God, or is there more to the singing stones than I have been told?*

Hugumki is once again facing a temptation he does not think he can resist. *I have heard them, now I deserve to see them.*

With his decision made, Hugumki quickly opens his bag to unwrap and pull out one singing stone.

With the desert about to erupt, Hugumki can feel everything around him pulsing as it waits to begin a new day. Inside, Hugumki's blood pounding heart is beating so hard it feels like a countdown as he turns to receive the first kiss of light from Father Sun.

Breaking free of the horizon, eager photon spirits race across the desert, all intent on capturing the singing stone in Hugumki's hand.

Hugumki, in turn, reaches for the sky and destiny itself. With that simple gesture, the singing stone is reveled in all its awe-inspiring glory.

Bright light meets cloth polished reflection and Hugumki's hand erupts in dazzling brilliance.

On high, hungry brother eagle is caught between the first fiery ray of a new day, and a blinding flash of gold.